HOPE EPTING LOSCHAK

Chasing the Sunset

Book One in the Vision Catchers Series

First published by Vision Catchers Publishing 2025

This novel is entirely a work of fiction. The names, characters and incidents portrayed in it are the work of the author's imagination. Any resemblance to actual persons, living or dead, events or localities is entirely coincidental.

Designations used by companies to distinguish their products are often claimed as trademarks. All brand names and product names used in this book and on its cover are trade names, service marks, trademarks and registered trademarks of their respective owners. The publishers and the book are not associated with any product or vendor mentioned in this book. None of the companies referenced within the book have endorsed the book.

First edition

ISBN: 978-1-969299-00-1

Cover art by Rachel Kelli
Editing by Samantha Stringert

This book was professionally typeset on Reedsy.
Find out more at reedsy.com

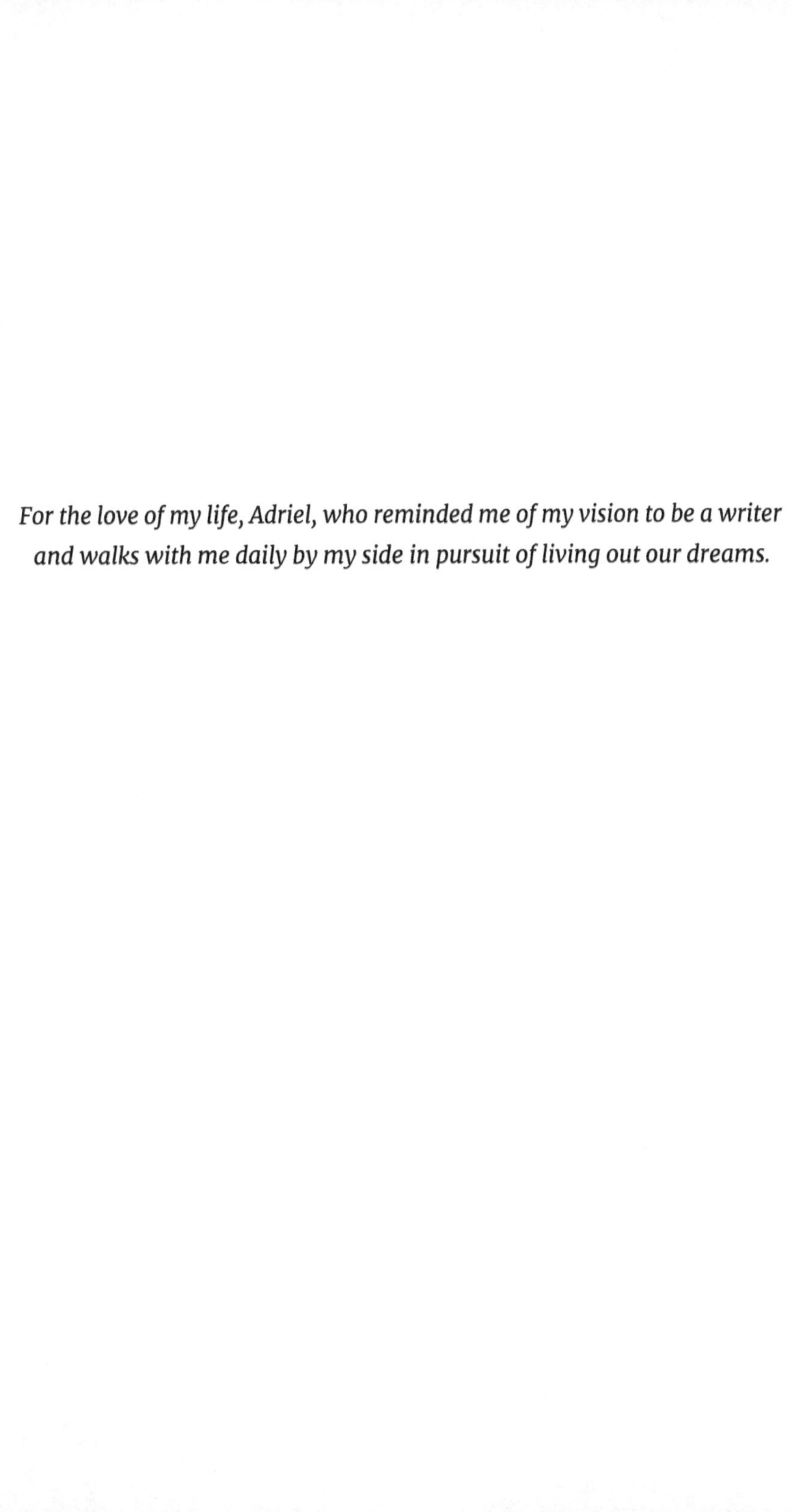

For the love of my life, Adriel, who reminded me of my vision to be a writer and walks with me daily by my side in pursuit of living out our dreams.

Author's Note about Content

Dear Reader,

This novel explores a woman's journey of reclaiming her dreams and rediscovering her sense of self. Along the way, it touches on difficult subjects that may be upsetting or activating for some readers.

This book contains depictions of domestic abuse (emotional, psychological, and financial) and gun violence. It also contains references to death by suicide, infant loss, homophobia, and racism.

These topics are not included for shock or sensationalism but rather to reflect the real and nuanced struggles many face while trying to survive, heal, and grow. If you need to pause, take care of yourself, or skip certain sections—that's not just okay, it's encouraged.

Above all, this is a story about **hope, healing, and the power of second chances**. If you're in a dark chapter of your life, I hope Lucy's journey reminds you that it's never too late to chase the sunset.

With care,

Hope Epting Loschak

Prologue

Gabe sat staring at the blank canvas as he had for the last few weeks. Growing bored, he walked over to water the plant in the small room he'd rented. As he gazed out the window watching the day fade into night, he lost hope that inspiration would ever strike.

In an attempt to rally himself, he closed his eyes, imagining the motto of his people—Catch the Vision, Empower the People, Create Lasting Change. Letting the phrase course through his veins, trying to draw power from it, he let the energy he gained push out of him like a sunbeam attempting to send inspiration her way.

A few moments later, he saw a faint vision hanging in the air. He grasped it gently, like catching a butterfly. The fragile dream sent a tingling sensation down his spine and restored his hope. He worked quickly, grabbing his sketchbook and making a plan before the idea was lost. She was finally ready.

1

The Golden Hour

It was just reaching the golden hour, and Lucy mindlessly washed a pan as she stared out the window and smiled at the warm glow that shone behind the willow tree. Dusk was her favorite time of day. The soft tones that photographers loved so much moved her soul and gave her goosebumps.

She'd cooked roast beef, mashed potatoes, and green beans for dinner for herself and Colt. This was the perfect meal for taking one last stroll through the acreage in their backyard. He wouldn't be home from work for another thirty minutes. The sides could remain heated on low on the stove and the roast could stay warm in the oven.

She opened the creaky screen door. Right before it slammed shut behind her, their cat Garfield darted out. He followed her as she walked along the stream that ran next to their house. She took a deep breath in and allowed the vibrations of the magic hour to enter her body, then breathed out all the tension and anxiety she was carrying. A soft breeze blew from the west, pushing back the wisps of her hair that had come loose from her bun. She watched the sun begin to set. It was a gorgeous and fragile moment—a daily wonder that so many neglected to bathe in. As the day was just out of reach of her, it was just beginning for another. She imagined herself chasing the sunset until she was one with someone else's sunrise.

As her body finally started to give in to the beauty of the afternoon, the car door slammed and jolted her senses. Her heart raced, and she ran back inside as fast as she could. Garfield followed, but the door slammed in his face before he could get inside.

Colt came through the door. "Hey," he huffed.

"How was your day?" Lucy inquired, not out of curiosity, but out of a routine obligation.

"Miserable. Same as every day."

As he walked through the room with a scowl on his face, Lucy forced a slight smile and spoke softly, "I made your favorites for dinner."

"Good. I'm hungry. I doubt it will help get off the stink of this shit day." Colt closed his eyes, shook his head, and let out an exasperated sigh.

Lucy knew no matter what she said, it would set him off. She decided not to say anything at all, but he was looking for a punching bag.

"Don't you have anything to say to me? Why are you looking at me like that? You think I shouldn't be complaining, right?"

"I didn't look at you ... I mean, I think it's fine for you to vent about your day. That's why I'm here."

"Yeah, right," he huffed again. "I'm gonna go vape on the porch."

Lucy stayed in the living room as he pushed by her. She heard the creak of the screen door.

"LUCY!!! What's Garfield doing out here?"

"Oh, yes, sorry. He must've gotten out when I took a walk before dinner."

"It must be nice to have time for walks. You have to watch him. The coyotes and hawks would love to gobble him up. He was my grandma's favorite companion. It means a lot that she entrusted him to me. Don't you get that?"

Colt picked up Garfield and stroked his head gently. He leaned his face into Garfield's and whispered in his ear, "I'm sorry she did that to you." Holding Garfield tight, he turned his back to her in a protective gesture. As he glanced back toward her over his shoulder, his gaze burned into her with vitriol. Under his breath, but intentionally audible, he said, "Fucking moron."

Lucy's stomach tightened. The tightness crept up to her voice. "Honestly, I didn't mean to let him out. He's fine now and I'll try to be more careful in the future." She hoped her words would calm his anger, but she knew this mood all too well.

"You better."

The sun had set, the magic hour was over, and all the light that had poured into her for a brief time just minutes ago had now, once again, turned to darkness. They said little at dinner. Colt didn't thank her for making it, or offer to help with the dishes as per usual.

The days had been going on like this. They'd continue like this—it felt as if to the end of time. Lucy had once thought if he'd change jobs or she found a job to bring in more income, things would be different. Both had happened. She worked as a bookkeeper at a local nonprofit and he left being an English teacher at a middle school to teach at a community college, which at least left him less depressed than teaching preteens. Lucy loved to watch him teach. She'd watch his lectures that were posted online sometimes. He seemed so different, so nice, so like the person she met and fell in love with. Only she knew the darker side that created her living hell.

After dinner, he told her he had an early meeting in the morning.

"Could you rustle me up a roast beef sandwich that I can grab on my way out tomorrow?"

Not wanting to set him off, she headed to the kitchen. When she opened the bread box, she froze and braced herself for a tongue lashing. The grocery store had run out of Colt's favorite bread the last time she went. Now, there was only one piece left.

"Colt, it looks like we're out of bread. Can you pick up something else for lunch tomorrow and I can swing by the grocery store in the afternoon?"

"No, that's a waste of money and your roast beef is going to go bad if we don't finish it soon. Just go to the store and get some more now."

With a sinking soul, Lucy turned away. She grabbed her keys and purse with a quiet burning frustration. She never had the energy to cry anymore. Taking a seat on the couch, she laced up her tennis shoes. While tired, getting out of the tension of the house also came with the ability to breathe a little. Her nerves were always so on edge. She knew she'd screw something up when Colt made requests of her, even something as simple as picking up a loaf of bread.

She put her hands on the doorknob and just as she was about to leave, Colt pulled her back, gently wrapping his arms around her. He whispered in her ear, "Could you also pick me up some blue e-cigs too? I love you."

And there it was. He always did this—Jekyll and Hyde. She turned and looked up at him. "Of course. Love you too."

Pecking him on the cheek, she slipped out. Joni Mitchell's voice came in to soothe her when she turned on the car. Backing up past their manicured lawn, she stopped at the mailbox to grab the mail. Their street was dark yet peaceful, so she hesitated for a moment before turning the lights on.

Driving past the local elementary school, post office, and drugstore, she soon arrived at Pete's Groceries. It was 9:00 p.m. and they'd just closed. She thought she could beg her way in. All she wanted was a loaf of bread after all. Pete and the staff knew her.

She stepped out of the car, walked toward the door and saw a family leaving—a young mother and father pushing a stroller of a two-year-old. She paused and just watched them. They probably realized they were out of something essential like bread and made a late-night grocery run ... together. They were chatting and smiling with one another, and Lucy felt a pang of jealousy.

She remembered learning that a black hole was a dying star—the light collapsing in on itself. Her insides felt like that—a vacuum of darkness that was pulling with all its might to rip her heart from her chest. She watched and stared as the family loaded up the car.

She couldn't convince the teenager locking up to let her complete this quick chore.

"Please ... I only need a loaf of bread. I can see it from here."

"Sorry ma'am, I closed out the last register. I got somewhere to be."

Lucy's annoyance at this youngster wielding power over her was short-lived. It melted away as she sunk into her current reality. As if the thought of going home wasn't bad enough, the thought of going home empty-handed and getting berated was absolutely deflating.

She drove a few more miles to the Walmart. A crescent moon accompanied her fantasies of an alternate universe where she'd chosen a different path. It was November and fifty degrees. She rolled down the windows and let the cool air hit her face. The westward wind from that afternoon had grown stronger. When she was close to the Walmart, she saw a man hitchhiking on the side of the road as she approached a stoplight. He couldn't have been more than twenty, so he was less of a man and more like a kid. He was Black, dark-skinned, on the taller side, wearing a shirt that read, "John 3:8."

Lucy grew up going to church and, as a teenager, took part in youth group. She didn't know that many Bible verses, but that one rang a bell. She couldn't quite remember it. The light turned green, but she hesitated to drive on. The man smiled at her and she looked into his kind eyes. There was a deep desperation she recognized. For a few seconds, Lucy felt like she was looking into a mirror. She considered leaning out the already open window and asking him where he was going, but she heard Colt in her head.

"You know better than that. What were you thinking, idiot? Picking up someone on the side of the road?"

She heeded the voice and continued to the Walmart. When she was just about to turn down the hill that led to the parking lot, a shopping cart manned by a large teenage boy darted in front of her. She was only going three miles an hour, but the sight shocked her and she reflexively slammed hard on the brakes. Shaking her head and catching her breath, she assessed the full situation. Another smaller adolescent had taken a ride in the basket and the boys were now laughing. "That was awesome dude," one kid shouted. Their game of chicken didn't faze them at all.

Lucy couldn't think of a time where she'd gone to the store and there hadn't been teenagers loitering about. How did all these kids get the memo that the Walmart parking lot was the place to hang? It wasn't just Booneville; it was every small town with nothing to do.

She pressed on and parked. As she exited the car, she looked back to see the commandeered shopping cart laying on its side. One boy was now attempting to jump over the cart on his skateboard.

She held her breath, anticipating that she may soon call 9-1-1 or at least need to grab the first aid kit from the car, but the kid actually made it.

Nostalgia swept over her as she remembered how she'd skateboarded as a teen for a brief time—even fantasized competing and going to the X Games. The memory brought a smile to her face. She watched these kids chomping on Cheetos and drinking Monster Energy drinks. Despite having no desire to join them, she would've been happier to just sit in her car watching them act like fools than return home to be with Colt.

With a sigh, she resigned herself to playing the role of the dutiful housewife and went into the store to buy the bread. She dawdled in the clothes section before making her way to the groceries. She touched the texture of a fuzzy robe, yearning to wrap her body in its cuddly warmth. Even at the low price of $19.99, she knew Colt would scold her for wasting their money. Her phone pinged. It was Colt asking where she was, but she ignored it. Instead of responding, she beelined to the bread aisle, her pace quickening.

Colt's preferred brand was out of stock on the lower shelves, but she saw a couple of extra loaves on the top shelf. At 5'3", even when she stood on her tippy toes, she couldn't reach it. There was a sign adhered to the shelf that read, "Ask for assistance for all items on the top shelf." She looked around for someone to help and was glad when she saw a tall man heading in her direction. As he grew closer, she recognized him. It was the hitchhiker, holding a bottle of water.

"Hi ma'am, do you need help?" he said as he pointed to the shelf.

"Yes, please."

The man had at least six inches on her, maybe more. He easily grabbed it and handed it to her.

"Thank you." Lucy read his shirt again. Her mind was reaching for the verse. She decided to just ask him. "What's that Bible verse on your shirt?"

He beamed at her. "The wind blows wherever it pleases. You hear its sound, but you cannot tell where it comes from or where it is going. So it is with everyone born of the spirit." The words fell off his tongue like poetry. They wrapped around her heart, tugging at a longing to be a free spirit. The desire wasn't strong enough to break her soul free of Colt's chains, but the stranger soothed her.

Her eyes met his. A memory stirred in her, and she didn't want to leave. Attempting to drag the conversation forward, she said, "Oh yes. You know, I used that verse in a Sunday school art project. We all had to pick one to go along with a self-portrait collage. I'd forgotten all about it until now." She glanced at his water and pointed. "You giving up on hitching tonight or have you just come in for provisions?"

"Just grabbing some crackers and water, then it's back to my post."

Lucy's phone rang. She didn't have to look to know it was Colt. The bread felt heavy in her hands, a burden weighing her down. She let the call go to voicemail and looked back at the man. "I have to go. Thanks again for the help." She left abruptly, brushing by him and rushing to the register to hurry back home, hoping Colt would go easy on her. She sent a quick text before driving away.

Lucy: *Had to go to Walmart, on my way home now.*

The stranger's words replayed in her mind all the way home. Her phone pinged a few more times. She ignored them, not even taking the time to check the messages after she pulled into the driveway—running into the house with the right bread as fast as she could.

Colt was standing a few feet from the threshold when she opened the door, arms crossed, glaring at her.

"About time. What took so long?"

She stepped in, attempting to navigate his landmines as best she could. "Pete's closed just as I got there, so I went to Walmart, and then I had to get someone to help me … "

"Help you get bread? Why?"

"Well, it was … " before she could get her explanation out, he interrupted.

"Did you get my e-cigs?"

The color drained from her face. BOOM. She'd failed. She didn't have to say anything. He could read her like a book.

"You forgot? Goddammit Lucy." He raised his voice. Lucy held her breath. "I mean, I texted you a reminder. You didn't answer my call. This could've all been avoided if you just paid more attention. Seriously, sometimes I don't know where your head's at."

She exhaled. "I'm sorry, I just got detoured. I'm going to make your sandwich." She held up the bread, then hurried to the kitchen.

Colt sat in his chair and sulked, occasionally shifting his eyes toward her. She called out to him, "You want mayo and mustard, right?"

"Of course not. Then it will get soggy. You know what? Forget it. I'll just make it myself in the morning."

"Are you sure, I ... "

"Did I stutter? Look, really, I just needed those e-cigs."

She stared at him blankly, a feeling of hopelessness clutching at her heart. In a measured tone, she said, "Okay. I'll go back out. I'll fix it."

"Thank you."

This was their pattern. A dance that made her anxious and feel dead inside, all at once. Sitting in the car, she stared at the house, lost in her thoughts. Her phone beeped. This time, she looked at it.

Colt: You know I can see you, right? What are you waiting for? Turn on the damn car and go.

She scrolled through the other texts she'd ignored earlier. She was delighted to see they weren't all from Colt. One was from her friend Anna.

Anna: How's everything? I was just hanging at Jittery Joe's today and missing you.

She smiled at the mention of their dear coffee shop, where they'd spent hours together as baristas. Anna was the only friend she still kept in touch with—one of the first she'd made in Athens.

She and Colt had started dating her senior year at UNC Chapel Hill. About five months in, he was accepted into grad school at UGA. Lucy followed him. Anna was a bright spot in her life after arriving in a town where she knew no one. They didn't just work together—they took long walks after their shifts and became fast friends.

Lucy thought she'd easily visit or at least keep in touch with her undergrad friends after the move. After all, Athens was only about a five-hour drive from where she'd been in North Carolina. But between her job and keeping house—Colt wanting things just so, even then— she lost contact with all of them.

Anna became her confidant when Colt's mental health started to decline when his mom died. She was a beacon of hope for Lucy as she tried to navigate Colt's unresolved trauma and complex relationship with his mother. When they moved again for Colt's teaching job, she vowed that she wouldn't lose touch with Anna.

And she hadn't. Anna had even planned a girls' weekend a couple of weeks back for Lucy's thirtieth birthday. Unfortunately, her birthday fell on the same weekend as the anniversary of Colt's mom's death. He threw a fit that she'd be leaving the house for a couple of days. He wallowed in the bedroom after she told him her plans, eventually behaving like a child and shouting, "Mean to me. Mean to me. Mean to me." When she finally answered his chant and entered their room, his eyes were red with tears. He told her he didn't know if he could go on without her by his side for the weekend. Guilt overcame her. She promised not to leave, cradling his head in her arms and rubbing his forehead. The relief in his face was instant.

Anna sent flowers, but it wasn't the same as the peace and solace the trip would've given her. Now, reading Anna's text, all the lovely memories of her support mixed with those of Colt's manipulation in a bitter cocktail—his anger overpowering any sweetness Anna had sent her way. Numb inside, she heeded Colt's demands once again and pulled out of the driveway.

She arrived at the gas station. Hypnotized by spinning thoughts of Anna, Colt, and the kind stranger while driving automatically on a route she'd taken so many times before. She took a moment to herself before she went to talk to the clerk. When she finally climbed out of the car, she stumbled. The exhaustion of the day had set in. The man at the counter recognized her and knew what she wanted before she spoke.

"Blue e-cigs?" he said.

She nodded, paid the man, and took her receipt. Still sleepy, when she stepped outside, her grip on the receipt loosened as a gust of wind blew it out of her hand. It rode the breeze for several feet, like a surfer catching a wave. The words from the verse on the man's shirt replayed in her mind while she watched the paper drift out of sight.

The wind blows wherever it pleases. You hear its sound, but you cannot tell where it comes from or where it is going...

Sitting back in the car, she looked toward her home and then back in the direction of the now-vanished receipt.

Not knowing where she was going, she drove in the opposite direction of Colt, soon arriving back at the intersection with the friendly hitchhiker.

Lucy rolled down the window and asked him, "Where you headed?"

"I'm trying to get to Nashville to see my aunt." As she looked into his eyes, there was no sense of awkwardness.

She pushed a lie out of her mouth that would soon become the truth. "Well, it's your lucky day, because that's exactly where I'm headed." While stunned at her excited utterance, she couldn't take her words back now. At that moment, she didn't want to.

Lucy grabbed the mail she'd placed in the passenger seat earlier that night and tossed it in the back. He climbed in. Then, just like that, she left with a stranger, in the middle of the night, freer than she'd been in years.

2

The Escape

Her mind raced. *What did I do, what did I do ... how do I even get to Nashville? It's northeast, right? Right. So l will just get on 145 North and maybe I can use my ... SHIT, my phone.*

She glanced down at it and was relieved to see that Colt hadn't called or texted yet, but she knew it was only a matter of time.

"Hey, can you grab my phone and turn it off?"

"Um ... alright ... I don't know many people who turn off their phones. Did you drop it?" he asked, examining the cracked screen.

The truth was one night when Lucy was talking to her mom, Colt came in angry and slammed it against the wall. He then accused her of cheating on him.

She glanced toward the man. "Yeah, I'm a bit clumsy, and I haven't wanted to spend the money to replace it. The battery is shit, so I turn it off when I don't need it."

The man held the off button and said, "Okay. Done." She exhaled a small sigh of relief, but her heart was still racing. She couldn't help looking in the rearview mirror to see if Colt was chasing her down.

They sat in tense silence for a few minutes, but rather than break it with awkward conversation, Lucy relaxed into the quiet moment. She put aside the worries about Colt, whether she was heading in the right direction, or if this man was dangerous. She just focused on the road and enjoyed aimlessly wandering.

The sound of the car became a lullaby. Her eyes closed, her head nodded downward, and she fell asleep. A few seconds later, she awoke to the man screaming her name as they drifted onto the highway's shoulder. She startled awake and braked hard, breathing heavily. Once she'd taken stock of her surroundings and realized she was physically safe, she put the car in park and drew in a deep breath to calm herself.

Swallowing hard she turned to him and said, "Thank you." In a flash, her heart sped back up and fear overwhelmed her as she looked at the man in horror.

"How did you know my name?"

He paused for just a moment and lifted a piece of mail from the floorboard that must have fallen when she cleared the seat for him.

Holding it in front of him, he said, "I took an educated guess."

Her eyes darted down and around the dark car, wondering if any other private information was lurking about, but the only thing other than the letter was his backpack resting at his feet. He must have sensed her nerves.

He looked down at his hands and then lifted his head to speak. "Lucy, I'm Gabe." He paused. Staring at his hands once again, he seemed to be thinking through something carefully.

After several moments, he looked at her with kind, smiling eyes and gently said, "I know I've asked you for this ride, but even though I don't have a car, I have money and a license. You're clearly tired. I'd be happy to drive and I can pay for the gas. I know the way. You could sleep."

Sleep. Sleep without worrying about being woken up by Colt needing something desperately like water, coffee, or a sleeping pill. Sleep, not interrupted by Garfield walking across their heads early in the morning and without Colt screaming, "This is all your fucking fault. If you kept him on a more regular feeding schedule, he wouldn't do this."

Lucy weighed her options. Gabe's proposal got her sleep and she didn't have to admit she had no clue where she was going. It also cost her a lot less money. She only had a bit of cash and this way Colt couldn't trace a credit card. But then again, what if a racist cop pulled them over, checked the plates, and then called Colt because the car was registered to him? Or even worse, do something horrific like shoot Gabe? Her head was spinning.

"You know what, you're right. I'm tired. I'll take you up on your offer to pay for gas, but how about you just navigate? I promise if I get too exhausted or feel like I might fall asleep again, I'll pull over."

"Okay. Deal. You just keep on this road for about twenty-five miles."

They were on the right track. She emitted a small sigh of relief that he hadn't said, "Make a U-turn." The car was quiet. To avoid small talk and falling asleep again, she turned on the radio to break the silence. The CD player in this used 2010 Civic had often transported her to the music she'd accumulated before she married Colt. Joni began singing "River."

Lucy let the words sweep over her. When she sang about wishing she had a river to skate away on, Lucy became on the verge of tears. She wasn't sure if they were tears of relief or fear, but she knew she didn't want Gabe to notice. She turned down the music and reluctantly sparked up a conversation to avoid the impending waterworks or another near accident.

"What were you doing in Booneville? Do you go to Northeast Mississippi? Are you visiting family for the holidays?"

"Yes ma'am, I've been going to Northeast Miss, but I'm going to my aunt's for good. I'm an art student and I um ... well ... don't need to be there anymore to do that. I have a room at my aunt's and a place to make my art."

Lucy found this to be a little cryptic and wondered if he was telling the truth, but then again, didn't blame him for not sharing his whole situation with her. She wouldn't be revealing much about herself either. She looked down again at his backpack.

"That's not a lot of stuff for someone who's moving. And not to sound like your mother, but you aren't wearing a jacket. Aren't you freezing?" Lucy scolded.

"Um...I didn't expect the cold snap. My cousin picked up my clothes yesterday. I was supposed to ride with her, but I had something to take care of first," Gabe said sheepishly.

"Oh." Lucy was unsure what to make of this, but she had the urge to continue to scold him, telling him he should know better than to get in a car with a stranger. Realizing that would be pretty hypocritical, given that she could tell herself the same thing, she held her tongue and quietly drove on.

After a while, she'd learned that Gabe had grown up in Tennessee and this aunt was like a second mother to him after his parents died in an accident, though he was vague about the details. She told him about being raised in North Carolina, her job at the nonprofit, and the normal small talk down to, "What's your favorite ice cream flavor?" After telling him that hers was Rocky Road, Gabe told her he didn't have one. "Are you insane? How can you not have a favorite ice cream?"

He looked at her and smiled a gentle smile she was beginning to really enjoy. "I just don't. Honestly, I don't have a favorite of much of anything. I like to choose what I feel in the moment."

She took a beat, thinking back to the verse on his shirt. "Like the wind, can't tell where it's coming from or where it's going?"

"Exactly." He threw her a knowing, soft smile.

The fuel light flashed on the dash. They'd been driving an hour and a half. Lucy guessed they were probably halfway there, if he was indeed taking them to Nashville. She pulled off to the first gas station she saw.

Gabe was staring out of the window. He seemed not to have noticed that they'd pulled off. She turned her body toward him with her gaze shifting up to the lighted gas station sign and said, "It's time."

"Okay. I have cash, I'll go inside and pay. Will thirty bucks do it?"

"It should."

When she put the car in park, she wondered if she'd actually done it. Had she escaped or was this a dream? The fear that Colt would've followed her had subsided, mostly. He wouldn't have any idea she'd been headed this way. She'd had no idea. Every time someone pulled behind them for the first forty miles, her heart raced and she feared Colt would run them off the road.

Gabe opened the car door and strolled into the station. She contemplated standing up and stretching and going into the restroom, but she closed her eyes just for a moment. Then suddenly, the car door opened and her senses jolted. Her heart raced as she oriented herself.

She glanced over and there was Gabe. "You're back. Did you forget something?"

"No, we're all set."

She glanced up at the gas pump and saw that the numbers read $30. She'd passed out cold. While it had been only a few minutes, it felt so good. Until Gabe had returned, it was probably the most restful sleep she'd had in weeks, or maybe even months. Exhausted, she looked toward Gabe and without thinking about it too hard asked, "Is it too late to take you up on your offer to drive?"

He smiled. "No Lucy. Happy to, you just sleep."

"Okay. Maybe I should go to the bathroom real quick before we go. I'll just leave the car on."

She climbed out and headed toward the bathroom door on the side of the station. To her surprise, when she opened the door it was relatively clean. There was some air deodorizer covering up any foul scent that might be there.

She hadn't realized how much she needed to pee until she did. It seemed to go on forever. After washing her hands, she spent at least two whole minutes looking at herself in the mirror. There were dark circles under her eyes and she examined her pale skin. It had been ages since she'd really looked at her face.

She closed her eyes, about to fall asleep again—right there in the bathroom. She gave herself a quick slap to her cheek, then headed back out to meet Gabe. He was in the driver's seat. In her exhaustion, she hadn't even thought about the fact that he could steal the car. It felt weird to put so much trust in a stranger, but her gut told her she could. Maybe it was just indifference. Even if they didn't end up in Nashville, she didn't care. She just didn't want to go back to where she'd been.

Half asleep, she stumbled to the car, buckled, and closed her eyes. She fell asleep to the sweet music of Joni Mitchell and hoped the soundtrack would continue on into her dreams.

"Lucy, we're here," Lucy heard as a hand touched her shoulder and shook her a bit. She awoke in a drowsy haze. Gabe was holding out the car keys for her to grab.

"This is my stop. I'm not sure you should drive. My aunt has a room that you can sleep in. Want to just crash here till morning?"

Before even looking up at where "here" was and still half asleep, she muttered, "Alright." She'd made so many impulsive decisions tonight. What was one more? She blinked a few times, stepped out of the car, looked around and was stunned. The house was giant, like one of those plantation houses from *Gone With the Wind*.

"Your aunt lives here?" She wondered if that was racist of her to say as the words fell out of her mouth.

"Yes. She owns it. It's sort of a bed-and-breakfast."

"Oh, so I need to pay her for the room?"

"No. You gave me a ride here. That's payment enough."

Excitement welled up in her. She'd never been to a bed-and-breakfast. It was probably not that different from a hotel, but the term seemed luxurious and scrumptious.

She turned to the car and instinctively went to open the trunk to grab her bag, but deflated when she realized she hadn't packed one.

Oh wait, she thought. Yes, she had. Few people knew how Colt treated her, but Anna did—even before the birthday weekend failed to launch. A few months ago, when they were on the phone, Anna encouraged Lucy to pack a bag and hide it, just in case. Lucy had completely forgotten about it, but she did it one day when Colt was at work. She'd stashed it with the spare tire in the compartment that was underneath the trunk.

She continued toward the trunk and pulled up the carpet to get to the spare tire area. In the middle was a small duffel. Gabe came up behind her to lend a hand. She looked up at him, embarrassed. "Old habits. My dad was a master at packing the car efficiently and the first thing would always go in the 'spare' space."

"Understood," Gabe said and then reached down to carry the bag. The door was locked and there was a bell, but right before Lucy could press it, Gabe said, "I have a key." He bent down to open up his backpack and as he fumbled to grab it, Lucy saw a familiar image in his bag. It was a painting—looking at it gave her goosebumps. It looked like a woman running toward a sunset, similar to what she'd imagined herself doing earlier that day. She thought perhaps this was a sign she'd made the right decision.

Gabe stood up, keys in hand, unlocked and opened the door with one arm and with the other guided her toward the entrance and said, "After you."

Lucy entered the large foyer where an opulent set of stairs greeted her. At the top of the stairs were hallways on either side, overlooking the lower level. She saw nothing resembling a check-in desk.

Swirling anxiety and excitement woke her up. She turned to Gabe to decline his invitation, but before she could, he said, "Come with me. I want to introduce you to Aunt Rae if she's up. She's a bit of a night owl."

She followed him despite her worry. Bookshelves lined the walls from floor to ceiling in a giant room that led into an empty dining room. There were chairs and couches in the room with the bookshelves and one of them was occupied by an older woman. Her mouth was agape and eyes closed. She stirred as they approached. When her eyes opened, a bolt of energy consumed her. She jumped up with joy, hurrying toward them, arms outstretched.

She embraced Gabe warmly. "Gabe! You made it. I was beginning to worry."

"Yes, Aunt Rae. This is Lucy. She gave me a ride, so I told her she could stay here tonight. Lucy, this is my Aunt Rae."

"Well, of course she can stay. Hope he wasn't too much trouble." Rae grabbed Lucy's arm lovingly, smiling from ear to ear and winking at her.

"Not at all," Lucy said. Rae radiated love. It overwhelmed Lucy. Colt had deadened her nerves and now she had goosebumps as Rae's warmth brought them back to life like candles burning with a small flame.

"You look exhausted. Let me show you to your room."

If Lucy had Rae's waking energy, she wouldn't need to stay the night. She could drive on for hours. Since she didn't, she followed Rae with Gabe as she climbed the stairs from the foyer. They took a right at the top of the stairs, passed a couple of doors, and took another turn. Rae opened a door and climbed another smaller set of stairs. These were much plainer than the foyer or hallway they'd just passed through. At the very top of the stairs was a single door. Rae pulled a key out of her pocket and opened it.

Lucy wondered if Rae always kept keys on her or if it was a master.

Maybe she was so tired she hadn't noticed her grab it before they'd headed up.

"Here we are. This is your room. We call it The Tower. There are clean towels on the dresser, and oh, here's your key." It was an actual key, not one of those fancy card systems. Lucy looked at the trinkets attached to it—a large keychain with the words "Rae's B&B" and another colorful charm with a quote from *Alice in Wonderland*. "I knew who I was this morning, but I've changed a few times since then." Reading it stirred something deep inside her.

Lucy looked around the room. It was a gorgeous bohemian paradise. Because The Tower was the highest room in the house, the ceiling slanted—covered by wooden slats painted white and in the middle was a large skylight. Lucy looked through it and saw the moon and stars. She imagined the sun would gently wake her up in the morning. The walls were white and adorned with a few soothing pictures and tapestries. There was a light with a large shade and tassels hanging over the bed and potted succulents on each of the two nightstands, which, just like the bed, were a lightly stained wood. The bed linens were shades of light brown and white. A shaggy white faux fur blanket lay at the foot, finishing out the look.

Lucy had wanted to design her and Colt's room just like this, but he wouldn't let her. "That look is for rich wannabe hippies," he'd scoffed. They went for the more practical and unpretentious interiors from the Walmart she'd visited earlier in the evening. She was so busy soaking everything in she jumped a little when Gabe looked at her and said, "Thank you so much again for the ride. I hope you have a great night's sleep."

Lucy looked at the young man, who was still a stranger to her, but also felt like a close friend. "You're most welcome."

Gabe and Rae turned around and shut the door and went quietly down the stairs.

When they reached the bottom and were out of earshot of Lucy, Rae smiled at Gabe. "Well, well, well, your first vision quest! This IS exciting. I am so proud of you for getting her here."

Gabe glanced behind him to make sure Lucy hadn't heard. He looked back toward his aunt and said in a hushed tone, "She wouldn't have come unless she was ready."

3

The First Step

Just as Lucy expected, she woke up with the sun as its beams radiated from the ceiling. The pleasant smell of bacon and coffee and the sounds of laughter filled the air. Torn between hiding in bed and not facing the realities of the choice she made last night, her rumbling belly won out and forced her up. The cold hardwood floors on her feet sent shivers through her body as she headed to her suitcase to grab clothes. Before she opened it, she noticed the clean towels sitting on the dresser. A shower was too intoxicating to pass up, despite her hunger.

The warm water on her body was a welcome friend, caressing her softly. For such an old house, it had surprisingly much better water pressure than hers. She wanted to get a plumber to check it out, but Colt said it was a waste of money. This rain style shower was like one she'd seen once in a movie and fantasized about having. It also had a detachable hose she could switch on to get her "tits, pits, and bits" extra clean.

The shower wasn't all relaxing. It also started her mind racing, as showers tend to do. What would she do next? Should she go back? This had definitely been a pleasant break from reality, but if she didn't go back, she was homeless. Colt was going to be furious. If he somehow found her in this luxury, she wouldn't hear the end of it. She decided to just take it "bird by bird," one step at a time—finish the shower, get dressed, eat breakfast, and then she could do the next thing. No harm in waiting until she had a full belly to decide how to handle the mess she put herself in.

The urge to turn on her phone and Google what to do when running away from home weighed heavy, but she resisted. She wasn't ready to be tracked. Not without a plan.

She opened the bag she'd packed months ago and put on a pair of jeans and a white T-shirt. Did they use to be this loose?

Catching her reflection in the full-length mirror in the corner, she examined herself. The bags under her eyes and pale skin she'd noticed last night were still there, but she must have lost at least ten if not fifteen pounds in recent months. Last she checked, she was 145, but she hadn't stood on a scale for a year. She hadn't really had much of an appetite lately, but she also hadn't focused on herself at all as of late. All her energy went into taking care of Colt.

Her ensemble and appearance were less than desirable. Knowing she didn't want to wear the same thing as last night, she scrunched her face in disappointment, exhaled, and made her way downstairs.

The aroma of breakfast became more heavenly when her foot hit the first step. She closed her eyes to take in the scent of coffee—it was a siren call, beckoning her onward. In the darkness, she stumbled over something furry, catching herself before falling. The furry resident was a tabby cat. It rubbed against her legs and when Lucy peered closer, she read its name tag hanging off its blue collar. "Penelope." Bending down to pick her up, she said, "Hello Penelope, you're just the cutest!" Penelope purred. It made Lucy miss Garfield.

Lucy gently placed the cat on the floor, and Penelope promptly ran away chasing after a nonexistent creature. Lucy continued downstairs and when she reached the dining room, Gabe greeted her with a warm smile.

"Good morning Lucy, I hope you slept well."

"Yes, I did, better than I have in a long time."

"I bet. You nearly slept the morning away."

"Oh no, what time is it?" Lucy realized she hadn't even looked.

"Ten thirty."

Worry replaced Lucy's tranquility. "Is there any breakfast left? What time is checkout?" Was she going to make a plan and face reality without a full belly?

"No worries. Aunt Rae always makes more than enough every morning and there's no rush to checkout. Follow me."

Lucy shook off her fear for the moment and followed Gabe to a dining table. There were three other guests sitting at the table who appeared to be finishing their breakfast. A smiling young Asian woman probably around Lucy's age in her thirties; an older Black man with gray in his hair and a purple and green golf shirt; and a white man who looked like a politician in a suit, who looked to be in his mid-fifties.

Gabe pulled out a chair for her next to the woman. Right when Lucy sat down, her stomach grumbled loud enough for everyone at the table to hear.

"You've come to the right place," the woman said. "The food here is exquisite. I'm Daisy. What's your name?"

"Lucy."

"This is Gerald," Daisy said, gesturing to the politician, "and Reggie."

Reggie waved and smiled and opened his mouth as if he were about to speak when Gerald interjected, "She's not lying about the food. It's probably one of the biggest things that has kept me here. Try the grits. Have you had grits? I had my doubts. I'm from New York and had never had them, but O-M-G, they're A-Mazing. Gabe, what are you waiting for? Get Lucy a plate!"

Gabe smiled with tight lips and drew a deep breath. His exasperation with Gerald made her like him even more. He turned his head toward her. "Lucy, how would you like your eggs?"

"Oh, sunny side up." Lucy spoke softly to counter Gerald's energy and to add calm back into her morning.

"Got it." Gabe turned toward what Lucy assumed was the kitchen.

Reggie cleared his throat, but before he could speak, Gerald got his words out first again. "Lucy, so where are you from? What brings you here?" Daisy shot him a look as if this was an inappropriate question.

"Originally I'm from North Carolina, but I live in Booneville, Mississippi now. And you said you're from New York? How long have you been visiting here?" Lucy asked, side-stepping the second question.

"Oh. I'm on day twenty, so I'm halfway through. I still haven't found my way. Yesterday I tried my hand at making a mosaic. That was a disaster, but I guess it was better than when I went to the Open Mic. I did that first and nearly shat myself. It was so embarrassing."

Lucy was so confused. Why was this guy doing all this artsy stuff? Almost seemingly against his will. Day twenty! Must be nice to have that much vacation. "What do you do in New York?" Lucy inquired, enabling his talkativeness.

"I'm a hedge fund manager."

Now that fit. He must be going through some kind of mid-life crisis, she thought. She was getting hangry. Gerald's presence felt like nails on a chalkboard in the middle of pure bliss. Attempting to shift the focus away from Gerald, Lucy turned her attention to Reggie so he could get a word in. "Reggie, what about you? Where are you from? What do you think is a must-do or must-see in Nashville?"

"I'm from New Orleans. Not sure what's a must-do, because I don't know you all that well, but for me, I love the Bluebird Cafe. My wife and I went there for our twentieth wedding anniversary to see our daughter sing. I've never seen either of them happier." He smiled and closed his eyes. "I can smell her perfume just thinking about it." He opened his eyes and his smile seemed to turn to heartbreak in a flash.

The conversation paused when Gabe came in with a smorgasbord of southern breakfast staples and coffee. Her plate had eggs, biscuits, hash browns, bacon, and, of course, the grits that Gerald raved about. The coffee smelled otherworldly and had notes of hazelnut.

It was the perfect breakfast, just what she would've ordered if she could've had anything. The food put her in a trance. She barely noticed when thunder rolled loudly.

As she continued to devour her meal, the others talked about how it was going to rain and debated which was better: umbrellas or rain jackets. Although their chatter was background noise, it occurred to Lucy that she had neither. As she ate the last bite, she knew she was going to need to stick to the decision she made earlier in the shower. Decide what to do next.

The answer became obvious. Get some cash. She looked down at her hands and looked at her wedding ring. Could she pawn it? It wasn't a real diamond but she was pretty sure it was gold. That should get her a place in The Tower for at least a week, an umbrella (the clearly superior option), and some clothes perhaps. Next, she needed to let someone know she was okay. She'd ask Gabe if she could use his phone to call Anna. One step at a time.

When she looked up after settling on this plan, she was shocked to see only Gabe sitting across from her. She'd been so deep in her thoughts she hadn't realized the others had left.

"Gabe, I didn't realize you were there." She contemplated telling Gabe about her predicament. He'd been so kind. Before she could get the words out, Gabe spoke.

"I'm sorry. I didn't mean to sneak up on you. I was just going to ask you if you had plans today."

"No, not yet, I was just trying to figure that out," Lucy said. She held herself back from adding, "I was just trying to make a plan for the rest of my life."

Gabe smiled and with shoulders shrugged, said, "Would you like to see some of my art?"

"Sure, that sounds nice. Is it in a gallery?"

"No. More like a studio. It's here, so it isn't far." Gabe smiled and then pulled out the painting from his bag she'd seen the night before. "I'm going to frame this one today to hang. Do you like it?"

Lucy stared at a painting of herself chasing the sunset. Hairs were standing at attention on her arm. It was definitely her and her vision—the stream by her house in the foreground was uncanny. She wasn't being narcissistic, or at least she didn't think so. Could she be seeing things?

Shaking the thought from her mind, she smiled at Gabe and said, "Could we swing by a pawn shop first?"

"Of course," Gabe said. "I know just the one. Follow me."

It was pouring, but Gabe lent Lucy the most beautiful umbrella. The inside looked like it was hand-painted in gold with notes of turquoise. The top was a turquoise gradient, and the handle looked to be made of pure gold. She felt like a wealthy Italian heiress carrying it. It was just like one she imagined in a book she loved and made her so happy. She almost forgot about the thunderstorm, but once they got to the car, she had to put the umbrella away. As she did, she realized the guests who claimed raincoats were better had a point. She got soaked anyway as she ungracefully slipped into her seat, but it was rare for Lucy to feel as fancy as she did with that umbrella. It's worth getting wet, she thought.

Gabe, once again in the navigator's seat, directed her through the neighborhood of the B&B and toward the pawn shop. He clearly knew the area like the back of his hand. The pawn shop looked ordinary enough. It was in a strip mall next to a nail salon, grocery store, hobby store, and a Mexican restaurant. When Gabe opened the door for Lucy, fear paralyzed her from stepping one foot into the store.

The fear was like what she felt as she was leaving Mississippi last night and glancing in the rearview mirror to see if they were being followed. If Colt yelled at her for letting Garfield out, what would he do if she pawned or sold her wedding ring? Leaving behind the symbol of her and Colt's love for one another wasn't just about the money. She was making a choice to leave him behind and move on.

"What are you doing out there? Come in, come in, why don't you? You're going to get all the merchandise wet," a small woman said as she approached Gabe and Lucy, ushering them inside.

She looked Lucy up and down. "You're here to pawn your wedding ring, am I right?"

"Well, I ... " Lucy stammered, having trouble finding the words.

"I'm right." The woman smirked. She grabbed Lucy's hand and pulled her quickly through the store toward the cash register. "I can always tell when a woman is thinking about parting with a promise. There's no mistaking it and no shame in it. No shame in it at all. You can be proud you made this decision."

Lucy touched her face, trying to feel the expression the peculiar-looking lady was talking about. She was a tiny old woman, about 4'10", with long white hair. She was wearing a green dress that looked like it was from a renaissance festival. Lucy tried to calm her nerves and was actually relieved that she didn't have to say anything to initiate the transaction.

The store breezed by as the woman pulled her through it, and she examined it as best she could along the way. The store itself was dimly lit and besides the "normal" items you'd expect to find in a pawn shop like TVs and jewelry, there were exotic trinkets and even a large, medieval knight's suit of armor. A musty smell wafted toward her from the old books in the rear of the store.

As they reached the counter, an enormous door opened in the back, and out came a tall man with thick white hair in a black-collared shirt and black pants. His face was long and stern as his eyes darted toward Lucy and the tiny woman. The man approached, and he revealed a surprising warmth, smiling and saying, "Welcome to the Last Chance Pawn Shop! Is Alice helping you?"

"Well...uh, she was just," said Lucy hesitantly, shifting her gaze toward Alice.

"I'm helping her, run along you're not needed here. This is a matter of a sensitive nature." She lifted Lucy's hand that she was still holding, tilting the ring in the man's direction.

"Okay then." The man nodded and then spotted Gabe behind them. "Gabe!" he exclaimed enthusiastically.

He sauntered toward him, and they hugged. Alice brought Lucy's attention back, and with shaking hands, Lucy asked, "How much do you think I could get for this?"

"Let me take a closer look. Can you take it off?"

Lucy didn't have to tug too hard. It had been on pretty much constantly for the last ten years, but the weight she lost recently had made it almost fall off.

Alice examined the ring carefully and went behind the counter to get one of those microscope things that jewelers have. "Do you want to pawn it or sell it?"

This made Lucy's head spin and her heart race. If she sold it, she feared Colt would ask her for the money when he found her. "Well, I'm not sure. What's the difference again?"

"Eh Gabe," Alice shouted across the shop, "she on a quest?"

Gabe nodded yes while shooting daggers with his eyes at Alice and made a "cut-it-out" motion across his neck. Her hand flew to her mouth, looking at Lucy like she'd told a child that Santa wasn't real. Regaining her composure quickly, she said, "I'd say pawn it, dear, just to be safe. I'll give you $750 for it now and then write you up a standard forty day contract."

"What did you mean by a quest?" Lucy inquired with her head tilted and brow furrowed in utter confusion.

"Sorry, I'll let him tell you about that bit. So do we have a deal? With the ring?" Alice said.

Lucy took a deep breath and tried to not let panic set in. "We have a deal." She was going to try putting one step in front of the other. Alice moved quickly and grabbed a contract out from under the desk. Lucy turned to ask Gabe about the quest, but he wasn't there. Alice had a quill and jar of ink—using it to fill in blanks on the contract.

She handed it to Lucy to read over the details. "It's all boilerplate. Basically, says that if you can give me $750 + ten percent in the next forty days, you can have your ring back. If you don't, I can sell it."

Lucy stared at the line where she was supposed to sign. Her palms began to sweat. All she could think about was how Colt would use this to hurt her or shame her if he ever found out.

Memories came flooding back of their wedding day, which was fraught with family drama. Colt's parents wanted her to have the ceremony at the church he grew up in, and she wanted to have it at the botanical gardens surrounded by orchids.

She did it their way in the end, but Colt had been angry—too angry— over the whole mess. When the minister asked, "Do you take Colt, to have and to hold for all the days of your lives?" she thought, "What if I say no right now?" She knew that wasn't the sort of thing she should be thinking right then, but she thought it nonetheless. Just as so many days after that, her thoughts and her words were diametrically opposite and instead of running away, she said, "With all my heart, yes." On the wedding day, despite that unhealthy thought, she still had hope for them and dreamed of their life together.

She looked down at the contract. Would this be a waste? How far could she really get on $750 anyway? Would she have to crawl back and ask Colt for forgiveness? Thinking back on what she had decided in the morning, she took it one step at a time. She needed the seed money to last her the next week and to decide her next move. She wiped her sweaty hands on her shirt and signed.

Alice then went to the cash register and handed Lucy the money.

Lucy put it in her purse and began looking for Gabe. She finally spotted him at the front, looking at a painting. When she came closer, she saw he wasn't looking at the painting as much as examining the easel it was sitting on. It had a small drawer that he was tugging on, but it appeared to be locked. He mustn't have heard her coming because he startled a little when she approached and asked, "Ready to go?"

"Um ... I think I'm going to see if I can get this easel. It doesn't have a price."

The man with the white hair came over and let Gabe know he wasn't really selling it, but Gabe sweet-talked him into selling it to him for forty dollars. Before he walked to the cash register, he turned to Lucy. "I've been wanting a new easel. I was going to order one online, but something drew me to this old one. You mind? I figured since we're going to the studio anyway ... "

"Yeah, sure," Lucy replied, though she was eager to get out of there. She kept thinking about what Alice had said about her being on a quest. The transaction didn't take long and as they exited, the rain had stopped and the skies had cleared. Lucy cranked the car, placed her hands on the steering wheel, and stared at them. Her fingers were naked for the first time in years. As the tears welled up inside her again—heart pounding with fear and excitement, she replayed everything that happened in the shop. She turned to Gabe. "So, what's this quest all about?"

"Let's talk about it in the studio."

4

The Studio

As Gabe directed her back to Aunt Rae's, Lucy started to spin. *What the FUCK am I doing? I've let this man hitchhike a ride, drive my car, and now he's directing me to his studio to tell me about some "quest."*

It occurred to Lucy that she may not even be anywhere near Nashville. He'd driven and encouraged her to sleep. If this was a horror movie, this is the point in the story where she'd be yelling at the screen: "Leave, get out—what are you doing? He's a stranger!"

She wasn't even sure why she let him do it, but his presence soothed her more than anything had in a very long time. Taking a deep breath in, she attempted to quiet her inner critic as much as possible. Right after this excursion, she decided that she really needed to call someone and let them know she was okay.

"It's right there," Gabe said with a big grin as he pointed at a small shack. "See the one with purple shutters and a green roof?"

Tucked away on a short gravel road, the little cottage was adorable. A small front porch with rocking chairs and two flower boxes with pansies on the outside gave it a southern artsy vibe.

"Oh, it's so cute, Gabe. Do you share the space or is it all yours?" Lucy asked.

"Right now it's just me."

When she parked and stepped out, a cool breeze brought with it a sense of calm. It enveloped her, melting her anxieties. She followed Gabe onto the front porch as he opened a screen door, unlocked the main door, and held it open for her to enter.

To say that she was awestruck was an understatement. A feeling of love—love for life, love for herself—a love both foreign and familiar overcame Lucy.

The space was so much larger than it appeared on the outside, as if she was stepping into Dr. Who's Tardis. In the first large room, there must have been hundreds, if not thousands, of paintings and sculptures. She wandered, awestruck. She turned a corner and her feet were on soil. The area was like a small exhibit at a botanical conservatory, with no rope to guard it and no larger than her kitchen. She stood in the beautiful garden with flowers alongside vegetables and some chickens in a coop. As she looked down at one cute baby chick, a dozen or more butterflies tickled her, landing all over her body. She closed her eyes and raised her arms slowly. She smiled and twirled, surrounded by art and nature all at once.

She took it all in and somehow, in this space, she felt more like herself than she had in years. She wept. There had been so many times in this crazy journey where she fought back tears, but the waterworks were turned on as she succumbed to the wonder all around her. After a few moments, she turned to Gabe and gasped, "What is this place?"

"It's all of your visions for yourself, your life, that you once had that you've lost." Somehow, his voice was matter-of-fact and whimsical all at once.

"My life? But I just met you yesterday. How is this your studio? Who are you really? What are you?" Lucy asked, mesmerized and confused as Gabe glanced at his feet nervously.

"You're...sort of, well, my muse. You see, I'm what's called a Vision

Catcher. We're charged to protect people's dreams, hopes, and visions for their lives. All Vision Catchers work in different ways, but my gift comes out in art. I've caught all of your dreams and made this for you." He gestured all around, grinning from ear to ear.

"Are you an angel?" Lucy thought back to the Bible verse that had drawn her to him last night.

"Not quite. You can think of me as a guardian of your dreams." He breezed across the room and landed in front of a painting, gazing at it serenely. Pointing to it, he said, "I painted this painting of you as a superhero, because that's what you wanted to be when you were five. There's a small library over there with ideas for stories you haven't written. I planted this garden because for a while in college you talked about how you wanted to grow your own food, surrounded by flowers and butterflies."

"I forgot about that!" Tears still streamed down her face.

"I know. That's why I brought you here. To remind you of all the dreams, hopes, and visions you once had for your life. I went to look for you in Mississippi because honestly, I was bored."

"Bored?" She laughed a little through her sniffles and tears.

"Yes. When you stop having visions for your life or new, exciting ideas, I have nothing new to create. I can come up with my own ideas, I guess, but right now I'm tasked with following you."

"Come," he said, gesturing toward a long table. "Look at this. Do you recognize these?" He handed her a handkerchief as she made her way beside him.

She looked at a series of pictures of herself and Colt with their imaginary future kids. They were pushing them on the swings. A boy and a girl. The boy had curly brown hair and bright blue eyes. The girl's pigtails swayed in the breeze. Their shirts displayed their names. Joshua and Madeline. The memory of picking their names out flooded back.

Lying naked in bed with Colt, relaxing in his arms. They were still dating. Things were still so fresh. Possibilities of their future together were starting to emerge. She asked him if he wanted kids. He said he wanted two, a boy and a girl. Before asking if she wanted them too, he asked what she'd want to name them. She was still unsure. She took his dream in and let it swirl in her mind. Let it take hold of her as she searched for an answer to his question. She settled on Joshua, after her grandfather, and Madeline, after Madeline Albright, the first female Secretary of State. Lucy admired her for her formidable presence. If she had a daughter, she wanted her to be strong.

She moved on to other joyous visions. There was one of Colt and Lucy playing Scrabble with her friends. A half-full bottle of wine sat on the table with brie and croissants. They were laughing, smiling, joyous. This is how she envisioned their life during the honeymoon.

Then Colt's mom died, and he retreated into a dark place. She'd caught brief glimpses of this darkness when they were engaged after slight setbacks, like getting in trouble at the middle school where he was teaching. He'd be miserable for a few days and short with her. It's why she hesitated at the altar. The honeymoon was over years ago. Lucy would never forget the day Colt first cussed at her and made her feel so small.

The last picture in the series was one of Lucy at their house making dinner with her bookkeeping work on the table. Gabe had captured her despair and misery in a way that she knew intimately. Painted in dark tones, it seemed hopeless. "This one, this one never left me," Lucy said, "so I don't know how you caught it."

"Yes, it did. I painted it this morning while you were sleeping. I don't normally paint these dark ones, but I knew I was taking you here today. I needed you to see how different this was from the light you're capable of bringing to the world."

Lucy looked back at the painting and then up at the dreams. She wanted to erase time, to go back. Her eyes shifted back up to Gabe.

"Is this a multiverse situation? Can you take me to different timelines? Ones where I didn't marry Colt or pursued another path?"

"No, it doesn't work like that. You have free will. There's only this timeline. As C.S. Lewis once said, 'You can't go back and change the beginning, but you can start where you are and change the ending.' I sought you out to invite you on a vision quest. That's what Alice was talking about."

"I'm going to ask again, what's a vision quest?" She was as stern as she could be, hoping that he wouldn't evade her question again.

"It's a journey that you travel to find your true passion for life, or at least start heading that direction. We often invite people who aren't living out their dreams or in your case, have stopped hoping all together." Gabe looked at her with sympathy and sadness. "What I'm asking you to do is to decide to walk toward one of your dreams. One of the many things that you've imagined yourself doing in your life, before Colt."

"How would I know which one to choose? I wouldn't know where to start," Lucy remarked as she perused the large room of paintings and sculptures. She saw one of her at a desk writing. One in a classroom learning from what appeared to be Albert Einstein. There was an abstract sculpture of no person, but a microphone, a stool, and a guitar that seemed to float in mid-air. A fantasy of being a singer-songwriter without having to perform, perhaps?

"Look, just start somewhere. You've been drowning and miserable. I'm allowed to reveal myself to you and guide you, but only for a short time. The quest, should you choose to accept the invite, is forty days."

Lucy thought back to breakfast. "So, when Gerald said he was on day twenty this morning, he was talking about a quest? Are they all on quests?"

"Yes," Gabe answered and smiled softly.

"How much does it cost?"

Gabe smiled and shook his head. "If you accept the invitation, we won't charge you anything. You can stay in The Tower while you find your way."

"Free!" She was dumbfounded. "Wait, you knew that and you let me pawn my ring anyway? Is this a scam? Did Alice even give me real money?" she asked and started digging through her purse for her wallet.

"Really Lucy? You think I'd create all of this just so I could steal your wedding ring? I know in my bones that you're ready for this." He moved closer to her and grabbed her shoulders and attempted to urge her onward. "Our visions for ourselves and what we want can be achieved as long as we hold on to them. You've let these go, and I want you to take as many back as you want."

Lucy pondered this and wanted so badly to give into this idea of a quest. "What happens after forty days? How will I survive after that? Will you still be my Vision Catcher?"

He hesitated. "I can't tell you that now. There are many factors. It's best if you just take this one step at a time."

One step at a time. That's exactly what she set out to do this morning. She looked at him. He was giving her puppy dog eyes. She sensed he needed this as much as she did. The whole thing was just too good to be true. "I'm not sure. How soon do I have to decide?"

"Within the next twenty-four hours. So, this time tomorrow, but you'd be doing me a solid if you could decide sooner."

"Alright, I'll try. Can I make a phone call first?"

"Yes, but you only get one." Gabe looked dead serious.

"Wait, seriously?" Lucy asked, eyes wide.

Gabe paused, then fell apart laughing. "No silly, we aren't trying to lock you up. We want to set you free."

Gabe's phone buzzed. He looked down at it briefly and then said,

"You think you can find your way back? I just want to do a couple of things here, but you can go on and make those phone calls."

Lucy looked out the window and could see the main house. "I think so, yes."

"I'll come check on you in an hour or so."

She did a 360, looking at all the visions and dreams Gabe had so beautifully captured. A pain that had blocked her from hoping for more from her life—more than Colt—began to melt away. There were now figurative butterflies in her stomach to accompany the few that had stayed on her head. She opened the door and stepped out onto the porch. The weight of the next step bore down, but she'd gone through a catharsis.

Gabe watched Lucy leave, making sure that she found her way, then turned back to his phone and pulled up the text he'd just received. "Congratulations, Gabe, on making it this far in guiding an Originator on a vision quest. Please watch the orientation video link below as soon as possible."

He placed his phone on his new easel, pulled up a comfy chair, and tapped the link.

The crest of the Vision Catchers Guild (VCG) spun in an animation accompanied by orchestral music. Then, the screen cut to Vance Gunderthorpe, the chair of the guild, sitting before a simple dark green backdrop in front of a formidable mahogany desk. He leaned in with his hands clasped in front of him.

Speaking in a friendly but serious tone, he said, "Hello, the Vision Catchers Guild is so excited about your quest. Because this is your first quest, you are receiving this video to remind you of the rules and point you to tips to help your Originator find their way."

Even though his tone was encouraging, Gabe's palms sweat as if he was a child about to get a talking to from Aunt Rae. Gunderthorpe's voice became firmer as he continued to list off rules. "You must invite your Originator within the first twenty-four hours of revealing yourself."

Gabe puffed his chest with pride. "Just did that, check," he said aloud to the empty room.

Gunderthorpe continued, "If your Originator declines the quest or leaves early, their connection to you will sever. Over time, their memories of you and the quest will fade, just as unclaimed visions fade from the mind. Their visions will drift—some may dissolve, while others may find a new Originator who is ready to act. You may not force them back onto the path, nor will you be reassigned to them."

Gabe's stomach tightened. He'd heard this rule before too, but hearing it again made him feel the pressure of his mission. He'd been following Lucy for years and losing connection with her would devastate him, though he always knew that was a possibility.

"You may not influence them to stay through promises, bribes, or coercion. The decision to complete the quest must be entirely their own. Be prepared to catch more visions and hopes. Quests are often a time of immense stimulation for Originators. Some will have trouble keeping up with all their ideas. Your job is to help them sort through what matters most."

Gabe smiled at this last one, hoping that Lucy would have more ideas than she could keep up with.

"If you encounter challenges along the way, contact your guild representative. Use the VC app to reach your assigned representative for guidance and troubleshooting."

The screen split. On one side was Gunderthorpe's face and on the other a mock-up of the VC app, highlighting the "Guild Support" button.

"We have compiled tips from some of the most successful leaders in our community, which you can locate in the app. Be sure to heed their recommendations, but also know that every quest is different and requires your unique perspective. Good luck, and may their wildest dreams come true."

The video ended, and the screen faded to black. He closed his eyes for a moment and drew in a deep breath. Learning the rules in school was one thing, but as the day of the quest approached, his nerves were getting to him. The app wasn't a thing when he began following Lucy.

Gabe received the link to the app immediately following the video. He explored the VC app to continue his preparations. He clicked on the tips and advice section. A playlist of videos was available as well as quotes like, "Be an enthusiastic cheerleader, a confidant, a sounding board, and give them space to make mistakes." He clicked on one entitled "Digging Out Their Passion," which featured Scarlett Kona, a Vision Catcher known for her directness and humor.

"Some people are absolute douchebags. No ifs, ands, or buts about it. But most people are pretty okay, and if you're getting frustrated with your Originator's personality or the choices they make, trust me, you're normal. Remember, those chosen and assigned by the guild as 'quest-worthy' have something deep inside worth offering to the world. If they can't see it in themselves, it's your job to dig it out. Most people have no clue what they want. Try to expose them to as many dreams and hopes as they've had in their life and pay attention when you see a fire in their eye. Simply saying, 'it looked like you were having the time of your life doing that' or 'you were on fire' puts them in a position of confidence, and they're more likely to succeed. Stay positive and keep dreamin'."

Gabe thought back to Gerald, the Originator at breakfast this morning, who had treated him like a waiter. This video was made for guys like that, not Lucy. He couldn't imagine getting frustrated with her at all—not after everything she'd been through with Colt. Looking around the studio in reflection, he knew her soul was just too beautiful.

The app sucked him in. After watching several more videos and exploring the app features, an uncomfortable tingling sensation hit him. His pair-bond with Lucy intensified in this close proximity— stronger than ever before. He'd only monitored her from a distance until now. She was clearly in distress. He needed to check on her.

5

The Phone Call and The Closet

Lucy was quiet as she returned to The Tower, still in shock by everything Gabe had just told her. Realizing how far she'd drifted made her sad. She was so far removed from the person who she'd been before she met Colt—a person with dreams. Now she was just an empty vessel, going day to day without hope. The little aspiration she had of coming back to herself emerged when she picked Gabe up last night.

Dreams deferred were now going to be forced into fruition at warp speed as part of the quest if she accepted the invitation. Part of her wondered if instead of pursuing them they'd let her just lie in bed forty days. Right now, that was all she wanted to do. She didn't want to face Colt, but she didn't want to face herself either.

She glanced over at the nightstand and the sunlight from the skylight struck the quote from *Alice in Wonderland*. It hit even closer to home today than it did last night. "I knew who I was this morning, but I've changed a few times since then." Right next to her keychain sat her phone. While she thought she could lie there for hours, she forced herself to grab it to call Anna.

Her stomach dropped as she turned it on for the first time in almost twenty-four hours. To her surprise and delight, she had no service.

Next step: jot down Anna's number, turn her phone off, and find a landline to call her. She drew in a deep breath before locking the door behind her, pushing aside the worry that even turning on her phone for a minute could've given Colt a trace. She headed downstairs toward the kitchen, where she thought she'd spotted a phone. When she reached the bottom of the stairs, she bumped into Daisy.

Daisy was wearing a fifties style polka-dotted dress and looked like she was ready to hit the town. "Hey there!" she said to Lucy with enthusiasm.

"Let me guess, does your quest involve a dream of being a swing dancer?" Lucy asked, captivated by the whole process.

Daisy smiled. "Not quite. I fantasized myself as a classy comic like the Marvelous Mrs. Maisel. There's an open mic tonight at The Laughery. I'm going to try my hand at it." Daisy's excitement oozed out of every pore. She was pure energy. Her chutzpah impressed Lucy.

"Wow! It takes guts to get in front of people and throw yourself on the mercy of strangers. How long did it take you to write the jokes?" Lucy thought back to the journals Gabe had pointed to earlier with all of her forgotten writings.

"Oh, that's the best part! Randy, my VC, snagged me this dress and gave me jokes that I totally forgot I'd thought of ... isn't this quest fabulous?" Daisy said, as she twirled from side to side in her FABulous dress.

"Well, I haven't quite started, but I'm sure it will be ... something. VC, is that short for Vision Catcher?" Lucy asked, curious to know if this was a term they used or just one that Daisy made up.

"Abso-tute-te-lutely!" Daisy replied with a wink. Lucy couldn't help but smile, but then remembered the task at hand as Daisy was turning to leave.

"Do you know if there's a phone around here? I need to make a call," Lucy asked, pointing toward the kitchen.

"Yeah, there's one in the kitchen, but I don't know if it works on calls to the outside. Here, use mine. Randy made it so I could make calls from here." She fished a cell out of a shiny red purse and held it out for Lucy to grab. "You won't be long, will you? The passcode is 1433, but here I'll unlock it." Daisy pressed the code into the phone and placed it forcefully into Lucy's hand. "I have to get ready for my set and really don't need the distraction anyway. Also, now you have to come to support me so you can give it back!"

"Um ... no, I mean ... I won't be long, but I don't know about the open mic."

"Oh ... please, please. Us girls got to stick together," begged Daisy. Lucy stood unmoving. Before she could respond, Daisy embraced Lucy and said, "You're a doll." Then she ran out the door.

Lucy looked down at the phone. Tornado Daisy knocked her off of her center. She'd breezed by before Lucy even had time to ask what she meant about Randy setting up her phone to work here. Here as in the B&B ... or was this place something else entirely? It was starting to feel like it.

She went back to The Tower and dialed Anna's number. The phone rang and Lucy worried she wouldn't pick up because it was a strange number. To her delight, Anna answered on the second ring.

"Hello?"

"Hi Anna, it's Lucy."

"Lucy, whose phone is this?"

"A friend's. Listen, I just wanted you to know that I'm safe and okay."

"Wait ... does this mean that you ... no ... you finally left that sorry ass?"

"Yep, I did. Last night and it has been, well, a little nuts."

"Nuts how?"

Lucy debated whether to tell her that she picked up a hitchhiker that also turned out to store all of her hopes and dreams away for her. But that would really sound like the opposite of safe and okay. Anna might think she'd joined some sort of cult. Instead, she said, "I pawned my wedding ring."

"What, really? That's great. I'm proud of you Luce."

"Do you think I should call Colt? Just to let him know I'm okay? I don't want him to file a police report."

"Just from your voice, you sound like you're in an okay headspace Luce. I don't want him to take that from you, but maybe … let me think." There was a brief pause on the line and then Anna exclaimed, "I know, YOU should call the cops!"

"Wait. What?" Lucy took a beat and before Anna could answer, Lucy recognized what Anna was getting at. "Ohhh … Wow, that's kind of genius. He's probably going to go file a missing person's report. If I call first and he comes in, they will have the answer."

Anna replied, "Exactly."

"Okay, I'll do it. Thanks so much Anna."

"Love you chica. Take care of yourself and come here if you need anything."

Lucy loved the idea of continuing to not deal with reality, though she supposed she should call her job too. Then again, she didn't really have a set schedule with them. She just came in one day a week to do the books and it could be any day she wanted. Plus, she hadn't decided. She'd maybe call them tomorrow.

She went old school and dialed 4-1-1 to reach the police. They could connect her directly to the Booneville police and then probably Daisy's number wouldn't show up on their caller ID. She was feeling pretty stealthy as the operator connected her. It rang once.

"Booneville Police Department, how can I help you?" The woman on the other end of the phone sounded like she'd been drinking coffee and smoking cigarettes for decades. She'd probably seen a thing or two, which hopefully leaned in Lucy's favor to help her with her current situation.

"Hi, um, my name is Lucy Rivers and my husband is Colt Rivers."

The woman interrupted. "Oh yeah, your husband was just here. He reported a stolen car," the woman said.

"Oh ... " Lucy should've expected he'd report the car stolen rather than her missing. She took a beat and continued, "Yes, um, well, you see, I took the car. I left him last night. My husband, he's not the nicest to me and I just couldn't go back to the house. I'm safe where I am, though, and not missing."

"But you have his car?" the woman asked.

"We have two cars. I have the one that I drive all the time. It's just in his name. I'm insured to drive it."

"Well, seems like this is a domestic matter and you may have a valid reason for taking the car. The DA may not prosecute since you're protecting yourself from harm, plus the fact that you drive it the majority of the time. I'd suggest you return it, though, since the report has already been filed."

"Prosecute? Isn't this joint property?" Lucy asked, feeling her blood rush to her head.

"In Mississippi, with a car, if it's titled solely in the husband's name, it may be considered his separate property, even if it was acquired during your marriage," the woman explained matter-of-factly with a tone of slight sympathy.

Lucy's heart sank. She was going to have to go back to Mississippi. She was going to have to face Colt because she "stole" his car. He'd basically made the choice for her about whether or not to go on this crazy adventure.

She'd wanted to get the car in her name, but Colt wouldn't let her. He said it was mostly his money, it should be in his name. It was just one more way for him to hold on to her.

Lucy stared out the window and said nothing. From this angle, she could see the gravel road that led to the studio. The emptiness inside started to overcome her again.

"Hello, ma'am, are you still there? Did you hear me?" the woman said, sounding a little annoyed.

"Yes. Um ... I'm here. I'll return the car," Lucy said begrudgingly.

"Okay, I'll let them know. And hey, even if you don't have a car, no one is forcing you to stay with him. I had a situation like yours years ago. It took a while, but I made it out. Hang in there," the woman said encouragingly, but Lucy still felt defeated.

"Okay. Thank you," Lucy said.

"Sure thing, sugar. Let us know if you need anything."

"I will, bye."

"Bye."

Lucy stood still, staring off into space. She didn't want to return the car. This wasn't the first time she'd attempted to leave Colt, but this was the furthest she'd ever gotten.

She'd left the house angry before and had felt like she had nowhere to go. Her mother and father lived in Oregon. She didn't have the money for a plane ticket and couldn't pay for enough gas to get there. It was at least a six hour drive away to get to Anna in Georgia. She hadn't really made any close friends in Mississippi.

So, even when she left, she'd just get space for an hour or two. She'd always come back with her head down into the house and apologize for whatever she'd done to set Colt off because she felt like she had nowhere to turn. One time she'd even hid in the neighbor's yard for a couple hours, just inside their potting shed. She hadn't even taken the car. She could hear Colt running up and down the street, screaming her name. It was like an angry game of hide-and-seek. Still, she returned, not knowing what else to do.

This time had felt different. Or at least it did until she told the woman at the police department that she'd return the car. The sinking feeling returned, and she cried in despair.

Amid her sobs, the image of her as a superhero swept into her mind. She dried her eyes and her mood shifted to determination. It didn't have to be the same this time. She had some sort of magic on her side through Gabe. He'd offered her a way out and she couldn't let this one go.

She looked down at the phone in her hand and, remembering that it wasn't hers, contemplated her next move. Returning the phone to her new friend and having some laughs didn't seem like a bad idea at all. She'd worry about the car in the morning.

Immediately after making that decision, someone knocked on the door. She heard Gabe's voice from the other side. "Hi, Lucy, just checking to see if you need anything."

Lucy looked in the mirror to make sure her face didn't look like she'd been crying. It did, but she opened the door anyway.

Gabe's presence was soothing. He repeated his question. "Do you need anything?"

Lucy thought for a moment, and then said, "Can you give me anything prettier to wear? I want to go see Daisy's set, but I want to look at least half as fabulous as she does right now."

"Oh, you need The Closet. Come with me."

Lucy followed Gabe into a library that was off of the dining room. She looked at all the books and wondered if these were people's lost visions. "What's The Closet? Is this it?" Lucy asked, perplexed.

"Does this look like a closet?" he asked rhetorically.

"Did I hear someone mention The Closet?" Rae's voice shouted from the other room.

"Yes, Aunt Rae. In here. Lucy needs an outfit to watch Daisy's comedy performance tonight."

"Oh, goodie!" she exclaimed as she joined them. "I love makeovers."

She looked at Lucy from head to toe, rubbing her chin, and asked, "What's your style?"

"I thought the outfit Daisy was wearing earlier was really cute," Lucy replied.

"Yeah, but what's YOUR style?" she challenged her.

"I don't know if I have one. I mean, jeans and a T-shirt now, but I'd love to have something nicer for the show tonight."

Rae smiled at Lucy and then turned to Gabe. "Let's show Lucy some outfits and have her tell us which one sparks joy."

"But Aunt Rae, I think I know."

"Oh come on Gabe, it'll be fun. You know what, I'll do it." She looked at Lucy and motioned for her to come closer.

"Um ... okay." Lucy moved toward Rae with a furrowed brow, simultaneously turning to Gabe and whispering, "What's going on?"

"It's okay, Rae's just going to show you some outfits." Gabe nodded at Lucy, urging her to continue.

"Are they in these books?" Lucy asked.

"No, they're up here," Rae said, pointing to her head. "This is a little out there, but just trust me."

Lucy nodded.

"Take my hands and close your eyes." Rae closed her eyes and held out both of her hands. Lucy did as she said, placing her hands on top of Rae's.

"Take a deep breath in," Rae whispered, "and let it all out."

Nothing happened for about fifteen seconds, and then Lucy was transported to a fashion show. One by one, models came strutting down the runway.

Rae spoke softly over the show, "Remember, which one of these sparks joy? Which one is you?"

The first model looked like a business woman with flair. She wore a black pantsuit with a hot-pink cropped blazer, wide-legged trousers, and high-heeled boots. The next model wore big round sunglasses, a printed jumpsuit with a plunging neckline, paired with strappy sandals. More woman in fashionable outfits strutted toward Lucy as she stood in amazement at the end of the runway. The parade of possibilities seemed endless from a flowy, pastel-colored dress with delicate floral embroidery and a cinched waist, paired with brown heels to haute couture looks, with one woman's aqua dress even having feather wings attached.

After several minutes, she saw an outfit that felt like home. It sparked something inside her. Could it be joy? The model wore a bohemian-inspired jumpsuit made of a lightweight linen material. The jumpsuit featured a wide-legged silhouette cinched at the waist with a braided leather belt.

"That one!" Lucy said as the model approached.

"Okay great. Open your eyes," Rae instructed.

Lucy opened her eyes and Rae grinned as she slowly let go of her hands. Rae walked over to the bookcase, pushed on it, and a secret door opened.

"The hippie boho closet it is!" she said enthusiastically, beckoning Lucy through the doorway.

Gabe pulled Rae aside. "I could've told you that."

"Oh, but this way was so much more fun! Sometimes you have to let them come to the answer themselves. And you never know, she could've surprised you." He didn't think so, but he tried to relax. It didn't take long as he watched her take in the sights with childlike wonder—transfixed by the racks of clothes.

Lucy dove into a sea of palazzo pants, wide leg cargo pants with deep pockets, soft v-neck tops with slightly frayed edges, and colorful flowy dresses. Even the jewelry section was all bohemian—bangles and beaded bracelets, some colorful and some more understated. It reminded her of some vintage boutiques in Asheville, but she could rarely afford more than one item, if any, in those stores.

"Can I borrow anything?"

"You can have anything. It's all yours and if you think of something else you'd like, let me know and I'll see what I can dig up," Rae replied.

"Wow!" Lucy was still drawn to the first outfit that sparked joy from the runway. It was on a mannequin near the entrance. She approached slowly. She looked back to Rae and Gabe and timidly asked, "Can I have that one?"

Rae replied with warmth and enthusiasm, "Why, of course you can! You hop into that dressing room in the back and I'll bring it to you."

Gabe hung back and just watched as Rae fussed over Lucy. Lucy headed for the dressing room, and soon after Rae had brought the jumpsuit. Lucy thanked her and closed the door. She'd felt self-conscious about her ratty jeans and T-shirt all day. Replacing them with the satin lined jumpsuit was exhilarating. It fit her perfectly. She fastened the belt and swayed side to side as she gazed at herself in the mirror. She closed her eyes and breathed in the moment.

Lucy knew why this style had sparked so much joy. It was the kind of thing her mom would wear. Growing up, she never thought she could pull it off like her mom could. She was a happy person and would spin around in the kitchen dancing in long, flowy, tiered skirts and dresses, all embroidered or having fringes with various sandals and ankle boots with lots of accessories. Her favorites of her mother's accessories were her feather earrings and bangles. As far as Lucy was concerned, her mother was the essence of fashion.

As she continued to examine herself in the mirror, she thought it needed something. She remembered the white feather earrings and this bracelet layered with turquoise and silver beads and had a small silver charm with a lotus on it that her mom wore. There was a knock on the door and Rae was standing there holding out jewelry very similar to the ones she'd imagined as well as a pair of knee-highs, ankle boots, and a long wool coat.

"It's a little cold out there. Forgive me for being a mother hen."

Lucy took the items from her, thrilled with the final look. She perused the closet a little further and grabbed some makeup and a couple of maxi dresses—one that reminded her of her mom's. "Thank you Rae. This is fabulous and feels like me."

"I can tell." Rae smiled.

She turned to Gabe. "Well, what do you think?"

"I think you're coming back to you," he replied, smiling softly.

Lucy felt tears prickle again. "Yeah, I guess I'm and I've only been away for twenty-four hours."

Gabe was both pleased and worried. She'd forgotten about the car. Picking out the outfit had been the perfect distraction. He tried to calm his nerves and hoped he could steer her toward the next right action. He looked at Rae and silently sent her thoughts.

"Aunt Rae, I'm worried. What am I going to do about Lucy? I think she's going to try to go back to Booneville. When she was trying on the dress, I caught a vision of her driving back and returning her car to the police station for some reason. I'm still trying to capture the whole idea. What am I supposed to do to get her to agree to this quest?"

She sent back words of comfort. "I caught that too. I can't give you all the answers, but I can tell you, the main thing you want to make Lucy feel is safe. Colt has torn her down so much. The safer you make her feel, the easier it will be to keep her on her timeline. I'm always here for you. Now, you just got to be here for Lucy."

Gabe looked back at Lucy, who was enthusiastically going through the purses. After trying several on, she picked a bamboo bag with a brown strap.

"Ohh ... makeup!" Lucy exclaimed as she headed over to a counter where Rae had pulled out just the right stuff to paint her face. "Can I go put this on in The Tower?"

"Of course," he replied.

Lucy could get used to this. Clothes that were "her." For free.

"Thanks so much, both of you." Lucy impulsively gave Rae a giant hug. Rae held on the way people do when they know you need extra support. The lingering comforted and relaxed her. Lucy felt at peace.

As they left the closet, she watched the secret door shut behind them. Only the bookcase remained.

"Okay. So, I guess we're going out?" Gabe asked.

"Of course." Lucy looked Gabe up and down. He looked like an artist. His shirt and jeans had paint splatters. Even though that was probably Gabe's style and she imagined The Laughery didn't have a dress code, she still asked, "Is that what you're wearing?"

Gabe laughed. "I'll change." He glanced at his phone. "We probably have some time. It's six. Have you eaten?"

"No." In all the excitement, she'd forgotten to eat. How was it already dinner time?

"Well, I'm sure Rae can whip something up for you. I'll go get changed and do a couple of other things while you get your face on and have some dinner. Meet back in an hour?"

"Sure," Lucy replied.

On the way back up to The Tower, her excitement calmed. When she pulled out the keys to unlock the door, her car keys dangled from side to side like a ticking clock. She'd attached them to The Tower keychain before she'd even called the police.

Her mind split in two and she froze. Torn between anxious realities and uplifting fantasies. Her eyes moved as the light twinkled on her new bracelet. She smiled and attempted to absorb the joy from it and her new outfit. She entered her room with a hopeful heart that was also scared by a past that just would not let go.

Gabe watched her leave and could sense her anxieties and worries returning to her. He could feel her slipping away and had to make a plan. Hopefully, his rep could help.

6

The Comedy Show

When Gabe got to his room, he got dressed quickly. He knew he needed to meet Lucy, but he couldn't resist checking in with his rep to see about a car, as Rae had suggested. From the app's home screen he clicked on "Contact your Rep." The options displayed: Video Call, Text, Leave a Voice Memo. Since he was in a hurry, he did a quick video call. It only rang once.

"Hey friend, I'm Ravi, your VC Rep. How can I help you?" The man was brown-skinned and had a mustache and a thick Australian accent. His giant smile made Gabe feel at ease.

"My Aunt Rae suggested I reach out. I need a car. Can you help me get one?"

"For a short trip or longer?"

"Longer."

"Of course, is that all? Your face read of such desperation I thought you needed much more."

Gabe was growing more confident and was excited about this white glove service. "Can you deliver it wherever and whenever I need it?"

"You'll need to pick it up from the Questing Car Lot and sign some paperwork. But, no worries, they're open 24/7. Let me just pull up your file. This is to help Lucy on her quest, I take it?"

"That's right. I think this will help us get her where she needs to go," Gabe replied.

"Well, I'll send you a message on the app with all the details. Looking at the file, I see this is your first quest. How are you doing with everything?" Ravi seemed genuine. Gabe felt he could be honest with him.

"Honestly, Ravi, I'm scared," Gabe said, letting himself be vulnerable, "but you just helping me with this is of great comfort to me. Thank you."

"I'm here for you if you need anything," Ravi said warmly. "Is there anything else you need right now?"

Gabe contemplated whether to use Ravi as a sounding board for all of his anxieties about the quest, but he needed to get going to make it to the show. He let Ravi know he was all set, confirmed he'd received the details about the car, closed the app, and headed for the door. Now, for the first time, he felt completely ready to guide her because he knew he had all the support he needed.

Lucy was trying to enjoy the window seat near the foyer that looked out to the circular driveway in front of the building. She was becoming increasingly impatient with Gabe. All dressed up with somewhere to go, but no idea how to get there. She'd hurried when she'd put on her makeup, thinking she'd be late after dinner. It turns out she didn't need to because Gabe was fifteen minutes late.

Within the first five minutes of waiting for him, she tried to summon him. She imagined him waiting for her when she came downstairs and then tried to forget it. Her thought was that he was supposed to catch lost visions. But the more she tried to forget about the thought of him actually being on time, the more it stuck.

Giving up, she tried to be patient and take in the sights. A framed saying hanging on the wall caught her eye: "Catch the Vision. Empower the People. Create Lasting Change." She liked the rhythm of it. She browsed the artwork and read the titles of the books on the bookshelves, but after several minutes of meandering around, she'd found this very comfortable seat.

She fetched Daisy's phone from her purse, thinking she could pass the time catching up on the news, but she couldn't remember the code. A forgotten magazine was sitting on the windowsill, so she picked it up to see if it could soothe her anxious desire to get to the club. It was called *Vision Catchers Quarterly*—dated three years ago but with a familiar face on the cover.

Rae stood in a stunning gown, posed with her hands on her hips in the foyer of the B&B. There were big letters next to her face - Rae Allard. In smaller letters, just under her name, were the words "Host Extraordinaire." The full-body shot framed Rae's body on the right of the page and on the left were headlines with subtitles.

- Vision Quests Enter the 21st Century—a new app, soon to undergo beta testing, promises to increase quest success rates
- Do Your Research—How studying successful relationships between Originators and Vision Catchers of the past can help us today
- Feranchin's Energy—Expanding our thinking about our origins
- After the COVID Crisis—How the Vision Catcher Community banded together to assist Originators in responding to the COVID Crisis
- The Black Market of Visions—An inside look at the seedy underbelly of stolen dreams and the forces trying to stop it

Lucy stared with excitement at the cover. She opened the magazine to the editor's note and hadn't gotten past the first few words before an out-of-breath Gabe ran into the room and interrupted her.

Doubled over with his hands on his knees, he struggled to say, "Hey, sorry I'm late, I … "

Lucy sat up from her reclined position and said, "It's okay. Catch your breath."

He took some labored breaths and then sat next to Lucy on the window seat. He looked down at the magazine in her hands. "What's that?"

She held the cover up, and Gabe's eyes grew wide.

"Oh, you aren't supposed to have that, I'm afraid. Give it to me."

"But I wanted to read it. Someone just left it here."

"Well, that was careless. Originators aren't supposed to dive that deep into our world. We need to focus on you. Besides, we're running late. No time to read, even if I could let you," Gabe said, reaching for the magazine.

Lucy pulled it close to her chest and replied, "Whose fault is that?"

"I know. I was trying to get a car, but they wouldn't check one out to me until the first day of your quest. Plus, I have to wait until you decide. I ran here, if you couldn't tell."

"I'm not blind," Lucy said. She had a sense of where this conversation was going and dreaded it a little.

"Can you drive?" Gabe asked in an almost apologetic tone.

Did he know what Colt had done? Known that she wanted to return the "stolen" car? Lucy hesitated. Surely they wouldn't be scanning license plates in Tennessee for a car that was just reported stolen in Mississippi, but her anxious brain worried anyway.

"Okay. Sure," she said with trepidation. Lucy loosened her grip on the magazine just enough for Gabe to pull it away from her and put it away.

In around ten minutes, they arrived at a small building with "The Laughery" in red neon lights over the door. "Barracuda" was blasting when they entered. It was a small dive bar. The walls scattered with signed posters of comedians who performed there in the past and a bulletin board scattered with flyers announcing upcoming acts. In the corner, there was a small stage with a wooden floor, a stool, and a simple corded microphone. Lucy felt her heart speed up just a hair, imagining herself going up there—sympathy, anxiety for Daisy.

There were maybe fifteen people scattered around the room's tattered bar stools and square tables.

Lucy leaned over to Gabe, shouting over the music into his ear, "Are we super early?"

He shouted back, "No, the show should start in five minutes. Open mics aren't super popular. Have you ever been to one where you didn't know the person performing?"

"Fair point."

Then, as if on cue, ten more people came in and the place looked decently full. Gabe said, "Well there you go. I guess someone has a lot of friends or a big family."

Lucy wasn't sure which would be worse, performing comedy for the first time in front of three people not laughing or in front of thirty also not laughing. Gabe headed toward the front and sat down at an empty two-top in the front row. Lucy hurried to his side and exclaimed, "What are you doing?! Everyone knows you can't sit in the front row at a comedy show. What if they make fun of you?"

He looked at her. "What if they do?"

"Well ... um ... that would be embarrassing. I honestly don't understand the question. Why would you want to make yourself a target?" The hypocrisy wasn't lost on her. She'd let years go by and remained a target of ridicule. Colt made her feel small all the time. Not in front of other people, but also not in jest.

Lucy looked around the room for less conspicuous seats. She spotted a table with a good view, but more off to the side. She looked at Gabe and tilted her head to the right. "Come on, let's move." He got up reluctantly. As they sat down, the music quieted and a small Latin man in his twenties hopped up on the stage, presenting himself with a cocky yet approachable confidence.

He gripped the microphone, waiting for the crowd to quiet down. "Hey there, friends. I'm Carl and I'll be your host this evening. Are you excited to see some comics?" Some people, including Gabe, clapped and shouted "Woo!"

Carl cupped his hand around his ear and said, "Oh what's that? I don't think you can hear me. Are you excited to see some funny people tonight?"

The crowd, including Lucy, gave the obligatory louder cheer to satisfy Carl. "That's more like it. Please put your hands together again and welcome our brave performer Daisy, who's stepping up onto the stage for the very first time."

Lucy and Gabe let out a "Whoop!" and clapped enthusiastically. Daisy strutted up the stage steps, smiled, and waved. The crowd continued to clap. As she gripped the mic, Lucy saw Daisy's hands shake just a bit. Lucy yelled, "Go Daisy!" as loud as she could to encourage her. "Thank you, thank you!" Daisy said.

"What's a first-time comic going to talk about? Well, of course I'm going to use this session as therapy and talk about my parents. Would y'all like that?"

The crowd responded by clapping.

"In typical Asian fashion, my parents really want me to become a doctor, but here's the deal: I can barely even take my own vitamins without gagging. And then there's the blood ... have you ever had to get your blood drawn or, even worse, gone to give blood? I don't mean that—it's not the worst—bless you for your service, all of you out there that do. But I can't do it. I pass out ...I mean out, cold. How am I supposed to deal with someone coming into the ER after his girlfriend's pet lion attacks him? Hey ... " she said, pointing to someone in the front. "Don't look at me like that … I can tell … you don't think I'd encounter that."

She took a beat and her face was stone-cold serious, with her eyes scanning the room back and forth.

"You don't. Well, I beg to differ! I just tried to study for the MCAT, but I accidentally ended up watching an entire season of Grey's Anatomy instead AND it happened—Doyle from Gilmore Girls was attacked by a freakin' lion! You might think, well, if you pass out at the sight of blood, how can you watch a show about surgeons? Because, dummies, I'm not stupid. It's not a reality surgery show. That stuff is ketchup or something. I don't know what they put in it, but my brain can tell the difference … apparently."

Lucy was laughing and looked around at all the other people laughing. She'd only met Daisy on a couple of occasions, but she was immensely proud of her. What guts it must have taken to get up there! Gerald had talked about an open mic at breakfast. She hoped this wasn't a prerequisite or some step she'd have to take.

"While studying, I did learn why I pass out from the sight of blood. It's called vasovagal response. You know when you're scared and your heart rate speeds up and you want to get away and jump out the window? Like when your parents show up for Thanksgiving and you hear the doorbell ring? Well, the vasovagal response is the opposite of that—at the sight of blood, you have a sudden drop in heart rate and blood pressure. This drop causes you to lose consciousness temporarily.

"So, I tell my mom all about this condition to justify the impossibility of me becoming a doctor and she says, 'You see. Listen to you, you sound like a doctor already.' They always have responses like that. They cannot get off of it—at all. I once told my parents I wanted to be a writer, and they were like, 'That's great, you can write prescriptions.'"

Lucy's mind drifted as Daisy continued, and she stopped listening to the act. She was just looking at all the joy on everyone's face. There was a man in the back whose laugh sounded like a cartoon. She saw a woman crossing her legs, clearly trying to keep from wetting herself. As Lucy turned her attention back to the stage, Daisy was wrapping up. "So I'm here, instead of being a doctor or studying to become one, talking to you, being a stand-up comic. I hope I was able to give you a laugh or two. That's my time. I'm Ms. Daisy, goodnight."

Lucy stood up, clapped loudly, and turned to Gabe. "I feel sorry for whoever has to follow that!"

Gabe looked at her and said, "Don't feel sorry for yourself. Just get ready." Lucy stared at him blankly for a few moments, and then Gabe cracked up. "I wouldn't do that to you." Lucy sighed in relief and took her seat on her way down, rolling her eyes at him.

A few moments later, Daisy was by her side. Lucy gave her a hug, congratulated her, and returned her phone. Daisy whispered into her ear, "I think I found my calling. Randy said I'm going to go to the next phase of my quest ... whatever that is." A feeling of anticipation swept over Lucy as she thought about all the things she could experience in the next forty days if she did her own quest.

The two sat together to enjoy the rest of the show. As Lucy suspected, none of them could follow Daisy.

When they arrived back at the B&B, a group was in the dining room, not eating, but playing some sort of game. Lucy peered around the corner in curiosity, wondering if she might join in the fun, but Gabe held his hand up. "I think that's for Vision Catchers only. Besides, tomorrow might be the first day of your quest. Have you thought more about whether you want to join?" He looked at her with the same hopeful desperation he'd had when he'd asked her for a ride the night before.

So many secrets. The scales seemed unbalanced. He could peer into her mind at least when she let an idea slip and maybe more. How could she know? Lucy looked up to toward The Tower. It was a free place to stay for over a month, but she had the ring money. She didn't have to do this, but what if she could find her calling like Daisy? Biting her lip, they stood in silence as Gabe gave her space to think.

She felt a slight tingle on the top of her hand. When she looked down, a ladybug was crawling toward her ring finger. It flew away after a few moments, landing on a beautiful potted plant near the door. She took it as a good omen. So many times she'd ignored the signs that she should change her life. The constant stomach aches, the weight loss, even Anna flat out telling her she missed the old Lucy. One night after Colt called her a bitch and screamed at her, she sunk into the couch. Garfield immediately cuddled up next to her, a rare posture for him. Even her cat was trying to signal that he knew what was happening wasn't okay.

This ladybug had centered her in a way those more obvious indicators hadn't. She turned to Gabe and felt him tugging on her heartstrings. With the same spontaneity as last night in Booneville, but this time with more conviction, she said, "Okay, I'm in."

"Yes!" Gabe drew his arms in a celebratory pump.

Lucy's adrenaline was coursing through her veins from the excitement of the decision. From the dining room, she heard Rae shout, "We win again!" Looking into the room, she really wanted to join in the fun, or at least read the magazine Gabe had confiscated.

He cut off her curiosity again. "We need to start early. I'll come get you around eight and hey, don't worry about the car. I've got a plan for that, too."

"How did you know about … " her voice trailed off. Of course, he knew. He didn't know Colt, though. Not completely. In the excitement, she'd lost sight of that obstacle. Colt had been stewing a whole day after her disappearance. Fear surrounded her heart.

Reading her, Gabe touched her lightly on the shoulder. "Seriously,

I've got you. You should go to bed." His eyes met hers and then looked over her shoulder with delight. She looked behind her, but couldn't find what he was fixing his gaze on. He stepped around her, crouched down to pick something up, but Lucy still couldn't see his object of distraction.

He turned around and held out the tabby cat she tripped over that morning, Penelope.

"Maybe she can bring you some comfort. She loves a good snuggle, and The Tower is one of her places to be."

Giddy, Lucy reached out and gingerly took the creature from Gabe's arms. "Awww ... hi Penelope. Do you want to stay with me tonight?" Penelope lifted her head toward Lucy's and purred.

"I think that's a yes," said Gabe.

"Okay. Thank you. Have a good night."

Lucy turned and climbed the stairs carefully, cuddling her new furry friend.

Gabe watched Lucy leave and was glad that he'd been able to distract her with the comforts of Penelope. She'd comforted him many times, especially moments when he missed his parents. As he turned to go to his room in the basement, he leaned in the doorway to observe the game. Rae spotted him and motioned for him to come to her. "Come on, Gabe, hang out for a bit." He was tired, but had also caught some of Lucy's curiosity. It couldn't hurt to just check it out.

7

The Game

Gabe approached Rae and the other three people still in the dining room. "Hi folks, you remember Gabe?"

"Oh sure," said Randy. Randy was rather plump, with red hair. Smoke from a cigar permeated the air around him. "It's been a while. So, it looks like you're starting your first vision quest, eh? Good luck," he chuckled.

"Yes. Well, she's ready," Gabe boasted, trying to hide his insecurities.

"But are you?" Randy replied as he took another puff on his cigar and blew a ring of smoke right into Gabe's face. Gabe coughed and then looked back up at Randy like a deer in headlights.

"Randy, stop that! Of course he's ready," Aunt Rae interjected. She turned to Gabe, grabbed his chin, and put her face close to his. "This is the moment we've been preparing for, sugar. Don't let him get in your head."

It was too late. He was in his head. Before yesterday, he'd feared his powers were weakening because it had been three weeks since he'd perceived any hopes or dreams from Lucy. He caught glimpses of nightmares she had for her life that were just miserable. Then, it came to him! An abstract dream, but a dream just the same, of Lucy chasing the sunset. There was hope in it—so much hope that, in fact, he knew she was ready to move on from her miserable life with Colt.

He drew the vision and then went to making a plan FAST! He came up with the idea of the shirt with Lucy's favorite Bible verse, at least one he knew that would ring a bell. He knew her mom had hung the youth group self-portrait art project in their house for at least a few years, if not more. And he used all of his powers to will her toward him. It felt so gratifying, and he was on such a high on the drive up from having beckoned his first Originator to go out on a vision quest.

As he looked around at all the others in the room, he felt so small.

Rae always said, "Fame and giant accomplishments aren't what we're trying to help our Originators achieve. We want to guide them to live their best life, whether that's being a novelist, a mom or dad, or a waitress. We want them to not lose sight of their dreams and have been given the gift to hold on to their dreams for them when they do."

Still, Randy was rumored to be pair-bonded with famous Originators that led to the creation of blockbuster movie hits and famous works of art. Next to Randy was Hannah. Hannah was a scientist. Aunt Rae told Gabe recently that Hannah had just finished a quest to help someone get on the path to be a researcher to develop a cure for lung cancer.

Then there was Theo. Theo was in the class above Gabe in Vision Catcher's school. Theo was one of the "cool kids" and an excellent artist. Gabe imagined Theo might be there on his first or second quest, though he seemed exhausted.

Rae turned to Randy and exclaimed, "Let's play!" and Gabe sat down. "Gabe, you can take my spot. Hannah and I were a team before you got here. I'll referee since we don't have even numbers," Aunt Rae instructed.

"You were referee and playing before; that's the only reason you were winning," Theo said smugly.

"Do you know the rules, Gabe?" Hannah asked. Gabe hadn't even bothered to see what was on the table. There were square cards on the table with the word "Visionary" on the back of them. He'd only played the game a handful of times in school when they were all still harnessing their powers, but he LOVED it. He smiled and nodded at Hannah.

It was sort of like Pictionary. Each card had the image or description of a realized dream. One player would look at the card and then try to transfer it telepathically to their teammate. The teammate would have ninety seconds to draw it. You couldn't project the words to your teammate exactly; you'd have to think of images that described it. The referee decided if the drawing really conveys what's on the card. The team with the most correct drawings at the end of eight rounds would win.

When he was younger, Gabe always had the upper hand when they played this game because it catered to how his mind worked in images. Others could often only write lost dreams. Remembering his victories from years ago, he looked at Hannah and said, "Oh, this is gonna be fun." He leaned back in his chair, raising his eyebrows mischievously.

Randy and Theo were first. Randy drew a card, looked at it, and placed it in the discard pile. Aunt Rae turned a sand-filled timer over, and Randy closed his eyes. Ninety seconds later, Theo had drawn a mouse, duck, earth, and roller coaster.

Aunt Rae looked at it and exclaimed, "Oh, going to Disney World! Good job, Theo, one point for y'all."

"Good job, Theo? I was doing all the hard work over here," Randy retorted and laughed.

"Okay ... good job, Randy too," she said as she patted him on the head. "I would've hoped a grown man of your stature didn't need that kind of validation."

He rolled his eyes and turned his focus to Hannah and Gabe. "Your turn!"

Gabe's hands were shaking as he drew a card. It suddenly felt like he was in the middle of his finals at the Essential School of Vision Catching. Hannah sensed this and whispered firmly, "Stop worrying, it's just a game."

The card read "Going to the Moon." Rae flipped the timer again. Gabe closed his eyes, imagined a moon with an astronaut walking on it, and tried to latch into Hannah's brainwaves to push it to her. He imagined the stars twinkling, and when he opened his eyes, Hannah had drawn a circle with a stick figure on top with a bunch of stars around. Time was up.

Aunt Rae said, "That kind of looks like one of those men who walks on the ball at the circus. Is that right? A man who had a dream to start a circus!"

"No, Aunt Rae, it was going to the moon," Gabe huffed in frustration at Hannah's artistic ability.

"Why didn't you send her a rocket ship, son?" Randy said. "Did he send you a rocket ship, Hannah?"

Hannah shook her head and laughed quietly with a sympathetic gaze pointed toward Gabe. "I'm a writer and scientist, not an artist. I think there's fault on both sides."

"No. That's clearly an astronaut on the moon surrounded by stars. I want a different ref," Gabe said while laughing along. "Seriously though, can I draw y'all what I was picturing in my head?"

"It won't count," Theo said.

"I know. I just want Hannah to tell me if what I draw is what she saw."

"Of course you can," Aunt Rae said reassuringly while turning the timer over.

Gabe drew quickly—an astronaut, standing on the moon, sur-rounded by stars—accurately, quickly, and beautifully.

When he was done, there was no joking anymore; everyone just sat in stunned silence at the masterpiece Gabe created so quickly. He looked at Hannah. "Well, is that what you saw?" Hannah smiled and nodded.

Satisfied, they continued to play. They lost when Gabe sent Hannah a vision of a writer being on the New York Times best-seller list and Rae guessed it was someone who fantasized about reading books all day.

He let out an enormous yawn. "Sorry, y'all, I've got to go to bed."

"Of course! Big day tomorrow!" Aunt Rae said enthusiastically as she stood up and embraced him.

Theo sighed and said, "I'm tired too, but I don't want to face tomorrow."

"Why's that?" Gabe asked.

"Because my Originator's a prick."

"Theo, language," Aunt Rae said, slapping him gently on the arm.

"You're having a hard time?" Gabe asked. His nerves about his abilities returned.

Before Theo could answer, Randy interjected. "That's what you get when you flunk your first time around. They assign you a lost cause. You're gonna have to dig deep to get Mr. Moneybags to embrace his purpose."

"Wait, that guy Gerald is your Originator?" Gabe asked, shaking his head slightly remembering how Gerald had treated him at breakfast.

Theo just nodded. "Yeah, I don't really want to talk about it."

Gabe was glad his Originator wasn't a jerk, but was curious how Theo flunked his first quest. "That sucks. I'd love to talk later. Maybe you can give me some advice."

"Sure thing."

Gabe said goodnight, gave Rae a hug, and turned to leave when Randy called out after him.

"Pay up. We won."

"Pay?" Gabe said, confused. "What were you playing for? No one told me there was a bet."

"Come on, Gabe," Theo retorted. "There's always a bet."

"Fine. What do we owe you?" Gabe huffed.

"You each owe us an idea. An invention from one of your Originators," Randy said with a tone of superiority.

"No way. I protect my Originator's visions, and you know I don't have full status. Until I finish this quest, Lucy is my only Originator. She's had a rough go of it lately; I'm not taking anything from her. Besides, she's not really an inventor."

"Please, I've peeked in your studio. She's got more visions than three lifetimes can hold. Like she hasn't come up with a song or an app idea I can give as kindling to one of my Originators? Everyone's got something," Randy said, still smiling.

Gabe stood up, frustrated, and slammed his chair on the ground. "You guys make me sick. You wouldn't give it to someone else in need; you'd just sell it on the black market. What happened to the oath we took? Selling people's ideas that you catch before they expire is just wrong." The words spewed passionately out of Gabe's mouth. Gabe glared at Theo and silently told him, "You can't think this is right, man?"

"How do you think your aunt paid for this place?" Randy said, holding his hands in the air, palms up, with his eyes directed at the chandelier that hung over the grand dining table. "We all got to bend a rule or two to survive."

Gabe looked around and realized he'd never really thought about it. Black market deals and bets on games weren't the ideals his aunt had raised him on, but he also hadn't asked her what she'd done to have such a nice place. He'd always assumed it was because of her role as a host. He stood unmoving, in shock from Randy's offensive implications.

Exasperated, Gabe turned his gaze toward Aunt Rae, who looked at him with what seemed to be a mix of empathy and remorse.

"Let him go to bed, Randy," Theo spoke up. "He can pay us later."

Gabe looked at them all in disgust and then hurried to his room. He needed his sleep. Tomorrow was a big day, and there was no way he was going to let Lucy fail.

In the hallway, he heard footsteps behind him.

"Wait, Gabe," Aunt Rae's voice called out.

He stopped and turned as she ran toward him. "Honey, I ... "

"You what? How do you have this place? I thought you earned this. You've served on the Guild, even. All the stories you've told me over the years about the Originators you've helped. Did you rip them off?"

"No. I never sold a vision on the black market or even through legal means." She let out a deep sigh and stepped toward him, grabbing hold of his hand gently.

Gabe said nothing, leaving space for a confession to fall from her lips. Aunt Rae looked toward the doorway to a small reading room to their right.

"Let's sit down for this."

Gabe reluctantly let her pull him to a couch and they sat. Aunt Rae closed her eyes, took a deep breath in and as she exhaled, she began to speak again.

"Many years ago, I was in your shoes. Pair-bonded with my first Originator. I knew he was special the moment I stepped into The Center when I was thirteen."

Gabe thought back to his own ritual at The Center when he was the same age. A place in the VC realm where lost ideas swirled in the air. He approached the sacred ground with trepidation. He knew the next two decades or more of his life would follow this soul. This ceremony had weight. If successfully pair-bonded, his aging would slow based on the amount of dreams that passed through him. If there was no match, his life would be shorter and he wouldn't have the role of a Vision Catcher. He'd heard the story of his family's legacy from Aunt Rae's stories. Now as she spun one more tale, for the first time, he felt the fear in her own experience from The Center.

The feelings of apprehension he sensed from her soon lifted as she spoke of capturing her first Originator's lost idea, mentioning the silence and the peace of the place. He'd felt that too. Something about the air shifted the moment he'd stepped on The Center. So many ideas zoomed around him, but when he reached out his hand, one floated to him—like it was riding the wave of a gentle magnetic force. Lucy's vision was simple and fantastical. She wanted to be a superhero. Rae described the dream she captured vividly. Etched in her memory. She felt a strong wind push it toward her. It was also simple, but more noble than Lucy's. Her Originator was formulating ideas on how to help his community through solar energy.

She continued her story. "As I went through the years of training following him, just as you have with Lucy, the brilliant and creative visions I captured for him along the way filled me with immense energy. His dream of powering his town with the sun took root in the 1950s. But as with many great minds, his was riddled with self-doubt. When his peers dismissed his dream as fantasy, he began to spiral. I tried to pull him into his vision before his ideas reached the point where I'd have to mark them as expired. No matter how much I pushed, his ideas kept slipping away as he listened to the naysayers. He settled into life as a researcher and grew a family."

"Why didn't you invite him on a quest?"

"I tried. I petitioned for a quest, but the Guild didn't think he was worthy or that I was powerful enough to help him reach his goal. So I bent the rules just a little."

"Bent them, how?"

"Well, I just held onto them. Like I said, they'd reached the statute of limitations."

"So, what happened then?"

"The Guild reclassified him from 'High Potential, but Drifting Away' to 'Passively Content - Not a Priority.' And I couldn't blame them, he was content with his job and family."

Gabe was sensing where this was going, but he hoped against hope that she hadn't done what he thought.

"I held onto his visions and waited for another soul to transfer them to. I didn't trade them at the Dream Exchange as required by Guild policy. Technically, the Guild allows vision repurposing after expiration by the original Vision Catcher, but only under strict documentation. Most Vision Catchers didn't bother. The purists thought it tainted the original dream. I thought it gave it a second chance. When I matched with another Originator around 1970 who had a similar energy to him, I passed the dream on. This time, progress was made. A Guild member who was retiring recognized this accomplishment and gave me their seat. Things just flourished from there. Once I finished my service with the Guild, they gave me this land, but also charged me with the responsibility to host Originators on quests and their Vision Catchers. Because all of this happened when I was relatively young in Vision Catcher years, rumors spread. They said my achievements and the B&B were obtained through illicit means."

"Oh, Aunt Rae, I'm sorry that people did that. It must have hurt. I guess they're still doing it," he said, thinking about Randy's comment that started the conversation.

"Yes, but I don't take it personally anymore. Like I said, I didn't file the vision for anyone to help someone. I kept it safe, but not for the recognition. That was unintentional because the Guild member who gave me their seat saw how my Originator's progress was effecting lasting change to the environment. I just wanted my first Originator's special vision to transfer to another special person. You'll learn too, in time, when bending a rule or two is necessary."

Gabe nodded and wanted to ask more, but then let out another yawn.

"You better get off to bed son, big day tomorrow."

Aunt Rae's confession had distracted him. He got up, gave her a big hug, and walked toward his room.

When he reached the door, he paused briefly at the threshold. A banging noise coming from upstairs stopped him in his tracks. After a few moments of quiet, he went to bed. Probably just Penelope knocking something over.

Lucy's sleep was deep until she heard the knocking at her door and felt Penelope wiggling out of their cuddle. Was it already eight? She looked up at the skylight and could still see stars.

She heard a voice through the door. "Lucy, it's Daisy. I need to talk to you. It's about Colt."

8

The Call That Gave Her Away

Anna jolted awake. Her dog was barking. Someone was pounding on her door, mirroring her racing heart. She drew in a deep breath and attempted to calm her nerves. She had a suspicion of who her late night visitor was and she knew she could handle him.

Sure enough, when she looked at her front door camera, her hunch were validated. It had been a few years. His gut had expanded, and his hairline had receded, but it was Lucy's husband for sure.

Before she went to bed, Colt had been blowing up her phone. She'd answered once and said that Lucy was safe, but she didn't know where she was. He called over and over and over, even though she kept dismissing the call. He was relentless. Irritated, she turned the damn thing off, which she never did. She'd thought about blocking his number, but played out a nightmare scenario in her head where his phone was the only one Lucy could get to and she needed her help.

She was a midwife and had been on call, but made a last-minute switch with a coworker just so she could get some sleep.

"Anna, where's Lucy?" He pounded on the door again and yelled more emphatically, "WHERE'S LUCY?!"

Anna sighed and ambled over to the front door, annoyed, but not worried. She refused to be intimidated. She opened the door and said, "Lucy's not here, Colt," her voice laced with exasperation.

"The hell she isn't." He pushed by her forcefully and wandered around her house yelling, "Lucy! LUCY!"

Anna's little dog, Charlie, was yapping away. Colt's head turned to him and he screamed, "SHUT UP!!"

Charlie whimpered a little and ran to Anna. She picked him up in her arms and stroked his fur. Holding him tightly to her chest, she followed the lunatic through her house. Colt went into the bathroom and pulled back the shower curtain. His breath was heavy and anger shot out of his eyes as he balled his fists in frustration.

"She's not here Colt, but as I told you earlier, she's safe. Go home before I call the cops."

He looked at her sternly. "You know she's safe so she called you," he asserted.

"Yeah, she called," Anna said, not backing down. She was a lipstick lesbian and Colt probably had a hundred pounds on her, but she was channeling her inner badass butch.

"What I can't figure out is from where? Where did she call you from? I track her phone. The last time my tracker saw her, she was heading north. You're the only friend she has this way. I've driven ten hours just to come collect her. She hasn't used her credit card so she couldn't have bought a plane ticket. I don't give her that much cash and she hasn't used the ATM."

"You need to leave." Anna used the most intimidating voice she could conjure.

"I'm not leaving until I find Lucy."

He stomped into Anna's room and got down on the ground, looking under the bed. He spotted her phone on the nightstand and grabbed it. He held it in his hand with sick delight, as if he'd just outsmarted her. He turned it on and said firmly, "What's the code?"

"I'm not giving you the code." She stared back at him, unwavering. He was about seven feet away from her, standing on the far side of the room while she was in the doorway. He walked toward her and said, "That's okay. I don't need the code."

Before she could react, he lunged toward her and grabbed her by the collar, holding the phone to her face to unlock it. She struggled to pull away. Arms flailing, she grabbed for the phone, but Colt pushed her away.

She put up a fight, trying to reach it again. He pulled back his jacket to reveal a gun holster. "Not one step closer bitch."

Anna stood frozen two feet away, her eyes fixed on the gun as he scrolled through her phone.

Colt smiled sadistically. "It looks like you've talked to a couple of people tonight. Your mom, a bunch of random numbers that you didn't talk to, Trish, and, of course, all the calls from me you so rudely failed to pick up. Oh, and what do we have here? A number not in your contacts, but you talked to them for five whole minutes."

"Yeah, it was my doctor. She was telling me about the results of a test," Anna said with a lump in her throat.

Colt laughed. "Your doctor calls you after five in the afternoon?"

"Yeah," she said. "It happens."

"Right, we don't live in Canada. No doctor is going to call you after five and talk to you about the results of your test. This was Lucy, wasn't it?"

"No."

"Then how do you know she's safe?" Anna stared stone-eyed back at Colt. "Anna, this is her, isn't it? What did she do? Get a burner phone or something? Is she cheating on me? I'm just worried about her. You should be too. Aren't you worried?"

"I'm more worried if she stays with you." The moment the words fell from her lips, she regretted them.

He took his gun out and pointed it at her. "I'm going to ask you one more time. Is this her?"

Anna looked at the gun and looked at Colt. What could he even do with that number? What was she protecting? She decided to tell the truth to get the madman out of her house.

"Yes," Anna said firmly. "She said she was calling me from a friend's phone."

The anger drained from Colt's face as he calmed into a cool but psychotic state. "All right. Wasn't that easy? No worries, I won't be bothering you anymore." He typed something into Anna's phone quickly, put it down, and left.

When she grabbed the phone, she saw he'd texted himself the stranger's number that Lucy had called from earlier. Anna called it as fast as she could to warn her as Colt's car screeched off in the distance.

9

The Return

Daisy came into Lucy's room in a frenzy.

"You talked to Colt? What did he say to you?" Lucy asked, horrified that Colt had contacted Daisy.

"He said you were missing and that he needed to know where you were." Daisy looked at Lucy with concern.

"Did you tell him?"

"No. I said I didn't know where you were. I pretended like I didn't know you at all. I said that I'd just lent my phone to you because you said yours ran out of battery. He asked me where I was when I lent you my phone. I said at a Starbucks in Atlanta. I hope you didn't want me to tell him the truth."

"You did good. How did you know not to trust him? How did he even get your number?" Lucy bit her lip nervously. She was a mix of emotions—confused, scared, but also relieved that Daisy had diverted Colt.

"Your friend Anna called. Apparently, you called her from my phone and he threatened her to give him the number."

Lucy closed her eyes and shook her head. "I'm so sorry you got pulled into this mess. This is supposed to be your big night and here

I'm screwing with your vibe. I shouldn't have borrowed the phone, I didn't think … "

Daisy cut her off. "If you recall, I insisted you use my phone. Also, Colt would've done the same thing if you called from a landline and then he'd know where you are. You don't need to apologize. And you can breathe. He can't tell where you are and he doesn't know who I am."

Lucy panicked anyway. She didn't feel like she could breathe. She went to her duffel and shoved her clothes in, putting her keys, wallet, and phone into her old purse.

"Wait, what are you doing? He doesn't know you're here. Don't go," Daisy pleaded.

"I have to return the car anyway. I'll be back. I don't want him screwing this up for me."

"So don't let him. What are you so scared of?"

Lucy found it hard to find the words because she wasn't sure what she was scared of exactly. His wrath frightened her, even though he'd never hit her. He was in her head and she didn't want him to be anymore. She just wanted him to disappear.

She looked at Daisy and spoke in a calm tone, not because she'd calmed down, but because she'd become numb. "You don't know him. He's relentless and angry. I don't want him to find me or you or this magical place. If I go return the "stolen" car, I can take it from there and hopefully get back here to finish the quest."

"You stole a car?"

"No." Lucy shook her head. "Colt reported it stolen. It's in his name. Anyway, the police told me I should return it."

"You're not going alone. I'm going with you," Daisy insisted, stomping her feet firmly on the ground.

Shaking her head emphatically, Lucy said, "No way, you were amazing tonight. I'm not going to let you ruin your quest."

"It won't be ruined. Who knows? Something funny might happen. I may look small, but I have a black belt. I can be your backup." Daisy put up her hands like she was about to do karate and tried to make an intimidating face.

Lucy laughed so hard she almost cried, and Daisy started laughing too. Once they both had caught their breath, Lucy relented. "Okay, meet me back here in twenty minutes."

Lucy sat on the bed, fiddling with her keys. She was happy that Daisy was going with her and that it would help her pass the time, but also she could still keep her phone off. It was five-thirty in the morning when Daisy once again knocked on Lucy's door. She had her hair in a ponytail and was wearing well-fitted dark blue jeans that hugged her small frame, the coziest soft oversized cream-colored sweater, and a pair of low-top Converse with socks that had some kind of print on them.

Lucy put on the same outfit she wore to the comedy show because it hadn't gotten that dirty and it made her feel powerful. She needed all the power she could get for the mission they were going to undertake. Thinking about finding Gabe to alert him to the plan frayed her nerves. He might try to change her mind. Determined to leave, she ignored the thoughts of his face of disappointment.

When they got outside, it was still dark and the B&B looked the same as when she'd arrived just last night. Lucy lingered for a moment before stepping into her car and then asked Daisy to set her GPS to the Booneville Police Department in Mississippi.

"The police department?! Didn't you say this was Colt's car? Why not just go home? He's probably going to Atlanta." Daisy's face scrunched up and her head tilted in confusion.

"I don't want to get stuck there with him. If we do that, how are we going to leave?"

"Um ... Uber," she said, holding up her phone. Lucy's hands sweat.

What if they ran into Colt? She didn't want Colt to yell at her, but Daisy's logic was sound. Why couldn't they just leave? She didn't want to get into it because she didn't fully understand it herself.

Lucy stood firm in not going home. "Let's just go to the police for now. We could probably run six to ten minutes from there and hide out in a church. We can call Gabe or a taxi from there, maybe. I don't want to go back home and I don't really want to talk about it."

"Are you sure there's a church?"

"You can look, but it's Mississippi. There's gonna be a church."

Daisy looked and said, "You're right, there's one a half a mile from the station. Okay, here goes nothing. Your plan, not mine." She typed in the Booneville Police Department into the GPS and they were off. Daisy started playing "Bad to the Bone" on her phone.

Lucy's eyes shifted slightly to the right, and she shot her a look.

She smiled at Lucy. "Oh come on … I was just trying to make you laugh. Don't be so serious."

"Alright, but let's not do music right now. Let's just chat. What were you doing before you started the quest? What's it been like?"

"Okay … " Daisy's posture shrunk. Her head was looking down toward the glove box and her eyes became distant and intense. Daisy paused and looked out the window for a few moments. She took a deep breath in and let it all out.

"Well, you heard my comedy act and, like many performances, it's not telling the whole truth. My parents did want me to become a doctor. I was even trying to do it for them in undergrad as a premed student. But I didn't stop because I was afraid of blood or because I never wanted to be a doctor. Both those things are true, but I quit school when I was twenty-one. When they … died." Daisy looked down toward her feet, her face heavy with grief.

"Oh, Daisy I'm so sorry." Lucy reached out to put her hand on Daisy's, giving a squeeze of comfort.

Continuing in a flat tone, she said, "They didn't even die at the same time. Just in the same year. One after the other. My dad went first and fast. He was older than my mom by about fifteen years. For someone so adamant about me being a doctor, he never went. It was skin cancer that was never treated. By the time he finally saw a doctor, it had already spread too much. He was seventy when he passed." Daisy paused again. "My mom didn't show how devastated she was, but I could tell. I took off for about a week from school, but went back for the distraction. About a month after his funeral, she was grocery shopping and some crazy person just came in and started shooting."

Lucy glanced over at Daisy. She wasn't crying. It was as if she'd told this story many times before and was just numb to it. "Oh my goodness. That's terrible. I hate guns." Lucy's mind drifted a bit to Colt's gun. It was only one, but one was all he'd need. Lucy glanced Daisy's way while still trying to keep her eyes on the road. "Do you know if she suffered?"

Daisy let out an exasperated sigh. "I hate that question. If someone's killed in an instant, people say 'well, at least they didn't suffer.' I would've preferred it not to be instantaneous, because if she had any chance, I know that she would've fought." Tears streamed down Daisy's face. Her voice broke as she said, "She was a fighter."

Lucy was in shock. She'd seen Daisy as so fun and lighthearted. Every person has their demons, she supposed, but some are harder than others. She once sought a therapist to talk about her relationship with Colt. Lucy remembered telling her, "It's not all bad. I mean, when I hear the horrors happening in Syria, I think how lucky I am." Her therapist had interjected that she had every right not to be miserable, even though other people had it worse. She could only control her own situation, not a tyrannical government. That was a year and a half ago, and Lucy still had to remind herself of the therapist's words. She didn't keep going to see her though, because she couldn't afford it.

After a few moments of silence, her mind wandered back to her present situation.

Lucy said the only honest thing that she could. "I'm sorry. I don't really know what to say."

"Don't be sorry. There's nothing to say. That was five years ago. Most of those years I spent drunk and living off their life insurance. I got pulled over and arrested for drunk driving a couple of months ago. That's when Randy bailed me out of jail before I'd even met him. He lied and said he was from a nonprofit that helped family members of gun violence. He befriended me, helped me get sober, and then invited me on the quest." Daisy wiped her tears and smiled a little. "I'm so excited about this new chapter. I've got a new motto."

"Oh yeah, what's that?"

"Embrace the Joy. Release the Guilt." Lucy could see a weight lift off of Daisy as she said it, her smile becoming wider.

"The quest, at least in this first phase, has been tough at times, but mostly a dream. The comedy you saw me do last night was the twelfth vision I pursued."

"Ohhh ... what were some of the others?"

"Well, there was archery—I didn't even remember that dream, but apparently I'd a brief fantasy of being an Olympic archer when I was ten. Singing—because you got to give it a shot in Nashville, right? I worked bagging groceries for a day. I'm not sure it was ever anything I envisioned for my life, but I did it because Randy said it would be good to have a job where I didn't have to use my intellect too much and then just come home and do whatever. I've tried my hand at so many things in such a short time: a chef, a dancer, a bartender—which, in hindsight, wasn't the smartest thing for me to do. What else ... honestly it's all kind of a blur. They guide you through it though."

Lucy was glad the conversation had turned back to lightness. Daisy turned to Lucy. "Look, I trust you feel you need to return the car, but we have to get back to the B&B as soon as we do."

While Daisy's companionship was voluntary, Lucy's stomach started knotting up with guilt for taking her from her quest. She was in awe of all the amazing things Daisy had tried. Lucy thought back to Gabe's studio with all the visions he'd captured for her. If she'd heard Daisy's list before she saw all the fabulous creations he'd made, she would've thought Daisy was a MUCH more interesting person than her, but after seeing Gabe's studio, she remembered how rich her inner-mind was before the past couple of years with Colt.

Lucy glanced over at Daisy. "Have you ever had something that you feel in your gut that you need to do and if you do it you'll just feel lighter? I feel like I know what's weighing me down and taking the steps to lift the weight off of me makes me feel freer already. Making this trip with you... it makes me lighter."

"I know what you mean. In orientation, they actually had us do an exercise where we had to write everything that's weighing us down or holding us back from being our true authentic selves," Daisy said.

Lucy crumpled her face for a moment in confusion. "Wait, what's orientation? I haven't done that yet. Oh my god, this trip is going to put me so behind. Am I going to miss orientation?" Lucy looked at Daisy with her mouth drooping open and eyes wide in utter shock.

Daisy frowned and said, "Honestly, I don't know. We may be taking a gigantic risk coming here. You on your quest and me on mine too. I didn't tell Randy I was leaving. All I know is that for the longest time I wasn't thinking about anybody but myself. When I saw I could help you, I just knew in my gut before I entered whatever this next phase is, which is honestly a bit scary. I wanted to do this for you. From everything I've experienced so far, they want you to succeed. I'm just putting my faith in the universe and hoping that everything will work out."

Lucy sighed and attempted to release the guilt of diverting Daisy.

"It's so crazy, until I saw those visions that I'd lost, I'd been too timid to name what was actually keeping me from a happy life, from pursuing my inner desires. I haven't wanted to admit that Colt was holding me back—with his insults and passive aggressiveness or even just following him while he chased his dreams. I moved away from a lot of my friends when he went to grad school. Now I see it clear as day, the poor choices I've made … marrying him … staying."

The GPS interrupted her thoughts again. She took a few more moments to concentrate on driving before continuing her thought.

"When this whole thing started, and I picked up Gabe, I kept telling myself that I just take it one step at a time. I do think that if I can drop off this car at the police station and they let me go … I think I can leave and never look back."

Daisy looked over to Lucy with deep sympathy. "You'll always have to look back. It's just the nature of life. Did you know scientists have actually found the cluster of cells in your brain that cause the persistence or disappearance of traumatic memories? If that's true, at the cellular level, we're truly a sum of all our experiences."

"Whoa that's deep." Lucy glanced down at the gas gauge and realized they were running low. She looked around for a gas station and saw one a mile ahead. "We're about out of gas and I don't want the cluster of brain cells that hold the traumatic memory of running out of gas in my twenties to be reactivated. I'm going to pop over to this station to fill up."

Daisy laughed and told Lucy the story of the time she was stranded on the side of the road, which passed the time until they pulled up to the BP. Daisy opened the door and ran inside as she screamed, "Sorry, have to pee like a racehorse." Lucy followed her into the station at a slower pace, took thirty dollars of the ring money and put it on pump six.

As Lucy filled up the tank, her mind wandered to the next leg of the trip. She started spinning and imagined herself being put into handcuffs and being put in a holding cell with a drunk, handsy, snaggletoothed man. The click of the pump shook her wandering mind awake. She went into the restroom to relieve herself and when she returned to the car, Daisy was already in the passenger seat, playing on her phone.

As Lucy climbed in, her mind went back to the jail. She needed a distraction. Turning to Daisy she said, "Hey listen, your presence here is very soothing to me, so please don't take offense when I say this, but do you mind if we just listen to music for the rest of the way?"

Daisy smiled and reached out for Lucy's hand and gave it a good squeeze. "I'd love that."

Lucy grabbed a small CD case and flipped through it, and then a giant smile stretched across her face. "This is perfect."

"What is it?" Daisy asked.

" '40 days' by the Wailin' Jennys. Someone told me one time that the title had nothing to do with anything biblical. It was actually the amount of time that the Jennys took to record the album. You can't let me forget to grab this when we leave. I think it'll be good luck."

Daisy agreed. They drove on, listening to the exquisite harmonies. Daisy fell asleep while Lucy let the trio wash over her repeatedly. "Heaven When We're Home" strummed at her heartstrings and she felt like they wrote it just for her—just for this moment. She repeated it at least three times. The song anchored on a line about not knowing what you're looking for, but knowing it when you get there, and it feeling like Heaven when you're home. She pictured herself arriving at a doorstep with old luggage and dropping it. All the weight of the past lifted off of her shoulders and her whole body calmed.

When the CD cycled through the songs three times, she heard the GPS say, "Your destination is in one mile on the right." Time seemed to pass slowly as she approached the station. Then finally, there it was, a converted retail store on the same road she'd ridden out of town on—Highway 45. She parked the car and took a deep breath in. It was eight-thirty in the morning, and she saw a woman standing on the porch smoking a cigarette and wondered if it was the woman she'd spoken to on the phone.

She began mapping out an escape route. "We passed the church about a half a mile that way," Lucy said, pointing to the right. Lucy looked around in the car. The mail was still in the back. She grabbed one piece. "Do you have a pen?" she asked, kicking herself for not thinking this part through.

"Um ... yeah, I think so." Daisy dug through her purse and handed Lucy a retractable pen. "You can pick one of four colors."

"Well, I only need one, but thanks."

"What are you doing?"

"I'm just going to write a note to leave on the windshield and tell them I'm returning it and that the keys are in the glove compartment."

"But what if someone steals it?" Daisy asked.

"Well, that'll be convenient, 'cause it's already reported stolen." Lucy smiled at the thought.

Daisy looked nervous now. "Why abandon it here? Why not just call and tell them where you left it?"

"Um ... well. The minute we call them, they'll call Colt." She lowered her head and looked around as if the car was bugged. She whispered, "And it's the police. They can trace our call. I say we make a break for it and walk as quickly as we can toward the church, but let's head into those trees behind us. If we play it cool, we'll at least have a head start and I've attempted to do the legal thing."

Daisy hesitated, biting her lip, but quickly rallied and cheerfully encouraged Lucy. "You got this girl."

Lucy turned off the car, put the keys in the glove box, grabbed her purse and gripped the note in hand. Her heart raced as she turned to

Daisy. "You ready?"

"Ready."

"Okay, let's gooo!"

Lucy quickly stashed the note on the windshield. Her adrenaline was pumping, and she ran before they were out of the eyeline of the police station. Her ankle boots weren't the most conducive to this, especially when they got to the woods. The wide legs from her jumpsuit caught on a small bush and she soon was face down in the dirt. Her new outfit was now ripped and beautiful coat dirtied. When she looked up, she'd lost sight of Daisy in the trees.

She got to her feet and was about to call out to her, but she heard footsteps behind her as she got on her knees. The hairs on the back of her neck stood straight up. She turned around slowly, hoping it was just her imagination, but it wasn't.

She froze and peered up at a tall uniformed officer stood over who was smiling. With a chuckle, he said, "You know, when people steal cars, they don't normally hand deliver them to us with a note."

Lucy looked down at the ground and then over her shoulder. When she looked back to the officer, he dropped the condescending tone and took on a more serious demeanor. "Come on, you're going to need to come with me."

She did as she was told and followed him back toward the station.

10

The Rescue

Since she complied with the officer right away, he was kind enough not to cuff her. He had completely dropped the jovial posture he'd taken with her a few moments ago. He was direct, but polite, in his instructions. "Follow me ma'am. Step through this door."

When she entered the main office of the station, the air was stale and the lack of windows or natural light reminded Lucy of her first job in high school working in the basement of a bank shredding paper—depressing and suffocating. The fluorescent lights buzzed and illuminated the drab gray carpet. There were eight worn-out, sparsely occupied wooden desks. The woman who Lucy had seen smoking earlier sat up front. Her eyes fixed on Lucy like a magnet following her as the officer led her to what was presumably his desk.

Gesturing toward a chair, he didn't mince his words. "You can take a seat right there. Now stay put while I get a few things." She looked up at him and read his name tag, "W. Hunter." Turning to the woman in the front, he said in a louder voice than necessary, "Sandra, will you keep an eye on this lady, please?" A simple task, given her gaze had not shifted.

Officer Hunter soon returned with another officer and a dog. He asked Lucy to stand as the dog sniffed her. "I won't pat you down. Our K-9 Officer says you're clean. You can sit back down."

"Okay. Am I under arrest?"

"Well, no, not right now, but let's have a conversation. So tell me, what happened here?" The officer pulled up the security footage from minutes ago. Lucy watched the black-and-white scene and cursed herself for being so frenzied. Her mind wandered to how Daisy was and if she'd made it to a safe hiding spot.

She was nervous for Daisy and her heart was racing, even though Officer Hunter said she wasn't under arrest. To get this questioning over with, she made a deliberate decision to play the "dumb wife" card and turned on a little bit of a southern accent to sweeten the pot. "Look, the car is in my husband's name. He reported it stolen because I left him a couple of days ago. I'm insured to drive it. I didn't know I was doing anything wrong. Honest to God."

"Ah, yes, okay. I think I remember this," he said.

Lucy's voice became higher pitched as she made excuses for her actions. "I called about it, and a woman I talked to said I should bring the car in. So I did."

"Did anyone take this call from this woman?" he called out to the entire room.

"Yes, that'd be me." Sandra got up from her desk and approached them. "I told her to return the car and that the DA would probably not press charges." She turned to Lucy, adding, "Now, I didn't tell you to abandon it here, did I?" She looked back up to Officer Hunter. "I told her these domestic matters don't usually go far."

"Well, I was worried you'd call my husband," Lucy said defensively and meekly all at once.

This gave Officer Hunter pause. He examined Lucy's face closely. His demeanor softened and his lips held together tightly, as if he was trying carefully not to say the wrong words. "Does he hurt you?"

"Not physically, no," she replied.

"Well, he's the one who filed the report, ma'am, so we're going to be calling your husband."

"Please, please, please don't," she pleaded. "I mean, call him and tell him you have the car, but don't tell him I'm here."

"Well, I have to be honest and tell him you dropped it off," the officer explained. "Do you need to file a restraining order? Are you sure he hasn't hurt you?"

Lucy considered this. She hadn't even thought of a restraining order. Her thoughts boomeranged back to Daisy. "I need to leave now. Am I free to go?"

"Well, we have more paperwork to do. What's your rush?"

Lucy thought for a minute, trying to come up with a believable lie that would have him take sympathy on her. "I've got to get to work."

"Where do you work?"

"I do the books for the Booneville Humane Society." She waited on pins and needles when he called to confirm her employment. Luckily, Wednesdays were the day she usually came in and he didn't ask if they were expecting her, just if she was employed there.

"Alright, that checks out. Before you go, you need to give me a number that I can call you at."

Lucy gave him her number. She didn't need to lie—she was just going to leave her phone off. Her hands sweat and her mind raced, thinking of all the trouble she could get into. With intensity and nervousness, she said, "I really need to get there. You have my info and the car. Can I just leave? Please?"

His face softened again. "Okay, okay. Sandra, will you be able to take her to work?"

Sandra frowned and scrunched her face. "I'd be happy to disrupt my day. It's not like I have to answer the phones or enter any of this paperwork."

Officer Hunter rolled his eyes and matched Sandra's sarcastic tone. "Fine. I'll see if one of the rookies can do it." He continued to type into his computer as Lucy's mind raced, trying to formulate a new plan.

Sandra's eyes shifted down, looking at Lucy with pity. "Fine, I'll do it. It's not that far. It's time for my smoke break anyway."

Officer Hunter nodded and then held his arm out to indicate Lucy should stay seated. He looked quickly toward Sandra and thanked her. Fixing his eyes back on Lucy, he raised his eyebrows and said, "Now, before you leave, I'm going to need the name of your passenger, too. The Chinese woman. Even though we didn't take her in."

"Why?" Lucy asked.

"She's an accomplice."

"Well, she was helping me return the car, so really, she was just an accomplice to doing the right thing. I took the car a couple of nights ago. You're not really going to take her in, are you?"

Every time she thought of Daisy, her stomach ached with worry. She gave him a fake name and number after he assured her they wouldn't contact her unless Lucy did something else illegal.

"Thank you for cooperating. Let me give your husband a call."

Lucy's heart raced as she heard the phone ring through the officer's handset. Sandra piped up unexpectedly after the second ring. "Let me go ahead and take her, Bill. You can finish up this paperwork without her." She gave Lucy a knowing look and nodded her head toward the door. Lucy was on a roller coaster of emotions, but she sensed Sandra may be on her side.

"Okay, okay. Have a good day at work," he said. As Lucy scurried away, she heard the officer say, "This message is for Colt Rivers. We have the car you reported stolen yesterday at the station. You can call me back at—"

Sandra drowned out his voice as Lucy approached. "You go wash up. Then we'll get going." There was no way to get the Mississippi mud out of her white clothes, but a wash up wasn't a bad idea.

She got as much dirt off as she could and hurried into Sandra's car. "So, you're not really going to work, are you?" she asked.

Lucy hesitated. "Um … "

"Look honey, like I told you on the phone yesterday, I've had a situation like yours. Where do you really need to go?"

"Well, I need to find my friend and then we need to get to … " Lucy paused. "Then we need to get the heck out of Booneville."

Sandra looked to her left, right, and glanced in her rearview mirror. She paused for what felt like an eternity. Finally, she leaned into Lucy and said in a soft tone, "Alright. Where's your friend?"

"Well, we were supposed to meet at this church down the road." Lucy glanced behind her toward the woods and saw a Converse shoe peeking out from behind a large oak. "But maybe she didn't make it." She pointed as discreetly as possible toward the woods, hoping Sandra could see what she saw.

They drove slowly to the edge of the woods. Lucy opened the passenger window and whispered loudly, "Psst—Daisy, hurry! Get in."

A frazzled Daisy walked quickly, opening the passenger door and sliding in. She opened her mouth to say something, but Sandra interjected.

"Well—that was easy. Now the church? Is that really where you want me to take you? Seriously, what's next?"

Lucy hesitated, thinking of the best place to go now that they didn't have to be on foot. "Actually, can you take us to Walmart?"

Sandra nodded her head and rolled down her window, lit her cigarette, and drove on.

Lucy turned behind her. "Are you okay? I was so worried."

"Worried about me? What about you? You were the one hauled into the police station. I was trying to come up with a story to rescue you. I swear, I was working up the courage to go in there and pretend to be your lawyer, but then that was a crime in itself and —"

Lucy reached out and squeezed Daisy's leg to calm her. "It's okay. They aren't charging me."

Daisy's posture relaxed. "Oh, good."

Lucy turned away from Daisy to see where they were. When they passed the same stoplight where Lucy had first picked up Gabe—what felt like a lifetime ago— Daisy let out a yelp of excitement. She played it off as a hiccup to Sandra while Lucy tried to control her smile.

Sandra pulled up to the back of the parking lot. As Lucy and Daisy climbed out, she leaned out the window and said, "Y'all be careful now, hear?" They nodded in acknowledgment and then she drove away, flicking her cigarette out of the window as she left. Once she was out of sight, Lucy and Daisy walked quickly away from the parking lot to see the best thing they'd seen all day. Leaning against a truck on the side of the road with his legs crossed and a huge smile on his face was Gabe.

Lucy ran out and hugged him. "You don't know how glad I am to see you," she said, tears welling up in her eyes.

"Right back at you. Thanks for having a scary vision about going to jail. That helped immensely."

Lucy remembered the frightening scene she'd pictured while filling up for gas. "Wait, we were about halfway here then. How did you get here so fast?"

"Turns out I have access to a helicopter. And I know a guy who lent me his truck. Come on, let's go. Orientation starts at one."

Daisy called out "Shotgun" and climbed into the front seat. Gabe opened the back for Lucy and she loaded in and then looked down at her hands. Daisy hung her head around the passenger seat facing Lucy with a giant smile on her face. "We're going to get to ride in a helicopter, Lucy! How cool is that?"

"Pretty cool," she agreed as she took a deep breath and then looked out the window.

Familiar sites surrounded her and a little bit of nostalgia set in as she thought back to the first time she encountered Booneville, when Colt and she first stopped at the college. When she stepped out of the car, she smelled the freshly cut grass of the well-manicured lawns. They walked down a pathway that was shaded by sturdy water oaks and magnolia trees. Colt nervously tried to find out where the administrative offices were, and she was just trying to soak it in. "You're going the wrong way," Colt snipped as she meandered.

They eventually found the administrative building where Colt filled out his new hire paperwork. They'd hired him over the phone, so the hard part was over, but he was still visibly nervous.

She asked the administrative assistant where the library was, and if there were any independent bookstores in town. Originally from Asheville, North Carolina, she'd spend hours in the Smith Family Bookstore—curling up and getting lost in the worlds of Terabithia, Wonderland, and Narnia. When she pulled herself outside of her books, she'd people-watch. Soaking in the artists, justice seekers, and university students that would gather there.

She wasn't surprised to learn from the assistant that there was no such indie bookstore in Booneville, but there was a library. "The George E. Allen library isn't too far from here. It's named after a lawyer for Presidents Franklin D. Roosevelt and Dwight Eisenhower. He was born in Booneville. He was one of the most famous people to come out of Booneville," the assistant said proudly.

Lucy spent hours in that library during her time in the small southern town, but it wasn't the same as the Smith Family Bookstore. It was quieter, unless it was children's storytime, but she couldn't do similar people-watching as she'd done in Asheville. There were, however, places to go to see all sorts of characters from the college campus to the Walmart. She actually loved the quiet nook she'd carved out for herself in the town and would miss it.

Gabe drove past the Cross of Booneville, a massive 120 foot cross that had recently been erected. It hadn't even been there the entire time Lucy had lived there. It had been a vision of an eighty-one-year-old man named Deryl. He said that God told him to build an enormous cross along Mississippi Highway 45 near his home between Booneville and Baldwyn. So Deryl made it happen. He had the vision, he formed a nonprofit called "Building the Cross" and he spearheaded the committee to fundraise for it. They started raising funds for it in 2020 and it cost $200,000. Lucy couldn't believe that they'd raised the money in just over a year. She thought that $200,000 would've been better spent on helping with the pandemic or hungry children in the county, but Deryl still impressed her. There aren't many people who say, "I have a vision of what I'm called to do" and just do it. He didn't let go of it, he just went for it. She'd never done anything like that before. As the truck turned down a small road and a helicopter came into view, she thought, perhaps she would now.

The bright orange helicopter sat in the middle of a pasture. Gabe parked next to a fence gate, got out, and gestured for Lucy and Daisy to follow him. There was a woman and a man next to the chopper. One had to be the pilot. She had gorgeous brown skin and was wearing a dark blue flight suit with three yellow stripes on each shoulder and other various patches and insignias slightly weathered from years of experience. She looked calm and collected in her aviator sunglasses and, as the group got closer, Lucy could see a patch that said Capt. Priya Desai.

The man was young, white, and considerably more out of shape than Priya. Gabe dangled the keys and handed them to the man. "Thanks so much for the loan."

"Anytime, y'all did so much for me. It's the least I can do."

Earlier that day, Gabe awoke with a vision of Lucy going to jail. He knew her so well, he just knew in his bones that she'd left. When he saw the missing car, he panicked. He began frantically getting dressed, grabbing the first jeans, T-shirt, and sweater he could.

He had the whole day planned, and Lucy ruined those plans with her escape. He was going to help her get the car back. Then, he was just going to follow her in another car ... after orientation. Gabe knew that those who had a good experience at orientation were more likely to be successful in their quest.

Now, he couldn't convince Lucy that she could hold off on returning the car and just stay. He had an entire speech worked out. Her impulsive decision to take matters into her own hands had made his plans irrelevant. He grabbed his phone and called his rep. Ravi connected him with the graduate helpers network.

It turned out that Gabe didn't have endless resources for quests, but there was a directory of Originators that would do favors for the Vision Catchers because of the success of their own quests. A loan of a helicopter and a car did the trick.

Gabe arrived at a small airport, his heart pounding with anticipation. His palms were sweaty as he approached the aircraft. Priya, who became a helicopter pilot following a quest, was standing by with a warm smile that was calming, but his nerves and fear of flying were still palpable within his body.

After he shook her hand, it was clear he could not hide his nerves from her. Her eyebrows raised slightly, her warm smile transformed into a sympathetic frown, and her head tilted to the left. She reached up and touched his arm and in a soothing tone she said, "It's going to be alright. I've done this hundreds of times before." He simultaneously let out a sigh and nodded his head.

With one graceful motion, Priya opened the passenger door, inviting Gabe to step inside. He climbed into the cabin and turned his head away from the large panoramic windows, not even wanting to gaze out of them even when on the ground. He took his seat, buckling his seat belt extra tight, and closed his eyes.

He heard Priya make her way to the pilot's seat. The blades above began to stir, slicing through the air. Once the engine roared to life, Gabe took deep breaths, doing a meditation exercise, shutting out everything until about an hour later when Priya's voice came over the telecom to inform him they were almost there. He still didn't look out. Once the engine had come to a complete stop, he finally examined his surroundings.

The car was there to meet them. The Originator was a student who lived in Booneville and was going to the community college. He didn't have his first class until noon, which gave him time to lend his truck for an hour to Gabe. He and Priya had swapped stories of each other's quests while they waited for Gabe to return.

Now, Gabe turned to Daisy and Lucy and made quick introductions. The student left and walked toward his truck.

"Can I call shotgun?!" Daisy blurted.

Priya smiled endearingly toward Daisy. "You certainly may."

The door was open. Priya instructed them on how to climb in and buckle their seat belt. Daisy bounced up and down with excitement and then climbed in. Lucy thought she'd be the most nervous flyer, but after settling in, she saw Gabe sweating profusely and his eyes squeezed shut. She wanted to comfort him, but she wasn't sure what that could be. She called out to Priya, "Is he going to be okay?"

"Yeah, he'll be fine. He was like this the ride over. Happens all the time. Barf bags under your seat if you need 'em."

Lucy felt under her seat to ensure the bags were there. Gabe took two deep breaths and seemed to go into a trance. Priya turned the engine on and Lucy looked out the window as they lifted off the ground. She looked down and could see the campus. She then looked up toward the horizon and was thankful to be leaving, hopefully for the last time.

They landed at 12:55 p.m. Gabe had informed Randy of what happened and he was there to pick up Daisy. Gabe had a car waiting for Lucy and himself and started running toward it. Lucy followed. She caught her breath as he drove.

"Why are we running? Is it bad if I'm late for orientation?" Lucy shouted.

"Well, they're most likely running on VCT, Vision Catcher Time and ... "

Lucy interrupted, "Please tell me that means they're always running late?"

"No, more like always fifteen minutes early. They could be stick-in-the-muds and make me send you back to Booneville, but Aunt Rae knows what's going on and ... "

She cut Gabe off again. "Wait, what?" Lucy's heart sank. She hadn't realized how much hope had been welling up inside of her since they got rid of the car. She felt like a balloon that was slowly deflating.

"It's an outside chance ... we're only going to be about ten minutes late. Just forget that I said that. It's me being nervous. This is the first time I've done this too."

"Okay. Okay." Lucy tried to calm herself down. Lucy hadn't really thought about Gabe's state of mind—not until he got scared in the helicopter. She thought he was supposed to have all the answers, but apparently he was just learning too. Why wasn't Gabe guiding her through everything? She hadn't expected to have to meet new people and go to an orientation.

"So what's orientation, anyway?"

"Well, it's sort of like a two day conference with all the other people that are starting their quests the same day as you." Gabe turned his eyes away from the road just for a moment to speak to her.

"Will you be there?" she inquired.

"We'll work together to set a plan for the next forty days and get you on the right path. We'll do some things like you did with Aunt Rae and the runway to determine where we might go."

"That sounds fun! Why can't I just do that with you?"

"Well, that's just not how it works. In life, you have many people and distractions when you're trying to find your path. By going through this process with others it will make you more likely to continue after the forty days are up when people continue to be in your orbit who have different goals than you."

"I guess that makes sense ... sort of." Lucy looked out the window as Gabe turned onto a road with a guard gate. A sign read "Must show VC credentials to enter, visitors must be on the pre-approved list." The guard rolled down his window and Gabe handed him an ID card. He scanned it and looked at his computer screen to see results.

"Is this Lucy Rivers?" he said, speaking to Gabe and gesturing toward Lucy.

"Yes."

"Can I see some ID?"

Lucy fished her ID out of her wallet. The guard looked down at it, looked at her, and then handed it back. Lucy wondered how strict the screening process really was.

"Okay. You'll make a right here—it's the first building on the left." The guard glanced at his watch. "You better hurry. You're late."

11

The Orientation

Quest Day One

Lucy watched the scenery breeze by as Gabe rushed in the direction the guard had pointed them in—going about forty-five mph on a clearly marked twenty mph road. They appeared to be at a classic small southern college campus with manicured lawns and red brick buildings. They passed by a typical-looking quad where a few people were throwing a frisbee and there was a line next to what appeared to be a coffee cart. Gabe turned into the parking lot next to one building that bordered the quad and parked quickly. He unbuckled his seat belt, bolted out the door, and ran. He slowed and ran backwards, looking at Lucy, who hadn't matched his pace.

"Come on. We're late!" He gestured in an exaggerated "hurry-it-up" motion. Gabe opened a door that had a sign on it that read "Orientation" and held it for Lucy. The door looked like an emergency exit at the back of the building. Lucy expected them to race through some back hallways, but when she stepped in she was in a room that was akin to a small playhouse with 150 or so seats surrounding a small stage. She looked around at the eager faces and saw that there were only two seats left. They were closer to the front than she would've liked.

Lucy wasn't sure what to expect from orientation, but it was reminding her of assembly at one of the summer camps she attended as a child. The lights dimmed, and the crowd grew silent when Rae walked onto the stage wearing a silver robe. She presented less like the heartwarming aunt Lucy had met the previous day and stood with more grandeur—a formidable presence, her rich, ebony skin glowing in the spotlight.

Rae looked across the audience with her arms outstretched and exclaimed, "Welcome, esteemed seekers of truth and self-discovery! We're so glad you've come."

Gabe shouted, "Whoop!" with glee and clapped along with others in the crowd. Following their lead, Lucy clapped too.

"Hello, I'm Rae and I help organize these orientations and host both Vision Catchers and Originators at my B&B. Some of you I've met already." She smiled and winked at Lucy. "I know it wasn't easy to decide to leave your home for over a month to pursue this quest. When contemplating chasing a dream, we too often let negativity have its way, whether it's coming from outsiders, people we trust, or from within us. Your quest is to find your path and determine what lights YOU up. This won't be easy and the most challenging obstacle you'll meet along the way for many of you will be yourself." As Rae said this, her eyes landed directly on Lucy and she immediately felt herself shrinking into her seat. Rae maintained eye contact as she spoke words of comfort.

"Ideas have been stirring inside you throughout your life—visions of inventions, books, art, a happy family, an ideal career. Those visions are powerful. They're the life force that created the guides that have brought you here today. We chose you because something has happened in your life to make you lose touch with yourself. Those seated around you are all going through something. This orientation is designed to help you get in touch with what makes you excellent and push past your demons. Lean on one another and on your Vision Catchers during this time to catapult you into success on this quest."

Lots of people, including Lucy, looked around the room at one another. It reminded Lucy of the first day of class or a typical college orientation when you didn't know if you'd make a friend for life. Maybe she would. Excitement bubbled within her.

"Now to get to the logistical stuff for the day, I'll turn it over to Gus, but before I do, I'd like to leave you with one of my favorite quotes from Louisa May Alcott—'We all have our own life to pursue, our own kind of dream to be weaving, and we all have the power to make wishes come true, as long as we keep believing.'"

The words gave Lucy goosebumps. Rae let them hang in the air for a few moments before the crowd started to applaud. As Rae waved and left the stage, a man wearing a burgundy suit came out. "Let's give it up one more time for our Vision Catcher Rae." The crowd applauded more and when it quieted, the man continued. "I'm Gus, your orientation director. For our Originators, your Vision Catcher will hand you an envelope with a room number and a map of the room you need to go to after lunch. Vision Catchers, please return here for your orientation after lunch. The dining hall is just out the door and around the corner. You can't miss it. There's a sign that says, of all things, 'Dining Hall.'" Gus chuckled to himself and a couple of others were nice and laughed along. "Now disperse, we'll see you all back here tonight during our evening entertainment."

Gabe turned to Lucy and handed her a bright red envelope, which bore her name in silver cursive. Inside the envelope there was a piece of paper directing her to go to Mason Hall Room 202 for small group. It also included an orientation schedule. Things seemed very organized.

Day	Time	Activity
1	1:00 PM	Intro Session
1	1:30 PM	Lunch
1	2:30 PM	Breakout Groups
1	4:30 PM	One-on-One with VC
1	6:00 PM	Dinner
1	8:00 PM	Evening Entertainment
2	9:00 AM	Breakfast
2	10:30 AM	Small Group
2	12:00 PM	Lunch
2	1:30 PM	Talent Show Prep
2	3:30 PM	One-on-One with VC
2	6:00 PM	Dinner
2	7:30 PM	Talent Show

She headed with Gabe to the dining hall, where they had a disappointing spread of sandwiches and bagged chips. As they went through the line, Lucy turned to Gabe and said, "I would've thought that they'd have something more elaborate. Something more of our dream meal."

"Well, the VC chefs are empaths and that is possible. But it takes a few hours to calibrate to everyone's desires. There are close to seventy-five Originators here. They'll be preparing meals to serve at dinner starting from the time you leave for small group."

Lucy grinned. "Well okay. I guess I'll settle for a turkey sandwich for now."

After the helicopter ride and the adventure in the morning, Lucy was tired. She decided to not mingle and stick close to Gabe. She sat in silence, studying the schedule. Her eyes kept being drawn in to the words talent show. She hadn't been much of a performer growing up. There was the church choir, and she loved watching *The Voice*. She even occasionally put an office chair backwards toward the TV and pretended she was one of the judges, deciding if the singer would be on her team, turning around when she did. It genuinely shocked her what some people looked like compared to their voice.

Looks can deceive, and she figured ears can too. Her mind wandered more to the biggest deception of her own life that had brought her here. Colt had wooed her and adored her. After their first date, he had flowers delivered to her office. No man had ever done that for her. They had talked about their favorite books and the ills of the world for hours on end. People have layers. Perhaps he hadn't deceived her at all, she thought. Maybe he was just lost, like her. Where had his dreams gone? Did he have a room full of paintings too? Their downfall had started when he had a mental health crisis—his mother died, he dropped out of grad school, and started teaching middle school. She was falling back into the thought patterns that had kept her with him for so long—guilt, justification of his behavior, and making excuses for his actions. A pinging sound interrupted her thoughts.

She looked up at Gabe, who was chomping on a chip and looking down at his phone, the source of the ping. When he wasn't talking to her, he was worse than a teenager, always staring into the tiny machine. Her mind continued to popcorn. She thought about how Gabe had deceived her when he brought her here. Yet still, she trusted him. Another ping. Her brain bounced again back to the schedule and the talent show.

"Gabe, does everyone perform in the talent show?"

Gabe shrugged a little and nodded in a way that silently apologized that she'd have to go through the inevitable embarrassment of performing. He wasn't unsympathetic to Lucy's objections. He told her he had to perform tonight and wasn't looking forward to it.

"So everybody who was here today, nearly seventy-five people, are going to have to perform? That's horrific. How long does that take? Haven't you ever been to a child's dance recital?"

"Well, no. I haven't, though I think I caught a vision of you sneaking out of one once. It must've gotten better because you forgot about the plan to sneak out. But to answer your first question, everyone who's still here has to perform."

"What do you mean, everyone who's still here? Can I opt out of orientation? I asked you earlier if we could just do this thing together and you said no," Lucy said, crossing her arms.

"The talent show is at the end of day two. We've got a lot of ground to cover between now and then. Some people leave before then, or that's what I've been told. Remember, this is my first time, too."

"Do they drop out because they have to perform in the talent show?"

Gabe laughed. "Not usually, although I'm sure that's happened."

Lucy seriously considered whether she could drop out. She thought of her room in The Tower and the inspiring words from this morning and figured a little embarrassment for three minutes wasn't worth derailing what she hoped would be an amazing forty-day journey. She wasn't sure she had talent, but then she thought that she may have forgotten something.

Leaning in closer to Gabe, she said, "Can we go back to the studio before this forced performance? I think I'm going to need inspiration. I'm not sure I've got much talent at all."

"Well, actually ... " Just as Gabe was about to answer, Gus's voice came over the intercom, just like in grade school. "Attention, please put away your trash and head to your small groups, Originators. Vision Catchers, back to the assembly room."

Lucy looked down at her map and studied it. She didn't want to be the last one there. She felt like a college freshman. Her map reading skills had gone out the window ever since the invention of GPS. She looked up at Gabe for guidance. "I don't have the best sense of direction."

"It's really simple. You're just going to need to go out these doors and make a left and it'll be the next building. You'll see a big sign."

"Okay. Well bye, I guess." She went out the door and saw a bunch of people making a right, not a left. Almost everyone was making a right, in fact. What if Gabe had a bad sense of direction too? She got out the map again and flipped it around. The group of people that had turned right blocked her view. Instead of taking a moment to figure it out, she ignored Gabe's instructions and followed them, just for a minute. When she saw the group head past the edge of the dining hall to a building on top of a big hill, she decided to trust Gabe knew what he was talking about and head back the other way.

Soon, she saw the big sign that said "red and green small groups meet here" with a giant arrow. She followed the very clear sign, breathing a sigh of relief that she was on the right track. She went up the stairs and found room 202. It also had a sign on the door that said the "red group." She turned the knob, opened the door, and said to herself, "One step at a time."

Gabe watched as Lucy entered the room and let his worries that she'd try to escape again dissipate for the moment. He'd momentarily kicked himself when he saw her turn in the opposite direction of where he'd instructed her to go. He contemplated calling out to her, but he gave her a minute to find her own way and felt satisfied with himself that he had as he headed back to the assembly hall.

Except for the opening ceremonies earlier that morning when there was a mixed group of Originators and Vision Catchers, Gabe hadn't gathered in a room with this many of his kind since he graduated from the school years ago. He looked around the room to see if he saw any familiar faces. Theo wasn't there because he was still in the middle of his initial quest, but then he spotted Cecilia. She was gorgeous. He'd always had a crush on her. It wasn't just her long brown hair or her smile, but she exuded this confidence that he envied.

A confidence that presented itself when they locked eyes and she motioned to him to come sit with her. Gabe's heart raced, and he felt the blood rush to his face. He tried his best to match her energy and strut confidently as he walked toward her. Unfortunately, he tripped over something and almost fell right on his face. He caught himself, but not before others took notice. He looked around to see what he'd tripped on and saw Kai, a VC about three years older than him, snickering with a smug smile.

He rolled his eyes and walked slowly toward Cecilia. Agitated, he slid into the seat next to her, avoiding eye contact. She touched his shoulder and turned toward him. "Are you okay?" she asked, tightening her lips in pity.

"I'm fine," he replied, smiling shyly. He was really fine—Cecilia Gray was touching him! She wanted him to sit next to her. What was this? He awkwardly looked down at his hands, clasping them tightly as if they were a stress relief ball.

He was trying to come up with the words to say to her that wouldn't make him sound like a dweeb when she said, "This is so nerve-racking, isn't it? I mean, I've been following my Originator for a while, but this is it—the last test before we get full status. And I can't believe I got her here. She's so closed off right now. Yesterday she came back to her room with a black eye. I don't even know where she went. I couldn't read her or pick up on anything."

"Oh, I can top that. Mine drove back to return her car to the police in the town where she lives at five-thirty this morning. Luckily, I could tap into the Vision Catchers Network, get a helicopter, and get her back here by orientation. My nerves are off the chart."

"Why was she returning? Was she ... " Cecilia stopped mid-sentence when footsteps stomped across the stage.

Gus walked up to the mic and said, "Greetings, friends. I see rookies and long-time veterans in the crowd. Some of you old-timers have taken a well-deserved hiatus from going on quests in the last few years. During this time some things have changed, so you'll want to pay attention to these announcements too." Some older people at the back of the room, who were whispering with one another, looked up.

Gus continued, "You should have received alerts on your phone to use our new app. We've been using it for a little more than a year and have found it to be a very successful and efficient way to track your progress and your Originator's. This data we're collecting will help us in the future to gain a real pulse on the good that we're creating in the world and that exists in the world at large."

An older gentleman in the back, who was bald with wisps of gray hair on his head, stood up and said, "I don't like where the Guild is going with this app. This isn't how we used to do it. All these alerts and buttons make this process so much more complicated than it needs to be. Give me your old-fashioned book or binder. Can I just have an option to do that? I have plenty in my library to choose from." The woman next to him said, "Here, here."

"Unfortunately, Don, no. This is the new way. You can take this up with the Guild, but this isn't the appropriate venue to air your grievances. The Guild took steps to get Vision Catcher input. Believe it or not, we trained the committee members to support the app's back-end. I think one of them is here today. She along with other tech and scientific minded Vision Catchers have put a lot of work into this and are sending reports back to the Guild." Gus put his hand on his forehead and squinted, searching the crowd. "Hannah, will you stand up?"

Hannah looked around the room, cheeks bright red, stood up and half waved. Gabe felt so sorry for her, but she was strong. *Hopefully, she won't get harassed too much*, he thought.

After she sat down, Gus said, "Now let's proceed."

Don huffed and sat down with a scowl on his face, mumbling something to the woman next to him, glaring at Hannah.

The lights dimmed, and a screen came down. The familiar Vision

Catchers Guild Crest appeared animated as the presentation began. "First a message from Vance Gunderthorpe for those who may haven't viewed it on the app yet," Gus said. The intro video Gabe had watched on the app yesterday played.

After it concluded, Gus continued, "The features of this new app include videos from esteemed VCs, a quick connection line to your rep, and this is also where you'll be required to record your Originator's progress. After your first one-on-one session with them this afternoon, the app will prompt you to do this." Gus talked about the technical aspects SLOWLY for the old-timers and demo'd how to navigate the app.

Cecilia leaned toward Gabe and said, "Well this part I'm not nervous about," giggling just a little. Gabe lightly laughed as well. After Gus droned on for at least five minutes on how to report errors in the app, he saw Aunt Rae walk in and started paying attention.

"While she cannot get to every one of you, Rae may come and observe your session for the first-timers out there. You'll need to be prepared to welcome her in as you guide your Originators on their journey." Wide-eyed, Gabe and Cecilia exchanged looks of nervousness with one another.

"No need to panic. This is just for advice and guidance, not judgment. Your Originators are judged through our scoring system tracked in the app."

Someone in the back shouted out, "How's that supposed to work?"

"I'm glad you asked. I was just getting to that." Gus moved on to the next slide and revealed a scoring system.

"Your Originators have a journey that's not always a straight path to achieve a fulfilling life. There are things on their journey that will reflect positively on their progress and, in turn, you as a Vision Catcher, but their journey also includes aspects that are negative. Some examples of positive and negative are on the following slides."

Gus read off things on each of the slides, adding these were just examples and they may be judged in other ways.

Gabe swallowed hard. He mustered up the courage to say, "How will you know if this is happening? In school, we learned about documenting the quest and submitting the materials to the Guild. Isn't a caseworker or Supporter supposed to review how the Originators are doing after that point?"

"The system has changed and is more automated and accurate now. After each session at orientation and at the end of each day of the thirty-seven days after, you will be required to check in with your rep and transmit what happened during the day to them telepathically. The app will calculate the points based on the visions you send to your rep. The software will analyze your submission. It's very sophisticated and its lie detector functionality will pick any deviation from the truth up. This has eliminated the need for so many Supporters."

Hands shot up into the air.

"Questions can be sent to me in a direct message via the app. I'd like to move on to our next activity as we only have a short amount of time before you need to go pick up your Originators." Gus paused and looked around as the hands slowly descended.

He continued, "I know that was a lot to sit through, so let's get our creative energy flowing through a quick pump up session. Some of you are more powerful than others in terms of how easily you can send telepathic messages. In a pump up session, every one of you in the room will think of a song to send to DJ Princess."

A curtain rose in the corner of the stage and a short woman with curly hair sat behind the speaker system. She waved to the group excitedly and bobbed her head up and down to the music that must have been going on in her head. Some people in the room must have already started trying to send her their songs because she yelled out, "Not yet. Wait for Gus to tell you to go."

"That's right." Gus took a couple of beats for dramatic effect and then shouted, "On your mark, get set, go!" Silence filled the air and DJ Princess's eyes were closed tight and her face scrunched up from concentration. After ten seconds, the song "Cecilia" by Simon and Garfunkel played over the loudspeakers. Gabe turned to Cecilia, whose cheeks were blushing. Despite Gabe's own nerves, he grabbed her hands to dance with her. She bashfully obliged. The music and Cecilia soothed his anxiety. He wondered how many people might have been thinking about that song. How many others thought she was the most beautiful one in the room? Though he'd always been told that his telepathic powers were strong, could he have done it all on his own?

The DJ played "Cupid Shuffle" next and everyone was called up onto the stage in a big clump to do the line dance. They got all mixed up in this process, so Gabe wasn't right next to Cecilia anymore. When the song ended, Gus said loudly, "We don't have much time, find a partner."

Gabe looked around for Cecilia, but Kai had already grabbed her. When he turned around, Hannah was standing right in front of him. They smiled and nodded at each other, silently agreeing to pair up. Hannah leaned in. "Hopefully, we'll have more luck than we had playing Visionaries."

"Are they scoring us?" Gabe whispered back, his nerves still shining through.

Hannah said, "Well, not now, but," and before she could explain, Gus interrupted with more instructions.

"Okay, it looks like everybody has a buddy. Now, this exercise is called the path to fulfillment. Knowing what you know about the person you're leading through this quest for the next forty days, hold your partner's hands and take turns projecting the feelings that you imagine your Originator will have at the end of this journey. This exercise allows you to feed off of one another's positivity. Remember, the ultimate goal of all of this is to create a world where people are happy in their lives."

Hannah and Gabe held hands. Gabe looked around and locked eyes with Kai, who smiled and winked at him. Someone shouted, "Do we just start?"

"Heavens yes, just go," Gus exclaimed, sounding exasperated. Gabe turned his focus back on Hannah.

"Have you done this before?" Gabe asked Hannah quietly.

"No talking, just thinking!" Gus shouted.

"Alright, alright." Gabe thought, projecting his thoughts to Hannah.

He imagined Lucy at the end of the forty days and imagined her energy as light and carefree. He visualized her giving herself a big hug of the self-love. The energy that Hannah sent to him felt more exciting. Like ideas that were shooting off from a sparkler surrounded by happiness and joy.

After a minute, Gus exclaimed, "Now stop!"

Gabe opened his eyes and came out of the exercise feeling energized. When he looked at Hannah, she looked relaxed. The people in the room turned back toward Gus, awaiting instructions.

"I hope everyone is in a positive space after that. Your Originators were divided into different small groups and assigned a color. If you handed your Originator a red envelope with instructions, they're in the red group. If it was green, they're in the green group, and so on. Before we pick them up for your one-on-one sessions, I'll need you to go to your designated group. Spotlights please!"

On Gus's command, various colored spotlights illuminated around the room. To an artist like Gabe, the myriad of colors were simply beautiful. He looked toward Hannah. "I'm headed over to red. You?"

"Blue," Hannah replied.

"I really loved the energy that you imagined for your Originator. If I have questions, do you mind me messaging you? I really admire everything that Aunt Rae has told me about your previous work. Plus, your scientific mind might help this artistic one in a jam." Gabe felt very comfortable around Hannah, like she was the big sister he never had.

"Of course, and I'll see you around the next couple of days. I liked your projected energy as well. I feel very at ease fetching Reggie from his small group."

"Oh, I met him at breakfast the other day. Sweet old man. I better go. See you around." Gabe waved and turned toward the red spotlight, seeing that many had already made their way over there, including Cecilia. Thrilled to get to spend more time with her, but as he approached, she looked almost queasy. Kai was also in the red group, but she had put a few people between him and herself.

"Are you all right?" Gabe said, touching her shoulder this time.

"Yes, it's probably nothing," she whispered softly. "That exercise with Kai was weird. It was like he sent me a happy energy, but there was something off about it. Like a masked happiness that depressed people sometimes exude. I'm just trying to shake it off."

"That sucks. I had a really great session with Hannah. This is all new. I'm sure there's going to be ups and downs for us just like there are going to be for Lucy and ... what's your Originator's name?"

"Emily."

"I'm glad we're in the same group. Let's definitely stick together."

Cecilia nodded in agreement, smiling at Gabe as he met her gaze with enthusiasm. "You don't know how much that means to me. I ... "

"People, people. Hush now," Gus said over Cecilia and the others chatting. "Go and get your Originators from their assigned rooms together. We want you to arrive at the same time. Check the app to see where that is."

All heads shifted down to their phones and Kai announced to their group, "Got it. We're going to Room 202 in Mason Hall." He started walking toward the exit. Gabe and Cecilia looked at one another and sensed the butterflies swirling in each other's stomachs. They followed in lockstep with the rest of the group, some of whom were still looking down at their phones.

When they reached the room, they were told to wait a moment for an event organizer. While they stood there, Kai came around to Gabe and Cecilia.

"Did you see the leaderboard?" he asked, holding up his phone. Gabe stared at the numbers taunting him. His stomach twisted in knots. Kai was near the top.

12

The Small Group

The room was small, with six other people sitting in a circle. Lucy sat down in the last empty chair next to a large white man in his fifties with a bald spot on the top of his head and the sides grown down to about his chin. He was wearing a button-up shirt where one button couldn't hold his girth and his undershirt was now peeking through. The armpits of the shirt were slightly wet and Lucy got a strong whiff of his body odor. Despite a little bit of disgust, she turned to him, smiled, and said hello.

As Lucy examined the faces around the room, one woman began to speak. She could've been the cover model for the game Old Maid. Her hair was white sleeked back in a bun, she was wearing a pink shawl, and a frumpy dress with flowers on it. Her stockings were bunching up at the ankles next to her blue buckle shoes that looked very comfy. Lucy wondered if this woman had ever been to Rae's closet. Judging from her age, she probably had. Maybe this was just *her* style.

"Can I have your attention, please? I'm Ms. Benedict, your small group leader for orientation. I've been a Vision Catcher for decades and have been leading these orientations for the last ten years. It might look like I'm just an old grandma, but make no mistake, I'll push you to your limits in my group. Do not doubt it."

She reached into a large patchwork bag and pulled out small spiral-bound notebooks, passing them around the circle. Then she grabbed a handful of pens and placed them in the middle of the circle on the floor. Some were blue, some were red, some had feathers and looked like quills, and there were even those retractable pens with multiple colors of ink.

Ms. Benedict instructed them to pick one pen that sparked joy. Lucy chose the one with the feather. It was heavier than she expected. "We'll get to this activity in just a moment. First let's do introductions. Please tell us your name and a time that you remember being blissfully happy. I'll start. My name is Ms. Benedict, and a time that I remember being blissfully happy was when I was a young girl getting ice cream with my friends in the summer. Our parents had taken us camping, and it was a scrumptious treat one day after we'd been on a long hike." She smiled from ear to ear and looked around the room at each one of them. Lucy hoped she wouldn't be called on to speak next. To her relief, Ms. Benedict said, "Can I have a volunteer to go next?"

The fat smelly man next to her spoke up. "I'll go. Hi my name is Gary, and it's hard to recall a time that I was blissfully happy, but the one thing that sticks out is this time last year right after my brother Steve died." Around the room, jaws dropped, and some stink-eyes headed in Gary's direction. "I know, I know, that's not the blissful part don't look at me like that." Gary looked around the room and took a beat before continuing. "See my brother Steve, he was about ten years younger than me. He had four kids. The youngest one was about three and you know she can only sort of get the fact that she wasn't going to see her dad again. I stayed with them at their house for about a week after the funeral. I was in the guest bedroom and I was looking at this picture of me and my brother when we were kids at our lake house. I'm not much of a crier, but something about that picture set me off in that moment, like things sometimes do when you lose somebody. Then, Mary Beth came into the room—that's the youngest kid's name, Mary Beth—anyway, she came in and she had a pair of underwear on her head and two pigtails sticking out of the leg holes. She was wearing the cutest little dress, and she said, "Uncle Gary, will you come to my dance party?" And of course I said yes, laughing at her hilarious hairdo and overall cuteness. Her tiny hand grabbed mine and pulled me into her room where she had "Brown-Eyed Girl" blasting. It was just me and her. Here I was thinking we were going to be dancing to "Baby Shark." It was great. She was swaying and dancing and holding my hands and having me dance with her. And for a moment, being there with her, dancing, listening to timeless feel-good music, looking into her adorable brown eyes with the ridiculous pair of underpants on her head, I felt joy for the first time in a while. I was laughing and being silly—making funny faces at her. Then she screamed out, 'My daddy sings this to me all the time.' That blissful happiness I felt turned to heartbreak for me—my little niece didn't know her dad had died. So yeah, that's my moment of blissful happiness, but it was just that," Gary snapped his fingers, "a moment."

Not even Ms. Benedict spoke for at least thirty seconds. They just took it in. Then she said, "Well thank you so much Gary for being so vulnerable and honest with us. Anyone want to volunteer to go next?"

There was another long pause before one woman whose jaw had dropped spoke, "Well that's very hard to follow, but my name is Myra and a time I remember being blissfully happy was when I went on vacation by myself and kayaked down this river and then went to dinner at this cute cafe, and watched *Fried Green Tomatoes* on the TV in my hotel room."

The raw honesty of these individuals shocked Lucy. The phrase, "don't judge a book by its cover" was running through her head. Myra was an extremely good-looking blonde who appeared to be in her twenties. Lucy would've never thought that she would've found bliss being by herself. As for Gary, she couldn't have possibly imagined he would've told such a poignant story. She racked her brain, trying to think of the blissful moment she'd want to share with the group.

"That sounds lovely, Myra. Let's just go in a circle now - counter-clockwise." The man next to Myra was Lamar. His memory of bliss didn't seem all that blissful to Lucy. He talked about how his parents never let him have pets and catching a frog in his backyard and secretly smuggling it into his room. He made a little environment for it, but he didn't know how to feed it. So the frog died shortly after. His blissful memory was in the week that he had it.

Flora introduced herself and talked about the blissful time she had hiking in the mountains and being at peace with nature. Lucy was glad for Flora's introduction because perhaps people would follow her lead and be a little less deep and more brief than Gary had been. There was one more person to share before it would be Lucy's turn. She still hadn't come up with a blissful memory.

"Hi, my name's Paul, but my dad and brother and occasionally my mom called me Stubbletop growing up. My mom would also call me Paulie, but my dad was relentless after I got a bad haircut one time. I remember being in a group sort of like this where we were asked to introduce ourselves. I said my name was Paulie. My brother was there. He said 'What's your real name though?' And he poked and he prodded me until I said Stubbletop. The group of boys that we were with—I think it was Boy Scouts or something—just laughed. Some nicknames are great and some just stick ... and they hurt. But when I got to college, my brother and dad weren't there. I could finally be called by my name. I remember being in the dorm and people were just being loud and noisy and playing some kind of bowling game down the hallway. I peeked my head out to see what was going on and one guy said, 'Hey Paul, you want to come to dinner with us? We're going to go grab a slice down the road'. Just the sound of my name filled me with joy."

"Thank you Paul, we've got about five minutes for our last two people and then we'll move on to the journal exercise." Ms. Benedict looked at Lucy and nodded at her to begin.

Lucy felt bad that everybody had chosen a memory from a long time ago. The only happy memories that were popping up into her mind had happened in the last forty-eight hours. Since Ms. Benedict had hinted that she needed to be brief, she simply introduced herself and said that she was blissfully happy listening to her friend do stand-up. The last woman to speak was sitting on the other side of Gary. Lucy hadn't even really looked past him to see her.

When Lucy peered around him, she saw a skinny woman with a black eye. The woman was frowning and staring off into the distance, clearly lost in her own thoughts. She shook a little as she realized all eyes were on her. With a little hesitancy and a voice full of sadness, she said, "Hi my name is Emily. I can't think of a time I was blissfully happy."

She and Lucy had definitely taken up less than their allotted five minutes. Ms. Benedict spoke directly to Emily with an encouraging tone. "I hope that your Vision Catcher can help you recover one of those memories." She clasped her hands, took a deep breath in and said, "Now it's time to use those pens that I had you pick out at the beginning. How many of you journal?" No one raised their hands. "Anybody a writer or want to be?" Flora timidly raised her hand and Gary followed.

"Well, that's okay," Ms. Benedict said, seeming to almost comfort herself more than the group. "Our first exercise is simple. I want you to write about your perfect day. What would it feel like, what would it smell like, what would you do? Some people get hung up on this exercise because of the word 'perfect', but try to quiet that inner critic. This is just a journal exercise. It doesn't have to be perfect. This is just meant to get you into a state of dreaming about your ideal life. I'm going to start a five-minute timer."

Lucy looked around as some were writing quickly. She regretted her choice of pen because it felt very awkward in her hand. She thought the feather really went with her new boho outfit, which Gabe had given her to change into when they'd been driving to the helicopter. It wasn't just the pen, though. She also hated hand writing anything, and she had horrible handwriting. She attempted to imagine a perfect day anyway.

I'd wake up feeling fully rested in a room a lot like The Tower, except it would be my own house. I'd be wearing a cozy T-shirt and pajama pants. I'd put on my shoes and go kayaking on the lake that would be just outside my house. I'd come back and my lunch of shrimp tacos, black beans, and chips would be delivered at my door and after I enjoyed that, a masseuse would show up to give me a two-hour massage. I'd sit down in a comfy chair in a fuzzy white robe and read a funny book. My second meal of the day would be at my door, maybe Indian this time, and I'd enjoy a great chick flick while I ate it. I'd top off the night with Rocky Road ice cream and go to bed.

Seeing that most people had put down their pens, Ms. Benedict said, "Okay, hopefully that was an easy one. Now, I want you to write everything that's weighing you down or holding you back from being your authentic self. In other words, what's keeping you from having this perfect day in the near future? What about tomorrow or one week from now?"

The question made Lucy uncomfortable. She broke the silence in the room timidly. "Are we going to have to share these?"

"Yes," Ms. Benedict said matter-of-factly.

Lucy's stomach started tightening up, and she squirmed a little in her seat. She knew that some of them had been so vulnerable with one another, but she didn't know these people.

"Lucy, this is a safe space. No need to worry," Ms. Benedict said in a soothing tone. "Everyone, put your pens down for a moment." The group did as they were told, and their eyes shifted from one person to another. "How many of you feel uncomfortable with this exercise?"

Lucy put up her hand slowly at half mast and a few others followed: Emily, Myra, and Paul.

"You see Lucy. It's not easy for anyone. What most scares you about it?"

"Never mind. Can I just do the exercise now?"

"No, please answer."

As all eyes were on Lucy, beads of sweat formed on her forehead and her legs shook nervously. After several moments, she ripped the Band-Aid off and spoke.

"Well, I'm scared that if I talk about my problems or what's holding me back, it will be so tiny compared to everyone else who's been invited to this quest. I mean, my friend Daisy was talking about why she was invited this morning and it seemed so much more intense than what I've been going through."

"So if I'm hearing you, you don't feel justified in having problems or complaining. Is that right?" Ms. Benedict asked.

Lucy managed a nod.

"Is that what some of you are feeling?" Ms. Benedict calmly looked around the room, and this time, all but Gary and Myra nodded. "Okay then. What if somebody thought your problems were trivial? Who cares what they think? Your issues are valid because they're stopping you from living your best life. Please take a deep breath and give it a go. What's weighing you down and holding you back from being your true authentic self and being able to have your perfect day?"

Lucy took a deep breath in and let it out. She closed her eyes, imagined herself as a superhero like the one she'd seen in the studio, opened her eyes, and picked up her pen to write a list.

1. **<u>COLT</u>**
2. Fear
3. Low self-esteem
4. Not living somewhere cool (i.e. no lake house)
5. Not having enough money to do something like the day I talked about

Lucy sat trying to think of more things, but Colt ultimately overshadowed everything. She waited a couple minutes until Ms. Benedict interrupted others who were still writing. "Pens down. Time to share." Her voice was singsong, like a kindergarten teacher. It grated on Lucy's nerves. "Lucy, you first. Read us your perfect day and then tell us what's keeping you from it."

Lucy frowned and took a deep breath in. She read her perfect day word for word. She glanced up and saw Flora with a giant smile on her face. Then Lucy continued reluctantly, "So, well, the biggest thing holding me back from being my true authentic self is my husband. He calls me names. I never do anything right, and I'm always walking on eggshells, hoping that he won't blow up at me. So, my list of why I can't be my true authentic self for have that perfect day is I guess fear, low self-esteem, I don't have enough money to do any of those things, and I don't live somewhere cool like a lake house. And I know what you're all thinking. Well, why don't you just leave your husband? Wouldn't that fix all of your problems? Well, I have, but he's still up here." Lucy made a gesture toward her head. "Honestly, I'm scared, but being here—I hope it will fix everything and I can really be free of him."

"Let me stop you there. It won't fix everything. We can't. We're asking these questions to see if YOU can get back to a place where you're creating joy in the world." Lucy shrank back, chastised. She'd heard this before and knew that it would be a recurring theme in her quest. It still hurt a bit to hear Ms. Benedict cut down her ideas.

Lucy knew she needed to muster the resolve to make the most of this for herself. She couldn't help but feel worried still and instinctively looked behind her to be sure Colt hadn't somehow heard the whole thing.

Gary went next, and Lucy was excited to see what he had to say.

"My perfect day would be waking up next to my lovely wife and snuggling with her in bed, making love, then getting up and having a breakfast of scrambled eggs and grits, sausage, and toast. There'd be multiple football games on that day and at some point my buddy Rick would come over to watch with me. I'd go to my mom's house for dinner and then come home and snuggle into bed with my beautiful wife."

"And why can't you have that perfect day?"

"Well, there's not football games on all the time. I don't have a wife. She left. I'd have to pick up the phone and call Rick for him to come over, and I rarely do that. My mom's dead. I have to take care of our disabled son. He's got Down syndrome. I have some relatives who've agreed to take him for this short time now, but that isn't the usual. I got to work. Go into the office, do the accounting, no one wants to talk to you and you're just the accountant, and then pick up my son from his adult day care, make him dinner as best I can or pick something up, and then watch TV and do it all over again."

"Both Lucy and Gary made some solid logical points. How many of you put you didn't have enough money to do all the things you wanted to do?"

Everyone but Paul raised their hands.

"How many of you imagined people that were dead in your perfect day?"

Flora, Gary, and Emily raised their hands.

"I think some of you have magical thinking. It's perfectly fine to imagine and dream about being around loved ones that are no longer here and even having a lot of money. We all do that. In both Lucy and Gary's stories, what are some things that the rest of the group think they can do to be true to their authentic self or have their perfect day? Doesn't have to be anything big."

Emily said in an almost resentful tone, "Gary can call his friend."

"That's great," Ms. Benedict said encouragingly.

Myra said, "Well, you know our perfect day wouldn't be perfect if it wasn't special. I get Gary has some heavy responsibilities with his son. Care can be expensive, but maybe you could budget for two days out of the month for his son to be in that adult care facility or stay with somebody else he knows, so he can at least get up and make that breakfast and enjoy some football. And like Emily said, call his friend."

Ms. Benedict smiled. "Thanks Emily. Thanks Myra. These are great suggestions. You see, the common thread is that it's just a baby step. What about for Lucy?" The question hung heavy in the air. Lucy knew the answer. They all did. It was just who was brave enough to say it.

To her shock, the words fell out of her own mouth. "I've got to let go of the fear that Colt will pull me back in." She spoke slowly and gazed off into the distance.

Flora snapped her fingers. The rest joined in. The sound lifted Lucy's spirits in an unfamiliar and delightful way. She felt a tingling in her chest—a layer of insecurity melting away, like butter meeting a hot skillet, light and golden.

Ms. Benedict opened her mouth to say something else when the door to the room opened and seven people, including Gabe, came through it. Ms. Benedict looked up. "Ah yes, your personal Vision Catchers have arrived. Now, my friends, you'll do one-on-one exercises to expand on what we've been doing here. Before we meet again tomorrow, I ask you to hold one question in your mind. You don't have to answer it, but just ask yourself: What is it I really want and what's keeping me from getting it? Okay? See you tomorrow!"

Lucy felt raw and was glad to leave the intensity and scrutiny of the group. Digging deep into the well of emotions she had long ago closed off was overwhelming. Unsure if Gabe would push her even harder, she looked up at him and meekly greeted him. "Hi."

Gabe smiled and held the door open for her. "Come on. I found us a perfect spot." He led the way and made a beeline to a beautiful patch of grass just past the quad on top of a hill next to a large oak tree and yet still basking in the sun's warm glow. There was already a picnic blanket. He sat down on the ground and gestured for Lucy to do the same.

"Well, looks like you may have picked the nicest spot on the campus."

"I think so," Gabe said. "At least the nicest near where all the action is." He smiled that giant smile that Lucy had become familiar with and it comforted her. Lucy let out a giant yawn. It was unintentional, but the lack of sleep from the night before and the intensity of the exercises they'd just done in the small group had made her utterly exhausted.

"Oh, yes, you must be tired. I'm a bit exhausted myself. Why don't I go get us a latte from the coffee cart on the other side of the quad?"

Lucy wondered how he knew her go-to drink was a latte, but then she remembered he knew so much about her. She gave an enthusiastic nod, and he was off.

Just as Lucy was about to lie down, a strange man in a black hoodie approached quickly and, without a word, sat right beside her. He crossed his legs to mirror hers. She was so stunned that she didn't even move at first. Gathering her senses, she backed away from him like a crab and demanded to know what he was doing.

"Don't be afraid." He cupped his mouth and whispered, "I'm here to help you."

13

The Strange Man and the Session

Lucy took a deep breath in and exhaled out. So many curious things had happened up to now. She tried to convince herself that the man sitting next to her was probably a Vision Catcher or something. She mustered up the courage to respond to his ominous statement. "Help me how?" she asked.

"I wanted to warn you about something."

Hairs raised on the back of Lucy's neck, thinking that Colt might be around the corner.

The strange man continued, "First let me ask you why did you decide to take part in this vision quest?"

"I needed a change in my life and they're offering me a free place to stay to figure that out. It was kind of a no-brainer."

"Don't you think perhaps it came too easy? Haven't you ever heard of people getting sucked into a cult? These people aren't here to help you. They ruined my life and they'll ruin yours, too. I didn't think my life could get much worse, but after this quest, it was hell."

"What did they do to you?"

"Well, he ... " The man looked around as if he was being chased or followed and needed to make sure that no one would see him. He spotted something or someone and simply got up and left.

Lucy walked around the quad, trying to find the man so he could tell her more. He was nowhere to be found, but she spotted Gabe heading toward her carrying her latte in her search. She quickly dashed into the building to her left and made her way to the ladies' restroom.

While in a locked stall, she ran through everything the man in the black hoodie had told her. Was it too easy? Lucy had never thought about it this way before. She assumed Gabe was only there to help her. Could what this guy was saying be right? What if they were actually trying to make her life worse? It WAS all too good to be true.

She tried to imagine the worst she'd ever felt with Colt. It was probably the day that he first called her a cunt. It was so shocking and heartbreaking and scary. The exercises they'd done today made her feel fear. How was this any different from that? She chose the quest, but she hadn't chosen to do the orientation. Gabe hadn't given her a syllabus when he invited her on this journey. She was so desperate; she hadn't asked many questions at all.

She heard footsteps pass in the hallway, and her heart raced. She was unsure of what to do, but that wasn't an unfamiliar feeling. It was just like the helplessness she felt every time she was returning from an argument with Colt after she'd hid for a few hours. She'd been stuck with him with nowhere to go—it always felt like the only thing she could do. Walk back in with her head down and apologize. At least with Gabe, she could just be on guard. She had nothing to be ashamed of, but now, the only logical next step was to go have her session with Gabe.

She took a deep breath in and exited the building. Gabe was looking for her. He was making a 360 slowly, being careful not to spill the coffee cups he had in his hands. "Hey Gabe, over here," she called. "I just needed to use the facilities."

"Ahh ... got it. Come on, let's go."

He motioned to head back to the spot on the hill. Lucy slowly made her way up the hill while continuing to look for the man in the hoodie along the way. When she reached Gabe, his presence soothed her and she couldn't help but to smile softly. Did he have her under some sort of spell? She shook her mind to a more alert state. Straightening her posture, she focused on keeping up her guard. She couldn't let herself succumb to a possible cult.

"Okay," she said, "so what do we do now?" He looked down at his phone intensely and held up one finger.

Gabe was reviewing the instructions on the app one last time. It was sunny, but only fifty-five degrees outside. Despite the cool breeze, beads of sweat formed on his forehead. He was so nervous that he'd screw this up. He hoped he could set the tone for Lucy's mind to open to any steps that lie ahead, which was the goal of the exercise, but now she seemed more closed off than she had ten minutes before.

He handed Lucy her drink, took a deep breath, and asked, "Are you ready to start?"

Lucy nodded slowly, not saying a word.

"Okay, once you get a few sips, I'm going to need you to put your coffee down, stand up straight, and put your hands in mine and close your eyes."

Lucy did what he said, still not speaking. A few moments passed and Gabe opened his eyes and in a concerned and nervous tone said, "What's wrong?"

"Me? Nothing?"

"Lucy, I'm an empath by nature. Did something happen? Is it Colt?"

"No, well, I'm just not sure I want to do this."

"You're not? You seemed so excited this morning after the opening ceremony. What changed? Did something happen in small group?"

"Well actually," she hesitated. "You know, maybe I'm just tired. Can

I just lie down for a little bit here?"

Gabe was uneasy about this new information, but looking at the schedule, he caved into her suggestion. "Okay, but I have to do this exercise with you before dinner."

Lucy laid down on the picnic blanket in the shade, closed her eyes, and within a minute or two was breathing deeply and asleep. Gabe watched her for a few moments and put his headphones in to watch more advice videos from the app. This one was a brief lecture from Vance Gunderthorpe:

"You are pair-bonded to the Originator you are guiding on this quest. This means that when you are in close vicinity to him or her, you can more easily transfer dreams and visions that they've lost back to them. You should feel your powers enhance when you are around them. If you succeed in your first quest and achieve full status, you will have a deeper understanding of humans, yourself, and your powers. However, as the quest goes on, your pair-bond with your Originator may actually weaken each time you fail to guide them on their path to fulfillment. So, as a reminder, let's review the basics of vision catching:

"Vision Catchers can catch visions, dreams, and ideas so that they aren't lost. Each person will have in their lifetime a Vision Catcher who is the guardian of the dreams and hopes one has for their life.

"You can give visions back to your Originators telepathically or the Originator may retrieve the vision themselves. However, if the Originator becomes shut down and in a rut or dies, the visions become nontransferable to the Originator. This means they can no longer retrieve the dream, hope, or idea and their Vision Catcher can not transfer it to them.

"When this happens, the Vision Catchers should file the idea in the Dream Exchange so it may be transferred to another Originator. Many times people will say, "I thought of that first," but by not executing, their idea was given to someone else. The statute of limitations varies based on what the vision is. Your duty and the oath that you took requires you to preserve dreams as long as possible.

"Not all visions can be filed for someone else, of course. These visions include things like one's vision for their life as a whole—whether to get married or have kids, for example. You, the Vision Catcher, document this. File these in our storage facility if they're taking up too much space.

"If you are reaching the end of forty days and your Originator does not seem to be on the path to fulfillment, you may be tempted to obtain an expired vision for them. This should only be done through appropriate channels and will only be successful if the vision that you purchase is close to a vision they had for themselves. For instance, giving them an idea for a novel when you've already identified that they are a talented writer could be the push that they need to have an amazing life. If you are caught buying or selling visions on the black market, the Guild will reassign you to a much less prestigious role in our community or even send you to a Rehabilitation Center. Heed this warning as you continue on your quest."

Gabe knew all of this, yet it served as a not so pleasant reminder of how much was riding on Lucy's success. Her success was his success. It would be so embarrassing if he had to tell Aunt Rae that Lucy had dropped out, or worse, returned to Colt. Just a few moments after the video ended, Lucy stirred, but then fell back asleep. Gabe checked his watch and laid down beside her, trying hard to send her soothing and comforting thoughts and images. He hoped their pair-bond would make her let go of whatever reason she was unsure she wanted to continue. He fought sleep, fearing that if he did, Lucy may slip away, but eventually lost the battle and drifted off.

Lucy woke first and saw Gabe sleeping. She made a conscious effort to ignore the man in the black hoodie. After all, why should she trust him over Gabe? Gabe hadn't steered her wrong thus far. He'd rescued her and brought her to orientation. Watching him, he looked so young and peaceful. She made a quick mental note to ask him how he could be her Vision Catcher when he looked ten years her junior.

There was a large clock on the top of one building lining the quad that read five o'clock. Wanting to keep her promise to him, she shook him awake so that they could complete their session.

Gabe startled a bit and then smiled when he realized Lucy was still there. Once he was fully awake, he sat up and asked, "Are you ready now?"

Thinking about the experience she'd had with Rae in The Closet, Lucy felt a sense of comfort, peace, and excitement for what this next step with Gabe would be like. She confidently said, "Yes, I'm ready."

Gabe smiled again, moved closer to where she sat, and said gently, "Now with an open heart, put your hands in mine."

Lucy opened herself up and put her hands in his hands, closed her eyes, then heard Gabe's voice again.

"Let's first imagine that perfect day that you outlined earlier in the small group."

Lucy woke up in a room more splendid than The Tower. The coziness of the space and the softness of her pajamas, she could feel all over her skin and all of her muscles relaxed.

She felt more alert and awake than she did before she'd put her hands into Gabe's. Her gaze drifted out the window at the lake. A deer was drinking from it at the shoreline and a fish jumped out of the water. She put on the shoes that were by the door and walked down a short, tree-covered path to get to a dock with a kayak tied to the side of it. She grabbed a paddle secured to the dock railing and glided gently into the boat with perfect balance and grace. Untying the vessel, she paddled toward the center. It was idyllic and more peaceful than she'd imagined.

The thought crossed her mind that perhaps she needed sunscreen. Would it be possible to get sunburned from a dream or whatever this was?

Gabe's voice came in and interrupted her thoughts. "Don't worry about sunscreen, don't worry about anything. Let's just live out your perfect day."

Lucy's body once again relaxed and she continued paddling. A few moments later, she heard a loud splash in the water. When she looked over toward the direction of the sound, there was a giant monster heading toward her. It was what she'd always imagined the Loch Ness Monster would look like—with skin and a body like a snake and a face like a dragon with red eyes that stared her down. She clinched up and screamed.

She heard Gabe's voice again. "Lucy, what's wrong?"

"Can't you tell what's wrong? There's a monster heading right toward me?!"

"Yes, and do you think this monster is going to hurt you?"

"Of course I do. IT'S a monster."

"Do you think it can eat you?"

"Well, I guess not because I'm talking to you, so I'm not really here. This is more like a dream."

"Right. So what would happen if you just sat there and let it come toward you?"

Lucy really didn't completely know what was possible, but since Gabe seemed to imply that everything would be fine, she said, "Nothing, I guess."

She sat still and stared at the monster. It slowly transformed into a human. It was Colt. Her heart pounded even harder than it had when the monster was approaching.

"What's wrong now, Lucy?" Gabe asked.

"Colt's swimming toward me."

"Yes, and do you think he's going to hurt you?"

"I don't know what I think. I'm just scared."

"Dig deeper," Gabe said with authority.

"Well, I'm talking to you so, I guess he's not going to hurt me either."

"That's good. What are you going to do now?"

Lucy, pondering this, turned around and headed back to the house. She set out in her mind that she was going to let go of the fear. When she did Colt disappeared. She continued her perfect day.

When she returned to the house, her lunch of shrimp tacos was at the door just as she'd imagined. Soon after a masseuse came, relaxed all the fear out of her, and made her muscles feel like jello. The coziest chair was next to a fireplace where she read *Born a Crime* by Trevor Noah, laughing out loud. The doorbell rang—another food delivery. She savored every bite as it danced on her tongue. She watched *My Big Fat Greek Wedding*, ate some ice cream, and then climbed back into the bed where she'd begun.

"Okay now, that's what I call a perfect day. Open your eyes," Gabe said.

"Oh wow. That was fun other than the monster and Colt. Why's it still light outside?"

"Well, time moves differently during transdreamosis."

"Transdream, what?" Lucy asked.

"Transdreamosis—it's the visualization technique that Vision Catchers can use to make you see the possible. Of course, your psyche is still involved—I'm not in complete control. That's why you saw the monster and Colt."

"Okay, so how much time passed?" Lucy looked at the clock and answered her own question. "Fifteen minutes? This whole thing has to be a dream. I'm going to wake up any moment with Garfield on my head and Colt yelling at me."

"Trust me, this is real. If you continue this path that we're on together, you'll never wake up like that again."

Despite the tasty food Lucy had in transdreamosis, her stomach growled. "I guess dinner's next?"

"Yep." Gabe smiled. "I think shrimp tacos might be on the menu."

Lucy jumped and clapped her hands with excitement and ran down the hill toward the dining hall. As she did, she heard Gabe off in the distance yell, "Don't wait for me. I'll catch up."

Gabe looked down at his app and saw an alert. "Please record your session by clicking here."

He clicked the link, and to his surprise, Ravi showed up. "Hello Gabe, are you here to record your session?"

"Yes, but I thought I was just going to write it down."

"No, we have you send a vision of what happened over to me and then I'll record it for you."

"Oh, okay."

"Just let me know when you want to begin," Ravi stated.

"I'll start now."

Gabe locked eyes with Ravi and visualized everything that had just transpired. Ravi took notes along the way and when the transfer was complete said, "Okay, that's all I need. Please let me know if you have questions once you receive your notification of your results. We've used the app system for a couple of years, but technically, it's still under development, so we really need your feedback to ensure it functions properly."

Shortly after this they said their goodbyes. Gabe was left a little baffled. In school, Professor McGuvers had taught them that they would be required to document quests. It was to be done in journals or through the Vision Catchers preferred medium, which for Gabe was art and painting. As he thought back on these lessons, he received another alert.

"Congratulations, Lucy has received a positive score of 100 points for overcoming her fear during your transdreamosis session. In order to pass the quest, she must obtain at least 5,000 points. More points are given to personal growth that is achieved through real experiences rather than simulated ones. Lucy also lost fifty points for the doubt she had about doing the session. Please refer to this score sheet to familiarize yourself further with the scoring system."

Gabe clicked on the link to the score sheet, but he thought the number of points assigned to certain milestones or setbacks seemed arbitrary.

Positive Points

- Overcoming Self-Doubt: 50-200 points
- Discovering Passion and Purpose: 75-300 points
- Healing from Past Trauma: 100-250 points
- Asserting Boundaries: 75-200 points
- Cultivating Confidence: 100-250 points
- Embracing Vulnerability: 50-200 points
- Forging New Friendships: 100-150 points
- Taking Risks: 50-200 points
- Embracing Creativity: 75-150 points
- Facing Fears: 50-250 points
- Accepting Imperfections: 50-150 points
- Finding Inner Peace: 100-250 points
- Cultivating Resilience: 75-200 points
- Letting Go of Toxic Relationships: 100-250 points
- Embracing Self-Discovery: 50-150 points

Negative Points

Minor Setbacks: Negative 50-100 points: These are relatively minor obstacles or challenges that temporarily slow down Originator's progress but can be overcome with some guidance and effort.

Moderate Setbacks: Negative 100-200 points: These setbacks have a more significant impact on your Originator's journey, requiring more time and guidance to address and overcome.

Major Setbacks: Negative 200-300 points: These are substantial setbacks that significantly hinder personal growth and require intensive intervention to aid recovery.

Critical Setbacks: Negative 300+ points: These setbacks are severe and have the potential to derail the entire quest. They represent moments of great crisis or regression in your Originator's development.

Examples of these setbacks include:

- Self-Doubt Resurgence
- Losing Sight of Purpose
- Relapse into Past Trauma
- Ignoring Boundaries
- Self-Sabotaging Behavior
- Losing Confidence
- Suppressing Emotions
- Isolation and Loneliness
- Avoiding Risks
- Blocking Creativity
- Repeating Past Mistakes
- Restlessness and Anxiety
- Resisting Resilience

- Staying in Toxic Relationships
- Avoiding Self-Reflection

Looking at the points Lucy had received, Gabe felt like a failure. He stretched his neck, tried to relax and let go of the negative feelings. He knew he had the training and the tools to help Lucy live a life of fulfillment. Still, Randy's words from the night before turned through his head. Was he ready for this? If he failed, it would just be that much harder the next time.

Wondering how Cecilia was doing, he decided to message her to check in and possibly see if they could sit together at dinner. His hand shook as he searched the app for her name, then DMed her. He kept writing one thing and deleting it and then writing another. He finally settled on, "Hey, how's it going?"

The phone rang, and to his surprise, it was Cecilia. Gabe's palms started to sweat as he answered, "Hello?"

"Hey. I wanted to talk to you, and I hate texting. I hope that's okay."

"Of course. How did your one-on-one session go?" Gabe took a deep breath in, attempting to calm his nerves.

"My Originator, Emily, is pretty closed off. I think we made some headway today. What about you?"

"Honestly, I'm scared. I was pretty confident that Lucy was ready for this new chapter in her life. Like I told you earlier, we had setbacks with her running away, but then, right before we were supposed to start our session, new doubts seemed to creep into her mind. I don't know if it was something somebody said in the small group, but she hesitated to do the one-on-one and lost fifty points because she was unsure of herself."

Right after he said it, he immediately regretted it. He wanted to impress Cecilia. Why had he revealed so much? Cecilia was so amazing. He thought that she probably helped her Originator get at least 250 points.

"That point system is stupid. I mean, sure you can score figure skating, but that score just reflects execution and how close to perfect the skater got. This is different. This is people's lives and people are going to fall. Even if that figure skater wiped out during a three-minute routine, they could've touched you profoundly. The music, their movement and grace. My point is, don't pay attention to the points. That's what I'm doing. I just need to focus on bringing her into an amazing life."

"How many points did she get?"

"I told you, I'm not paying attention to the points." Cecilia's voice was calm and firm. Gabe felt the blood rush to his cheeks, embarrassed at asking such a stupid question.

"I don't understand that. I just feel like a failure. I mean, you know my aunt. She's successful. If Lucy doesn't pass her quest, it's going to be harder for me the next time. I mean, what if they'd been counting points before the beginning of orientation? Lucy would've been in the hole for taking the car back to Mississippi."

"Yeah, and Emily would've been docked for whatever trouble she got into last night. None of that matters. You have to stop focusing on whether Lucy's quest is successful and focus on what the NEXT best choice is for you and for her. The points will happen if you do a good job. That's how they built the system."

Gabe thought about his next best choice. "I wish I had your confidence."

"Do you want to continue this conversation at dinner?"

"Sure."

14

The Dinner and the Evening Entertainment

Lucy skipped into the dining hall, excited for her custom meal, hoping it was just as yummy as the one she'd just imagined. She heard someone shout her name. It was Flora. She waved her over to sit with her.

"Hi Flora. What are you eating?"

"Oh, it's this marvelous chicken pot pie my grandma used to make. They got it just right, so flaky it's perfection. Sit with me." Flora gestured to the empty chair across from her. "How was your session?"

"It was okay I guess. Actually, the session itself was enlightening and at the end, I felt pretty good. But confidentially, some weird guy came up to me and told me that this was some kind of cult and they ruined his life."

"Get out of town. Really?" Flora didn't seem like someone to suspect anyone of wrongdoing. She seemed like what Lucy imagined as a stereotypical Midwestern nice person—friendly with no social inhibitions. Flora's eyes darted back and forth, then she leaned in closer. "Is he here now?"

Lucy feigned stretching her neck so that she could look around without drawing attention to herself. It didn't work. During this process, she spotted Paul, who waved and headed in their direction. Before he reached them, Lucy said, "No, I don't see him. Do you think it was some sort of test?"

"I don't know. I hadn't really been that suspicious before now. I was kind of desperate for a change when Rosa approached me about the quest," Flora replied.

Paul sat down next to Lucy. "Hey, you mind if I join you?"

"Of course not. Lucy was just telling me about this guy who told her that Vision Catchers are a cult and they ruined his life," Flora said with enthusiasm to spread the gossip.

Paul's eyes widened. "Was he wearing a hoodie?"

"Yes! Did he talk to you, too?"

Paul nodded. "Yeah, he introduced himself to me. His name was Waylon. I remember because I had some of the best sex of my life one night in Cabo with a guy named Waylon." Paul paused for a moment, silently reminiscing in his mind, presumably about his tryst.

Flora, with intrigue and urgency, said, "Don't stop there, go on."

"Anyway, he just snuck up on me right after my one-on-one session. It feels a little too easy. He may have a point."

"Easy!" Flora exclaimed. "This isn't easy at all. I had to leave my kids behind and give my husband a bogus story about why I was going to be away for so long. Plus, they've been really pushing me psychologically to places I don't want to go, and this is just the first day! But hmmm ... cults do that, right? They make you leave your family behind and 'reprogram' you. I was just listening to a podcast about this just the other day. Lord, I've got chills all over."

A man came up behind Lucy and handed her a plate of shrimp tacos. She was so engrossed in the conversation; he startled her causing her to jump a little in her seat. She'd forgotten all about them and licked her lips in excitement. "Yummy. What are you getting, Paul?"

"Filet mignon with mashed potatoes and asparagus." Paul closed his eyes and seemed to imagine the dish. A woman came behind him and placed before him a hamburger, french fries, and a milkshake. Paul looked up at the woman. "But this isn't what I-"

"What you ordered?" she interrupted. "This must be hanging out somewhere in your subconscious because it's what our chefs picked up."

Paul nodded at the woman, bewildered, and then looked down at the meal. The woman hurried back to the kitchen. He looked back up at Flora and Lucy with a frown on his face.

"Well," Flora prodded, "does this bring back a happy memory? It looks like a Happy Meal!" Lucy was perplexed. Outwardly Flora seemed like one of those "always look on the sunny side of life" people, but her statement about her one-on-one session hinted at some inner demons.

Paul looked deep in thought and then Lucy saw a single tear fall from his cheek. "I guess it is. My grandfather used to buy me Happy Meals when I'd go visit him. My mom would never get us fast food." He smiled a little. "I'd always be so excited to go over to his house for the weekend because we'd get Happy Meals and then go to Blockbuster and rent any movie that wasn't rated R that I wanted. He'd heat up some popcorn, and we'd watch it. In the morning we'd get up and go fly-fishing. It was so much fun. I haven't thought about that in a while. He died when I was nine."

Paul looked serene as he took a bite out of his hamburger. He closed his eyes and soaked in the memory.

Lucy looked up at the ceiling, pondering Paul's situation, and said, "So they can't really be a cult. I mean, you hadn't thought of that in a long time or that's what you just told us. There are so many things they have known ... and how could they unless some of this magic that they're talking about is true?"

"They could be a magic cult," Paul replied with his mouth full of burger and ketchup dripping down his chin. He wiped his mouth, taking a swig of milkshake before continuing his thought. "I take back what I said before. It isn't too easy. Also, I'm not going to let anybody ruin my life. What does that even mean? Isn't this process about teaching us we can do whatever we want? If you ask me, he just couldn't cut it and is looking for somebody to blame."

Lucy nodded and Flora said, "That makes sense to me. I know so many people who are unhappy with their life and blame other people or things. I mean, I bet that's why a lot of people are here. I vote for guy in hoodie is pathetic and the Vision Catchers aren't a cult."

Flora's enthusiasm in her logic made Lucy laugh.

"Right. Maybe he's not pathetic. Like I said, he just couldn't cut it," Paul reiterated.

"Speaking of cutting it, Gabe told me that a lot of people drop out before the second day. Before the talent show."

Paul took a stress-filled bite into a french fry. "I wonder if they'd let me be a stagehand or something?"

"Gabe said we all had to perform. What do you think you'd do?" Lucy asked Paul.

"I think I'll recite a poem. A haiku. Those are short. It goes five, seven, five, right? This talent show stinks. I would not perform tonight. But they are making me."

Flora applauded and then said in a teacher-y voice, "That last line was six, not five. It will work though if you just change, 'they are' to 'they're.'" Flora held her hands up, waggling her fingers when quoting Paul. "I think I'll do that too. I'll write one about our group. The red group is best. Though I know of no other. I feel it in here." She ended the poem, laying her hand on her heart. "What about you Lucy?"

"You want me to write a haiku?"

"No, what's your talent going to be?" Flora said in a way that reminded Lucy of a parent asking a kid what they wanted from Santa

Claus.

Lucy took a beat, a bite, and with a mouth full of taco said, "I've got absolutely no fucking clue."

The three laughed hard. It was one of those contagious laughs where everyone knows it wasn't at all funny, but something in that moment makes you laugh so hard you can't catch your breath. After about a minute, Lucy smelled a familiar aroma. She turned around and there was Gary. Through laughter Lucy said, "Hey, Gary! How's it going? How was your session?"

"Well, I'm not sure as good as yours. What are y'all laughing at?" Gary looked at the three of them, perplexed.

"We were just discussing the talent show."

"Oh yeah. I think I know what I'll do," Gary said happily.

Paul had caught his breath and stopped laughing. "What's that? It can't be reciting a haiku, that's mine."

"I can't tell you what I'm going to do. It'll ruin the surprise," Gary said with determination.

"Oh please tell us, we're in your group. We're supposed to share. You can surprise everybody else," Flora pleaded.

"Nope. My lips are sealed." Gary smiled at the three of them still standing. "I was just going to the auditorium for the evening entertainment. Want to join me?" he said, mostly looking at Lucy.

"Sure, let's go!" Flora exclaimed.

The four went together to the auditorium happily. When they entered, someone had transformed the room into a wonderland with what must have been thousands of twinkling lights hanging from the ceiling and running up the walls like vines. Large paintings hung on the walls with single words on them like "believe" "passion" and "dreams." One had the phrase Lucy had seen earlier at the B&B: "Catch the Vision. Empower the People. Create Lasting Change." They'd removed the chairs and there were colorful cushions and blankets with clear pathways between them leading up to the stage. The stage curtain was drawn shut.

The lights dimmed, and a spotlight hit the center of the stage. The curtain opened to reveal Rae. Lucy hoped Rae would sing and dance, but she had a hard time imagining it.

Suddenly, a full orchestra played, and sure enough, she sang in a typical Broadway show tune fashion. "This song's for you, yeah, that's right, you. We've been waiting for you." She gestured to the crowd and her voice became more staccato as she continued.

"We're inviting you to our cocoon to give you the opportun-ity, to see what you're meant to be. So, I'd like to introduce you to our team."

She opened her arms wide, backed up, and turned right. As she did, dozens of people appeared in a cancan line. Some wore tuxedos and some wore red dresses. Lucy spotted Gabe, who looked a tad bit uncomfortable.

The music swelled as Rae called out in a roll call style, "Where are my writers?" Nearly half the stage hurried to the forefront. The band continued to play softly as Rae's voice cut through, "Yes, that's right, seventy percent of our Vision Catchers are writers. Want to witness the art of writing? How would that work, you ask?" She paused for a moment, looking around at everyone, then slyly smiled. "It won't. We promised ENTERTAINMENT. Let's captivate, not bore, our audience." Her gaze hardened as she addressed the line of Vision Catchers, her voice filled with joy, but still cutting sharp. "Dismissed!"

The spotlight disappeared and the whole theater was pitch black. Lucy could barely see her own hand in front of her face. Rae's voice boomed like a narrator on a movie trailer. Her words peppered with notes of the Genesis chapter of the Bible. "In the beginning, there was darkness and silence. The Universe seemed boring."

Lucy became transfixed by the colorful, swirling lights that appeared on a screen at the back of the stage. The colors bounced around off of the walls in a frenzy.

Somewhere from the back of the stage Rae continued, "As life took form, something else was also brewing. Ideas and visions began to form and swirl in the air. Some visions took up residence in plants, who used them to flourish and survive."

The overhead lights brightened the stage and illuminated an intricate set to reveal a forest. More colorful lights bounced around, but some dimmed in the dark corners of the forest.

Rae went on, saying, "The Universe noticed that some ideas having nowhere to land started to dwindle into nothing, but as this happened a miraculous energy took shape."

A large white and translucent balloon lowered from the ceiling and hung above the audience.

"We call this energy Feranchin. Once formed, Feranchin served as a vessel to hold all the ideas, visions, and dreams. It gave them a safe home."

The lights darted toward it until the balloon became a colorful mass, and it inflated more. Rae walked into the crowd.

She looked up at the balloon as it inflated and spoke gently into a microphone, "The thing about visions and ideas is they don't like to be alone. As people and creatures developed visions, they also lost them. This force collected the lost ideas. They began to combine and grow until Feranchin could not hold them all."

Lucy watched the balloon inflate even more, approaching her face. With a gentle pop, it burst like a bubble rather than a balloon, and colorful confetti fell all over everyone in the room. Lucy looked over at Flora, who was delighting in the spectacle, collecting extra confetti off the floor and throwing it over her head again. She looked like a child playing in the snow for the first time. The bright lights returned and bounced around everywhere.

"The ideas released all over the world and found homes in humans and animals alike. Great inventions were created, empires were born, dreams were achieved." A bird came onto the stage and built a nest. A cat entered and looked up at the nest. It was Penelope from the B&B. Her eyes fixed on the bird, but it flew away.

Crew members in black came out onto the stage, bringing a large stone and a fake fire with bright orange and yellow streamers. The spotlight illuminated Vision Catchers dressed as cavemen painting on the walls, creating stone tools, and speaking a language Lucy had never heard before to one another.

One of the caveman actors who had painted on the wall mimicked dying and Rae said, "But creative ideas were also lost to despair, disease, and death." Colorful lights left the dying actor and bounced around once again. A grieving female Vision Catcher who had been drawing on the wall as well looked distraught and lights left her as well.

"The Universe knew Feranchin could only hold so much, it needed something more. A keeper, a guide. From the fabric of Feranchin, the first Vision Catcher was born, taking human form." The lights swirled together and from the middle of the stage, with fog surrounding him, a man stood holding some kind of clear vessels that the lights went into.

Gary leaned over to Lucy, smiling, and whispered, "That's my Vision Catcher, Kai."

Kai walked over to the grieving woman and poured some of the light from the vessel over the woman, and the lights appeared to enter her. Uplifting music swelled from the orchestra as Rae's voice crescendoed. "More and more Vision Catchers burst forth into life, but not all ideas were easy to protect. Some dreams were fragile, others stolen, and still others abandoned by Originators who feared their own potential." As Rae spoke, more people carrying orbs walked around the stage, but as she described the fragility of the dreams, the music turned darker.

One Vision Catcher grabbed an orb and smashed it on the ground. The lights from the vessel dimmed.

Rae's tone was serious. "The story of the Vision Catchers has always been one of hope ... and of conflict. For every dream realized, there is another that's lost. For every Originator guided, there is one who resists."

Goosebumps. The chills Lucy felt from the dreams lost shot straight through her spine. Even though it was just a play, she felt a dark energy cloud the room.

"The Vision Catchers, over time, joined together and formed our own society. The Universe has given us and others like us, part human, part creativity, a clear directive. We have a mission of storing and restoring visions and creating lasting change in the world. We organize, hoping one day everyone will live a life of joy." Kai walked on the stage and grabbed Rae's hand and raised it.

The audience sat silently, taking in Rae's words. From the back a man's voice called out: "Imposter, imposter, he won't help you. He ruined my life and they'll do it to you, too." He pointed to Kai. He started walking through the crowd. "I was once a hopeful. On a Vision Quest, just like you. But that man didn't deliver hopeful dreams." The shouting man came into Lucy's view. It was Waylon from earlier in the day!

Kai dropped Rae's hand and shook his head. "Will you please remove him?" Kai said, gesturing toward Waylon. Rae left the stage to Waylon's side to calm him. She seemed to have comforted him because he stopped shouting and started crying. Through his tears, he just kept repeating, "He ruined everything." Soon Rae escorted him out in a gentle and caring manner.

Kai was angry. His nostrils flared, and his face filled with disdain. His feelings didn't seem to be just toward Waylon, but to all the Originators in the room. A familiar fear ignited within Lucy as he looked around.

A fear she felt with Colt. Her eyes shifted to Gary and she could sense his anxiety. Her mind and heart raced as she tried to decide her next move. Just as she was about to lean over to Gary and suggest they try to leave together, a firm hand touched her shoulder and she froze.

A familiar voice whispered in her ear. "It's okay Lucy. The show must go on." She turned her head slightly to see Gabe and, once again, his presence soothed her. She turned her attention back to the stage.

Kai was pacing, but then stopped center stage, ran his fingers through his hair, closed his eyes, and shook a little. This seemed to readjust his anger, and his mood completely shifted. He turned to the audience, smiled, and said, "We had a closing number prepared, but our host has had to deal with one of the more negative aspects of this job. Let's just leave you with some orchestral music."

The crowd looked around, stunned at one another as the house lights abruptly went up. The orchestra played "Sunny Side of the Street." Flora, still seated cross-legged on the carpet, leaned over and said, "Well, that was entertaining, I guess."

After much chatter and conjecturing of what may have happened to Waylon, Gabe told Lucy, Flora, Gary, and Paul that to his knowledge, this was rare.

He also said, "I'm not sure how he even got onto the campus. We're in a secret realm, which Originators can only access while accompanied by a Vision Catcher. I'm sure there'll be an investigation. I promise to let you know when I know more."

Their group dispersed one by one as their Vision Catchers came to consult with them. Gabe continued to speak words of comfort to Lucy, but eventually directed her to ride back to the B&B on a small bus, arranged for herself and other guests. The VCs had to stay behind to reset the auditorium. She said goodbye to him and boarded the bus as thoughts about leaving raced through her mind, despite genuinely believing Gabe. Thoughts interrupted when she noticed Gary at the back of the bus.

She hurried next to him and whispered, "Are you okay? What did Kai say?"

"He said that, that guy's name was Waylon. He said he had some mental health issues," Gary whispered back. He looked around to see if anyone else was listening and spoke softer—almost inaudibly, "Schizophrenia."

"Oh my gosh, really?"

Gary just nodded as the bus moved. Doubts still crept into Lucy's mind. She dug through her purse to ensure she still had her ring money, making alternative plans to the quest in her head. It was all there, except what she'd spent earlier that day, but her heart dropped when she realized what else was missing—her keys. She looked up at Gary, fear in her eyes, and dug deeper into her purse—mints, Kleenex, her wallet.

"What's wrong?" Gary said softly.

"Oh no oh no oh no," she said. A crumpled receipt, a napkin, a half-eaten cookie, but no key to The Tower. Tears began streaming down her face. She looked out the window as the bus turned down the driveway to the B&B.

Gary touched her lightly on the shoulder and asked her what was wrong again.

"I lost the keys to The Tower. Or rather, I didn't lose them. I know exactly where they are." Her words were barely audible through her sobs.

Gary tried to comfort her. "Well, if you know where they are, then why are you crying?"

"They're in Booneville. I left them in the car when I left it there this morning. It has the keychain, the one that says Rae's B&B. Colt. He's going to find me."

Each tear drop was a little epiphany. Despite the uncertainty of whether she'd leave the quest, this realization solidified everything in her mind in an instant. She wanted to stay and see what happened next—one step at a time, but she knew she couldn't do it if Colt knew where she was.

"You heard Gabe. Only invited guests can find their way to Rae's B&B."

"Waylon found his way. Colt's relentless. You don't know him."

Gary looked at Lucy with eyes that seemed to be made of empathy. He touched her arm and gently said, "Well, that Waylon guy was here before. He could've made a friend on the inside who helped him find his way back. Colt has no clue about this place."

She nodded, wiping off the last of her tears as the bus came to a stop. She didn't want to say more to him. He was just as in the dark as she was. They disembarked along with others and entered the lobby. Lucy wished Gary a goodnight and went to look around for someone to help her with the key situation.

15

Lucy and Rae

Lucy didn't have to look long to find Rae sitting on what appeared to be a yoga mat on top of the dining table. She was in full lotus position with her eyes closed. Lucy hesitated to interrupt her. She had a long night of performing and then handling a crisis. Even Vision Catchers needed to meditate and unwind, she supposed. As she dug through her purse one more time, Rae broke the ice.

"Lucy dear. You lost your keys?"

"Um ... well ... yes. I can't believe you could read my mind that fast. You looked like you were in another world."

"I was, but you're digging through your purse. Even the most unperceptive person knows that's the universal sign for looking for keys." Rae smiled softly and gracefully hopped off the table and said, "Don't worry so much. I have another key. Let me just grab it for you."

Rae bent down at the threshold between the foyer and dining room. She walked over to a drawer handle bolted to the floor. Rae pulled up on the handle to reveal a giant vertical drawer with keys hanging from hooks.

Last night, Lucy had felt safely tucked away in The Tower, but seeing the keys on display made her feel exposed. Her anxiety was rising, and she blurted out in a judgmental tone, "You keep your keys out for anyone to grab?"

"No child. This is a floor safe. It's programmed to only respond to my touch and a few others." She grabbed a key and quickly put the floorboard back in its place. Looking at Lucy, she said, "See you try."

Lucy tried to pull up on the board just as Rae had, but it wouldn't budge. Satisfied, she stood up and Rae held out the key for her. The key had a different keychain that had a new quote on it: "Go confidently in the direction of your dreams! Live the life you've imagined." ~Henry David Thoreau.

In a normal frame of mind, Lucy knew this would empower her. Still haunted by the idea that Colt would find her and make her leave, she confessed her worries to Rae. She told her about leaving the key in the car in Booneville. With every word, her breath grew more rapid. "What if he finds me here? I know he's looking for me. It's only a matter of time. He could already be here. Nashville is only a few hours from Booneville," Lucy said as she looked all around her.

Rae touched her gently on her shoulder and spoke in a comforting tone, "We're Nashville adjacent. The B&B and some of the other places you've been, like the pawnshop, the VC campus, and the studio, are all in what you might call another dimension. We won't have to drive far to get to Nashville city center, but only those on quests or who are in the Vision Catcher community can see the roads to get to this entry point."

"What about Waylon? And will I not be able to come back here after I finish my quest?" Lucy pouted her lips and looked up at Rae with big, sad eyes.

"If you're invited at least once, there are ways and channels that can get you into this dimension," Rae said in a soft tone. "In Waylon's case, he somehow got his hands on these." She pulled a pair of eyeglasses out of her pocket. "Someone who has been here before and has these can see the path to get here. Years ago, these were made for an Originator on a special quest."

"This is all really confusing. You're sure that Colt wouldn't be able to come here?"

"I'm sure. He's never been here, so even if he had these, it's impossible," Rae replied.

Lucy felt like she was being ripped apart at the seams and didn't know up from down. Depleted, she'd stopped crying. All she wanted to do was just curl up in a ball and sleep. She wasn't sure who she could trust.

After a minute of silence taking it all in, she said, "I just want to go to bed."

"I think that's a good idea. Go ahead." Rae drew her into a hug that was as comforting as the softest of blankets.

As they pulled apart, Lucy thanked Rae. Holding the key tightly, she looked Rae in the eyes and said, "I'll keep a close eye on this one."

"I know you will." There was a warmth to Rae's words, putting Lucy at ease. It was no wonder Waylon had calmed in her presence. "Get to bed," she instructed. "You have orientation tomorrow morning at nine. Gabe will take you to head that way at eight-thirty."

Lucy nodded. She began the long climb to The Tower at a slow, methodical pace. Her worries had subsided for the moment except for one: whether she'd pass out before she reached her bed.

16

The Smaller Group

Quest Day Two

Breakfast at the B&B had been relatively uneventful, which was a welcome change over last night. The gossip from the previous night fascinated Daisy. She promised Lucy she'd cheer her on in the talent show, but they soon learned that Daisy wouldn't be permitted. Because of Waylon's outburst, only Originators taking part in orientation could be on the campus. Security officers checked IDs at every entrance.

Despite this disappointment, Lucy was excited to see the members of the small group from yesterday. She already felt a close bond with some of them and hoped no one had dropped out. Unlike yesterday, she was the first one through the door.

The circle of chairs was gone. The chairs had been moved and were lining two large six-foot tables in the middle of the room, along with arts and crafts supplies. There were tiles stacked at one end and on the other Sharpies, paint brushes, various acrylic squeeze bottle paint, cups of water, and paper plates.

Lucy went to take a seat. "Oh, fun! Arts and crafts!" a man's voice called out behind Lucy. She turned around. It was Paul.

"Good morning Paul. So besides writing haiku, you're a fan of finger

"

painting, I take it?" Lucy smiled and winked at him.

"I'll have you know I was a prolific finger painter in my younger years. But I quit altogether when my mother told me that my work had become derivative of another kid in my class. Little did I know that drinking wine at art galleries and calling out things as being derivative is a rich person's Disney World."

Lucy laughed. She watched as Paul grabbed one of everything at the end of the table. His brow furrowed in concentration. His pensive nature caused Lucy to stay silent instead of butting in and saying, 'Are you supposed to be doing that?' He squeezed one blob of every color onto a plate and took it to his seat. Flora, Gary, and Emily had entered the room while he was doing this. Lucy contemplated following his lead, but made pleasantries with Flora instead, interrupted when the door in the back opened.

"Good mooorning!" Ms. Benedict waltzed in with a bright, shining positive attitude and a singsong voice. "Well, I see someone's an eager beaver."

Paul nodded enthusiastically.

"Okay then. Everybody follow Paul's lead." The group took supplies and their seats. When Lucy looked around, she noticed they were short a couple members. It took her a while to remember who was missing. There was Myra, who had had a lot to contribute yesterday. Then there was Lamar, who told the story about the pet frog he had for a short time.

"Ms. Benedict, will Myra and Lamar be joining us?" Lucy asked.

Ms. Benedict shook her head no. "Unfortunately, they chose to leave. This quest is not for everyone."

"How will we know if we should quit?" Gary asked.

"I don't think anyone should quit. If you feel like quitting, think about why you felt compelled to accept the invitation in the first place. Think about your life, where you were, and what you were feeling when you chose to join us. Remember that this whole endeavor brings you on a path to fulfillment. Were you fulfilled before you began here? From some of what you shared yesterday, there are things you're still searching for in your life. This path and journey isn't easy, but our vow to you as Vision Catchers is to get you to a place where you love your life and feel at peace. Sound good? Are you ready to move to our first activity?"

"Yes," Gary said a little sheepishly. His brow was scrunched and he was looking down at the ground. He didn't seem ready.

Lucy wasn't ready. The conversation about quitting was causing a ping-pong of thoughts in her brain. Despite the moment of clarity last night after losing the keys, Myra and Lamar leaving so soon shook her. Were they approached by Waylon too? Did they know something she didn't? She shook her head in an attempt to release the doubt from her mind. She tried to clasp hold of the epiphany from last night. The desire she had to stay.

The color of the tiles varied for each person. Lucy had yellow, Flora had white, Emily had black, Gary had orange, and Paul had light blue.

"Please flip your tile over," Ms. Benedict instructed. The group did as they were told in spite of apprehensions. Paul looked around, disappointed. He seemed obsessed with digging into the paint. The back of the tile had a white, slightly textured surface, in contrast to the colorful, glossy front. Now with the tiles flipped over, everything was uniform.

Ms. Benedict continued with her instructions. "Now, in life, there are things that hold us back from getting exactly what we want. We talked about some of them yesterday. Gary mentioned his son, making it hard to give himself time for self-care, and some of you mentioned not having the funds or resources to get to where you want to be. I want you to dig a little deeper today. Those things I just mentioned are very much in the present. Is there anything in your past that's causing you to not take action on finding solutions to your present problems? For example, this can be regrets, guilt, shame, or sadness. Once you have those in your mind, I want you to write them with the Sharpie on the back of your tile. I'll give you five minutes. I'm starting the timer now." She took out her phone to start the timer.

Just like yesterday, some people began writing right away. Flora wrote immediately, as did Paul and Gary. Lucy was more pensive and hesitant. Emily sat and looked off into space for the first couple of minutes and then started writing.

When Ms. Benedict's phone's timer beeped, most of the group seemed to startle and looked up, except Flora, who was still writing. "Okay, time's up. Time to share," Ms. Benedict cheerfully sang. Emily groaned and rolled her eyes, which made Ms. Benedict say, "Okay, Emily, you're first."

"Hard pass," she replied.

"I'm sorry, but that's not an option. This is not so we can 'get up all in your grill' as you might say. This is for connection. Didn't we all feel more connected with Gary after he shared yesterday? It's important to know that even if you live a solitary life, part of a fulfilling life is about relying on and being in a community with others. It makes life richer and takes us further."

Emily shifted her eyes to the left and pouted in anger. "Well, I lost my community. My person. His name was Daniel. He died last year— shot himself in the fucking head." Emily's voice grew intense and her anger spewed in Ms. Benedict's direction. "I'm doing just fine on my own. If I'd realized there would be group work as part of this quest, I might not have accepted the invitation."

Despite Emily's anger, Ms. Benedict's tone remained calm. "Okay, but if you were doing just fine on your own, you wouldn't have been invited, so you wouldn't have had the option to accept. People don't tend to venture to someplace new, if they're content. You're here for a reason. Let's focus on what you wrote on the back of the tile. We'll sit here quietly until you're ready." After thirty seconds, Paul began anxiously tapping his foot, crossed his arms, and pouted. They sat in silence for another couple of minutes. Lucy thought Emily would stonewall them all, but finally she caved.

"Okay, okay, fine. You talked about regret, guilt, shame, or sadness. That's what I wrote, but I don't think any of those words express it fully. For me, it's all of those things rolled into one. Ever since Daniel's death, it consumes me. I can't even dream anymore. I don't know what I did wrong. He left a note where he said it wasn't my fault. He was in medical school and he lost a patient. He'd made a mistake or that's what he said, and he blamed himself. The hospital had to settle some malpractice suit. There was nothing I could do to comfort him and I tried. I just haven't been able to find joy. I have no clue where I'll end up after this quest. I honestly just accepted the invite for the escape."

Flora snapped her fingers. The rest joined in to support Emily's share.

"Thank you, Emily. How many of you accepted the invite at least partly to get away from your current lives?" Ms. Benedict asked.

Everyone raised their hands. "See dearie, you're not alone here. We'll support you."

After a few moments, Flora said, "Remorse. That's the word you're looking for — regret, guilt, sadness all rolled into one. I wrote it on my tile. Before I got here, I was suffering from what the doctors said was postpartum depression mixed with I guess regular depression. My youngest would have been two this month. He died suddenly at seven months. Caught pneumonia and spiked a fever quickly. I had a babysitter, but I was only going to be gone for a few hours to run errands. There were the other kids to take care of too. I feel remorse because why did I hire a babysitter? Why didn't I just hire somebody to run the errands for me? The truth is, I was already having postpartum depression, which I felt guilty about because I hadn't had it with the other kids. But I just wanted to get out of the house. The babysitter did pediatric CPR, but it didn't work. It wasn't her fault, and I told her that, but I still blame myself that I wasn't there for the last moments of my baby's life. I just haven't been able to break free of this. I wrote remorse, depression, overwhelm, heartbreak, and guilt."

As tears welled up in almost everyone's eyes, Emily snapped. The rest joined to support the brave sharing that had just taken place. Lucy could feel the empathy emanating all around and the snapping warmed her soul, a much more gentle show of appreciation than clapping. Ms. Benedict looked down at her watch. She reached into her purse and pulled out a hammer and four Ziploc bags. Lucy saw everyone's body tense up and eyes go wide. "I'm sure the rest of you wrote similar words to Flora and Emily. Self-doubt, perhaps? Maybe you wrote about the actual regrets or memories that are holding you back. Whatever you wrote, while your feelings are valid, they have no place in this quest." She handed out the Ziploc bags and told them to put their tiles inside. She handed the hammer to Flora. Flora looked up at Ms. Benedict with confusion and concern. "Seal your bag really tightly and hammer the shit out of that remorse. Let it all go." She put a hand on Flora's shoulder. "But don't pulverize it dear. We're going to paint some on the other side."

Flora slowly and carefully put her tile in the plastic bag, placed it on the table, and narrowed her focus directly on it. Her chest rose as if her breath was winding up both her arm and courage to break it apart. The whole table shook when the hammer hit the tile. The paint bottles and cup of Sharpies fell over from the vibrations. Ms. Benedict quickly swooped in and grabbed the supplies as the others held onto their cups of water. She hammered again and again, over and over, sometimes missing the bag entirely. Then Ms. Benedict instructed her to hand the hammer to Paul and for him to do the same. After Paul went, it was

Lucy's turn, and she hesitated.

She'd written "self-doubt, enabling Colt, feeling like I can't go back to who I used to be, feeling my friends and family are mad at me." Since she'd been with Colt, she stopped calling her parents or friends as much. She'd declined invitations to weddings or going home to visit her parents because if Colt came, things would be unpredictable in the car, in the hotel room, and anytime they were alone. He may be in a good mood, but trips were hard even in healthy relationships. He'd most likely end up drunk and shouting vile things to her when they were in private. If she went without him, she'd still deal with him constantly calling her and accusing her of cheating on him.

It wasn't until she truly got angry—angry at how Colt had made her feel like every fight, every problem, everything was her fault—that the hammer came down hard and shattered the tile into pieces.

Gary was last and, despite being the largest one there, probably the most gentle. When he was done, he handed the hammer back to Ms. Benedict. She turned to Paul and asked, "How did that feel Paul?"

"Liberating."

"Gary?"

"Hard."

"Why?" she asked, her sincerity shining through.

Tears welled up in his eyes. "I'm not sure."

"That's okay. It isn't supposed to be easy, but hopefully helped to at least let loose those feelings that are keeping you from your authentic life. Let's move on to something a little more aspirational." Ms. Benedict looked at Paul and smiled widely. He was looking up at her like a puppy about to go for a walk. He was still eager to paint.

"For this activity, we'll paint symbols of who we want to be. Think about a person who you admire, someone that you'd like to be like? There's no reason you can't." She handed out gloves to everyone. "You want to be careful not to scratch yourself on the tile. Turn over every piece, shiny face up, and paint the symbols of the person you want to be. I'm giving you fifteen minutes."

After a few minutes, Ms. Benedict broke their concentrated silence. She walked over to Flora. "What are you painting?"

"Well, I know, at my core, part of who I am is always going to be a mom. But I want to do better at that. A mom whose family sits down to dinner together. That's why I drew the table and the mac and cheese. I'm also thinking of drawing things that I don't do now or don't do enough, but I think about. A journal, music, a river with rocks for space and time and nature's beauty."

"That's wonderful." Lucy smiled at Flora's visions. She'd been a little stumped and had trouble getting started. Ms. Benedict gave Lucy a knowing look. Lucy recognized that Ms. Benedict might have just asked Flora that to jump start her. It worked.

Lucy thought back to the studio and the garden. She drew flowers and butterflies. She really didn't know the person she wanted to be. All that ran through her mind was the person she didn't want to be. She embellished the sunflower and felt a tingle of happiness and peace. She let the feeling guide the paint brush and drew a peace sign. When she glanced over at Flora, she saw she'd drawn music notes. Lucy, for a moment, suppressed the urge to copy her.

But then she thought back to a performer who played acoustic guitar on Friday nights when she was a barista. He always opened his set with the same line. "Bono said, 'Music can change the world, because it can change people.' That's all I can hope for tonight, folks. Do my very small part to change you for the better."

She sunk into that sentiment and let go of her fear of being unoriginal by copying Flora. She painted music notes too because she wanted to change. Thinking back to the comedy show, she attempted to paint a mouth laughing to represent wanting a life full of laughter, but it just looked like a red blob.

The activity put her into such a trance that she nearly spilled her paint water when Ms. Benedict said, "Alright! Paint brushes down."

Lucy looked up and saw that Paul wasn't heeding Ms. Benedict's instructions. He just kept painting and Lucy strained her neck to see what he'd put on the tile pieces. They were small and it was hard to tell what anything was except a sun and a moon and stars.

Ms. Benedict brought out a wooden piece in the shape of a quarter circle. Lucy hadn't noticed, but as they were working, Ms. Benedict had slathered it in mortar. She instructed them to lay their tiles face up on the object quickly and not to think about it too hard.

Everyone chipped in, with Paul taking the lead as an artistic director. "Oh, I see a spot for that piece, Lucy. I think it should go right there." He pointed to an empty section of the board. Once they'd set all the pieces, they stepped back from it.

"Do you see it?" Ms. Benedict put a hand on Lucy's shoulder, looking over to peer at the art. "Our collective pain is still underneath, but we've smashed its power and coupled it with our hopes and aspirations."

Paul whispered, "It's beautiful."

Others snapped and when they stopped, Ms. Benedict perked up and ran over to her bag. "I have one last thing. This is the room number of where you'll go after your next sessions with your Vision Catchers to rehearse for the talent show."

Lucy's stomach dropped, and she felt a surge of panic. She hadn't given much thought to the talent show today, and now it loomed before her like an insurmountable mountain. The fear of public humiliation washed over her, and she imagined a crowd of people laughing at her as she stumbled on stage or forgot her lines. Her breath quickened, and she desperately scanned her mind for any talent or skill she could showcase.

Unable to contain her anxiety any longer, Lucy excused herself abruptly, leaving the room in a hurry. She found a quiet corner, her heart racing, and her palms sweaty. As she tried to regain her composure, she wondered how she'd ever find the courage to face the daunting challenge that now seemed impossible to conquer.

17

The Talent Show

Lucy walked into an empty dance studio with a piano in the corner. She hadn't played the piano since she was seven. Were they going to have her try to play a concerto or something? She hoped not.

She went over to the piano and touched its keys, trying to remember how to play "Chopsticks." As she was just finding her groove and getting the hang of it, the door opened and Emily walked through. She leaned out into the hallway and then turned back around. "My card said to go to room 104. What are you doing here?"

Lucy pulled out her card and held it up to Emily. "Do you think we're going to have to do an act together?" Lucy asked, knowing that the answer was probably yes.

"What talent do you think they were going to ask you to perform? Not piano, I hope," Emily smirked.

"I don't know. If it were up to me and I had to pick something, I guess I'd sing because I love music. I mean, who doesn't?"

"Same," Emily said, not elaborating at all.

The door opened again. Gabe and a gorgeous woman with a sharp pointed chin, high cheekbones, and long brown hair entered. The woman sashayed into the room with a giant smile on her face. Gabe introduced himself to Emily. Lucy soon learned that the woman was Cecilia, Emily's Vision Catcher.

"Okay. They don't do this for everybody, but they paired you two up to do your talent together. Consider yourselves lucky," Cecilia said with a soft smile.

"Lucky how?" Emily asked.

"Well, you're not going to have to perform alone. You'll get to rely on one another," Gabe said.

"What are we gonna do?" Lucy asked.

"Emily, come here," Cecilia said with authority. "Hold my hands."

Cecilia took Emily into a transdreamosis and they stood unmoving for a few minutes. Only Emily's face changed. At first she smiled, then she looked scared, and then she opened her eyes.

"Why did you show me that?" she asked Cecilia.

"For inspiration. I believe you got a standing ovation then and you can do it again."

"That was a seventh grade play. There were mostly parents in the audience. Of course we got a standing ovation." Emily rolled her eyes and let out a deep sigh.

"You were good," Cecilia encouraged. Lucy saw such love in Cecilia's eyes. She really cared about Emily.

Emily crossed her arms and looked off to the side. "I don't know. It was kind of embarrassing when I screwed up, though."

Cecilia repeated, "But you were good."

Lucy, unable to take the suspense anymore, interjected, "What the heck is going on?" She turned to Emily. "What did she show you?"

"She showed me a vision I had of being the star in the seventh grade musical. I was in the musical, but I wasn't the star. It was a silly twelve-year-old's dream to be a main character and not just in the background cast."

"Okay, what was the musical?"

"*Rent.*"

"What do you want us to do?" Lucy looked toward Gabe. "That's a giant production."

"You can sing one song," Gabe said.

"So you want us to sing?" Lucy said, her eyes darting back and forth between the three others.

"Yes," Gabe and Cecilia said in unison.

Emily rolled her eyes, but also smiled a little.

Lucy turned to Emily. "Well, it was your vision. What song do you wanna sing? That one about the minutes in a year?"

"No, that's overdone."

"Well, which one then?"

Emily paused for just a moment, and then with slight hesitation replied, "Take Me or Leave Me."

"Remind me how that one goes again?" Lucy said.

Emily sang the chorus softly and Lucy immediately knew Cecilia was right. She was good, even with the lack of confidence. "Do you know that one?" Emily said. She looked conflicted on how she wanted Lucy to answer the question.

"I'll need the lyrics, but yeah, I know the tune."

Gabe looked down at his phone and started typing. He said he was ordering up the sheet music and asking for one of their on-call pianists that had volunteered to help with rehearsal today. They were conveniently going to be delivered to the room in five to ten minutes.

Cecilia said, "Wonderful! So glad we could settle on this. Now let's warm up. Follow me."

She reached her arms in the air and stretched them. Lucy and Emily did the same, and Lucy's arms began to shake. Cecilia vibrated her lips as if she was blowing a raspberry. Lucy remembered a music teacher in school calling this a lip trill.

Cecilia moved her body all around and shouted, "Okay girls, just sway your body back and forth and wiggle it, wiggle it, wiggle it. Lucy, Emily—you're too stiff! Loosen up. Move your body all around. You're going to need to dance when you sing this number. It's a musical after all. This song will be a tug and a pull." She walked over to them and placed Lucy's hand in Emily's. "Now, Lucy, brace your feet and pull on Emily. Now Emily, you pull back."

Lucy and Emily did as they were directed. "That's it! Pull back and forth. Lean into one another when you're the one who's being pulled. You're getting it! Good! Good! Now just dance any silly move you can think of," Cecilia exclaimed. As she shouted words of encouragement and demanded they continue to dance to no music, she sashayed over to the piano and played a note. She ended her shouting and sang,

"Repeat after me: la la la la la."

Emily and Lucy looked at one another with apprehension. Emily shrugged taking the lead and sang, "La, la, la, la, la, la." Lucy joined in and they went back and forth repeating anything that Cecilia would sing which ranged from "Do re mi fa sol la ti do" to the "Itsy Bitsy Spider." A knock on the door interrupted them.

Gabe opened it, and a short man entered. He was wearing a tuxedo with a bright red bow tie and cummerbund, as if this was a dress rehearsal. The man was carrying a folder and made a beeline to the piano. He opened the folder and placed the sheet music in front of him. He handed Lucy and Emily song sheets. "Now, who's going to be Maureen and who's going to be Joanne?" he asked.

Lucy quickly scanned the music and saw that Joanne's part was much smaller and quickly shouted, "I call Joanne!" It was louder than she intended.

The man chuckled. "Alright then, I guess you're Joanne." He looked toward Emily. "You ready, Maureen?" Emily nodded as her hands shook, holding the song sheet. He smiled and then turned back to the piano. "Let's get started."

Just a few hours later, as they entered the hall, a woman stood at the door and handed out a small leaflet and checked their badges. Lucy looked around for Emily, but saw Flora first. She waved and beckoned Lucy over. Lucy sighed. Flora chose to sit in the front row, which always made her feel so exposed. She approached Flora with hesitation. "So, you're sitting in the front row?" Lucy asked.

"Yes, I always do in these general admission situations. I mean, when else do you get to sit in the front row?"

"Well, it's not *Hamilton*. What if there's a stand-up comic? They always pick on the people in the front. Or," Lucy paused as she opened her program. "Look. The third act is a magic act. They could ask one of us to get on stage."

"So?" Flora said. "You're going to have to get up there and perform later. It will get all your jitters out."

Flora continued to look around and waved Gary over. He walked up. "Front row. Really?"

"Oh my gosh, please people, you can't beat the view."

"Yeah, but you also can't fall asleep. Have you ever been to a children's dance recital?" Gary replied.

Lucy and Gary laughed, but Flora rolled her eyes and let out a big, exasperated sigh. "Well, if you want to move, you can, but I want to be here to cheer you guys on and I'd appreciate it if you'd extend me the same courtesy. Pleeeeease ... I need to look out and see a friendly face."

"What are you going to be doing, anyway?" Gary asked Flora.

"I'm going to be reciting a spoken word piece that I wrote."

"Oh wow. That's brave," Lucy said and glanced down at the program again. "Oh my God, you're first!"

"Yeah, I know. I'm nervous. So please stay here, so I have a friendly face." They agreed, and the lights flickered, to indicate it was time for everyone to take their seats. A woman approached and took Flora by the hand to guide her backstage.

Gary leaned into Lucy, holding out his program, and whispered, "I think my act is going to look pretty juvenile next to these other performances."

Lucy touched Gary's arm in an act of comfort and solidarity. "You'll do fine. Even if you don't, it's not like they're grading us."

"I don't know. I get the feeling they are," Gary replied.

Lucy was trying to think of words to comfort Gary when the lights dimmed. Gus came out onto the stage in a circus outfit—he wore a long red coat and a top hat. The bright red curtain drew back to reveal an entire orchestra playing music from *The Greatest Showman*.

"Welcome and thank you in advance for putting your humility aside and sharing your talents with us tonight. We have a lot of acts, so I'll get right to it. If you see your name in the program as one of the next two acts, please enter backstage through the door to my right. Please welcome to the stage Flora as she performs an original spoken word piece, *Lost Things*."

Gus handed the mic to Flora, and Lucy saw her hands trembling. She yelled out, "You got this girl!" Flora looked at Lucy and smiled. She then closed her eyes, bowed her head for a moment, and reopened them with a look of determination on her face.

"There are so many things that you don't expect out of life.

And.

There are so many things that as a society—as a collective we do expect. Growing up, it was always the question: what do you want to be when you grow up?

For women and even little girls, it's how many kids do you think you want to have?

And later.

Where do you think you're going to settle down?

I played with wedding Barbie and just assumed I'd get married and have kids ... "

Flora's voice pounded in a staccato rhythm, taking pauses, but with the consistency of a drumbeat. Lucy imagined Flora's heart beating quickly and then pausing. The pattern seemed not to be just for emphasis, but because it was what her whole body needed to continue. It was beautiful.

She spoke of motherhood, of sorrow, of dreams buried beneath diapers and dinner prep. Of the terrifying weight of joy and grief held in the same hand. She named some of her dreams, which deepened Lucy's understanding of Flora.

No more dreams of writing.

No more dreams of living in New York and being able to see Broadway shows.

They slipped away ...

And then she talked about the idea of someone finding all the lost things. Her words tugged at the fear many on quests must be feeling. The weight of the expectations of the Vision Catchers.

She ended in a whispered tone. The crowd remained in silence for several seconds. Lucy was sure those seconds must have felt like eons to Flora, but the air seemed thick with connection and understanding. Tears were streaming down Flora's face. Gary broke the quiet when he began clapping. Lucy joined in, and then the entire room started. Everyone stood to their feet. Standing O. The expectations that the Vision Catchers had for the Originators and the Originators had for themselves swirled around and lifted into the air. The crowd simmered down and Gary leaned in to Lucy and said, "How is anybody supposed to follow that?"

"Just be extra prepared. You better get backstage. Looks like you're fourth."

Gary sighed. He left his seat and went through the door.

The show continued on, more like the elementary recitals that Lucy expected. There was a pianist playing "Canon in D." The magician followed her, and as predicted, both Flora and Lucy were called up on stage to "assist."

As Lucy and Flora returned to their seats, Gary walked out onto the stage with a red ball on his nose and clown makeup in a clown outfit. Lucy could hardly believe that he only spent the last two acts making himself up. He even had the large clown shoes flopping on. The circus music played. He smiled and pulled out three clubs from his giant pockets.

Holding them in one hand, showing them to the crowd, urging them to say "oooh" and "awww." He juggled two, then added a third. When he dropped one, he made fun of himself. Putting the clubs away, he switched to balls. After about thirty seconds, he started tossing one ball up in the air very high. It was almost like he was acting out the three stooges as a one man show, having a football bump him on the face, tripping and falling and then successfully juggling some. The crowd whooped and hollered and laughed. He'd wrapped them around his finger with his levity and his humor.

Lucy had a sense of pride well up within her. She wondered if he'd done this kind of thing for his son in the past. She imagined him making his son laugh when it was just the two of them. Gary ended simply by walking off the stage, juggling while he was walking.

Was this his calling? Lucy thought. *Being a clown?* Lucy imagined it wouldn't fit within his lifestyle. She imagined finding your calling on the first mini quest of this forced performance was probably one in a thousand, at least.

They had to suffer through a few other acts. She hoped the suffering wouldn't extend to when Emily and she performed. She checked the program. There were two more acts before her, and she needed to go backstage. She had a different outfit picked out for this performance, trying to really embody the character she was playing: Joanne. A suit because Joanne seemed serious, but she kept some jewelry out of sight that was more "her" because it gave her a sense of bravery. She closed her eyes and breathed in and breathed out and tried to relax.

She was ready, but when she looked around, she didn't see Emily. They were up next, but everywhere Lucy looked, no Emily. She got nervous that she'd have to do the performance all on her own. She visualized how she'd approach the duet singing on both sides. Did she even know the words? Her heart raced as her anxieties rose. Her spinning thoughts were interrupted by a rustling coming from a door labeled Storage. She opened it and there was Emily puking into a trash can.

"Are you okay? Are you sick?" Lucy asked.

Emily shook her head no. "I'm nervous. I always puke when I'm nervous."

Lucy tried to be encouraging. "I don't want to go out there. I'm nervous too, but remember, this is just a talent show for what's basically a camp. This isn't an audition for *American Idol* or *The Voice*."

Emily said, "I get that, but I don't think I can do this."

Lucy replied, "You can and you will. I refuse to do this by myself." Lucy didn't know what the consequence would be if they didn't, but she didn't want to get sent home. She'd rather die. She looked at Emily with as much sympathy as she could. "I've got to take this chance. Look, let's do some deep breathing. Hold my hands."

Emily held Lucy's hands. Lucy tried to recall a meditation session she'd done years and years ago, before she was with Colt. It was really simple and it had a really simple cadence. "Breathe in and know that you are breathing. Breathe out a smile." She repeated this ten times. "Breathe in and know that you are breathing. Breathe out a smile."

On the tenth time, she heard their names called by Ms. Benedict. "Lucy, Emily, it's your turn. Get out there. They've already called your names! We're waiting!"

They rushed away and took their places on the opposite side of the stage. They waited for the intro music.

Emily sang the first words of the song, "Ever since" and then stopped.

Lucy looked at her and whispered, "Breathe in, know that you are breathing. Breathe out a smile." Emily took a deep breath in, breathed out a smile, and the piano started the intro music again for her.

And she let it all out. It was quiet at first, but then she gained her confidence and momentum. She was in flow and sounded beautiful. Lucy's part didn't come until at least forty-five seconds into the song, if not more. She was so mesmerized by Emily that she almost missed her intro cue. By the end, they were looking into each other's eyes, singing confidently, and locked in. Lucy felt the energy between Emily and herself being amplified by the audience, but somehow simultaneously had forgotten that they were there.

It was a connection that she'd never felt before. When they finished, they looked out into the crowd and received a standing ovation. It was nice to see friendly faces like Gary and Flora in the audience cheering really loudly.

After the show, at the reception, the mosaic from the small group hung on the wall. The leaders of all the small groups had combined them to make one large circle. It drew Lucy in momentarily, but the chatter of the room interrupted her reflection.

Everyone was coming up to Emily and saying things like, "This is your calling, you should do this. You've found it, girl. I've never heard somebody sing as well as you."

And no one said anything to Lucy ... except Gabe.

He was kind of obligated to come up to her, she thought. But all he said was, "You did a good job." Lucy's heart sunk. It had felt so great on stage, shadowed under Emily's light. Now, she was just embarrassed.

She looked up at Gabe, her eyes begging for reassurance. "It wasn't how I envisioned it at all."

He looked back at her with sympathy and took a deep breath in. After a moment, he said, "It never is. That's why so many dreams go unfulfilled. You imagine the finish line and it takes time to get there. And some visions are just not possible, but beautiful just the same. If you tried to chase the sunset, you'd end up lost in the darkness, but your vision made a beautiful painting or would make incredible poetry. Singing is probably not your destiny, but it's along your path. It's a part of this quest."

"Why do I only have forty days then, if everything takes time?"

"It's a Vision Quest. It isn't going to get you to a dream fulfilled. Is your vision for your life with Colt? Do you want to walk on eggshells every day and have him call you names? You were miserable doing that, weren't you? The impossible visions were all that I could catch while you were with him. Fantasies of lives not possible, not with Colt. You're amazing and if you choose, you can do amazing things. I'm not saying to give up on singing, but perhaps we can revisit it after you try out some other dreams. This was a talent show assignment, after all."

"Okay. So what next?"

He glanced over to where Emily and Cecilia were chatting and said, "I think you know." Gabe and Lucy headed toward them.

Gabe struck up a conversation with Cecilia. Lucy swallowed her pride and went up to Emily and gave her a big hug and said, "You were fabulous."

Emily looked back. "I couldn't have done it without you. You were great."

Lucy felt pride and a gladness in her heart for what she'd done to help Emily with her nerves. She smiled at her and asked, "Well, is this what you're gonna do? Everybody's saying that you should."

"I don't know," she replied. "I have to talk to Cecilia, but yeah, maybe."

Lucy encouraged her. "I mean, we're in Nashville, right?"

"Right," Emily said with more confidence and a smile that beamed from ear to ear.

Lucy let out an enormous yawn. "I better go to bed. I'm exhausted." Lucy glanced over at Gabe and didn't want to interrupt his flirtation with Cecilia. She headed back to the B&B with a lifted spirit. Butterflies flitted in her stomach as she tried to envision what would be next on the quest.

18

The Vibanator

The sound of Gabe's alarm blared. He hadn't set the tone. The app set automatically to the 500 miles song, "I'm Gonna Be" by The Proclaimers. Normally, it hadn't bothered him, but today the effects of yesterday's events presented themselves as a pounding headache. He rubbed his eyes and groaned, realizing he'd let the pressure—and maybe Cecilia's energy—get to him. He'd never lost control like that before.

Last night after the talent show, after Emily had blown people away with her vocal acrobatics, Cecilia was on cloud nine. She was smiling and radiating happiness. When Gabe went to Cecilia to congratulate her, she invited him to celebrate with her.

"Where are you celebrating?"

"Well, where else? The Vibanator. I even have a special invite to the VIP Room."

"What's The Vibanator?"

"OMG, Gabe, you must really keep to yourself. It's only the best exclusive club for Vision Catchers. I can't believe you've never been there." Still beaming, she grabbed his hand and pulled him out of the room. "Let's goooooo!" she shouted.

Cecilia drove. She had a baby blue Thunderbird convertible with a black top. When Gabe climbed in, he noticed the mess in the back seat— balled up papers, books scattered about, along with the occasional empty Big Gulp.

Cecilia noticed his gaze and said, "You know what they say, 'creative minds are rarely tidy.'" She shrugged at him. Her cavalier attitude actually impressed him. Most messy people were extremely apologetic and embarrassed about their mess. She owned it.

They pulled up to a familiar area of the VC campus. "I didn't know there was a club around here?"

"It's a speakeasy. You know the Truett Library?"

"Yeah, I've been there. Does it transform to a club at night?"

"Well, sort of. You'll see." Cecilia parked and once again grabbed his hand and ran toward the library doors. There was an emergency exit steel door to the side of the entrance. She knocked three times with one knock, a space, and two quick knocks. A large man came to the door. He must have been at least 6'7". He had a box cut throwback haircut, which made him even taller.

Gabe would expect a bouncer, especially one of his stature, to be serious, but he had the same infectious energy as Cecilia. He smiled and excitedly said, "Welcome, welcome, my friends. I'm Glacious. Come in. I'll be your concierge for the evening. Let me know if you need anything, anything at all." Gabe tilted his head at the strange man.

Cecilia looked at him and said, "I got a special invite to the—"

"Friend, I know," Glacious interrupted. She didn't even have to finish her sentence. He gestured at his own eyes and Cecilia's a few times. They were in sync. He could read her thoughts. "Follow me," he said joyfully.

He quickly raced up the stairs and then trotted down a hallway that was covered in books. Cecilia was skipping like a little girl on the playground. Gabe tried to slow down to read the titles of the books, but he had no idea where they were going. Every time he dawdled, he lost them.

They stopped at a wall. Gabe knew better than to think this was a dead end. Glacious's energy calmed, and he closed his eyes. The wall then opened up like pocket doors, and music pumped their way as they stepped in. There were hardwood floors, purple spotlights flashing around, and a disco ball above.

Cecilia started dancing to the music. It wasn't your normal club music. It was a mash-up of "Dancing in the Moonlight" and "Do You Believe in Magic."

Cecilia turned to Gabe. "All the songs are remixed versions of songs written by Originators."

He looked all around, taking it all in. His heart was pumping and his hands started to sweat. Glacious sensed this and grabbed a drink off the tray of a passing waitress and whispered in Gabe's ear, "Here, my friend, a little liquid courage to ease those nerves." He pulled back and winked at Gabe. Turning back to Cecilia and Gabe, he motioned for them to continue following him, turning sideways and galloping. "This way!"

He led them to a traditional velvet rope. At first, Gabe thought it was a little pedestrian and less dramatic than he was expecting—given the lead up to the entrance of the club itself. Then he saw there was another hidden door people were crawling through.

As Glacious undid the rope, Gabe saw someone that threatened to put an end to his night. A stern-faced woman with arms crossed. She took a stance that was more of what he'd expect from a bouncer. Even though she was tiny, her presence loomed large.

She nodded toward Gabe. "He isn't on the list," she said without even looking at a list.

Cecilia jumped in, "He's with me."

"Well, this room is only for people who are on the list."

"But I got this invite with a plus one." Cecilia pulled out her phone, pulling up the app, showing her the invite.

"Yeah, this space is for Vision Catchers whose Originators have found their purpose on a quest."

"My Originator wouldn't have found her way without his," she said, gesturing to Gabe. She pulled up her app again and scrolled. She pulled up the video of Lucy and Emily singing together. Pointing to Lucy, Cecilia said, "She gave my Originator the boost she needed to get to her true path."

The tiny woman glanced up toward Gabe, still menacing, but her defenses seemed to ease slightly. "And this is your Originator?"

Gabe nodded timidly, not wanting to anger her.

"Okay," she said reluctantly. "Show me your app and pull up your Originator's ID. If it matches, I'll let you in. I'm a bit of a sucker for musicals and I caught that performance. Your girl was phenomenal," she said, tilting her head toward Cecilia.

Gabe pulled out his app, clicked on the "Your Originators" tab, to show the tiny woman Lucy's ID. She opened a door that looked as if it had been built for her. They squeezed through and he almost hit his head. Gabe looked back to Glacious and with raised eyebrows. Glacious said, "Yeah, I can't make it back there. You guys have fun and join us back out here in a bit. DJ Princess can really spin. You don't want to miss it."

The room was full of velvet chairs and couches and even had a short red carpet at the entrance. A woman approached Cecilia and Gabe and handed them both a large drink. They were fishbowl size and blue with a red curly straw. It was sweet, but then burned on the way down.

"Yowzer, that's strong," Gabe shouted.

Cecilia laughed and replied, "Yeah, they don't skimp on the good stuff for the VIPs." They walked toward a table and some of Gabe's sloshed out. He wanted to drink it slowly. He was a lightweight, and didn't want to embarrass himself in front of Cecilia. Whoever was hosting this party must've been pretty high up. Possibly even a Vision Guild member, or at least a super cool Vision Catcher.

They were some of the first people there other than a few women sitting on a couch and a man receiving a shoulder massage.

The alcohol helped shake Gabe's nerves. They danced, and they laughed, and they talked and talked. He was over the moon when he held Cecilia tight and she pressed her body against his. The pulsing of the music vibrated through them and they were all in sync.

He thought the club was probably just for young people, but then he saw Randy. His plump old self actually had moves. It was kind of surprising.

But now as the alarm blared, Gabe realized he must have blacked out. He grabbed for his phone as he tried to recall the events of the evening and how he had ended back up in bed. He looked at his app and his eyes widened. "Oh, shit."

A message appeared. "You havent checked in with your VC Rep about yesterday's performance of your Originator. Please check in now to avoid point reduction on this quest."

He needed a moment. He took a deep breath, head pounding. He needed to go find some coffee. Once he was fully caffeinated, he could think back on Lucy's day yesterday and what had happened clearly and carefully. A notification alert on the app distracted him. "A fellow Vision Catcher has left you a review." He hadn't even noticed this feature and his palms started to sweat as he looked at what it said.

It was from Cecilia. She said, "Lucy was a dream last night with my Originator, Emily. She really stepped up so that Emily could shine during their performance. My Originator's nerves were through the roof and I feel glad that Lucy stepped in to help."

Below the review, there was a score.

Forging New Friendships: 100 points

Cultivating Confidence: 100 points

Gabe smiled. He heard a knock on his door and from the other side, Aunt Rae said, "Bing! Your coffee is ready!"

He opened the door and took the cup of coffee from her. His first words of the day came out hoarse. "What are you ... "

She interrupted. "Good morning! I saw what time you came in last night and figured you need a real life alert, not just that app. You better get a move on. I let Lucy into the studio a half hour ago."

"Geez, I wanted to do this my way. Do you hover over all your Vision Catchers this way?"

She shook her head. "Well, a hangover is no way to start out. Come on, chop chop!"

Gabe hurried to get dressed and out the door. Annoyed, head throbbing, but knowing she was right.

19

The Skateboarder

Quest Day Three

Lucy was sitting on the bricks that lined the studio garden. She buried one hand in the soil near a beautiful peace lily. Butterflies tickled her arms while roosters crowed nearby—they knew it was time to begin.

When she heard the creak of the door, she looked up at Gabe and said, "Oh, hey, guess I'm the one running on VC time today."

Gabe smiled. "Ha ha."

Lucy studied his face. "You look rough."

"I'm fine," he replied defensively.

"Okay ... so how does this work? Do I just pick one of these?" she asked, looking all around the studio.

"Actually, no. I have an idea about where we should begin. Just hold on one sec." Gabe darted to a closet and came back with enthusiasm to Lucy, carrying a painting of her as a teenager on a skateboard. "What about this one? You remember this? I think it'll be a good start."

She doubled over in laughter. When she looked up, his eyes were lit up with excitement and expectation, as if Lucy becoming a professional skateboarder was still an option at her age.

"Wait, you're for real? Was this because I was just thinking about this dream the other night?" The wheels spun in her head, thinking about the possibilities. "Will you take me somewhere where I'll get to meet Tony Hawk?"

"Well, no, I don't have those kinds of connections, but I have already designed and painted a skateboard for you."

Lucy smiled endearingly. "Oh, so you've been planning this for a while. Can I see it?"

Gabe got even more excited and ran to the back of the studio to retrieve it. While she waited, she thought back to the time she had her eyes glued to all the hot skater boys and rad girls in the X Games. She had massive crushes on all the skater boys with their long hair and flannel shirts. It took her weeks to learn how to pop an ollie, but she was persistent and focused, eventually mastering the trick. Then this boy in her neighborhood laughed at her and that's all it took. No more practicing or trying. She put away the dream of going to the X Games just because of one stupid boy's opinion.

Gabe returned, beaming, with the skateboard painted like the night sky. The background was made of deep purples and brilliant blacks, peppered with stars. Thin silver lines connected some of the stars. When Lucy took a closer look, she could almost make out her face.

Lucy shouted, "Oh, I love it!" She took the skateboard from Gabe and was giddy. Cradling the board in her arms, she ran her hand over the glossy painted side, the surface contrasting starkly from the rough and abrasive top covered in grip tape. Lucy spun the wheels with her hands. She closed her eyes and smiled as she pictured herself on the top of the X Games podium. The skateboard filled her with goddess-like power.

"I also have these," Gabe said as he handed a helmet, wrist guards, and elbow and knee pads to match.

"Right boss, safety first!" she said while giving Gabe a half salute. She buckled the helmet on her head and put the elbow pads on and went outside to begin practice, but everything outside the studio was dirt and gravel. "Can you take me somewhere to practice?"

"Of course. Let's goooo!!!" Gabe shouted enthusiastically and sprinted toward the car. Lucy followed him gleefully.

After driving for a couple of minutes, Gabe felt a familiar tingling in his spine—a vision reawakening. Lucy may have not noticed, but Gabe had placed the painting of this vision in the back, alongside the skateboard and pads. His eyes moved toward the rearview mirror. He saw the Feranchin energy he'd infused into the canvas years ago float into the air and reabsorb into Lucy as she sat beside him. Her psyche was calling on the dream. As her passion swirled around, it also passed through him. He could feel it strengthening him.

The memory of the day he'd first captured this vision flooded back to him. He'd had a miserable morning. Kids at school teased him when he had to read a vision he'd caught in words in front of the class. Their brains worked differently than his. He could capture everything with brushstrokes, but all the school exercises were in writing.

Later that day, during a shadowing session, his mentor had asked him, "Do you know how special you are, Gabe?"

Gabe had looked away. He'd heard this kind of pep talk from his aunt too many times before. He just wanted to be like everyone else—not special.

But with a father and both maternal grandparents born of a brainstorm, expectations had always weighed heavily.

"You're powerful. The images that you see and can project are more vivid and clear than ones I've ever seen with any other student. Your imagination is woven into the visions you catch. The details are amazing. You're not a writer, you're an artist."

Gabe sighed and nodded.

The mentor turned and said, "Follow me." He took him down the gravel path to a building that became his studio.

The mentor left him to paint alone for the first time. Previously, he'd always been by his side. Gabe felt nervous, but also free. He stared at the blank canvas for an hour. Then the door blew open and a lost vision blew in.

It was different from those he'd captured of Lucy before. Less childlike. It was full of Feranchin, but he could also see the negative forces that blew it in his direction. They hung off of it like a tail of a comet. The self-doubt born of the ridicule of the boy teasing her. Before his paint brush hit the canvas, he took his mentor's words to heart and shook off his own self-doubt. He let his bullies and demons leave his consciousness. He only focused on the power of this vision. He painted Lucy standing on the podium at the X Games. With every brushstroke, he felt her power. It was a pivotal moment in his training.

When he showed Aunt Rae later that day, she cried. She knew he'd had a breakthrough.

The vibration of the side of the road jostled his wandering mind. He gripped the wheel tighter to realign himself in the lane.

Lucy looked at him. "You okay?"

"Yeah, just a little hiccup."

He focused back on the road and pondered whether he was being selfish in this first adventure. The vision was more special to him than to her. But what if it worked?

After driving for about fifteen more minutes, Lucy became impatient. "There!" Lucy exclaimed and then whined, "Come on let's just pull over. Look, there's a park right there."

"You'll be happy you waited when we get there."

They got there, and Lucy wasn't happy. It was a skate park and there were tons of kids going down hand rails, small ramps, and gliding in and out of concrete pools. While mostly preteen and teenage boys, she was glad to see some girls in the mix.

Lucy turned to Gabe. "This is a little much. Shouldn't we be starting in a deserted parking lot? That's how I learned how to drive. Why did you take me here?"

"This is Two Rivers Skate Park. It's one of the best free skate parks in Nashville. You can learn a lot just by observing. You wouldn't get that in an empty parking lot. Try to approach this with an open mind. What if you could really train to be a skater?"

Lucy tried to reset with an open mind, scanning the park again. She saw signs requiring helmets, which she was glad of, but when she perused the skaters, only half were wearing them. She turned to Gabe. "Where are the parents? Look at all these kids not wearing helmets."

"Don't get distracted. Focus on your journey."

"Come on, man. You just told me to watch them." She smiled at him playfully and shook her head at his ridiculousness.

"Well, I haven't come empty-handed." He looked around and then waved at a man covered in tattoos, in a flannel shirt, a white undershirt, and cargo shorts. How these folks could wear shorts in the winter was beyond Lucy. The young man's hair was wavy and brown. He looked just like the kind of skater Lucy would've had a crush on when she was a teenager.

As he approached the skater said, "Hey Gabe."

"Hey man. Thanks for coming." They greeted each other with a bro hug—starting with a handshake and ending with the two patting each other on the back.

Gabe made introductions. "Alex, this is Lucy, Lucy this is Alex. Alex is in our alumni network and he's agreed to give you an intro lesson to get you started."

She looked at Alex. "Thanks so much for doing this. Where should we start?"

"Well, you see that big pool over there?" Alex came close to her and pointed toward an empty pool full of skaters doing tricks. "I thought

I'd have you skate down it and then back to me." She froze in fear. His giant smile didn't ease the blow of his proposal.

Eyes wide, she finally managed to say, "Excuse me, what?"

"I'm kidding. Come on, follow me. Let's get away from these kids." He turned toward a path that had trees hanging over it. As they left the main area, Lucy noticed a little girl about eight-years-old with a French braid sitting on the ground and watching the action. She was all alone and looked sad. She paused, forgetting about Alex for a moment, and knelt down beside the girl.

"I'm Lucy, what's your name?"

"Brittany."

"Hey, are your parents here? Are you okay? You look sad."

"I'm okay. My brother's over there. He's babysitting."

Lucy looked to where she was pointing and saw an older boy.

"That must really stink when he's supposed to be playing with you and you just have to watch him skate. What do you like to do?"

"I want to skate too, but we can only afford one board and he says since he's older he gets it."

Lucy's heart sank. She wanted to hand the girl her board right then, but Gabe tapped on her shoulder and she turned toward him. "Hey, I only reserved Alex for the next couple of hours. We got to go."

"Wait a minute," Lucy said, but when she turned back to talk to the girl, she'd left. Somebody probably taught her about stranger danger. Two men lurking and a woman talking to her, Lucy should've known better than to approach her, but the girl just drew her in—she didn't know why.

She stood up and jogged to catch up with Alex. Gabe had been carrying her board and helmet. Alex made a turn, and they were in a flat, almost abandoned parking lot. It wasn't completely empty. A couple of guys who had set up a small wooden ramp were skating and filming their tricks.

Lucy turned back to Gabe who was still a few paces back and whispered, "See, I told you, empty parking lot."

Gabe held his hands up still holding the board and helmet and said, "You got me. But hey, that's why I commissioned the expert. Go on."

He handed the helmet to Lucy. She secured it on her head and then grabbed the board—nerves buzzing as she approached Alex.

She felt the pressure. It was one thing trying this out in front of Gabe. But out here? With strangers watching? What if one of those guys caught her falling on camera? One of them even looked like the jerk who had teased the desire to skate out of her decades ago.

His eyes looked directly into Lucy's as he said, "So, have you done this before?"

"Not for a long time."

"Okay, well, it's not quite like riding a bike. Let's look at your board."

Lucy handed him the board and in the corner of her eye, she could see Gabe beaming with pride. Alex examined the board and spun the wheels. "Gnarly design, you do that Gabe?"

Gabe nodded a goofy smile. Alex continued, "Alright, Lucy, first things first. Let's make sure your board feels just right. You want to have a good balance between stability and maneuverability. Check the tightness of your trucks—that's these metal things right here." Alex pointed to the skateboard's undercarriage.

Lucy nodded, eager to learn. "Got it. How tight should they be?"

Alex grinned. "Good question. It really depends on your preference, but since you're just starting out, let's go with medium tightness. That should give you enough control without making it too twitchy."

Lucy adjusted the trucks as instructed, using the skate tool Alex had lent her. She wondered what "twitchy" meant. She really didn't want to ask too many questions, though. "Okay, how's this?"

Alex inspected it. "Perfect. Now, step on the board with your non-dominant foot first."

Lucy hesitated but eventually placed her right foot on the skateboard, gripping Alex's bicep for balance.

Once she'd gotten back her focus and actually balanced, Alex continued, "Good. Now, keep your weight centered over the board, and place your back foot on the ground for stability."

Lucy did as instructed, finding the initial balance challenging.

Alex reassured her, "It might feel wobbly at first, but that's normal. Now, practice pushing off gently with your foot while keeping your weight over the board. Imagine you're pushing your way into a gentle glide."

Lucy took a deep breath, let go of Alex, pushed off lightly with her left foot, and felt the board move beneath her. She wobbled but didn't fall.

"Nice job!" Alex encouraged. "Now, to steer, lean your body gently to the left or right. Your trucks will turn the board in the direction you lean. Try it."

Lucy tried steering, making a few wobbly turns, but she was getting the hang of it. Just as she was gaining confidence, she hit a pebble and stumbled off the board, and it darted in front of her. She caught herself from falling and then grabbed the board.

When she turned back, defeated, Alex was still positive. He nodded approvingly. "You're doing great. Remember, the key to skateboarding is balance and control. Practice pushing and steering until you're comfortable. And don't forget to practice stopping too—you can drag your back foot on the ground to slow down."

Lucy practiced turning and going straight for at least thirty minutes while Alex and Gabe just watched her. She was surprised by how tired she was just from pushing her foot, but the endorphins were pumping, too. Her energy and excitement powered her along. She was feeling confident when Alex shouted to her from the other end of the lot, "Okay, ready to learn some tricks?"

Her stomach dropped. She rolled back to them and said, "But what if I fall?"

Alex shook his head and said, "Don't fall."

"That's your coaching instruction. 'Don't fall'?"

"Pretty much, yeah. I could say what some coaches say, which is 'Everybody falls, even pros. Don't get discouraged if you fall.' But I say screw that. My philosophy is don't fall. If you have it in your head that everybody falls, it makes you fall more, in my opinion. Look, see that fence over there." He pointed to a metal fence at the end of the lot.

"Yeah."

"We're going to start over there. You'll get to hold on to the fence, so no worries. Remember, it's all about balance and not being afraid of falling."

Alex and Lucy skated over to the fence. She was impressed with how well she'd done in just a short period. Some muscle memory from her brief time in middle school had kicked in. *Was this it? Am I going to be a professional skateboarder?* she thought.

She was definitely feeling joy, but it soon shattered with frustration after her fifth attempt at an ollie. An ollie is a trick where you and the board leap into the air and land back down. When she learned how to do it in middle school, it had taken multiple falls over multiple weeks. She hadn't thought about holding onto something then. Every time she attempted it, she didn't fall exactly. She used the fence as a security blanket and held onto it so tightly.

Every time she failed, she'd blame something—the board, the fence, the wind. She even thought maybe the wrist guards were getting in her way, so she threw them aside. After a while, the metal cut her hands in a few places when the board would get away from her.

Alex was patient. "In order to do an ollie, you've got to feel comfortable leaning back on your tail," he said.

It was easy enough for them to practice just leaning on the tail while holding the fence, but that wasn't the trick.

Alex's calm voice made it sound easy. "So if you want to lean back on your tail, you want to put pressure down toward the ground and not backwards. If you go backwards too far, you're definitely going to fall. So remember, you want to put pressure on the tail, slide that front foot up, get your knees up as high as you can, lift the board up off the ground, get it up high, level it out, land, feet over the bolts of course. You can hold on to the fence for a bit, but my goal is by the end of the hour, you'll be confident enough to let go of the fence."

Lucy didn't mean to, but she rolled her eyes. Alex was losing his luster with his positive attitude and belief that one could just will themselves not to fall. She was growing physically and emotionally tired, but Alex persisted in his encouragement.

For the next thirty minutes, she attempted to follow his instruction. Her hand was being scratched so much by the fence that she let go of it. She turned to Alex. "Okay, I'm going for it. No fence."

Alex went into a half squat and clinched both his fists and shouted, "Alright! Let's goooo!" He drew the attention of the few boys in the parking lot, interrupting their amateur filmmaking.

Lucy was nervous and looked down at her partially bloodied hand. She secured her helmet as tight as she could and then drew a deep breath in. Lucy got on the skateboard and pushed off just to get it moving some. She put pressure on the tail, but not too much, pushed her foot forward and jumped. The second she was in the air, she thought, *I'm doing it. I'm actually doing it!* Her loss of focus caused her to lose her balance and as the ground came toward her, she heard a crack.

She'd done exactly what Alex told her not to; she put out her arms to brace herself. A sharp pain traveled up her arm as Gabe made his way to where she lay. She looked up at him. "Uh-oh."

"Are you okay?" Gabe asked anxiously.

"I think I'm," Lucy moved her wrist slightly, "ow. No, I don't think I am."

"Don't worry," he said. "We're going to take care of you."

"Are you sure you don't have some kind of magical time machine? I'd really like to start today over and maybe not dream of being a thirty-year-old middle schooler."

Gabe laughed. "I'm sure." Alex and Gabe helped Lucy up, and they walked over to a bench that was scratched up from years of skateboard tricks and sat down. Lucy's wrist was throbbing. Gabe asked, "How's your pain on a scale of one to ten?"

Without hesitation, Lucy replied, "Eleven."

Gabe instantly responded, "Let's get you to the hospital."

Lucy agreed and thanked Alex for his time.

"No. Thank you! This was so much fun. I hope you stick with it. It takes a few weeks to get the hang of even a trick like an ollie."

"I'll think about it," Lucy said, somewhat genuinely. She really loved the fantasy of her being a badass skater. The reality, though, had her headed to the hospital, so they parted ways. At least for now.

Gabe held the car door open for Lucy as she gingerly climbed in. He'd thought skateboarding would be a fun start to the quest, but was regretting it now. Lucy seemed to have calmed down from the shock, transfixed by what was happening outside of the car—her eyes appearing to be searching over the skateboarders.

"What are you looking for?" he asked

"I'm looking for the girl. The one I was talking to earlier. I think that's her, but I'm not sure. Can you give her my board?"

Gabe sighed. He wanted this to be it. How cool would it be if this unexpected, crazy suggestion was Lucy's destiny? He looked out toward Lucy's gaze. Sure enough, that was her, and she looked just as sad as when they'd encountered her before. He grabbed the board from the back of the car.

"Don't forget the helmet and pads." Lucy winced as she attempted to take the knee pads off. "Oh, and the wrist guards I threw off by the fence before I fell."

"Okay. Okay. I'll get those." Gabe went over to Lucy and gently pulled her knee pads and elbow pads off. With the skateboard in tow, he said, "I'll be right back."

He retrieved the wrist guards and hurried toward the little girl. When he reached her, he quickly gave the board plus the safety equipment to her. "Here, the lady I was with before wanted you to have these."

Her jaw dropped, and she stared at the board with excitement. She tilted her head and scrunched up her face. With a pinch of whine in her voice, she held up the helmet and pads and said, "These won't fit."

"You'll grow," Gabe said matter-of-factly, and left. His worry about Lucy overwhelmed him. He picked up the pace and ran toward the car.

20

The Hospital

"Mission accomplished," Gabe said as he climbed in. Lucy smiled, and her entire face lit up.

He grabbed his phone to punch in Central Nashville Hospital to the GPS and saw a message notification from the VC app. He didn't want to look at it and began to wonder if this physical setback would lose Lucy points. As he set off, he glanced over at Lucy. She was holding onto her wrist and gazing out of the window, and he saw a single tear stream down her face.

When they reached a stoplight, he turned to her and said, "Well on the bright side, you're right-handed."

"No, I'm left-handed."

Puzzled, he replied, "I could've sworn I saw you eating with your right hand the other day."

"Well, we live in a right-handed world, so sometimes I switch, I guess, but yeah, I write with my left hand." Her single tear became a sob. Gabe tried to find the words to comfort her and was just about to lay a hand on her shoulder when the car behind him blared its horn.

Gabe let out a deep sigh as his foot hit the accelerator, his stomach turned and he could feel his blood pressure rising as he tried to imagine what would be next on their quest. He spun on how he'd possibly get 5,000 points if Lucy couldn't even use her dominant hand.

When they arrived at the hospital, there was construction in the parking lot outside the emergency room entrance. Gabe circled around several times before deciding to drop Lucy off at the front and venture to find parking farther off. When he put the car in park briefly in front of the entrance and went to open Lucy's door, a man in scrubs yelled at him, "You can't park there."

She turned to Gabe and said, "I'll wait for you."

It took Gabe ten more minutes to find parking and come back to the entrance. He didn't see Lucy, and he panicked for a moment that she may have fled again. Taking a deep breath, he entered the ER and spotted her waiting in line to check-in. There were three people in front of her and three people behind her. When they reached the front, they asked her what the problem was. She explained, and they handed her a clipboard to fill out, taking it with her right hand and then handing it to Gabe straight away.

Construction outside the hospital made it impossible to find a quiet area to sit. He hated to talk so loud, asking her private medical questions. He felt the blood rush to his cheeks when he asked, "When was your last period?" As she replied a little nervously, the man in scrubs who had fussed at them about the parking approached, giving Gabe the stink eye as he passed by. Gabe looked around, more conscious of his surroundings, and saw a few more people looking at them with suspicion.

He was frustrated, but hoping to ease the tension in the room, he code-switched. He shifted his tone to be more formal. "Well, Miss Lucy, I think that's it. Do you need my help with anything else?"

She leaned in and loudly whispered, "What the hell are you doing? *Miss Lucy?*"

He didn't answer. Instead, he tilted his chin slightly, letting his eyes scan the waiting room. When she followed his gaze, she saw what he saw. An elderly white woman was watching them intently. Lucy gave a small nod, her expression shifting with recognition. She understood.

They handed in the papers and waited for what seemed like an eternity. When Lucy was finally called back by the man in the scrubs from the parking lot, Gabe stood up and followed.

When Gabe reached the door, the man put his hand out. "I'm afraid it's patients only."

Lucy pleaded with him. "Please, um" pausing for a split second to glance down at his nametag, "Fred, he's my friend."

"Sorry, ma'am, relatives only. I'm afraid it's policy."

Gabe nodded and gritted his teeth as he watched Lucy disappear into the depths of the hospital.

There was no such policy and Fred knew it, but he was protective of women and had just got out of a lecture that all the nurses had to attend about signs of abuse or human trafficking. A physical injury and an unlikely pairing. Something just seemed off. He guided the woman with the hurt wrist into a triage station.

"Lucy, just give me one moment while I start your chart. Can I have your license and insurance?"

Central Nashville Hospital's e-charting system connected to other hospitals. He searched for her name and found a person who matched the address on her license in the system from their sister hospital in Jackson, Mississippi. He typed in the pertinent information and then turned to do a quick exam.

"So what happened? You hurt your wrist?"

"Yes, I fell doing something stupid."

Fred looked down at the intake packet. "It says here that you were skateboarding?"

"Oh my gosh, he wrote that?" Fred tried to judge if there was any fear in her face. "Yes, I fell skateboarding. What difference does it make?"

"Well, none … I suppose." Fred was becoming more and more convinced that there was something shady happening here.

"And what brings you to Tennessee? Your license is from Mississippi."

She swallowed hard. "Just visiting a friend."

Fred wasn't convinced. He noted her answer and put an order in for X-rays.

"Wait here. Someone will come to get you for an X-ray soon."

Fred walked away to the nurses' station and dialed the number that was listed as Lucy's emergency contact in the Mississippi system. He just had a funny feeling about that Black man.

"Hello?"

"Hello, yes. Is this Colt Rivers?"

"Yes, this is he. Who's this?"

"I'm a nurse at Central Nashville Hospital. I'm calling because your wife has come in with what may be a broken wrist and her Mississippi file lists you as her emergency contact. Wanted to let you know."

"Was anyone with her? Did she come in alone? Is she going to be okay?"

"She was with a Black man. She called him her friend, but I think you should come here."

"I do too. I'm on my way now. It'll take me a few hours. Don't let her leave."

Fred was relieved that his tone sounded genuinely worried. He'd made the right call. Something wasn't right.

When he passed by the triage station, Lucy was sitting still waiting for X-ray. Fred hated inefficiencies. He normally would have checked on the holdup and made sure his orders had made it to radiology, but he wanted to delay. Even though his shift was ending, he hung around.

After she finally returned to the room, Fred checked her chart again and saw that the doctor had ordered a sedative and a surgical consult. Confident that the process would take several more hours, he clocked out.

Lucy's eyes opened, and it took her a minute to remember where she was. She looked around the room and was surprised to see Daisy seated by her side.

"Daisy," she said, still a little groggy. "What are you doing here?"

"When I found out you were in the hospital, I came straight away."

"How'd you find out? Where's Gabe?"

"They didn't let him in at first. I bumped into him when he came back to the B&B to get you a change of clothes. I think he should be back soon."

"That painkiller cocktail they gave me was strong. Before they gave it to me, the doctor said I'd have to have surgery."

"I'm sorry, that really sucks. At least this makes for a good story," Daisy said with a pitying smile.

"I guess," Lucy replied softly.

"Well, hey ... speaking of stories. How was your first adventure? I mean, besides the broken wrist, of course."

"Well, actually, it was pretty great. I'm still thinking about possibly going back."

"Really? I cut my fingers on one of my first quests and I hopped ship right then."

"No, I'm messing with you. I gave the board away to this little girl. How about you? How's it going with the comedy?"

"It's rough, but at this point I've kind of settled on it. Randy is giving me some good material, but I'm kind of concerned that it might not be on the up and up."

"What do you mean?"

"Well, I really really really don't remember any of these visions and comedy that he's giving me. I'm starting to doubt that it's something that he got from me. I heard some other Vision Catchers talking about a black market where you can buy visions."

"Wait what? So you can just purchase the dream? Why would Randy do that for you?"

"I don't know. Maybe there's some kind of bonus scheme if they successfully get somebody on a new path. I mean, I am on this path, but I'm not gonna have him forever. I'm only going to be on this quest for another fifteen days. What's going to happen after that?"

Lucy felt drunk, slurring her words, but managed to find something encouraging to say. "Does it light you up? Is it what you were put on Earth to do?"

"Well yeah, it's nerve-racking as all hell, but it's the best feeling after I step off that stage when I've made people laugh. It's exhilarating."

Lucy smiled and continued to slur her words. "You sound enthusiastic. Do you know where the word enthusiastic comes from?"

Daisy shook her head no.

"It comes from the Greek word enthousiasmos and means 'possessed by a god' or 'inspired.' I tell you what you let the gods possess you this afternoon and write jokes about this." Lucy pointed to her wrist, which was temporarily braced.

"About what?"

"I give you permission to make fun of me for being a middle-aged person pursuing a career in skateboarding. In fact, I challenge you to write it. Don't talk to Randy. Even if there's some kind of black market of jokes, I bet this is a first. Do it while I'm in surgery and then you can perform for me when I wake up! If the drugs are anything like what I've got now, then I'll be in hysterics."

Lucy started laughing and couldn't tell if it was because of how high she was or the idea of a comedy show in a hospital room. The laughter was contagious and Daisy began laughing too.

Once they both caught their breath, Daisy grabbed her hand and squeezed it. "You know, what you said earlier about being possessed by gods ... that reminds me of how they explained this whole thing in that play at orientation. Did they do that for you guys?" Daisy asked.

"Yes, but we didn't get to see the end. It got interrupted by this weird guy. I think I saw the part you're talking about. There were lights all around and we got to the part where one of the actors poured the light over a woman and it looked like they entered her. That's what you're talking about, right?" Lucy was loopy, but she heard the beeping heart monitor pick up a bit, fueled by the gossip.

"Exactly. I can't remember the whole thing, but what made me think of the whole possessed by gods thing was how the VCs were first formed. So as I understand it, when like a genius had a brainstorm, like say, Isaac Newton, they couldn't keep up with their thoughts. The ideas were just like swirling around them. Then the universe swooped in to collect the ideas for safekeeping. And like eventually, there were too many of these ideas for the Universe to hold. So the Universe created Vision Catchers to hold on to the visions. So Randy and Gabe are half human and half creativity or ideas or whatever. They are literally possessed by gods, in a way — or whatever the Universe and our collective unconscious are made of."

Lucy's heart monitor slowed back down, but she forced her eyes awake to continue talking to her friend. "I get what you're saying. I saw that part. With those glowing orbs. They were talking about how they formed a society to ban against the forces that causes us to lose dreams." Her voice trailed as her impaired mind tried to fetch the memory. She spoke excitedly when she retrieved it. "But then this guy, Waylon, started shouting. They just dismissed us after that and played some music."

"Really? That's the part that hit me the most. I've talked to Randy some more about it since then. They call the light energy Feranchin, but they also warned about this dark energy called Infrassin. That's like self-doubt, greed, despair that can consume and kill ideas. I definitely was filled with some dark energy when Randy rescued me. The VCs capture light visions and banish dark ones. I find the whole mythology fascinating, but Randy can be pretty tight-lipped, like there's some things they won't let us know."

"Yeah, I found this magazine with Rae on the cover that had a headline about Feranchin, I think. But Gabe took it away."

"I've been able to pry a little more info from Randy. I kind of pestered him with questions. I told him I couldn't possibly perform if I didn't have some of my curiosity answered."

"Did it work?"

"Only a little. He did say they can procreate with each other just like us—the VCs, that is. And that the further they get away from being created by a brainstorm the less powerful they get." Daisy's face lit up with excitement, but Lucy was fading. She blinked a long blink as Daisy said, "And he also said ... "

A nurse came to check on Lucy before Daisy could finish. The nurse said visiting hours were over.

Daisy gave Lucy's hand a squeeze. "Okay I better go then. I hope everything goes well with the surgery."

"I better go too." Lucy's eyes closed, and she went into a drug-induced sleep.

21

The Confrontation

Lucy's eyes slowly opened. Only moments ago an anesthesiologist was talking to her before surgery. Things were fuzzy at first and she wiped the goop that was clouding her vision. When she looked down at her arm, she could see that her wrist was now braced more firmly than it had been before and an IV was placed on the other arm. She looked to the chair where Daisy had sat before, but it was empty. Lucy was confused, but every time she tried to focus, she felt a force pulling her eyes shut. She relented and gave in to her body.

A few minutes later, a nurse walked in and checked her vitals. As the blood pressure cuff touched her skin, Lucy stirred and became a little more alert. She turned to the nurse and asked, "When are they going to take me in for surgery?"

"The surgery is already done, dear."

"Really, I couldn't have been asleep for long. It only felt like a minute."

"You've been out for a few hours. Do you want juice or crackers?"

Lucy nodded and closed her eyes. What felt like a second later, the nurse returned. The juice rallied her somewhat, and she wondered about Gabe.

"Is there a man in the waiting room? I let them know he'd be my ride home before the surgery. His name is Gabe."

"They probably won't discharge you for another hour or so. Let me check. I'll be right back. You just rest. The TV remote is right beside you."

Lucy turned on the TV and the weather channel came up. A snow storm was hovering just north of Tennessee. The anchorman's voice grated on her a little and she tried to turn it off, but the power button didn't seem to work. She changed the channel, but decided it was all too loud, so she just muted it. She closed her eyes again and sleep came fast.

Gabe had been waiting for hours. He'd brought his sketchbook so that he could take his mind off of Lucy's pain. Drawing pictures of her succeeding at skateboarding and talking to the little girl. When he paused to take another swig of his coffee, an interior door to the patient area opened slightly and he heard a nurse call out, "Anyone here for Lucy Rivers?"

He stood up and before he could say anything, he heard a man say, "Yes, I'm her husband." Gabe stood stunned as he watched Colt follow the woman into the back. He quickly followed, but couldn't catch the door before it was closed and automatically locked.

Frantic, he ran up to the front desk, but the line was three people deep. He waited, heart racing, and took a deep breath before trying to lock his mind into Lucy's. He knew she'd grown so much, but was sending her thoughts of strength and comfort. After a few minutes, he was just one person away from the front of the line. He'd talked to the woman earlier, and she'd told him that Lucy was in surgery. From his observations there was a lot of repetition in her job—answering people's questions, taking people's IDs, giving them visitor passes, sending messages to nurses ...repeat. Gabe sensed her exhaustion from her twelve-hour shift.

"Yes, sir. How can I help you?"

He was direct and hoped the woman would be sympathetic, though he was hesitant because of the racist stares from people he'd received earlier in the day.

"I'm here to see Lucy Rivers. I brought her some clothes."

She glanced up. "Oh yes, I just need to see some ID." She turned back to her computer.

Gabe pulled out his ID and handed it to the woman. She took it, barely looking away from her computer. He leaned in closer to the woman and said softly, "Lucy's in danger. Her husband just went back there. He's abusive. Can you do something?"

At this, the woman startled from the routine of her job and looked at Gabe seriously. "Okay. I'll handle it. Best you not go back. I'll give these clothes to her nurse. Hold tight." She turned and left before Gabe could ask anything else. He turned to see the line that had formed behind him and returned to his seat, hoping he could will the system to work in his favor.

Lucy awoke once again, feeling a hand stroke her forehead. She turned her head slowly toward the person. Her jaw dropped, her eyes grew wide, and she wanted to scream, but no sound came out.

Colt was standing over her bed, gazing at her with a sinister smile. She closed her eyes again and then opened them, hoping that it was just a hallucination, but there he stood, rubbing her head gently.

Colt, in an emboldened voice, said, "Well, well, well, looky what I found."

Lucy shrank back and the words "I'm sorry" almost fell out of her mouth reflexively, but she corrected course and instead said, "What do you want, Colt?"

"I want you. I've been all over the place looking for you. Why are you doing this to me? I even had to miss some classes, so I'm going to get docked for that."

"No one asked you to do that. Look, I needed this time to get my priorities straight."

"Your priorities? Your priority is with me. You're coming home. I need you." Colt went to the corner of the room and pulled a wheelchair around, motioning for her to get in.

"I can't leave now. They haven't discharged me and I've got a broken wrist. I don't need a wheelchair."

"Lucy, you know it's hospital policy." His condescension rang in her ears.

"Yeah, well, it's also hospital policy that they discharge you before you leave. You want our insurance to deny the claim for a surgery?" She knew this would resonate with him—he'd had to deal with hospital bills after his mother's death. Colt capitulated reluctantly and rolled the wheelchair back to its spot.

"Look Colt, I've got to continue on this quest. I promised." She didn't mean to let the word "quest" slip. *Damn drugs,* she thought.

"Promised who? What are you talking about?"

"No, I ... " Lucy struggled to find the words.

Colt's nostrils flared, his fists clenched, and in a loud tone he said, "I think I remember you promising me something, too. To stay by my side, till death do we part—or have you forgotten that?"

"No, I remember," she mumbled in a reluctant tone. She felt herself caving to a pain inside that ran deeper than her wrist.

Colt pulled a chair up next to her and rubbed her shoulder. If someone who didn't know them had walked in, they'd think he was being very loving. Crocodile tears welled up in his eyes. "Please don't leave me," he cried.

"I didn't say that I was leaving you. I just need to finish this thing. I'm not really allowed to talk about it," she said. Gabe had never told her what the rules were about talking to people outside of those on the Vision Quest, but she liked this idea and was going to run with it.

His voice raised again. "This is crazy. You're not allowed to talk about it. That's when you know shit's insane. Have you joined some sort of cult?"

Lucy moved her wrist a little, and though numb, a slight pain still shot through her arm. On the muted TV, she saw an advertisement for a game show and an idea sparked. She couldn't help but grin.

She leaned in close to Colt and spoke in a hushed tone. "Look really, I'm not supposed to talk about it, but I've got a chance to win some real money for us if I continue," she lied. She glanced around to act like she wanted to ensure no one was listening. She leaned into him and whispered, "The people who do the best can win up to a million dollars. But if they caught me telling you this, I could get kicked out. I mean, you've seen these kinds of challenges on TV. Do you really think I would've skateboarded unless it was for money?"

Colt's voice lowered, and he leaned in with intrigue. "For real?"

"Seriously, you need to leave. I got about a little over a month left and we weren't supposed to be interacting with people outside. It's a lot of money. Enough to pay off your student debt and for you to write that book you've always been talking about. That's why I had my phone turned off. But I'm turning it back on now that I've told you. You just can't contact me unless it's an emergency."

Colt took a beat and shook his head. "You're high and crazy. I don't know why you have to lie to me. You're coming back home with me."

Lucy stared at him, feeling helpless, in pain, and inebriated. Under her breath she said, "Try to make me."

With pure evil in his voice, Colt hissed, "I don't even have to try, bitch." He reached for her IV as if he was going to rip it out, but the nurse returned and he drew back his arm.

"Hi again, I just need to run a few tests. I'm going to need you to go back to the waiting room, sir.”

Colt's posture straightened as he looked down at the nurse and asked, "Why? I'm her husband." He looked back at Lucy, grabbing her hand, smiling at her insincerely.

The nurse replied in a friendly tone, "I'm sorry. It's a HIPAA compliance issue, I'm afraid. If you just step out into the waiting room. I'll be back to get you soon."

Colt's lips held tight together. He rubbed his chin, feigning an itch. Lucy had seen these microexpressions before when someone angered him in public. He was attempting not to misstep. He nodded and then looked back at Lucy. Still holding her good hand, he squeezed it hard and said in a sweet tone laced with a touch of psychopathy, "I'll be back in just a few minutes. See you soon." As Colt was leaving the room, he took one last look back at Lucy. His icy stare filled her body with fear.

The nurse took her blood pressure and noted that it was higher than before in her chart. She paused and sat down in the chair next to Lucy.

"Lucy, I'm Kara. I have to ask you a few questions, which are procedure. Is that okay?"

"Yes."

Kara looked at Lucy seriously, but with compassion. "We want to make sure you feel safe and supported before discharge. Do you feel safe at home?"

Lucy looked at the shut door, worried that Colt was listening, but the drugs seemed to serve as a bit of a truth serum. She leaned into Kara and whispered, "Not exactly."

"What do you mean by that? Is there anyone at home who makes you feel afraid or uncomfortable?"

Lucy nodded. Her breathing quickened and her eyes darted around–paranoid that Colt may have seen her.

Kara touched her softly on the arm. "Is it your husband?"

Lucy nodded again.

"Has he hurt you physically? Has he slapped you, kicked you, or injured you in any way?"

Lucy thought back to the time they were in the middle of a heated argument. Colt was calling her names and blaming her for something that wasn't her fault. She couldn't even remember what he was mad about now. What she did remember was trying to leave the house and him blocking the front door with his body. When she ran to the other door, he grabbed her arm to pull her back and then pushed her to the wall holding onto her neck. She could barely breathe. He didn't let her go until she agreed to stay. She had to wear turtlenecks when she went anywhere for three weeks because of the bruising. It was the middle of July.

She looked up at Kara and found the courage to whisper, "A couple times, but he hasn't ever kicked me or punched me or anything."

Kara took a deep breath in and looked straight at Lucy with a face full of pity. "How long ago was the last time?" Kara glanced down at Lucy's broken wrist and then back up at Lucy with a raised eyebrow.

Lucy knew what she was getting at and replied, "A while back, months ago. I really did break my wrist skateboarding ... as implausible as it sounds. Hand to God." Lucy raised her broken wrist and laughed a bit—half nervous giggle, half still high from the drugs.

Kara smiled a little, but then continued her line of questioning, walking the fine line between being firm and compassionate. "Does he insult you, belittle you, or try to control your actions?"

Lucy nodded. She lost her ability to hold it together. Tears streamed down her face, as memories of Colt calling her a cunt or moron or made her feel that she was less than flooded back.

"Oh sweetie, we got you." She brought Lucy a box of tissues. "It's protocol that I call a social worker. She may ask you some of these questions and a few more. In the meantime, you don't have to worry.

I'll go tell your husband that the neurologist came in to do a neuro exam and we're taking you to head CT to buy us some time. Meanwhile, we'll move you to a secure room. How does that sound?"

"Okay, I guess. Are you going to have security escort him from the building? I'd rather there not be a scene."

"I understand. This kind of thing happens more than you'd think. We have a process." Kara picked up the room phone, dialed some numbers and to the person at the other end said, "Hello. Yes, this is nurse Kara. I need a security warning issued on Room 232 and a consult with social services."

She turned back to Lucy. "Now, do you have somewhere to stay? What are you doing in Nashville, anyhow? I see you're from Mississippi."

"Yes, my friend Gabe has been helping me leave Colt. I don't know where he is, but he should be here. My friend said he had trouble getting in at first. I'm staying with his aunt."

Kara looked at her computer for a moment. "He's here. Looks like he's the one who alerted us to the security issue with your husband. We take everyone's picture when they check in as a visitor. Let me just pull it up."

Lucy waited nervously.

"These damn computers run so slow." A minute went by. "Okay, got it. I'll get him from the waiting room after I tell your husband we're taking you for the tests."

She stood just outside the door and called another nurse over. Ostensibly, the second nurse was to protect Lucy, but the woman was tiny and Lucy was worried what violent actions Colt might take when Kara told him he had to wait longer. She imagined he was fuming already sitting in the waiting room.

Within ten minutes, they moved her. From there, time seemed to crawl. Keeping true to her word, Kara fetched Gabe discreetly. His presence comforted her—along with the fact that she had a dedicated security guard. Despite this, she was anxious, but when she asked if she could have something to calm her nerves, Kara said they couldn't give her any more sedatives. She needed to be fully alert for the next steps.

Someone asked Gabe to wait outside while the social worker, Samantha, asked Lucy questions about Colt's behavior. It was emotionally draining, and she hadn't even touched on the worst of it. Crying commenced again. Wasn't there a limit to this well of tears? She was patient with Lucy, giving her the space she needed to process.

After she finished answering all Samantha's questions, Samantha explained to Lucy that they could file an Emergency Protective Order. It would last for fifteen days. If Colt violated the order, they could arrest him on the spot.

"Is that something you'd like to do?"

Lucy froze at the question—she could see clearly in her mind's eye a police officer serving the papers and the anger and anguish on Colt's face. She worried it could send him over the edge. He'd threatened suicide if she left him in the past. It's one of many things that had kept her from leaving him. Her heart sped up and beads of sweat formed on her forehead.

After a few moments, Samantha broke the silence. "You have to do this voluntarily. I can help you with the paperwork and get the process rolling, but it's your decision."

Outside, Gabe was feeling Lucy's emotional turmoil intensely. He tried to contain himself, but he couldn't wait any longer. He knocked on the door and stuck his head in. "Is everything okay in here?"

Lucy's voice cracked as she responded before Samantha could, "Gabe, she says I can file an Emergency Protective Order. If Colt violates it, he could go to jail."

Samantha motioned for Gabe to come in and said, "It's not mandatory. I told her that it's her decision."

Gabe entered and went beside Lucy, touching her arm softly and looking her in the eyes. He wanted to say the right thing and soothe her, but was having trouble finding the words. Finally, he said, "I think this is the best thing. You'll never be able to find your true path if you're always looking over your shoulder, worrying about Colt. The nurse said they do this all the time."

"Can I just talk to him again? I think I can just convince him to leave. We won't need to get the cops involved and then I can just stay with Gabe. He almost bought the ridiculous story that I was on a secret game show."

Gabe and Samantha both glanced at each other with the same worry in their eyes. He asked Samantha if they could have a few minutes. She agreed to step outside. He pulled up a chair next to Lucy and said, "Let's play a couple of different scenarios out in a transdreamosis session. Then you pick the choice you want. If you still want to just talk to Colt, we'll do that. Sound like a plan?"

She agreed, clasped his hands tightly, and closed her eyes.

22

The Protective Order

Samantha looked into the room, and Gabe and Lucy were holding hands, their eyes closed. She said a brief prayer of her own for God to guide Lucy to leave that bastard of a husband. She'd seen too many women who told stories like Lucy's only to return. Samantha wanted to be respectful and give them a couple more minutes, so she started the paperwork in case Lucy chose to file the EPO.

"Now let's first imagine filing the protective order," Gabe said. Lucy was still in the hospital with Samantha seated at her side. Lucy heard Gabe's voice say, "What's Samantha saying? Think about what she told you about the process and imagine that."

Lucy sunk more into the scene.

Samantha's voice was gentle, but firm. "It's not necessary, but it will make it easier when we try to make this a more permanent restraining order. Do you have anything in writing or any witnesses that can show Colt's behavior toward you?"

"Yes, I mean, I usually delete texts, but I think I have some emails. He threatened my friend Anna when he was looking for me the other night."

"That's good."

Just then Colt burst through the door and yelled, "What the hell is going on here? It doesn't look like she's getting a CT. Who the fuck are you?"

Colt and Samantha froze like a video that was paused. Gabe's voice came in, "Lucy, Colt's not here. There's a security guard outside the door. He doesn't know where you are."

Lucy argued, "Well, he sort of does. What if he finds me?"

"Okay. Let's say this happens. What are you going to do? Are you going to let him hold power over you? Let's take it where we left off."

Colt shoved past Samantha and ripped the sheets off of Lucy. He pulled a wheelchair around as he'd done earlier.

"Get in. We're leaving this second-rate hospital."

Lucy's pulse raced, and she was having a hard time breathing, but then she calmed. She reminded herself that this wasn't real.

"No. I'm not going anywhere with you."

"The hell you aren't."

Samantha shouted for security and pressed a button that set off an alarm. Two armed security officers escorted Colt away.

Samantha asked if she was okay. Lucy nodded and once they both calmed somewhat, Samantha said, "Now where were we? You ready to fill out these forms?"

"Yes, let's do it."

When Gabe let go of Lucy's hands and the transdreamosis session ended, she opened her eyes and could still feel the power of the scene. Her mind felt strong and she was ready to work through the system. They called Samantha back into the room. While the session felt like at least five minutes, the actual time must have been much quicker.

Samantha smiled softly at both of them. "That was fast. Did you reach a decision?"

"Yes, let's do it. Let's file the protective order." The actual events unfolded much less dramatically than Lucy had imagined. It took about a half hour to fill out the paperwork. The hospital staff assisted her in getting into Gabe's car without alerting Colt, and they got away.

As they drove, Lucy thought back to the keychain she'd lost. "I knew who I was this morning, but I've changed a few times since then." She felt a newfound courage from standing up to Colt, even if it was just on paper–putting it in writing may have made it even more powerful.

As they pulled up to the B&B her whole body relaxed, glad to be back in the VC realm, where Colt definitely couldn't touch her. Gabe walked her to her room, but before she could thank him, his phone rang. Distracted, he apologized and left her alone.

Ravi was calling. As Gabe headed to his room, his stomach was in knots. A check-in notification popped up a couple of hours ago, but he ignored it. He wanted to focus on Lucy and not worry about the points or the system. He hoped it wasn't to his detriment. Questions began swirling in his head, *Why's Ravi calling me? Am I in trouble?*

On the fifth ring, Gabe placed a shaky finger on the green button and answered. Ravi's face popped up on the screen. "Hi Gabe, according to our geolocation you spent several hours at the hospital today. Is everything okay? What happened?"

"I'm sorry. We had a mishap." His anxieties eased, knowing that Ravi's call was out of concern. With some apprehension, Gabe told Ravi the whole story. From how he'd pushed Lucy to a crazy skateboarding vision, hurting herself, the hospital, the surgery, Colt finding her, filing the protective order—all of it.

"It's all my fault. Lucy's traumatized enough and because of my stupid, naïve idea, she had to see her husband again. If I hadn't pushed her to a vision from more than a decade ago, we could've avoided all of this. I'm an idiot."

"This is par for the course, my friend. No matter what you did, Colt would have probably found her, eventually. Better it be in a hospital with security and social workers than when you were in the park."

He knew Ravi was probably right, but the image of Colt coming into the room during their transdreamosis session haunted him. His heart broke for her.

Because Ravi was being so nonjudgmental and comforting, Gabe continued to open up to him. "I'm not sure where we go from here. I mean, she's hurt now, so she's limited in what she can do. And now we have to deal with getting a more permanent restraining order. I'm feeling overwhelmed."

"Look mate, fifteen days buys you plenty of time to get the legal situation worked out."

"Yeah. Okay. I suppose that's reasonable, but … "

Ravi cut him off. "Slow down, I advise you to take the next few days to direct Lucy to a vision that uses her mind and heart," he paused and smiled mischievously, then added, "rather than hurling her body toward concrete."

"Ha. Ha. Noted."

Through a playful laughter, Ravi said, "I kid, I kid. So, I think you've told me enough for me to record what happened and assign points, but just to make sure, let's do an official transmission session."

Gabe took an open stance, locking in to Ravi's mind. He transmitted everything, referencing in his mind's eye some sketches he'd made in the waiting room.

When he was done, Ravi said, "Thank you, Gabe. I'll let you know if I need anything else. Take heart in the fact that, out of this pretty shitty situation, Lucy had a day of much spiritual growth. You're a good Vision Catcher."

Gabe needed to hear that. Sure enough, fifteen minutes later, he received an update from the app. "625 points have been awarded to your Originator. Click the link for a detailed report."

Detailed Report of Originator's Points

Achievements -Positive Points

1. **Revisiting a Childhood Vision** (Skateboarding Dream): +100 points
2. **Persistence and Bravery** (Learning to Skateboard): +75 points
3. **Empathy and Connection** (Interacting with Brittany-Young Girl Aspiring to Skateboard): +50 points
4. **Generosity** (Donating Her Skateboard): +150 points
5. **Overcoming Fear** (Filing the Protective Order): +200 points
6. **Emotional Growth** (Transdreamosis Session-Standing up to Colt): +100 points

Challenges-Negative Points

1. **Losing Sight of Purpose** (Trying to deceive Colt with a lie): -25 points
2. **Hesitation and Self-Doubt** (Wavering Before Filing the EPO): -25 points

Net Score= **+625 points**

Overall Score in quest: **+875**

Gabe was feeling more confident in reaching the 5,000 point threshold. If Lucy kept up this rate, she'd exceed it in the next couple of weeks.

23

The Painting Session

Quest Day Five

Gabe and Aunt Rae insisted Lucy rest for one additional day before pursuing her next vision. It had been a slow start. The painkillers were doing their job, and she slept until eleven in the morning the day after she left the hospital. She awoke quite hungry both for food and adventure, despite the weakness and pain she felt in her wrist. There was a lightness within her she hadn't felt in a while. The protection of the B&B itself, combined with the protective order, wrapped her in comfort, melting away the ball of anxiety that had set up a home in her stomach for so long.

The sun was shining. It was a beautiful day. She grabbed a fruit and yogurt parfait and enjoyed it while strolling the property, heading toward some gardens she'd admired while first driving to the studio. She was literally smelling roses when she spotted Gary sitting on a bench, staring off into the distance, looking pensive and maybe a bit sad. Sensing her eyes on him, he turned and the light inside him seemed to spark on. He flashed a broad smile and then furrowed his brow in confusion, tilting and scratching his head simultaneously.

As she approached, he said, "I'm confused."

"Confused by what?" Lucy replied.

"You have a pep in your step, but it appears since we last saw each other, you've hurt yourself pretty badly." He turned his gaze toward her wrist.

"Oh ... yeah. My dream to become a skateboarding pro took a nosedive or should I say a wrist-dive." She chuckled.

"For real, you skateboard? That's so cool!" he said with excitement, but then quickly changed his tone. "But, ugh, did you break it?"

"Yeah, and I had to have surgery to fix it."

"Oh, wow ... that's intense. Are you going to keep doing the quest?"

"Hell yes, broken wrist and all." The enthusiasm and determination in which the words fell from Lucy's mouth surprised her. She rarely cussed with such positivity.

"That's so cool that it hasn't gotten you down. You're making me feel a lot better."

Opting to skip sharing the setback with Colt, she kept the focus on Gary, looking at him with compassion. "Why would I make you feel better? Are you feeling bad? How was your first quest?"

"Well ... it was strange."

"Strange how?"

"I thought this process was supposed to be gut-wrenching in a way, but I really hoped each adventure would make me happier. My Vision Catcher, Kai, said I did amazing. But I don't know ... I feel like shit. Then again, seeing you," he said, pointing toward her wrist, "I shouldn't feel all that bad."

Lucy laughed a little. "Don't use me as a yardstick. What did you do?"

"Well, Kai told me to pick whatever dream I wanted and, well, in general, I'm someone who has trouble making decisions. So I spent well into the night reading what he'd wrote after the last day of orientation.

"Then I woke up late and Kai was really mad at me. He had all these things lined up for our day and I didn't know. Then he asked me what I wanted to do. The conversation got even more heated because I hadn't decided yet. I was going to consult with him, but then I got flustered."

"Oh, I'm sorry Gary, that must've made you feel awful."

"Yes, then it got weirder. He said that he told me about plans he made and accused me of not paying attention or forgetting. I don't know, maybe I did."

"What did you do?"

"I drank some coffee and then got on with what he had planned. Apparently, I had a vision of being a ranch hand. He took me to this commercial place for tourists, not a real ranch. I was totally uncomfortable. I didn't have any memory of the vision. I mean, look at me. Do I look like someone who would work on a dude ranch?"

Lucy looked at Gary, whom she'd come to know and love in a short amount of time. He was right, but she chose words of encouragement anyway. "Well, yes, you have a ways off to get to dude ranch, but it's not completely impossible. I mean, I went after a dream to be a skateboarder, so no judgment here."

"Anyway, he took me to The Closet, have you been?"

"Oh yes! Isn't it fabulous?"

"Maybe for you folks of the feminine persuasion, but I haven't really ever been into looks. Not much to look at, no matter what you put me in. Anyway, I had the whole getup. From the cowboy hat to the boots."

"Oh wow! Did you take pictures?" Lucy giggled a little and hoped Gary didn't think she was laughing at him.

"Thankfully, no." He let out a short, nervous laugh and then continued. "So, we get to the ranch and let me see ... " Gary looked up in the air fetching the memory. "I was too heavy to ride a horse, which made me feel like shit, the lassoing technique I was okay at, but not the best. I mean, you saw me juggle. Then they had me try being a rodeo clown and ... ugh, it was just NOT me. I hated it and just felt shitty after the whole day. Nothing about it was enjoyable."

"Wow. I wonder if that was what Waylon was talking about? He said that Kai ruined his life."

"Yeah, that's what I was thinking, but like I said, Kai was super complimentary at the very end of the day, even though he was kind of mean overall. I don't get it. I'm not sure I'll stay. Maybe he'll let me do something less active. Something like painting."

"There you go! That sounds relaxing. Are you artistic?"

"Not in the slightest," he snorted, "but it sounds better than falling into mud and having dudes in cowboy boots laughing at you."

"You know what? Why don't you take a walk with me? I want to show you something."

Lucy stood up and, with her unbroken wrist, reached out her hand to invite Gary to pull himself up and join her. Together, they walked to Gabe's studio. Lucy wasn't sure if the door was locked. However, when she turned the knob, the door opened and Gabe was inside painting a canvas resting on his new easel with earphones on.

He was facing them, so they couldn't see what he was working on. Lucy tried to make eye contact with him, but he was laser focused. Gary looked around with his mouth agape as he explored the visions Lucy had forgotten. "Wow. This is so much cooler than reading through books or watching video explainers."

Gary's voice snapped Gabe out of his trance and he jumped back, startled. "What are you doing here?"

"Well, Gary was feeling a little down after his session yesterday and was talking about the possibility of painting as his next adventure, so I thought he might enjoy seeing your gallery. Is that okay?"

"As long as it's okay with you. He's sort of seeing inside your mind."

Lucy went over to Gary and gave him a tour of her visions and dreams. She'd wanted to visit the studio anyway because she needed to pick her next dream. They saw a painting that looked like Lucy's perfect day at the lake house. One painting was of a newspaper article where they could only read the headline and subtitle. The actual body of the article was just squiggles. The headline read, "Woman Saves The Planet From Global Warming" with a subtitle using Lucy's maiden name, "Lucy Humphries, a leading climatologist, has just made a breakthrough discovery that could reverse climate change." Gabe had painted a picture of a woman looking into a microscope next to the words.

"Wow, you think you can save the world?" Gary asked.

"Well, I mean no, but it doesn't mean I don't fantasize about it. Or I used to, at least. Before … " Her voice trailed along with her thoughts of before Colt. When she was studying environmental science and she was full of big dreams.

"Even if it was just before. Most people never have that kind of optimism." A butterfly flew in front of Gary and his eyes pivoted to the garden and chicken coop. "What's over there?"

"Oh yes, come see this. Gabe made this. Isn't it awesome? I just love the baby chicks and the butterflies. In that optimistic period I thought about starting a community garden in a food desert."

"Wow, that's really admirable, Lucy."

Lucy smiled. His kindness kept her from sinking into a darker memory. She wanted to help him. While he was admiring the garden, Lucy quickly snuck over to Gabe. He was once again on his phone as she approached—it seemed like he was always on that thing, so she had no problem interrupting. "Gabe, I'm worried about Gary. His Vision Catcher said he did great yesterday, but he doesn't seem great. You lift me up in everything I do, even with this," she said, holding up her arm.

Gabe looked down at his phone again and then up at her with a confused look. "And you're saying Gary is feeling bad? Bad how? Did he hurt himself too?"

"No. He's really down on himself and feeling worthless. His Vision Catcher is the same one that was interrupted during orientation by that guy saying he ruined his life. I'm worried."

"Well, I don't think there's a need to worry. It looks to me that Gary's doing great."

"What do you mean? You've barely talked to him. Or is this one of those empath things? Can you see his aura or something?"

"No. Well, yes, something like that."

Gabe was pretty sure he wasn't allowed to tell Lucy about the scoring system. He tried to think back to the rules, but couldn't remember. He just assumed it wouldn't benefit anyone if the Originators found out they were being scored. What Lucy was saying about Gary didn't make sense. When he looked at the leaderboard, Kai was still ahead and Gary had 1800 points—almost double Lucy's. On paper, Gary was thriving. He wasn't sure what was going on, but he tried to put it out of his mind. He needed to focus on Lucy and her quest.

The painting he was working on when Lucy interrupted him wasn't one of her visions, but it was an abstract of how he was feeling about the quest so far. He really didn't want to let her down.

"So, did you find something to do next?" he asked.

"I saw the vision where I fantasized about being a climatologist and working to end global warming. I'd like to do something in that vein without, you know, going to school to relearn what the heck a climatologist actually does."

Gabe smiled. This was exactly what Ravi had told him to do, direct her toward something that used her heart and mind. He quickly typed a message to Ravi on his phone for an assist. Ravi immediately sent him a link to the volunteer page of an environmental nonprofit that one alumnus had founded after her quest. "Okay, what do you think about volunteering for an environmental nonprofit tomorrow?"

"Um ... I think that sounds amazing! Is that why you're always on your phone? Like, how magic *are* you?"

Gabe felt imposter syndrome crash over him like a tidal wave. Was he relying too much on this tech and not enough on his abilities?

Lucy must have sensed his insecurity. She laid a hand on his shoulder and said, "I'm sorry. I didn't mean to upset you. You're doing great. I wouldn't have gotten this far without you." With a sly smile, she leaned in and whispered, "But seriously—how do you have a cell phone? Do you conjure it up from the realm or something?"

Insecurities about his choices so far in this quest were rising—the skateboarding, the broken wrist, Colt showing up. He needed to tell her something that would keep her focused without revealing everything.

"It's ... complicated." Gabe hesitated, scanning his memory for what he was actually allowed to say. The app's disclosure rules flashed through his mind like a checklist:

> *Okay to mention the gifts. Don't explain the trust in depth. Definitely don't say anything about expired visions being valuable ...*

He took a breath, choosing his words carefully. "Some Originators—over the years—have shown their gratitude in big ways. Gifts. Land. Sometimes money. It's all pooled into a kind of trust that helps support our world and, well... helps us to mirror life in your realm."

"So your cell plan's powered by karma?" Lucy teased, raising an eyebrow.

Gabe laughed, grateful for the shift in tone. "Something like that."

He was relieved when Gary wandered over to them and interrupted their conversation. Gary's jaw was slack, still mesmerized by the studio. "I still can't believe all of this. You're quite the dreamer, Lucy. And Gabe, I mean WOW! I wish Kai was an artist and not a writer. I'm not sure my visions would be quite so incredible." A butterfly was resting on his shoulder.

"Well … are you ready to paint one and see?" Lucy asked, smiling at Gary's wonderment.

Gary looked around. His eyes widened as he shook his head. "I mean, I don't know."

Gabe was thrilled. "Do you both want to do it this afternoon? I've already got the materials. I can get you all set up!" Gabe may not have ever led someone through a successful quest, but he knew how to paint. He was so jazzed about the whole thing he was practically skipping through the entire studio—grabbing aprons, water, paint, canvases, and easels. He led Gary and Lucy to seats that faced the only small blank wall in the place.

Once they sat he said, "Okay, we're going to do a little meditation exercise. This is going to help you decide what to paint. Close your eyes. Feel your feet touch the ground. Breathe in and know that you are breathing. Breathe out a smile." Gabe was happy to see that Lucy's smile was bright. He had a feeling that if he used the words she used with Emily at the talent show, it would resonate.

He repeated the mantra four more times and continued in a calm tone. "Now, imagine the place where you could find perfect peace. What would it smell like? What would it look like? Would it be outside or inside? Look around this place and notice all the beauty around you. What colors do you see? After you're done exploring, open your eyes."

After a few moments, Gary and Lucy opened their eyes. Gabe was just about to instruct them on the next steps when his phone dinged.

It was a DM from Kai.

Kai: *What are you doing with my Originator?*
Gabe: *Nothing … Lucy brought him here, and we were just doing a meditation exercise and then we were going to do some painting.*

Kai: *Do whatever you want with your Originator, but keep your mitts off of mine.*

Gabe: *What?*

Kai: *You heard me. I don't want you tanking his progress. Do you see how high my score is compared to yours? You aren't equipped to handle two Originators at once.*

Gabe: *They're just painting.*

Kai: *Fine. Just this once … next time give me a heads up.*

Gabe turned back and shot a forced smile toward Gary and Lucy. "Alright, I hope you held on to those visualizations of your places of peace. There's no judgment here. Try to just let the paint brush be an extension of your mind's eye. Relax into it."

Lucy turned to Gabe. "Well, I can't quite relax … remember left-handed." She held up her casted arm.

"Maybe keep your painting abstract, then."

They both hesitated to put the initial brush stroke on the canvas, but just as he had done in the first orientation small group, Gary made the first move. He smiled softly at Lucy and raised his eyebrows slightly. "Your turn."

Lucy mixed blue and white and splattered it on the canvas. Gabe bit his tongue as he watched her jump up and down enthusiastically. He wasn't going to point out that her peaceful place couldn't possibly look like a bunch of spots of paint because she'd clearly found her happy place, and that was good enough for today.

Gabe gave them space to create. After a while, he went over to Gary's painting and was stunned. It was beautiful and lifelike. Gabe smiled at him and asked, "Have you done this before?"

"A long time ago in high school, but no, not recently."

"You're fantastic," Gabe encouraged.

Gary laughed in delight. "That's definitely a compliment coming from you."

Gabe pulled out his phone and took a snapshot of his painting. Kai probably knew that Gary was creatively gifted, but he thought he'd send it back as a peace offering. Hopefully Kai wouldn't be as upset once he saw the great progress his Originator had made. The joy Gary was feeling would surely score him some points on the app as well. He sent the picture over with a message.

Gabe: *Thanks for letting me borrow him. He's really talented. Hope you caught some creative visions because Gary is clearly artistically talented.*

He added a winky face. Gabe waited as Kai typed a message back. The three dots on the messaging portion of the app seemed to stay up forever. Finally, the phone pinged with Kai's reply.

Kai: *Maybe, we'll see. There are other factors to consider.*

While difficult, Gabe let go of this vague comment and turned his attention to Lucy. He wanted to do another transdreamosis session with her and continue to get her into a good state of mind so that when he checked in with Ravi, her point total would be higher. He was trying not to think about the points, but Kai's taunting was getting under his skin.

His phone pinged. It was Kai again.

Kai: *Are you a moron? Look at the app. Our scores have both dropped. I'm coming there to get him. Don't say anything else to my guy.*

24

The Point Drop

Quest Day Six

It was two in the morning and Gabe's eyes remained fixed on Lucy's point total-350. How had it dropped from 875? It baffled him. Unlike previously, when the points changed, and he knew why, the app didn't give a reason as to why her points dropped. He closed his eyes, replaying all the events of the day, and couldn't figure out where he'd gone wrong with Gary or Lucy. He flipped over to the leaderboard. Kai's smug profile pic taunted him—surrounded by other images of people that Gabe had admired all of his life. After completing eight quests, and even taking into account the negative points from earlier in the day, Kai's point total was even higher than Randy's.

Bewildered by how that was even possible, he tried to reach out to Ravi, but there was something wrong and it wouldn't connect. Unable to stop his racing mind, he accepted the fact that sleeping was an impossibility tonight and moved over to his desk with a pen and paper, trying to work out the math on how he could get Lucy to 5,000 points.

After two days in orientation, skateboarding, the hospital, a rest day, and a day painting, it was now the sixth day of the quest. There were thirty-four days left, including today, to get 4,650 points. Could they get there? The math worked out to be in his favor, roughly 137 points per day. He leaned back in his chair and sighed. It was totally possible, but the stress of it all was so intense that sweat dripped from his face. A moment later, Aunt Rae was standing in the doorway. Gabe turned as she cleared her throat. "Need a hug?" she asked.

When they embraced, Gabe began to sob and Aunt Rae knew exactly what was bothering him. "Oh, honey, it's not that serious. There's still time for Lucy to find her way."

Her words came as little comfort. "What about the points? They dropped for no reason that I can see. Maybe I took my focus off of Lucy and that's what happened. What am I going to do?" Gabe asked.

"Well, I didn't have to deal with all that in my day, but it's my understanding that if you don't get 5,000 points, you'll just have to repeat the first quest. It's not the end."

"I don't want to repeat. I want to be respected like Mom and Dad were. The Guild is just going to going to make me go back to retraining. Plus, I've heard most receive an even more challenging Originator the next time around."

"That mostly happens because people think it will happen. It becomes a self-fulfilling prophecy. Our thoughts can dictate the energy we attract. Keep a clear head and you will do fine."

"What about Lucy? If I don't get enough points, they'll make me transfer her visions to a maintenance VC. I don't want to lose my connection with her. I know after the quest, even if I succeeded, I wouldn't be able to work with her as closely as now, but still ... to be completely cut off. Nobody knows her dreams like I do, even if they can tap into the Feranchin I put into my art." Gabe's voice trailed off and his eyes shifted to the ceiling.

"Oh honey, that's tough. We won't let her fail," Aunt Rae said softly, drawing him into another hug.

Gabe wasn't sure if the 'we' she was referring to was the two of them or the Vision Catcher society at large. He thought of the overused cliché—*If you love someone, sometimes you have to let them go.* He mumbled through a few final sobs, "I don't know. Maybe she's better off without me. Nothing I'm doing seems to help."

Aunt Rae grabbed his chin, forcing his eyes to meet hers. "What would Lucy be doing right now if you hadn't given her the nudge to leave Colt? How would she be feeling? I don't know much about this point system, son, but I know she's better off because of you."

Gabe wiped his face and nodded, just as his alarm buzzed. Time to get Lucy. He drew a long breath, steadied himself, and walked to her door, heart heavy but just steady enough to knock.

As she brushed her teeth, Lucy faintly heard Gabe's voice. "Can I come in?"

"Sure. Just one minute." Lucy opened the door slowly and greeted Gabe with a warm smile.

"How'd you sleep? How's your pain?" he asked.

"Not the best, but the pain is definitely less than yesterday. Rae brought up extra pillows last night, and that made a world of differ-ence."

"Oh, wonderful."

Gabe looked around and Lucy instinctively tensed, becoming anxious that he'd get mad at her for something being out of place. She relaxed a little when he only enthusiastically commented on the painting she had hung on the wall from yesterday's session. Gabe wasn't Colt.

"I know it's nowhere near your level, but it reminds me of helping Gary more than anything. Thank you again for that."

"You're welcome," Gabe said softly, looking away from Lucy.

For the next hour, they did various exercises to prep for this next leg of the quest. After some journaling, they did a transdreamosis session where Gabe placed her in an awards banquet and made her give an acceptance speech about her work in saving the planet.

"Seriously, me, saving the planet? Isn't that a little presumptuous?" Lucy asked.

"That's the point. If you picture yourself doing the impossible, it will help you find the inner-strength you need to get close to your dreams. Just go with it," Gabe urged.

Lucy actually had fun accepting the fake award and left the session ready to kick this vision's ass. She grabbed another outfit from the closet, a loose peasant blouse with embroidered details, high-waisted flared jeans, and comfortable suede ankle boots. On their way over to the nonprofit where she'd volunteer for the day, she told Gabe how sparkly it made her feel.

They pulled into a small parking lot with an old brick building that almost looked like a house. When Lucy stepped out of the car and headed to the door, Gabe didn't follow. "Aren't you coming with me?"

"No, I have some other things to do. I'll pick you up at five. I made you an appointment. They should be expecting you."

Lucy pouted her lips and replied, "Alright, fine, but next vision, you're going to come along right?"

"Depends. I'll see you soon." With those words, he hopped into the car and drove away.

Lucy paused in front of the small building, opened the front door, and walked into an empty lobby. No one was sitting at the front desk. She heard voices coming from the hallway.

"Hello?" Lucy called out. She started to doubt that Gabe had actually dropped her at the correct place, but then she saw brochures on the front desk for the Tennessee Environmental League and a sign that read "volunteer check-in" with a clipboard in front of it. She wrote her name on the clipboard and took a seat, waiting patiently. There was a video playing on a loop describing the Tennessee Environmental League—called TEL for short—and its mission. It had been about ten minutes and anxiety was creeping in. The short clips showed very active volunteer assignments like picking up litter, planting trees, maintaining community pollinator gardens, and collecting compost, among other things. How was she going to do any of that with a broken wrist?

She hoped her volunteer experience wouldn't be working at the front desk. She wanted to get a little more hands-on or, in her case, a hand-on. Plus, if she had to listen to the ten minute video on loop all day, she'd definitely want to move on to another vision—this would've all been a waste of time. After sitting through two cycles of the video, a woman in jeans and an orange T-shirt with the logo of the TEL on it came out.

"Hello, may I help you?"

"Yes, um, I'm here to volunteer."

"Did you sign in?"

"Yes."

Without a word, the woman left and went down the hall. Lucy got up and peered around the doorway and shouted after her, "Did you want me to follow you?"

The woman replied a quick, "No." Lucy walked back into the lobby and watched the video for a third time. She looked down at her clothes. She'd definitely overdressed. A different woman came out wearing the same outfit as the other woman and holding an orange shirt.

"Deborah said you're probably a medium. Is that right?"

"Well, yes, that will do. I did just break my wrist. Is that going to be a problem?" Lucy gestured at the TV. "All your volunteer activities seem pretty active."

"Yes, you mentioned that in your sign-up form, we took note. You'll be canvassing with Sebastian." A young man with bright red hair stepped out from the hallway, waving and smiling awkwardly, wearing the uniform she was no doubt about to don.

"You'll basically be getting signatures for our petition to stop the needless destruction of trees near power lines. They don't pose a threat to the lines. It's just the power company being overzealous. We also want you to encourage folks to register to come to our open house in a couple of weeks. Does that sound like something you can do with your wrist?" Her tone was a strange mix of condescension and concern.

"Uh ... yes. Of course." Lucy accepted the shirt and went into the bathroom to change. She examined herself in her sparkly feeling outfit one last time before she removed her beautiful top and noticed some new bruises on her arm. She was so focused on the pain from her wrist injury she hadn't taken stock of how some of her other falls in her skateboarding adventure had come to the surface. She put on the T-shirt, opened the door, and found Sebastian waiting for her only a few feet away.

"Hi, it's Lucy, right?"

"Yes."

"Cool. Come with me. My car's all packed. I'm driving us to the site."

As Sebastian drove, he told Lucy about himself with excitement. He talked all about his experience volunteering with the organization and how passionate he was about the mission. His energy was oozing out of him and it was contagious. Lucy's energy began to soar as they finished setting up their table in a local park—their "mission control" for the day. As they chitchatted, she learned Sebastian was waiting to hear whether he or another volunteer would receive a paid position in the fundraising department the following week.

Sebastian was fearless and had no shame in approaching the strangers passing by. Most of the people didn't want to take a flyer and avoided eye contact. His opening lines didn't seem to work at all. He alternated between several.

"Did you know that planting just one tree can provide enough oxygen for a family of four?"

"We're losing trees every year to unnecessary removal, putting our air quality and green spaces at risk? Would you like to help?"

"Without the Tennessee Environmental League's efforts to clean up rivers, our waterways could become polluted, putting your family's drinking water at risk and endangering their health."

He wasn't making much headway. After a couple of hours, his enthusiasm seemed to wane.

They'd only gotten five signatures and one sign-up for the open house. Intellectually, Lucy knew that she alone couldn't help solve pollution issues or save all the trees that were in danger in her few hours of volunteering, but she was feeling like a failure and wanted to help Sebastian who she'd quickly grown to adore.

"Sebastian, how successful is canvassing normally?"

"Well, I've only done it a few times before. Those times it was part of a volunteer fair or community festival. People were a little more receptive. These folks have places to be."

Lucy racked her mind on what would entice more people to sign the petition. Some documentaries and reality shows she watched seemed to have a lot of success talking to people and she always thought it was because there was a camera. It added a little bit of authority. Of course, they didn't have a real video camera, but they had phones, though she was still trying not to use hers.

"Sebastian, would you mind if we changed tactics?"

Sebastian didn't seem to have an ego. He said, "Not at all" with desperate enthusiasm.

"I think that if I film you and you pretend we're doing this for social media or a YouTube channel, which we could actually post on, then we can make this more of a man on a street interview."

"What questions would we ask?"

"Well, do you think that there's anything that we can do about the climate crisis? Does it concern you? Start out with something like 'we're surveying people for our YouTube channel on global warming. Is that something that you'd be interested in talking to us about? We only have three questions. Do you have a couple minutes?'"

"Brilliant! Let's go for it." Sebastian was almost giddy as he handed his phone over to Lucy.

Soon, Lucy was enticing mostly Gen Z folks to talk to them. But they were talking. In just an hour and a half, they had at least thirty interviews. Even the people who didn't want to be on the channel or filmed signed the petition. They now had forty-five signatures and twenty-five people register to come to the open house. Filming and saying that they were going to put something on social media somehow added legitimacy to what they were trying to do.

Lucy was filled with a sense of pride when they returned to headquarters to tell the director about their results. When they walked into the office, the first person they saw was the volunteer coordinator, who handed Lucy her bright orange shirt at the beginning of the day. "Back so soon? Did you hand out all the flyers?"

"No."

"Well, how many signatures did you get?"

They told her about their success. Sebastian and Lucy enthusiastically talked on top of each other as they showed her the footage they took. She wasn't impressed.

"The truth is, I can't use any of this footage because you didn't have anyone sign releases and your goal was to get fifty registrants. Come on, Sebastian. You know better. Get back out there."

Sebastian's whole body deflated. "Yeah, okay. Let's go Lucy."

She followed Sebastian, but then right before she was going to step out the door, she snapped back around and said, "Wait! Can we have some releases?"

The supervisor sighed and slightly rolled her eyes like a sullen teenager.

When they returned to their station, Lucy reluctantly pulled her phone out of her pocket. She hadn't turned it on since she'd grabbed Anna's number a week ago. They'd been using Sebastian's phone to film the videos, but now she needed to get some release forms signed and didn't want to interrupt Sebastian's interviews. At least she'd thought to put a star next to the names of the people they filmed after they signed the petition. All she had to do now was text each person to see if they could stop by the table again.

She was excited and envisioned them getting releases signed, gathering more signatures, open house sign-ups, and when they came back triumphant, Sebastian would get the good news of getting the job. The moment she powered the phone on, it blew up, pinging like crazy. Missed texts, voicemails, and notifications flooded in. When the digital symphony finally ended, she assessed the damage.

There were 153 new texts and twenty-six new voicemails. Most of them were from Colt, but some were from Anna, her mom, her dad, and work. A wave of guilt swept over her as she realized how thoughtless she'd been. She was so distracted by the quest and obsessed over whether Colt would find her; she hadn't thought to touch base with the people who actually cared about her.

From a vantage point only fifty feet away, Gabe saw Lucy's posture change the minute she turned on her phone. She went from laughing and smiling to looking catatonic, staring down, unmoving. He knew it was time to step in.

He walked up to the table and gently said, "Hey there." She was in such a trance, he had to speak again. "Lucy, you okay?"

Lucy looked up, shaking her head like an Etch A Sketch that needed to be cleared. "What are you doing here?"

"It looked like you needed help. I think you should turn off your phone."

"But I've worried all these people." She pointed to her phone sharply, looking at him with wide eyes. "I need to get back to them. I just." She looked back at Sebastian, who was in the middle of taking an interview—selfie style.

Gabe thought back to the app's advice about boosting an Originator's confidence and said, "You looked like you were having the time of your life before. Your idea about getting more signatures by getting people to talk to you about their opinions was brilliant. You were on fire."

Her body seemed to relax and Gabe could tell she was coming back to the present instead of thinking of the past. "Look, Lucy, I'm proud of you for putting your fears aside. You need to get back to the quest. You can deal with these texts tonight. This," he gestured to Sebastian and the flyers, "was making you happy." He grabbed Lucy's phone and turned it off. As he put it in his pocket, Lucy reached out her hand to get it back from him.

"But I ... but I," Lucy stuttered.

"But you need to go help Sebastian," Gabe said, more sternly than he'd intended.

She looked at Sebastian and then back at Gabe and relented. "Okay."

Smiling gently and in a softer tone, Gabe said, "I really think that this may be your calling. It's been years since you've felt this level of joy ... truly." He walked away, saying nothing else, hoping he'd pushed her in the right direction. He watched her for about fifteen minutes as her spirits soared again.

When he went to pick her up, she thanked him. She told him all about how they were able to get more signatures and sign-ups than required, and the previously cranky coordinator told Sebastian that she'd tell the hiring officers about his success. She was beaming. As she went up to The Tower, Gabe reluctantly handed Lucy her phone.

"Don't turn this on without me, okay? I've got something to do and then I'll be right up."

She nodded. "I think I need a nap, anyway. See you soon."

25

Tug-of-War

Gabe wasn't much for socializing through the app. He'd seen some virtual get-togethers, but he imagined a worst-case scenario where the video feed displayed their point total above their heads as they talked in the online experience. Somebody would make fun of him—he just knew it.

He started to spiral and needed a distraction. He just couldn't shake the fact that Lucy's score had decreased so significantly when she was painting. Was it because she never had a vision of being an artist? Did Gary never see his own artistic ability?

When he saw that there was an in-person happy hour happening at The Vibanator, he decided to go to get his mind off everything. Lucy was resting, what was the harm in one drink?

Glacious greeted him with a smile. "Hey Gabe! How's the quest going?"

Lucy's score and her backsliding when she saw Colt's messages were playing on a loop in his mind. With every replay, a new knot formed in his stomach. He almost word-vomited all his fears to the tall bouncer just to get it off his chest, but in the end, simply replied with an obligatory, "Fine."

Glacious put a hand on his shoulder and with a sympathetic gaze said, "I'm sure it's not that bad."

He'd been so distracted by his own doubts about his abilities that he completely forgot the empathic nature of this community. He thought back to the tremendous strides Lucy had actually made—simply making it here and accepting the quest. Not to mention how she'd helped Emily or that little girl at the skate park.

He looked up toward Glacious and conceded. "Well, it's been a bumpy ride, but she's actually doing really great, considering where she came from."

"That's more like it! Well, don't let me stop you. Come on in, come on in." Then, leaning in closer, he whispered in Gabe's ear and pointed to the dance floor, "Cecilia's here." She was dancing with a group in the distance.

Gabe's palms sweat and he felt the blood rush to his cheeks as a smile became plastered across his face.

He began walking timidly toward her, not to dance, but to get a closer look. She was dancing in a group doing a line dance. The steps were simple enough, but he'd actually prefer a tune where he could be a little less constrained—he held back. A waiter offered him a drink, and while tempted to partake, he thought better of it, remembering his hangover from the last time he was at this establishment. Thinking back to that night made him beat himself up all over again. Was his drinking what led him to make the stupid decision to have Lucy skateboard? God, what had he been thinking?

As he approached, Cecilia's eyes met his, and she beckoned him by miming a person reeling in a fish. Gabe summoned his courage and answered the call by pretending to be a fish as he inched his way closer. The entire group was laughing, with one loud woman crossing her legs and shouting, "OMG, you made me almost pee!" She ran off the dance floor to relieve herself, and just as she did, the music changed to "Unchained Melody," and Cecilia wrapped her arms around Gabe, forcing him into a slow dance.

She had the power to clear his mind while also making his pulse race. He pulled his body closer toward her, giving in to the intimate moment. Her hair smelled of lavender, and as he breathed in her luscious scent, his shoulders dropped and his body relaxed. His cheeks were hurting from smiling so much, and he pulled back for a moment to look deep into her eyes.

"Oh, Gabe. I just caught a vision of your day; seems like you had a rough go of it. I told you not to worry about the points." Damn. He'd melted into the moment so much that he forgot to keep a wall up. Disappointed that he couldn't just shake off his troubles, he opened his mouth to reply when he felt a tap on his shoulder. He turned around. It was Kai.

"Can I cut in?"

Instead of saying, "No, you may not. If she'd wanted to dance with you, she would've," he shrunk, said nothing, and stepped away. Cecilia shot Gabe an angry look before looking up at Kai and insincerely smiling. Gabe frowned and tried to send her a vision of a cute dog holding up an "I'm Sorry" sign. Cecilia didn't reciprocate.

The group that had been dancing with Cecilia before the music changed had claimed a table nearby and had ordered some drinks. They beckoned Gabe over. He tentatively slid in beside a woman he thought he recognized from school but couldn't remember her name. She was bubbling with schoolgirl energy and said, "So, you and Cecilia ..." Trailing off, as if that was a statement that Gabe could've had some kind of response to. His pulse raced. He looked back at Cecilia and Kai before turning back to the group of gossipy women and shrugging his shoulders.

"Hey now, stop ... you're embarrassing him," said a blonde fifty-something seated across from him. Just then, the music changed, Kai and Cecilia parted, and she headed over to the table while Kai went to the bar.

"Cecilia really? Kai?"

She rolled her eyes and then darted them back to Gabe. "Gabe gave me no choice. I mean he abandoned me with him. I didn't want to be rude, despite the fact that he's a royal a-hole."

"I'm so sorry," he said. "I know he can be a jerk."

"Forget jerk," one gossip named Rosa perked up. "He must be a royal asshole. Has anybody found out what happened with that guy at the orientation? I mean, it doesn't make any sense. Kai's close to the top of the leaderboard. You look at that guy who was making a fuss at orientation and his quest ended with like 12,000 points."

Without meaning to, Gabe got sucked into Rosa's strong gossip energy. His voice mirrored Rosa's. "Right? I can't figure it out and I was trying to help his Originator the other day, and the dude went off on me. Then it was so strange—my Originator, Lucy, and Kai's, Gary, points just dropped. I really don't think I did anything wrong, but I don't know. I kind of think Kai had something to do with it, but then why would he make his own Originator's score drop?"

"I told you not to pay attention to the points," Cecilia said while gently placing a hand on his shoulder, warming back up to him.

"I can't help it. They're right there." He gestured to his phone. "If we don't get 5,000, we have to start over and won't get full status."

Kai came over with his drink. "You guys were talking about me, weren't you?" The VC spidey sense struck again.

"Yeah, we were," Rosa piped in and boldly interrogated him. "How are you so high on the leaderboard after just a handful of quests? I mean, your family isn't even VCs. No way you could do that good and that guy at orientation ... "

He cut her off. "That guy was just sour because he thought this process would be easy and he didn't have to put in any work. It's the

Guild's fault for selecting him in the first place. If it wasn't for him, I'd be number one on the leaderboard." He shook his head, a cocky smile plastered on his face.

He continued his diatribe. "So I don't come from a long line of Vision Catchers? They were Supporters, that's the same powers, just a different role. I pushed like hell to break that tradition. My parents certainly wanted me to follow in their footsteps. They saw the Guild wanted to eliminate their role, lucky for me, and they laid off."

"Did they lay off or step in? I heard your mom stepped in after your role assessment and begged the Guild to switch you from Supporter to Vision Catcher." Rosa smiled, and glanced around the group smugly.

Kai's fists clenched. He took a couple of deep breaths in as he glared at the others at the table. After a tense moment, his body relaxed, a smile swept over his face, and he said calmly, "You may not think I have what it takes, but the points don't lie. Maybe you should focus more on your own work rather than questioning mine."

Rosa shook her head and started in on him again. "I've been doing this for fifteen years, you arrogant wannabe."

Gabe, trying to diffuse, put up a hand and interjected, "Hey, hey, hey we're all doing our best. I'm sure your points are well deserved."

"Indeed, they are. Do me a favor and stop gossiping like a silly schoolgirl behind my back or you'll need to watch yours." Kai's contempt for Gabe was palpable as he glared at him.

The group was silent as the music changed, which they took as their cue to leave. Cecilia stayed and grabbed Gabe's hand. Kai's eyes shifted to the gesture. He shook his head and walked away.

Moments after he did, Gabe received a reminder to check-in from the app. Gabe checked the score; Lucy's points had mysteriously dropped again—now it was down to 150.

He looked at Cecilia's gorgeous brown eyes, and when the music slowed down, he wanted to ask her to dance again. But after the encounter with Kai and the point drop, his mind was split. He was still trying to figure out why the points had dropped in the first place—that was part of the reason he'd come down here. Now, he'd just made it worse.

Was it because of Lucy's mindset when she turned on her phone? Or maybe he was just late reporting to his rep? That wasn't his fault though, because when he'd tried, he wasn't able to connect.

Gabe changed the subject, briefly chatting with her about Emily's journey. Even though Emily had tapped into a true talent, Cecilia was constantly having to pump her up and reassure her. It sounded like they had a breakthrough today when Emily wrote a song about her best friend who had died. Cecilia still hadn't been able to figure out what had happened the night Emily came back with a black eye. Gabe was selfishly glad to know he wasn't the only one doubting himself.

He was emotionally and physically exhausted. His split mind turned to determination after receiving yet another text from the app telling him to check in. He parted ways with Cecilia and opened the app to connect with Ravi and clear this up. Still unable to, he closed his eyes and recorded a thought-message manually. He reported the bug of being unable to reach his rep and minutes later, was relieved to receive a call from Ravi.

"Hello, Gabe. What seems to be the problem?"

"Listen, I think I'm doing something wrong or there's something seriously wrong with the app."

He told him the whole story, and Ravi assured him he wasn't crazy. He'd escalate the case, but warned that he'd still need to get points. Gabe still didn't understand the point drop from the previous day or today, but he had thirty-three days left. Maybe reporting it to Ravi would clear the whole thing up.

When he came back home, it was two in the morning, and he sensed Lucy was crying and upset. When he got near her bedroom door, he no longer needed his powers. He could hear her sobs loud and clear. He could feel her pain in his chest. He closed his eyes and banged his head against the wall. What had he been thinking, dancing and gossiping while she was falling apart? He'd let himself get distracted again, just like after the talent show.

Lucy had some setbacks when she finally checked her phone the evening after her first day of canvassing. Gabe had told her to wait, but her guilt won out. She found a spot where she got cell service outside. The texts brought up the fear that Colt would find her and she hated to be out in the open by herself. Aunt Rae assured her that no one from the outside could track her down. The Vision Catcher realm was only accessible to people in their community and their guests.

Her hands were shaking when she called Anna. Shame swept over her, knowing Anna had faced an angry Colt days before and she hadn't bothered to check on her. She tried to excuse it. She'd been distracted by the mission of returning the car.

Lucy hadn't realized how bad the experience was when Daisy relayed what Anna had told her. It was like a game of telephone, with details either not shared or not heard in the frenzy of it all.

Anna hadn't told Daisy about the gun.

"It's okay. It's not your fault. I'm just glad you're safe," Anna had said.

Lucy was sinking despite Anna's forgiveness. It was her fault. He wouldn't have even gone there if she'd just come back to the house that night.

When she spoke to her parents, they told her Colt had harassed them, and they were relieved she had the protective order. Hearing their warm, relieved voices on the other end of the line was of little comfort. It made Lucy regret cutting them out so much. She'd been so embarrassed by the way Colt treated her. She realized then, as she felt their love radiating toward her, that she missed them so much and wanted to be in their lives more meaningfully. As they hung up, Lucy said, "I'll be in touch. I promise. I'm sorry I worried you."

"We'll call too. You just take care, okay?"

Her voice shook. "Okay."

"Bye sweetheart. We love you," her mom said.

"Love you too. Bye."

As she pressed end on the call, the guilt swept back over her for how Colt had treated them.

Colt. Reading and hearing his messages was the worst.

So much had happened in the last week, but his voice, his words, made her retreat inward—staring off into space, overcome with a deep sadness. The first messages were from before he'd called Daisy, then after he'd headed to the hospital with the nurse who told him she'd checked in with a Black man. Next came the anger at getting served the protective order—those were the worst.

His voicemails rang in her ears. "You're a selfish bitch. Gotta give you fifteen days, apparently. You'll have it your way now, but the clock is ticking."

She curled up in bed, frozen with fear and confused about what to do next.

Sensing her pain, Gabe came in with a gentle knock. She stayed in bed, unmoving, under the covers. Her sobs were faint, but broke Gabe's heart. He'd been so selfish and obsessed with the points. He wasn't even sure that anything he could say would help. Sitting down next to her, he spoke anyway.

"I'm so sorry I wasn't here sooner. It was stupid."

Lucy didn't respond at first. When she finally spoke, it was clear she'd not even expected him to support her in this moment. He felt awful.

"It's okay," she said, still under the covers. Through tears—barely audible—she continued. "I'm the stupid one. I broke everything with everyone who actually cared about me. Maybe … " Her voice cracked. "Maybe I deserve Colt. I'm the one who's stayed. Who'd want me now?"

He tried to choose his words carefully. He wanted to pull her back from the edge.

"Lucy, I know to you, we've only known each other a short time, but I've seen you here before. You're leaving the bright, sincere force of nature that I know you are at your core. I'm not so naïve as to say Colt's words are just that—words. Words have the power to hurt and tug us into our deepest insecurities."

Lucy pulled the covers back and met his gaze as he continued.

"You're now in a place where you can play a game of tug-of-war within yourself. On one side, your true self, and on the other, all your misbeliefs about yourself—that you're not good enough, that you can't keep going. Dig deep. Is the life you want back with Colt?"

She knew the answer, and her trembling, anxious body calmed slightly as she shook her head—no.

Then he asked, "Do you believe you can find what lights you up? Can you find the strength to get up tomorrow and continue this journey with me? One step at a time?"

Gabe's sincerity seemed to break through the noise of her pain, and she managed to reply softly through tears, "Yes."

They made a plan. She'd give her friends and family the heads-up that she would be out of reach, and then Gabe would give her a burner phone in case they needed to call in an emergency–he felt like an idiot for not thinking of that before. She needed time to heal, and Gabe knew that. As he buoyed Lucy's spirits, for the first time in a while, the points hadn't distracted him. She fed off of his healing energy. He was singularly focused on helping her. He didn't even notice when his phone buzzed in his pocket and went to bed without looking at it.

After a quick check-in with Ravi in the morning, his phone pinged to deliver a pleasant surprise:

Lucy has earned 1,000 points!

+150: Overcoming Self-Doubt

+200: Healing from Past Trauma

+175: Asserting Boundaries

+200: Facing Fears

+150: Embracing Vulnerability

+175: Cultivating Resilience

+200: Letting Go of Toxic Relationships

-100: Self-Doubt Resurgence

-150: Relapse into Past Trauma

Her new total is 1,150 points.

With weeks to go, Gabe was feeling more confident than ever.

26

Lighting the Way

Quest Day Twenty-Seven

The system of putting one foot in front of the other worked for a while. Her new volunteer post didn't go to plan every day, but she was finding her rhythm and felt she'd carved out a niche for herself at the small but mighty organization.

Her creative approach with Sebastian on the first day had been a boon to the marketing team. They'd used the footage and had a boost in engagement and continued with the style of interviews as a technique to increase real life engagement.

Each day felt like forward momentum toward something bigger. They'd even found some manual tasks she could do despite her wrist injury. She felt a sense of purpose she hadn't felt in years when simply pulling weeds and being in the sunshine of the community gardens. Small victories were coupled with the staff giving her greater responsibility, and it felt amazing to be seen and appreciated.

After a few weeks, as she was leaving the office, Sebastian asked her to come into the break room. There, to her surprise, were other staff members and a cake for her! They had named her Volunteer of the Month.

The accolade thrilled Lucy until she learned that the social media department had posted the announcement and tagged Lucy on Facebook. When Sebastian showed it to her, she saw some of her friends saw it and left positive comments, but her stomach tied itself in knots. Worries of Colt finding her bubbled to the surface again. They hadn't got the temporary restraining order, the court date was set for next week and the Emergency Protective Order had expired. Her fears proved valid when she dug deeper into the post and saw Colt had liked it.

She returned to the B&B with a heavy heart, uncertain of what she'd do if Colt found her again, but certain of what she wanted. On a walk, she encountered Gary at the same bench she'd bumped into him weeks before.

He told her he'd been waiting there all day because he wanted to spend some time with her. She sat down and he continued, "The best day I had in this quest was the day I spent painting with you and Gabe."

Lucy was worried about him. He looked like he'd lost weight, and not in a healthy way—he was pale and possibly even sick.

"You know people leave these quests. No one is forcing you to be here. This is supposed to be helping you. Why haven't you quit and gone to see your son?"

"I can't quit. Kai said that if I went back to my old ways, something bad could happen to my son. He said finding my path would mean a better life for him. He seems to have my best interest at heart."

"Okay, but what's he doing that's making you so miserable?"

"Kai is constantly lifting me up after making me do something that makes me feel completely crappy," he added. "I keep doing these things that I don't remember ever having a dream about. I don't think that I had a dream of being a rapper. I mean, look at me, that's even more absurd than the dude ranch. Still, he practically forced me into this lesson with a man and at first we were having fun, but then this other guy came and totally made fun of me, even though it was just my first lesson."

"That sounds really rough and it kind of sounds like Kai is gaslighting you. Gabe said you were a really amazing artist. Why don't you ask Kai to let you do that?"

"I have, and he just said that Gabe was wrong. That I'd never make the money that I needed to make for my son and me to be happy."

"Do you believe that? Do you have any dreams you'd like to pursue? That you could pursue? Do you think you'd be happy as an art teacher? Why do we have to pick something that we've lost? Maybe exploring what we've wanted to do in the past is just sparking an idea of what to do in the future."

"Wow. Maybe you're right. I'm my own person. You know what I was thinking would be cool?"

"What?"

"I think I'd like to start a program kind of like this one ... I mean, obviously, I don't have magic empath powers. What if we led art therapy camps? Like a more intensive version of those places where people paint and drink wine. We could have things like that, but they'd be more like the day you and I had with Gabe."

Lucy listened intensely as Gary got more passionate and an avalanche of ideas came pouring out of him.

"Paint your perfect day. Make a mosaic after writing all the garbage in your head holding you back on the back of the tiles."

He went on and on. He talked about how he'd have special sessions for people with disabilities. Lucy loved his idea of making sophisticated vision boards using old windows as the frame. He was clearly an artist, and it was an awesome idea.

"Yes!" she shouted encouragingly.

"Wow, Lucy. You light me up."

Lucy's soul sang as Gary's words echoed in her mind. Gary came closer to Lucy and embraced her. "I won't forget this."

"You better not. I'm not sure Kai would give the memory or vision back if you lost it."

Gary paused, reflecting on Lucy's comment. "I'm not sure." More silence.

Lucy could see the wheels turning and determination building on his face.

"I'm going to go for it." He smiled. The moment of decision was so clear, Lucy thought it almost needed a sound effect. *Bing.*

He said he had a friend who could help him write a business plan. "I'm so jazzed!" he said as he left, hugging Lucy one last time. Lucy felt his energy transfer to her. Gabe walked up just moments after Gary left.

"Hey, Lucy, you look happy," Gabe said.

"Yeah, I just helped Gary figure out what his next move is. I'm so happy I could lift his spirits," Lucy replied.

"What's his next move? You're not his Vision Catcher," Gabe tried to say lightheartedly, thinking back to his conversation with Kai.

"I know, but you don't need to be a Vision Catcher to encourage somebody to live out their dreams. I mean, sure, you've captured ones, but hey, I did one from a long time ago—and look how that turned out," Lucy said, holding up her wrist with a playful smirk.

"How's that really going to work out?" Gabe asked, raising an eyebrow. "Kai's going to be pissed at me. Last time when we were painting, he told me not to interfere again."

"Well, Kai doesn't need to be pissed off because you didn't interfere. I did. Besides, Gary's going to quit the quest."

"Wait, what?" Gabe asked, surprised.

"Yeah, Gary's just going to do his own thing. Kai's been really mean to Gary, gaslighting him."

"Lucy, I can't believe you did that to Kai."

"What? I can't believe Kai. Gary's got a lot going on at home, and he doesn't need somebody telling him he needs to do all these things he doesn't even remember ever dreaming of—it's not right. Gary's creative. He's cool. I made a snap judgment about him when I first met him—his smell, his looks—but I was wrong. You can't judge a book by its cover," Lucy said with conviction.

"Okay." He looked down at his phone as he seemed to always do. "I suppose it doesn't matter."

"Yeah," Lucy replied, somewhat miffed that Gabe had ruined her perfectly good mood. She had just forgotten about her worries about Colt, but now her anxiety coursed through her body like an army of ants crawling inside of her, stinging her along the way.

She rebuffed Gabe when he offered to do a meditation exercise with her to calm her nerves. He walked away with his head down, looking ashamed. She almost called after him, feeling guilty that she'd pushed him away, but she really did just want to be alone. She went to her room, crawled under the covers, and fell asleep.

27

Without a Shadow of a Doubt

Quest Day Twenty-Eight

When she got dressed that morning, she'd braced herself for the day. Worries filled her mind. Colt knew where she was, but she didn't want to give in to fear. She told herself she was done with that. If he showed up, she'd be brave. She knew what she wanted.

Her resolve slipped away as she buried herself in the work. It only took a few hours of handing our flyers for her to stop looking over her shoulder. She'd done this so many times over the last few weeks that she was in a state of flow. Happily talking to interested people about the cause and fine with most who brushed her aside.

When Colt did finally show up, despite the morning's anticipation, she was stunned. Her reaction was a familiar one. It was always the same. Not flight, definitely not fight, but freeze. Her brain locked her body as still as a deer blinded by headlights. Though this wasn't a blindside. She'd hoped he wouldn't come—dreaded it—but had expected it.

"Hey there Lucy."

The air in her lungs was unmoving as she tried to find the words that she'd rehearsed in her imagination over and over again. "Go away. If I wanted to be with you, I would. You don't make me happy anymore." It wasn't a soliloquy or complex, yet still the words didn't come. As her heart raced, she finally managed to let out a simple hello.

"Now, what did you say in the hospital? You were in a contest to win money … not that I ever believed it, but I'd say this is the opposite. Is that cult helping you somehow? How are you spending your days just volunteering … to what … save the environment? How realistic do you think that is as a long-term plan? It's not sustainable. Come back to me. I can provide for us. We're going to have a happy life." He smiled, wearing an "I got you" look on his face.

"I … I," she stuttered. Colt came closer and grabbed her good arm, pulling her with him. The grip Lucy had on the brochures released as he pulled with more force and might. They went floating to the ground.

"Some environmentalist you are. Look, you're littering." He smirked.

Lucy looked back at the trail of paper behind her and met eyes with Sebastian, his mouth agape and his body frozen just as Lucy's had been moments ago. His failure to act shook something loose in Lucy and she screamed, "HELP!"

"Shut up, cunt." Colt's anger now, instead of silencing her as it would have in the past, made her scream even louder. As she looked around, people were recording what was happening on their cell phones. She pulled back her arm, but Colt's hold on her was too strong. She closed her eyes as tears streamed down her face and her cries for help were getting weaker. Her eyes opened when the tug of Colt's arm released, and his whole body jerked to the left. As he released her, Lucy's momentum sent her tumbling toward the ground.

She fell on her broken wrist and the pain shot through her arm. Everything around her seemed to happen in slow motion. Someone came up to her and helped her up. As an officer put handcuffs on him, Colt glared at her.

After the cop secured Colt in his car, he approached her. "This man is saying he's your husband. Do you want to press charges?"

Confidence swelled inside her, filling the hole that had slowly grown over the last several years. Sealing off the self-doubt that Colt had implanted in her. She looked the officer directly in the eyes and said, "without a shadow of a doubt."

She wept as the officer walked away. Still in shock, she asked, "What happened? I mean, what made Colt let go?"

"You have this young man to thank for that." She turned, expecting to see Sebastian. He was there, but the officer was pointing at Gabe.

"I was on my way here to check on you." He looked down at his hand, shaking it out. "Man, I've been wanting to do that for a long time."

"You two know each other?" the cop asked.

"This is my friend, Gabe."

"I just assumed you were a stranger. Well, glad you're in good hands. I'll give you a moment and come back to take your statement." The cop went back to the car.

Lucy looked at Gabe, still shaken. "I told him I wanted to press charges."

"I heard. I'm proud of you." They walked over to sit for a moment at a nearby picnic table.

Gabe was immensely proud of the courage Lucy had shown. He briefly thought about the points Lucy would gain from this. She'd been coasting along at 3,500 after the last two weeks at the nonprofit. He shook the thought and turned off his phone so his full focus could be on Lucy.

After he accompanied her to give her statement, they returned to the B&B. Back in the privacy of his room, he stared at his phone, contemplating whether to record all the events that had just unfolded into the app. Hesitantly, he did. He'd received several new notifications and messages. There was a reminder to record today's progress, a message from his aunt about a family dinner, but most of the messages were from Kai. Gabe's stomach turned as he read them.

Kai: *Gary just quit his quest. Looks like your little "darling" Originator pushed him over the edge. I warned you about meddling, Gabe, and now you're going to pay.*

Kai: *Oh, you have nothing to say? Typical wallflower. Cecilia was right, you're just a "big ole softie." You know what another word for softie is? Loser.*

Kai: *Never mind, looks like I won't have to do a thing. You're tanking this quest. Lol. If Lucy hasn't hit 5,000 points by now, do you really think you're guiding her? What have you been doing? Painting in your little art studio while she goes off to "save the environment"? You're a disgrace to our kind.*

Kai: *Still no response? Fine. Just know that when I get on the top of the leaderboard and am a Guild advisor, I'll tell them all about how you sabotaged Gary's quest. You'll hate your assignment. I'll make sure of it.*

Stunned, Gabe's mind raced, and he thought back on everything he'd done wrong. Lucy slipped through his fingers before orientation even began, in their first transdreamosis session he wasn't able to help Lucy with her perfect day, and he regretted just taking Lucy's phone from her when she finally turned it on instead of helping her through her feelings. Lucy was doing all the heavy lifting. What was he even doing? He'd been painting a lot, just his own stuff while Lucy was enjoying being at the nonprofit. He wanted her to have that time. To have some peace and happiness after so long of being under Colt's thumb.

The messages from Kai were pinballing in his mind. He'd try to sleep, but he kept going back and reading them. He almost replied and then just deleted them. It's what he'd advise if Lucy was in the same situation. Don't give him the satisfaction of engaging.

He went to the studio and painted. Lucy's face, fierce and determined, took up most of the canvas. Over it, he painted the words, "Without a shadow of a doubt." He sighed as he felt the release of Colt's grip on Lucy's mind that she experienced in that moment.

He took out his phone to study the points system more carefully. Before he transmitted what happened that day to Ravi, he wanted to calculate what points he thought Lucy could get. He got out a pencil and paper to figure out the minimum and maximum points that he thought Lucy standing up to Colt justified.

Minimum Total

1. Overcoming Self-Doubt: 50
2. Healing from Past Trauma: 100
3. Asserting Boundaries: 75
4. Cultivating Confidence: 100
5. Taking Risks: 50
6. Facing Fears: 50
7. Cultivating Resilience: 75
8. Letting Go of Toxic Relationships: 100

Minimum Total = 50 + 100 + 75 + 100 + 50 + 50 + 75 + 100 = **600 points**

Maximum Total

1. Overcoming Self-Doubt: 200
2. Healing from Past Trauma: 250
3. Asserting Boundaries: 200
4. Cultivating Confidence: 250
5. Taking Risks: 200

6. Facing Fears: 250
7. Cultivating Resilience: 200
8. Letting Go of Toxic Relationships: 250

Maximum Total = 200 + 250 + 200 + 250 + 200 + 250 + 200 + 250 = **1,800 points**

Kai hadn't been wrong. Lucy hadn't made large gains while she was coasting along, doing her part to help the environment. He also knew that a volunteer job would not lead to long-term success for Lucy. However, this major step today, with putting Colt away, could put her over the 5,000 point threshold.

Feeling more confident, he went to check in with Ravi. Once again, the app was faulty. He couldn't DM Ravi and the check-in button was grayed out. The option to report the bug like he did before was faulty, too. He looked back at his painting and just hoped that they'd fix it by tomorrow.

28

Scored

Quest Day Twenty-Nine

Lucy slept well mostly, but pangs of guilt occasionally swept in to her consciousness as she thought of Colt lying in a prison cell. She was grateful for the restraining order that would be official soon. Why give Colt a record and ruin his life? If she could just file for a divorce and keep the restraining order, maybe that would be enough.

She couldn't wait to get to work today and get her mind off the whole thing. When she got there, the looks of sympathy from her colleagues and new friends made that almost impossible to do.

Sensing Lucy's setback in her mindset, Gabe went to find her. He approached her while she was collating a mailing.

"Hey there, Lucy," he said. "I'm sensing you're having a little bit of remorse about your decision to press charges against Colt."

"Oh God, why do you always have to read my mind?" she replied. "I don't know, Gabe. It seems a little too much. Maybe if I don't press charges, it'll be easier to get on with my life."

"I can see that. And I totally understand not wanting to go through official channels to punish Colt. But he committed a crime. You did nothing wrong."

"I know, but really, he just needs help. It's … just not the right thing, I think."

"Well, you don't have to decide this very minute. I want to talk to you about your quest here."

"At TEL? I love working at the nonprofit. It's the only thing that's kept me sane over the last couple of weeks."

"I know, but I think we should probably try some other visions out. Just until this whole thing with Colt blows over."

"Oh no, everybody's been super nice to me here," Lucy said.

Gabe interrupted. "I recognize that. But how about you come back to the studio with me? Just for a bit. And we can talk about it there."

"Oh, but I'm in the middle of this mailing."

"They can get somebody else to do it."

Lucy felt as if Gabe wasn't taking her job seriously. Her work didn't matter to him as much as it did to her. Maybe he was right, though. Maybe the work she was doing didn't make a difference.

Mind spinning, she thought, *I mean, if I wasn't here, somebody would collate the mailing. If I wasn't here, there would be somebody handing out flyers. And what did flyers do, anyway? The Amazon is burning. I'm not helping with that.*

Lucy couldn't make sense of all the swirling thoughts in her brain. Reluctantly, she agreed to go back to the studio with Gabe. As they walked out of the room, she looked back remorsefully at the mailers. Guilt set up camp in her mind with almost every decision she made. Whether it was something as large as pressing charges against Colt or as small as not finishing stuffing envelopes.

She knew that she'd committed to explore what made her happy, but at the moment being at TEL did make her happy. She didn't want to let them or Gabe down. Before walking out, she checked in with the development coordinator to make sure they'd be okay with it.

"Of course. Thanks so much for all your help. See you later."

Lucy let out a sigh of relief. The kindness of the TEL staff helped her to release the guilt of leaving them hanging as they left the office.

Every time Lucy stepped into the studio, a feeling of belonging overwhelmed her. She'd been there many times in the last few weeks. And if she could just stay looking at the visions she'd lost for the entire extent of her quest, she would.

Going back to the garden and the chicken coop reminded her of her work at TEL. The community gardens were such a place for peace for her as well. After seeing the familiar paintings, she stopped dead in her tracks, looking at the one that she hadn't seen before.

Gabe had so perfectly captured her feeling and her face when she told the cop yesterday without a shadow of a doubt. She was so sure then. But the shadows of doubt felt like they were crawling all over her. Like spiders.

"Oh, Gabe. Is this why you wanted to bring me here? This is just ... " She went up and touched the painting as tears crept down her cheek.

Gabe hadn't even thought of the painting. He still didn't want to tell her about the points, but that was all he was thinking about. He thought that if she just picked a couple more things, then he could meet that 5,000 point threshold, he could move on as a Vision Catcher, and Lucy would find her way. She'd come so far already.

"Actually, yes," he lied. "That's why I wanted to bring you here. I sensed you were doubting yourself, and I just wanted to remind you of the confidence you showed yesterday."

"Thank you, Gabe." She stared at the painting, and Gabe could almost see the doubts float away.

"Alright, so let's pick something else. What's another vision you'd like to pursue while we still have some time? There's only ten days left.

Can you believe that?"

"Okay. Well ... Let's try ... I don't know, Gabe. None of it seems like me anymore. I mean, a little, but ... Is there anything else we can pick from?"

"Well, I could go to the Dream Exchange. There's a lot of unclaimed dreams from people who are dead or who have just given up. These become nontransferable to the Originator. A lot of Vision Catchers use the exchange to feed their Originators ideas, but I don't think you should live out someone else's dream."

"That makes sense, but can't it be something new?"

"That's not exactly how this is meant to work. Let's just find one now."

"Okay. Alright."

She looked around at all the visions and her eyes fixed upon the large statue of the stool, floating guitar, and microphone. They were in Nashville, so why not try out her musical chops?

Putting caution to the wind, she said, "Alright, let's put my creative hat on. Let's go after the singer-songwriter vision."

Gabe smiled and nodded. "This will be fun."

Though Lucy thought songwriting would be "fun," Gabe had put her in a songwriting class. It was awful; the teacher just droned on and on and on. They didn't even get to write anything on the first day—"all talking about technique"—and she felt like she couldn't quiet her mind enough to even reflect, to write a poem or try to write some lyrics to a song. It wasn't the right fit.

She complained to Gabe, but he told her, "Give it one more day." And again, on day thirty-one of Lucy's quest, the teacher was no fun.

Gabe felt conflicted. Lucy seemed miserable, but her score went up for trying new things. Wasn't part of his job to push her? She'd scored more points in the last two days than she had in the last week at TEL.

Lucy felt like she was going to pull her hair out. *Why couldn't they just get to the meat of it? Didn't this woman know she was on a deadline?* She'd always wanted to be creative, write songs, do something that was outside of her comfort zone. But studying the technique and how songwriters go about their work was taking away the beauty and the magic of it.

At the end of one of the days in this class that had felt like years, she made a decision. She'd take the journal she'd received at orientation—which she hadn't really touched since then—and write a damn song. She even called Daisy to get some ideas. "Why not write a funny song?" She didn't want to dwell anymore on anything that Colt did.

She got Aunt Rae to make her some classic southern food. Daisy and she talked about romantic pursuits Lucy had prior to Colt, and the family reunions she attended as a child where she was always first in line to eat. Daisy said, "It sounds like you were on a seafood diet—you see food, you eat it!" They were in stitches. But Lucy believed a great country song could actually come out of it.

"I'm on a seafood diet.

I see food, I eat it.

It fills my soul, it heals my spirit.

So fillet me a fish, fry me up some okra.

If you don't give me chocolate, I'm libel to choke ya."

At first, they had the word "I'm bound," and Daisy said, "No, no, no, 'libel.' That's more southern." Even though they knew the correct spelling of this meaning would be liable, they spelled it phonetically how someone with a southern accent would say it. They knew exactly who to call to help them with the music and chords.

Lucy had a new energy, but she still didn't think songwriting was the direction she should head in her whole life. She really wanted to help people. After she sat in the class the next day, still studying technique, still not writing anything, she found Gabe in his studio and said, "I'm done. I can't do this anymore. You've helped me a lot. I've gotten through a lot. And I don't think I need this anymore."

Gabe's face was just so much more devastated than Lucy had ever expected. Why was he so disappointed? She'd found her way. Wasn't that his entire job? He looked down at his phone again.

"Why are you always looking at your phone? Eyes up here." She grabbed the phone out of his hands and saw something that resembled a profile on a social app, but it was about her. It had her name, a picture of a painting of her, then it read: "Total Quest Points: 4,900"

"You're scoring me?"

In a defensive tone, Gabe replied, "No, it's not like that. I'm not scoring you. The Guild is."

"Who the hell is the Guild?" Lucy said.

"It's the governing body of the Vision Catchers. I really need you to stay until you get 5,000 points. Please. I know you haven't liked the class the last few days, but your point total's been creeping up ... way more than it was when you were at the nonprofit."

"So you think this is what I should do? Songwriting?"

"No, I didn't say that. Let's look around for another vision." He searched the studio and landed on the chicken coop. "You liked community gardening? Maybe you can start your own community garden."

"Gabe, I know what I liked. I liked helping people, but I tell you what." She paused and looked at Gabe's pleading face. "I want to help you. So let's take a break for today, and tomorrow morning I'll come back—not going to the class again—and we'll go through the studio, vision by vision, and we'll find one to get you the points you need."

"Okay, thank you. You only need 100 more points. It may just take another day."

29

Ground Zero

Quest Day Thirty-Three

Gabe opened the door to the studio, and Lucy gasped. Her visions and dreams had been violated. The chickens in the coop were dead—their limp bodies adorned with lifeless butterflies. Lucy couldn't even wrap her mind around the cruelty. Taking in the wreckage, she uttered in a hushed tone, "Why would somebody kill the butterflies?"

They walked around. Dreams were just missing—gone. The statue of her dream to be a singer-songwriter, the pictures of her unborn children, and even the vision that had kicked off this whole crazy journey—her chasing the sunset.

As they approached the corner where Lucy knew Gabe kept his own personal artwork, she saw many of those pieces were still there. But as they drew closer, they saw that they'd been stabbed—straight through the heart of the canvas.

Bare easels stood as monuments to what had once been. One of them was the old easel Gabe had found at a pawn shop. Seeing it brought Lucy back to the first day he'd brought her here—to this magical place. Her eyes filled with tears.

"Why would someone do this?" Lucy asked, turning toward Gabe.

He'd fallen to the floor and was shaking, gasping for air.

She didn't want them to both freak out. Steeling herself, she attempted to speak words of comfort. "Gabe, it's going to be okay."

"Do you know how much time it took me to make all this? How can I help you recapture anything now?"

She tried to remain hopeful. "This is what I've been saying. I can make new visions. I don't need to look at the past."

His phone pinged an alert.

Seven days left, and you are not at the 5,000 point threshold. If you do not reach 5,000 points in the next seven days, your progression as a Vision Catcher will be in jeopardy.

"It might be too late by then." Gabe held up his phone for Lucy to see.

To Lucy, his anxiety seemed to be out of proportion with the consequences. "Gabe, you're talented. Even if you don't succeed in this quest with the points, you've helped me."

"You don't understand. My parents belonged to a special group of VCs—the game changers, who led important quests and safeguarded fragile ideas. Dreams that had a domino effect to entire shifts in how your culture operates, like my aunt. She's always told me stories of how she helped with the civil rights movement in America."

"Whoa there, you're putting some big time pressure on me now. Is that why you had me give that acceptance speech for an award for saving the environment? Wait ... why the heck did you have me skateboard?" She looked around and saw those visions had been taken too.

"It's not like that."

"What's it like, then? I'd really like to know."

Gabe tried to compose himself and clear his mind. He felt weak to her inquiries and didn't have the strength to resist them. He wanted to tell her, but he knew he wasn't supposed to talk freely about his process—not mid-quest. If she was going to understand what was at stake, she needed to know.

"When you lost your skateboarding vision, it was one of the first ones you lost because someone else diminished it. Others you just grew out of like kids do. You were very imaginative. During my training with my mentor, I had lots to capture in your early years. Your dream to go to the X Games was also special because it was the first one I captured by myself—without my mentor by my side. It was so full of Feranchin."

"Feranchin, that's the light energy, from the play, right?"

"Exactly. We infuse it in every creation we make. The writers do it with the words they choose, I do it with brush strokes. The more passes through us, the more life force we have, and the longer we live. Not that we keep it—we capture it, like I did in my studio. But it lingers in us. When it fades, it's like we do too. I may look like a teenager, but actually I've been in existence longer than you."

"Really?" Lucy's eyes widened. "How old are you?"

"Thirty-seven."

"Wow. So how long do you live? Twice as long?" Lucy asked, her head tilting and face full of wonderment.

"It depends. The aging process slows down as Feranchin passes through us, but it doesn't make us immortal. Our bodies still age. The aging process can even speed up if we're tied too closely with an Originator who has too much Infrassin—the dark energy of self-doubt or greed. I aged a lot when you were with Colt."

Lucy looked away. Her face fell, and he could sense her shame.

"It happens Lucy. Infrassin is an integral reason we exist—to fight it. We need to feel it to know when to transfer back some of the Feranchin we held for you. Most of the time, it's a gentle nudge and sometimes it's more direct, like this quest. But you've been doing so well. This setback isn't your fault." He gestured to the ransacked studio. Gabe's phone pinged again.

"Oh God," he said.

"What is it?"

"Well, you're on a good path, but it might be too late for me. You might as well leave. Soon, my connection might be severed from you. I just got another reminder about the point total."

"Oh Gabe, I'm not quitting now. What's 100 points?"

He looked down at the app. "It's not just 100 points anymore."

"What do you mean?"

"Something's gone haywire. Now you have zero points."

"What? Why? What did I do? Just because I didn't like the songwriting?"

"No ... I don't know. It's not your fault. It has to be something I did."

He closed his eyes. Silence lingered between them. Gabe thought back to all that had happened. What he felt now was 200 times worse than her points had mysteriously dropped. That day had been so great before that happened, before Kai had ripped into him for messing with Gary.

He began to connect the dots. Still deep in thought, he spoke one name out loud without intending to. "Kai."

"What about Kai? Wait ... do you think he did this?"

"I'm not sure, but every time your quest points have mysteriously dropped, he's been angry at me or you."

"I've never even met the dude. I just know he's a grade A asshole."

"Well first he was mad because of that day I painted with you and Gary. Then, I was talking about him behind his back. And then ... " Gabe paused as the wheels in his head were turning. With a furrowed brow he looked Lucy directly in the eyes and said, "I think you pissed him off when Gary quit the quest."

Lucy looked at him skeptically. "So, how does this work exactly? Is it like his anger management problem? The force of his rage is getting tangled up in whatever kind of magic tech the app works on?"

Gabe sighed. "It doesn't work like that. I mean, for a long time, I thought it was me that was screwing up. Our tech and innovation is basically created from the same resources you have. We've evolved our tools alongside humans. I don't think Kai's anger can have that kind of effect on an app."

"Well, forgive me. Until a month ago, I didn't think there were mystical beings capturing people's ideas for safekeeping."

"Sorry. I get your point. I didn't mean to dismiss you."

"It's okay."

His brain was still circling back on Kai when Lucy asked, "Could he have hacked the app?"

"I don't know. It doesn't make any sense." Gabe pounded his fists on the ground. When he looked up, the emptiness of the studio consumed his thoughts. His breath quickened. Panic set in again.

Lucy looked at Gabe and wanted desperately to solve his issue. "Well, can you unhack it?"

Lucy thought that this was an extremely logical question given that he could basically read her mind and transport her to her perfect day just by holding her hands and projecting it into her consciousness. Although, he'd so quickly rejected her idea about Kai's emotions crippling the app.

"How could I ... " Gabe's voice trailed off, clearly thinking about her question—taking her seriously. Lucy saw an epiphany flash across his face. He jumped up and headed toward the door, running. "Come on, I have an idea."

When they reached the main house, Lucy and Gabe were both out of breath.

"Why didn't you just hop in the car?" Lucy asked. "Why did we have to run across the field to get here?"

Gabe turned to her. "I thought this would be faster."

Lucy rolled her eyes, huffing, trying to catch her breath.

Aunt Rae came out. "Oh, children, what's going on here? Why are you so out of breath?"

Then Rae sensed what Gabe and Lucy saw in the studio.

"Gabe, what's going on in your head? Are you okay?"

"I need to find Hannah."

"Hannah? Why?"

"I don't have time to explain. Do you know where she is?"

"Actually, yes, I think she just went back to her room. Her Originator is at one of those songwriting workshops, I think."

"Oh God. Well, thanks. I hope I can catch her."

Gabe was about to run again toward Hannah, but paused and looked back at Lucy. He'd already brought her into the drama and away from her path. He wanted so desperately for Lucy to find her way.

"Lucy," he said, "I've got this. I'm going to try to figure this out. In the meantime, though, I think you should try to figure out what's next for you."

"Wait, what? I think … don't I need you for that?"

Gabe paused, thinking back to all they'd been through—the hills she'd conquered in a short amount of time. "You've barely needed me on any step of this journey, especially recently. I've seen you grow so much—from finding your bliss, to standing up to Colt, to standing up to me when you weren't happy."

Lucy looked at Gabe and smiled so softly, with tears prickling behind her eyes. Their pair-bond was so strong in that moment, he could tell she was thinking back to the night she picked him up.

"Here, come with me." He walked into the dining area and grabbed a notebook and pen from one of the bookshelves that lined the walls. "I'm going to have you do a journal exercise."

"A journal exercise?" Lucy said. "Why?"

"Think of it as catching visions on your own. When you get an idea, write it down. What do you really want to be doing? I mean, you envisioned your perfect day, but in terms of the life you want to lead, think back to everything you've done recently or witnessed from the visions I caught in the past. Then think of where you want to go next."

"Alright. What happens if I can't think of anything? I mean, those visions from the studio are gone. I'm having trouble remembering them all."

"Listen, the only repercussions for you, if the app doesn't score you with 5,000 points, is that you won't have access to me or our network. I know you can do this on your own, but those visions can still be retrieved—by you. They're still tethered to your consciousness. So write it down. There's a week left in this quest and you're not done yet. Dig deep."

"Okay. Okay. I'll start." As Gabe left, music filled the room. It was "Heaven When We're Home" by the Wailin' Jennys. Lucy let the words and gentle voices swirl around her like the soft breeze from behind her home just a month ago. As the memories and dreams flooded her soul, tears flooded her eyes. It was as if she was grieving for herself. She'd let herself get so far away from who she once was, but as she wiped her face, a new excitement renewed within her for the journey ahead.

Gabe reached Hannah's room just as the song ended and he sensed Lucy had begun to write.

30

The Backend

The door was slightly ajar. Through the crack, he blurted, "Oh, Hannah, I'm so glad I found you."

"Gabe, what's wrong? You look awful."

"Well, a lot's happened, but here's the short of it: somebody's hacked the app, Hannah. Someone is trying to ruin Lucy's score."

"Who?"

"Do you know Kai?"

"Yeah. Wait, he's hacked the app? What did he do?"

"I don't have time to get into it right now, but I can't even get in touch with my Vision Catcher rep. Can you somehow ... do a hack back?"

"I can try, no promises. I have admin rights to the backend, but I'm not a coder."

Hannah opened her laptop and clicked on an icon that read, *VC Quest App*. Once inside she said, "Okay, yeah, I see it. Somebody's placed a 'communication lock' on your user. I'll just ... unlock it ... okay, you should be able to reach out now."

"Oh, thank you so much, Hannah. You're a lifesaver. Can you also tell what happened that made Lucy's score tank?"

"I'll check. Well, that's weird."

"What?"

"I can see a record of when users log the activities that generate the scores. There's your VC Rep's ID tagged to most of Lucy's scores. But then ... there's this other user."

"What other user?"

"It's strange—they look like a VC Rep, but the ID is slightly off. See here." Hannah clicked over to a user list labeled 'VC Reps' and pointed to the screen. See how all of them start with 82 and they all have 737 within the 18-digit ID?"

Gabe scanned the screen. "Okay, yes, I see that."

"Well, this one," she said as she flipped back to Lucy's record, "the one that changed Lucy's score negatively, most significantly this morning, must've noticed they all start with 82, but it doesn't have the 737 pattern in it. Also, I can normally just click on the User ID to get to the profile, like here when I click on the legitimate scores. I see Ravi inputted the initial log."

"Okay, what happens when you click on the other one?"

"It pulls up an anonymous user. It's almost like it's hidden behind encryption layers."

"So, can you tell if it's Kai manipulating Lucy's points?"

"I'm afraid that's above my skill level. I can only do so much from here. But I can see something else that's strange."

"What's that?"

"See, if I click on Lucy's profile, all of her dreams were cataloged when you recorded them."

"Who did that?"

"An accountant."

"What? I didn't know about that."

"Really? I can't believe they didn't teach you about this at school. Maybe it was something I just learned along the way now that I think about it. It's a newer technology. Who was your primary teacher?"

"Mainly Professor McGuvers. He told us about Supporters who would assist and what to do with the visions if they became legitimately transferable."

"Ohhhh ... well he was old school. Teaching was a side-gig for him while you were in school. He's also served on the Guild for years and argued for disbanding the computer cataloging project."

"So he just didn't tell us about it?"

"Either that or you're a terrible student." Hannah smirked.

"Okay. So somebody came to the studio and cataloged this in the computer system."

"Yes. And see there are only a few that are still active. There must be hundreds here that the system or some user has set to expired status and deleted the details. That happens when the idea or vision has reached the statute of limitations and the Originator has not used it, but these shouldn't have all expired at the same time."

"Well, where are they? Where's my art? Did the accountant also secretly put a tracker on it?"

"No, the process of the accountant is quick. They work at lightning speed to scan a room, or flip through books, and then they're trained to hook into the mainframe and create the vision records."

"Can you undelete the details?"

"I can put in a request for an accountant to go to your studio and re-record them."

"That's the problem. Someone stole them." Hannah looked at him in shock with her mouth agape.

Gabe took a deep breath, attempting to control his anger and stay in problem-solving mode. "Are you absolutely sure there's nothing you can do to figure out who this anonymous user is?"

"Really, I'm sorry. I don't code, I just know how to navigate the system. I'll reach out to one of the lead developers for the system, Warren, and see what he can find."

"Okay. Thank you, Hannah." Gabe was about to leave, but caught himself. "I just barged in here and didn't even ask—how's your Originator doing?"

"Well that depends, which one?"

"Oh God, I forgot for a moment this isn't your first quest. I interrupted you and you have a caseload and … "

"Nonsense." Hannah cut him off. "You're in crisis, I'm happy to help. Of all of them, the one I told you about at orientation, Reggie, is doing the best. He's really working through his grief of losing his wife. Finally finding his bliss. He was brilliant at this Open Mic last night. He's at a songwriting class right now."

"Oh, Lucy hated that class."

"If I've learned anything through the years, it's different strokes for different folks. That class takes patience, which Reggie has in spades." Hannah looked down at her watch and apologetically said, "I do have to go though."

"Okay. Again sorry for taking up your time and thank you."

She clasped Gabe's arm gently signaling she wasn't in a rush. She looked him straight in the eyes and said, "No worries. It's my pleasure."

He left Hannah and went to his room. He was eager to finally touch base with Ravi. The contact VC Rep button was no longer grayed out.

"Hello Gabe … you look … " He paused, seeming to search for the right words. "I'm sensing something isn't quite right. What's wrong?"

"Ravi, somebody is messing with the app. And I think I know who that somebody is. I'm trying to find some proof. But Lucy's score is now at zero. And I know you didn't do that."

"Of course I didn't. Lucy's been doing well. I mean, some setbacks and some things you could've done better." Gabe frowned at this.

Ravi perked up his voice. "But overall, she's a star student. I'm sure we can fix this and it's a technical glitch. Just give me a moment."

Ravi typed on his computer. "Oh ... I'm so sorry, my system is running slow. Just hang on."

Gabe's mind raced, and his heart sped up. Of course, Ravi's computer was slow, that was probably Kai too. Impatience felt like it was encasing his entire body and his foot began obnoxiously tapping until his nervous energy could no longer be contained in his body and escaped through his mouth. "Look, honestly, I don't care too much about the score anymore. Remind me, what's going to happen to me when I don't get the 5,000 points? And how often does that happen?"

"Well, I don't know the statistics of how often that happens."

"Isn't that the whole point of the app, so you can track things like that?"

"Oh, sorry, sorry. We're still just getting used to it. It's only been a year or so that we've been using this points system. But yes ... oh, I see. I see where you've gotten negative scores. I don't remember these."

"Yes, yes, you see the ID? It's different."

"Oh, how do you know that?"

"Hannah was investigating it for me. She's raised a case to Warren to try to figure it out."

"Warren? This must be serious. What does it say about me that my client is in jeopardy?" Ravi shut his eyes, shaking his head. It was the first time that Gabe realized that the score probably wasn't just used to evaluate him. Ravi also had to answer for the scores.

Gabe attempted to redirect Ravi to the immediate issue at hand. "Is there anything I can do? Can I get in front of the Guild? Can I do it the old-school way where we just have a journal and a Supporter? Is there any kind of thing where we can not use the app for Lucy to officially pass her quest or me to pass as her Vision Catcher and guide?"

"Well, we're only authorized to go back to paper or an older way of doing things if there's a power outage. You have seven days left to get 5,000 points. It's possible. There are certain things that just ... "

"Even if it's possible, this issue has to be solved." Gabe was shouting now.

"Give me a moment," Ravi said with a steady voice, not matching Gabe's tone. Gabe's foot began tapping again. "I'm not seeing an opening on the schedule for a while for the VC Guild. And I don't have the ties to really get in front of them. I can see what I can do to escalate the case, but if you already have Warren working on the bug, you probably should be fine."

"Probably isn't good enough." Gabe's voice raised to a higher volume than intended, but Ravi's response was calm and collected.

"If you want to speak to someone on the Guild, you'll need to find someone who has connections. Mine don't go that far up the chain."

"Okay. Thanks." His voice was more curt than Ravi deserved. "I'll be in touch, hopefully, if our communication lines aren't locked again."

"Alright, Gabe. I'll let you go."

When they hung up, a message popped up on Gabe's screen asking him to evaluate his session with Ravi. He shook his head and let out a grunt of frustration before putting his phone back in his pocket. He began running again, back to Lucy.

Lucy heard footsteps in the distance and looked up from her journal, which had gotten quite full in a short amount of time. Gabe, once again out of breath, darted into the room.

Lucy was actually feeling quite calm. In a very short amount of time just by journaling, any devastation she was feeling about the studio being violated had transformed into motivation to meet the challenge of the quest. She was excited to move on and through, but still felt she owed it to Gabe to make this a successful quest. She was unconcerned if they could find his art and recover these points or not.

Gabe's frantic energy seemed to relax a little to match Lucy's sereneness when he met her eyes. She felt the light inside herself shine brightly by being able to anchor him in this manner.

"How's it going, Lucy? It seems like you're getting a lot done."

"Yeah, I've really been able to reflect on what I might want to do next. I thought about how I encouraged Gary to move forward rather than look at old visions. Not that capturing old visions isn't valuable but ... I think," Lucy hesitated, "I think I want to work at a domestic violence shelter—there are a lot of women and even men who are way worse off than I was with Colt. I'm pretty sure they have volunteer positions on phone call lines, and they need those at all times of the day." Excited at this idea, Lucy rattled on. "So if I could just do that for three or four hours in the evening, and work during the day, maybe I could get a position, eventually. The only thing is, I think I need to line this up fast, because I'm worried that I won't have a place to stay in a week. I still have most of the ring money, so that can last me for a little, but ... "

Gabe interrupted, "I get it, but we're on a time crunch. Are you sure this is the best move? Your wounds are pretty fresh. I'm not sure you'd be ready to help someone else being abused."

"This is what I want. I helped Emily and Sebastian and Gary and even you. I'm ready." She was confident in her decision and drew power from her decisiveness.

"Yeah, but you weren't dealing with ... "

"Gabe, seriously, can you make this happen or not?"

"Well, I'll see if I can set something up right now."

"Thank you. How's the point issue? Were you able to work it out? Do you need to handle that first? I can just hang out in The Tower while you ... "

"Lucy, you're my priority. I forgot that for a little bit, but my priority all comes back to you in the end."

Lucy felt a warmth in her, nervous but excited for the next step.

"Stay here or go to The Tower and I'll let you know what I work out in an hour."

31

Racing the Clock

Gabe smelled almond cookies baking in the oven, and knew Aunt Rae was making one of his favorites, probably to comfort him after what happened to the studio. He was tempted to just let her take care of him.

As he followed the delicious scent, the app pinged at him, reminding him of the point total that had not been met. He approached Aunt Rae hesitantly. He wasn't sure what to expect or what she'd do.

She turned to him as he walked into the kitchen and gave him a big smile. "Oh, Gabe, are you feeling any better? How's Lucy doing?"

"Well, Lucy's doing all right. I think I'm going to get her situated for the next or last piece of this quest."

"Oh, that's wonderful. I called the VC police about the studio."

"You did what?"

"Gabe, you need to report stolen visions. Plus, the chickens and butterflies were slaughtered. That kind of violence is usually not isolated to animals."

"I know, but what can they do? They're already dead, the visions are gone, and there's no security camera in the studio. I don't have time to make a statement anyway. I have to get Lucy going on her next steps and I have to ... " His voice trailed off just thinking of how ridiculous it sounded to say that he had to investigate the crime himself.

Could the police do anything? He already had the evidence that something was screwy on the app. The cops wouldn't care about that. They'd be more concerned with him inventorying everything that was stolen. Everybody knew they'd been working on clamping down on the black market for years. He took a breath and reminded himself of why he'd come there in the first place.

"Can you get me a meeting with Vance Gunderthorpe or the Vision Guild?"

"Why? The police are better equipped to handle this situation." She studied Gabe's face as he hesitated for a few moments and then she said, "Oh, I see." She was such a powerful Vision Catcher, and the family bond between them was so strong that she could read Gabe's mind. "Oh, honey. I told you not to be concerned about the points on that silly app."

"Aunt Rae, they're using the app to judge us. To make it so that I might not be able to go on a quest again. I don't even know if I'll be able to live here or do my art or … "

"Sweetie, it'll be alright. Do you really want to mess with the Guild? Can't you just talk to your rep about the points? That's what they're for," she said in a compassionate voice, but Gabe heard it as if she was a nagging mom.

"Pleaaasse," he begged.

Aunt Rae pushed back a couple more times, emphasizing that Gabe would be playing with fire by questioning the Guild's actions and decisions regarding the app.

"Aunt Rae, what are you really scared of? What could they really do to you?"

She looked down at her feet, and he could tell she was taking the question seriously—that he was breaking through. Gabe considered begging, as he'd done with her as a child. He used to just repeat,

"Please, please, please, please, please," hoping she'd relent. But he thought better of it and restrained himself. He eventually saw the Vision Catcher motto on the wall behind her. "Catch the Vision. Empower the People. Create Lasting Change."

He closed his eyes and projected these words to her, surrounded by images of the heroes that their relatives had guided. This broke her.

"Fine. I'll make the phone call for you, but I'm hands off after that. I left committee work and quite enjoy my current role of playing host and running the B&B. I'm still going to talk to the police."

Gabe nodded. "Thank you."

She pulled out her phone and dialed Vance Gunderthorpe's secretary. "Vance Gunderthorpe's office, Lisa speaking."

"Hi Lisa, this is Rae. I was wondering if Vance or someone on the Guild had some time to speak to my nephew. He's on his first vision quest, and he just has a few issues with the app."

"Oh, issues with the app should be reported within the app," Lisa replied.

"Yes, he's done that and is still needing to speak with someone. Can anybody just spare fifteen minutes, please? I sat on the Guild for so many years, and I don't want to interrupt the chain of command or process. I understand how important that is and how many quests you're managing at once, but if you could just do me this favor ... "

Lisa paused. "Well, I'll ask. It looks like he's had a couple of cancellations this afternoon, so a fifteen-minute meeting may be possible."

"Oh, thank you so much. We appreciate it. Any mentorship that Vance can provide to Gabe would be amazing. I think you know our family has done a lot for the Guild over the years."

"Yes, yes, I'll be sure to put that in the note," Lisa replied.

It was only ten minutes later that Lisa called back, but it had felt like hours. Gabe's appointment with Vance was later in the afternoon. He had a myriad of things to do to get ready.

First, he needed to find Lucy a volunteer position at a domestic violence shelter, which he still really didn't think she should do. Then he had to get her a job or find some kind of placement. He was going to turn to the alumni network for help with that. And finally, he needed to meet back up with Warren and see what he found, if he'd had time to investigate the points issue before he met with Vance.

He worked quickly to get Lucy set. He lucked out, and the domestic violence shelter had an opening for volunteer orientation today. She'd need to come in the next hour.

He let his intuition guide him and painted, attempting to recapture a vision Lucy had. When he messaged the network, letting them know he was looking for a paid gig for his Originator, he also posted a picture of the painting. He received responses within minutes and one person could see Lucy anytime that afternoon or early evening. They needed help right away and were eager to get someone on board. He was squeezing a lot in, but he had no choice. He was running out of time.

He went to tell Lucy. She was ecstatic and hugged him. "Thank you. I can't believe you worked so fast. I'm going to help someone just like me."

"Of course. I've arranged for a car to pick you up, so you don't have to worry about directions. I've got to deal with this app situation. You going to be okay?"

"Yes. I think so. You go, I can take care of myself."

As they parted ways, his adrenaline was pumping. Singularly focused, he wasted no time to observe his surroundings or plan what he was going to say as he rushed to Warren's office at VCG headquarters. "Warren, have you found anything?"

"I'm sorry. Who are you?"

"Oh, I apologize. I looked you up previously. I knew what you looked like, but I'm Gabe. I'm having trouble with the app. Hannah told you about me?"

"Oh, yes, Gabe. I've been investigating this. It's very interesting. I'm not sure exactly what's happening, but I've figured out who hacked the system."

"Who was it? Was it Kai?"

Warren paused, furrowing his brow. "I don't know if I have the authority to tell you that."

"Well, I'm going to meet with Vance Gunderthorpe in the afternoon to talk to him about the system. And try to get him to fix it so that Lucy, my Originator, will have a successful quest. I only have fifteen minutes to talk to him. Don't you have some kind of proof I can show him?"

"I don't know. I feel like it needs to be investigated even further." Warren was clearly a careful and diligent developer. But he wasn't meeting the moment with the same urgency as Gabe.

"Well, there isn't a lot of time left in this quest. I don't think we have the time for a full-on investigation. Can't we just bring the preliminary proof to him?"

Warren seemed hesitant. He wasn't interested in stepping outside the chain of command or upsetting the status quo.

"I get that this isn't my place of expertise, but I'm the victim here. I'm the one whose points were stolen."

"Yes, I see that. But I'm not sure this person is legitimate."

"What do you mean by that?"

"Well, I see they masked their ID to log in. But someone above me programmed it—somebody on the Guild. So, you can see my dilemma. Who am I supposed to trust? What if you, for some reason, are trying to crash the app? Or maybe you've behaved badly, and that's why your score went to zero? What if you're just trying to blame the app when she could've done something really wrong?"

"Well, which Guild member is it?" Gabe blurted, hoping that Warren would crack.

"I can't tell you that."

"Can you at least put some kind of lock on Lucy's record so my VC Rep, Ravi, is the only one who can give her or take away points?"

Warren contemplated this for a moment. "Well technically, it's the app giving out the points, he's just the user recording progress in the system. However, I can make it so he's the only one who can record progress on Lucy's case. That wouldn't break any rules."

Gabe was feeling encouraged, but still frustrated with Warren's resistance to give him the proof and info he needed for his meeting this afternoon. He pushed on to try to get Warren to give him the evidence.

"I get that you have more security clearance than me, but please try to understand. I have a lot riding on this. I'm not just asking to show you this because I'm nosy. This hacker has really messed with my future."

"Look, let's both stay in our own lanes. I'll handle technical glitches. You just help your Originator. She needs a lot of points."

Gabe's nostrils flared. He drew a deep breath before responding flatly. "Yeah, duh, I know. That's why I'm talking to you. The meeting is in a few hours, at three. Come on, man."

Warren paused briefly, looking at his screen and then back up at Gabe, scrutinizing him. Gabe stayed quiet, hoping that the silence would cause Warren to cave. He relented a hair and asked, "What if I met with Gunderthorpe?"

Gabe hesitated. "Well, I don't know. I used my family connections to get the meeting. He's expecting me." Gabe tried to calm himself from the frustration he was feeling. He needed to be in the meeting. This was *his* fight. But then he felt a pain in his stomach and sensed Lucy in distress. He relented and gave up on the idea of presenting the evidence himself. "You'll report back to me? Let me know what he says?"

"I may not be able to give you all the details if you don't have the security clearance. But yeah, I'll let you know what happens."

"Okay. Thank you." Still sensing Lucy's anguish, Gabe hurried out and hoped he wasn't too late to help her.

32

Planting New Roots

Lucy walked in for her orientation at the Safe Horizons shelter. The receptionist led her to a conference room with a table that sat eight people. She handed her an informational folder and was told to wait for the others. Left alone in the room, she opened the folder and pulled out a brochure labeled "Recognizing Signs of Emotional Abuse." As she scanned the signs, she felt her body tighten, realizing that so many of the traits described her relationship with Colt. She began putting mental check boxes next to each.

The brochure began with a heart-wrenching statement. *"Emotional abuse can be subtle, but it has lasting impacts on self-esteem, mental health, and overall well-being."* The words "lasting impacts" weighed heavily on Lucy as she read on. Isolation-check, Monitoring Communications-check, Constantly Checking Whereabouts-check, Excessive Jealousy-check, Belittling and Criticizing-check, Guilt Tripping-check, Abuser plays the role of victim-check, Mocking, Ridicule, Gaslighting, Taunting-check, check, check, check!

The list went on and on, with almost every single characteristic describing her relationship. She'd always said that Colt had never hit her. She realized now that he'd threatened her physically, even if he hadn't punched her in the face. The brochure described physical intimidation as breaking objects, and she thought back to her cracked phone screen and the time he threw his keys at her so hard that it hit a framed poster behind her and broke the glass.

"Are you okay?" A woman in a purple sweater set and slacks had entered the room without Lucy noticing. When she looked up, she felt tears running down her face.

She looked into the stranger's eyes and said, "Honestly, I don't know."

"I'm Pam. I'll be your instructor for this orientation. These sessions can often be very emotional for survivors."

Survivor. The word played on repeat in Lucy's head. "If I'm a survivor, am I still allowed to help?"

"Of course. In fact, having people who have been through something similar to what the person on the end of the line has experienced can aid us in getting someone the help they need."

Lucy wiped her eyes and, with a nervous giggle, said, "Okay. I guess I can help then."

Three other prospective volunteers joined the training and when it began, memories of her time with Colt flooded back.

During a role-playing exercise, Pam was pretending to be a caller, and another volunteer was practicing what they'd say. Pam said quietly but audibly, "I'm hiding in the closet." Lucy's mind rushed back to a fight she had with Colt.

She'd run back into their room, exhausted from trying to reason with him. She looked at the bed, but it felt too exposed, too vulnerable for some reason. Her eyes fixed on a small space between the bed and the wall in front of the nightstand. She moved her pillow to that space and covered herself with a blanket. The space was the only thing that helped to hold her up and prevent her from falling into the dark abyss.

"What the hell, Lucy? You're just going to lie on the floor?" Lucy kept her eyes shut. "You want me to feel sorry for you? Fucking cunt. You can stay there for all I care. I'm going out, and when I get back, maybe you'll be ready to apologize."

"Lucy? Lucy? Are you with us?"

Lucy awoke from her day-nightmare, becoming aware that she'd missed something. "Yes. What was the question?"

"It's your turn to role-play. Are you ready?"

Lucy hesitated. The four sets of eyes fixed on her. She found the words hard to find, but eventually, they came. "I don't think I am. I'm sorry. This is too much." She got up and walked out of the room toward the lobby. She sat on a couch in a semi-catatonic state. When she shook off the memories once again, she reached for her phone to call Gabe, but before she could, he was standing right there.

"Hey."

She looked into his kind eyes and smiled. "I thought that this is what I wanted, but it's too much. Too soon."

"I get it." He sat down on the couch, putting a hand on her shoulder. She leaned in on him, hugged him, and the floodgates broke again. Gabe's shirt was soaked by the time she caught her breath.

Lucy approached Pam, who had just left the conference room. Before Pam could say anything, Lucy looked up at her and said, "I think I need the help you give here. I thought I was ready to volunteer, but everything's just too fresh."

"How about you schedule to speak to one of our counselors before you leave?"

Lucy agreed, but she was eager to leave the flashback-inducing facility with Gabe.

As they walked through the parking lot, Gabe kindly shifted focus away from what had just happened and said, "I've found you a job. I think you'll have a lot of fun with it."

Lucy felt the hope in his words. They were a sweet elixir that seemed to permeate her raw nerves and relaxed her very soul. His calm eyes comforted her, and in his presence, she knew she was safe.

Within minutes of getting in the car with Gabe, Lucy had fallen asleep. Gabe knew she hadn't wanted to talk about her experience at the shelter, but he was glad that she was going to have support—especially if he wouldn't be allowed to contact her if he didn't get the points situation worked out.

He was sick of the damn points and was contemplating just packing up his art supplies and living a solitary life with Originators. He turned his focus back to Lucy when the GPS told him they'd arrived.

"We're here!" Gabe shook her gently awake.

Lucy opened her eyes and was taken back to the first time that Gabe had woken her gently when they'd arrived at the B&B. She looked to her left and right. All she saw were other cars. She had no energy for surprises so simply asked, "I forgot to ask, where is here?"

Gabe reached into the back seat and pulled out a small canvas. The scent of freshly dried paint wafted her way as he presented the painting to her. It looked like the garden Gabe had made in the studio, but more colorful and dense with plants. It seemed to be created in haste and had similar brush strokes to the painting of her chasing the sunset. She turned her head to the left and right, still disoriented in a sea of cars on top of the asphalt. With scrunched eyebrows, she looked back at Gabe. He was smiling brightly, as if she should know what was going on just by seeing the painting.

"I'm still a bit confused. Where are we?"

Gabe's face sunk and looked down at the painting as if searching for the answer there. "I'm sorry, I didn't use my words, thought the art could speak for me." He put the canvas back. Stepped out of the car and motioned for her to come with him. Lucy followed his lead and saw a small building in the distance next to four greenhouse structures. In front of the buildings were rows of potted plants with yellow tags and vibrant blue pots, adding a splash of color.

"This is a garden center. They need an assistant sales associate. You'll be helping with weeding, all sorts of caretaking of the plants, and recommending plants for customers. So you'll be able to learn more about flowers and plants. It's sort of like the vision you had of planting your own food and being surrounded by flowers, minus the chickens and butterflies, although I'm sure there might be a stray butterfly here and there."

Her mind went blank. She couldn't remember the names of any plants. Every time she tried to pull one up, the word would be just out of her grasp. How would she ever help a customer pick one out?

Gabe rattled on. "It pays pretty well, and it has benefits, so you may be able to stay at The Tower, but if you can't, you'll ... well let's not think about that. Just focus on interviewing well and then ... "

"Oh, I have to interview?" Her palms began to sweat instantly. "Gabe, I don't know. My nerves are pretty shot."

"Well, I'm sure it's just a conversation to test your knowledge and your passion."

"I'm tired. I don't think I'd be able to have a coherent conversation with anyone right now and I ... "

Gabe interrupted her nervous thoughts. "Here, let's do a little transdreamosis session just to get you prepped and feeling confident, alright? If you don't feel like it after that, I'll take you straight back to The Tower, promise."

She looked into Gabe's eyes and sensed his desperation. Reluctantly she murmured, "Okay."

Lucy closed her eyes and took Gabe's hands. Gabe spoke softly as he projected the image of the garden from the painting with a beautiful, colorful stone pathway. Butterflies were everywhere.

"Walk down the path. You see those flowers to your left? Those are Black-Eyed Susans. They bloom in the spring. This is the perfect time of year to plant them—after the last frost. Take your time and look around."

The soil was rich. Everything was blooming as if it were spring. She smiled when she saw all the funky yard art—from pink flamingos to metal sunflowers.

"What are those called next to the Black-Eyed Susans? Those purple ones that look like they're wearing a ballerina skirt, not quite a tutu, with the brown center."

"Those are Tennessee Coneflowers."

"Coneflowers," Lucy repeated softly. Her soul was lifting from all the beauty Gabe was placing around her. He played music overhead—"Hammer and Nail" by the Indigo Girls. The sweet harmonies relaxed her even more. She roamed around the garden, learning about many native plants. Lucy tried to hold them in her mind and memorize their names—American beautyberry, wild bergamot, azaleas, and rhododendron. There were flowering trees surrounding the garden.

"What's that tree with the purpley-pink flowers?"

"That's the Eastern redbud. They're really low maintenance. Now, they only live twenty to thirty years, but their inner bark can treat colds, sore throats, and skin infections."

Lucy went over and touched its bark. "You're a healing tree," she whispered into its branches. She stroked it like she was petting a cat and stood in silence for several minutes—taking it all in.

"I think you're ready," Gabe said gently.

Lucy opened her eyes and gave Gabe's hands a tight squeeze before releasing them. "Just ask for Claudia. She's expecting you."

With a deep breath, she walked toward the front of the garden center, smiling as she recognized the Tennessee Coneflowers on a poster hanging on the door. She walked up and waited behind two customers in the checkout, glancing around to see if anyone else working there.

It was probably a good sign that there weren't tons of employees milling about. Lucy hoped it meant they needed her. She was patient and after a few minutes she reached the front of the line.

"Hi, I'm looking for Claudia. I'm Lucy. She should be expecting me."

The clerk said nothing while he looked over her head, scanning the shop. His eyes soon fixed on a point and flashed recognition. He pointed toward the back of the store. "She's over in the perennials helping a customer."

Lucy turned behind her and saw a sign marked "Perennials," but there were two groups of people talking in that area. She turned back to the clerk. "I actually haven't met her before. I'm here for an interview."

"She's the one in the overalls," he said curtly, while motioning for the next customer in line to come forward.

"Oh … okay," she said a little timidly, trying to head toward the general area that his eyes had been fixed on. Nothing around her was blooming. She knew that a lot of the plants she'd just seen during her session with Gabe were perennials, but it was December. They wouldn't look the same. Her palms sweat yet again.

Lucy slowly approached a woman in overalls who had just picked up a couple of seed packets that had fallen to the ground. The woman placed them on a nearby display and started straightening others. Lucy took a deep breath before introducing herself.

"Hi, I'm Lucy. Are you … "

"I just hate it when these things get shuffled around and out of order. Don't you?" the woman interrupted.

Lucy swallowed hard, uncertain if this was part of the interview. She nodded yes and chipped in to straighten the display. Some seeds were out of place, but mostly, things seemed to be in order.

The woman picked up some Black-Eyed Susan seed packets while asking Lucy, "If someone buys these, when do they need to plant them so they'll bloom this spring?"

Lucy was relieved that the question was one she knew the answer to, but was a little flummoxed by this interview style. She ran with it anyway, telling her she'd need to plant them after the last frost for the best results. Lucy added with enthusiasm, "This is the perfect time to buy them."

"Well, it's settled then. I'll get them."

The woman walked off quickly toward the register and Lucy called out after her, "Wait ... are you Claudia?"

"No, dear. Thanks so much for the tip. It's usually so hard to get help around here."

Lucy closed her eyes and took a beat to reset. She took a deep breath in and before she could exhale, she heard a voice from behind her say, "Are you looking for me?"

Lucy turned around and saw another woman in overalls, but this one had a name tag that read Claudia. Her cheeks felt hot from embarrassment, but she managed a smile and replied, "I am."

"Are you Lucy?"

"Yes, I'm so sorry. The man at the counter said that you were back here, and that you were wearing overalls. I just assumed the woman I was speaking to was you because she was straightening up. I didn't think a customer would do that and ... "

"Calm down. No need to fuss. It's not your fault. Somebody should've taken you to me. Besides, I saw you with that customer just now. Looks like you made her pretty happy, which is what this job is all about."

Lucy breathed out a soft smile and followed Claudia through the store to a back office, where Claudia instructed Lucy to take a seat. Claudia went to sit too, but stopped short when over the in-store speaker someone said, "Manager to the front register."

She pointed up at the air. "Ahhh ... that's me. I swear he knows I'm the only manager here. He could've used my name. Gotta love the holiday shopping season. It's always something." She plastered on a smile and told Lucy to stay put, handing her an employee handbook to peruse on her way out.

Lucy flipped through the pages without looking at them too hard. The handbook contained your typical boilerplate stuff like non-discrimination statements, late policy, sick leave, but she froze when she reached the "Workplace Safety and Personal Security" section. Under the sub-sections that talked about topics she expected, like Medical Needs, Emergency Contacts, Workplace Incidents or hazards, there was one she must have breezed over in jobs she'd held in the past. She propped her elbow on her armrest and laid her head in hand as she read the section labeled "Restraining or Protective Orders" repeatedly.

"Your safety is our priority. If you have a restraining order or are aware of any personal circumstances that could affect your safety at work, please inform management so we can take appropriate measures to protect you and maintain a secure environment for all employees and customers."

It was non-threatening and kind, but the words made Lucy spin. Would she ever be able to escape Colt? Tears rolled down her face. She closed the book and wiped her eyes just as Claudia returned.

"Oh God. Are you okay? Something in the handbook upset you? Was it the drug test section?" She chuckled. "Don't worry about it. We don't test for weed. Hell, half the staff grows it." When Lucy didn't laugh, Claudia paused, her held tilted with sincere concern.

"Um ... it's not that. It's, well, I ... " Lucy closed her eyes, searching for the words. When she could find none, she looked up at Claudia, who was continuing to wait patiently. Just behind her, Lucy saw a picture on the wall. There were many pictures of flowers and plants, but the one just above Claudia's head was the Eastern redbud. Seeing the healing tree helped her regain her confidence. "I'm getting out of an abusive relationship. I have a restraining order and I wasn't planning to tell you, but then I saw it in the handbook and I just don't lie and … " As Lucy felt the tears fall she shook her head and got up to turn away, unsure if she should just leave. With her back to Claudia and in a broken voice, she said, "I don't want to put anyone else in danger or bother you with my problems."

Claudia came behind her and put her hand on her shoulder. "You, my dear, aren't a bother at all. We need the help, honestly, like I said, the holidays. I wasn't lying before. I saw you help that woman. This interview is more of a 'when can you start' conversation, not an interrogation. Gabe reached out on the alumni network, and I responded. Didn't he tell you that?"

"Well, no," Lucy said with a half laugh as she turned to look at Claudia. She drew strength from the redbud again and said, "Can I start now?"

"Yes, let's get the boring paperwork done, and I'll see you on the floor in half an hour to get you settled in." Though emotionally exhausted, Lucy pushed through, siphoning strength from Claudia and the beauty all around.

Later, from a distance, Gabe calmly looked on as Lucy was being given a tour—the peaceful moment made brief by a ping on his phone.

Warren: *I have an update.*

33

The Breaking Point

Gabe paced nervously as he waited for Warren. He hadn't said much over text. They just arranged to meet at his studio. He stopped and stood still as he saw a car come up the driveway. Warren stepped out with a solemn expression on his face. As soon as he was within three feet of him, Gabe blurted out from the porch, "How did it go?"

Warren said nothing and walked inside the building. When they were both behind the closed door, Warren paused and looked over his shoulder, leaning in and speaking softly. "He talked about how much effort they'd put behind the app and that it would look really bad if they shut it down temporarily to debug it, because there was already such pushback on it."

"Did he see the proof you found?"

"Yes. He said the savings from not having the Supporters probably wouldn't be seen for some years because of all the money, time, and energy that went into making the app. He didn't want to look bad because he'd pushed for the change so hard."

Gabe's face fell. He honestly thought that Vance would be sympathetic and want to put things right. He was the figurehead, after all.

"Didn't he care that there were Originators who were suffering, not because of their own decisions?" Gabe asked.

"Listen, I think he cared. I could see it pained him a little, but I don't think it was a massive enough problem for him to put his ego aside."

"What do you think?"

"Catch the Vision. Empower the People. Create Lasting Change." Warren smiled a little. He took a deep breath in as he opened his carrier bag and pulled out a thick folder full of paper. "I don't know if it's the right thing to do, but here. Here's your proof. You were right. Kai was manipulating the app. I also think someone on the inside, whether that's a developer or someone on the Guild, had to help him. This was a rush job. I haven't been able to look through all of this. I summed it up as best I could." He handed Gabe the report he'd written up for Vance.

Gabe looked at it, then looked back up at Warren with determination. "Thank you. Do you have any ideas about what we should do next?"

Warren shrugged, shook his head, and held up his hands. "I'm just the messenger. You can figure that out. Either help Lucy get the points that she needs in the next several days or bring this to light. I fixed the bug of someone messing with her points and did all I could to increase the security on her record so your VC Rep's the only one who can update it. I don't want to be involved anymore." He turned and walked out, saying nothing else.

"Wait ... " Gabe's words were useless. Warren was gone. His phone buzzed again, reminding him to check in with his VC Rep. Of course, it didn't fail to mention the fact that Lucy hadn't reached her point threshold. He threw the phone across the room as anger coursed through his veins. Immediately regretting it, he chased it down and picked it up. Luckily, it still worked, but the screen cracked. He froze for a moment and took a deep breath in and then attempted to exhale away his anger. He craved comfort and looked around his studio.

It was still in shambles, and he cleaned it as an act of meditation. He threw out the damaged art. Once he was done, he painted—not caring what was on the canvas—clearing his head and trying to figure out what was next for him. His phone buzzed yet again, and he decided to take Warren's advice. He could at least check in and see what he could do to get Lucy's score up.

He rang Ravi. "Hey there, Gabe. How can I help you?"

"I wanted to check in with you about Lucy's progress."

"Okay. You haven't checked in a while. Let's have a transmission session so I can record what's been going on in the system."

Gabe closed his eyes and projected Lucy's fear at Safe Horizons shelter, but also her strength and vulnerability in that moment. The realization that she needed help. He thought about how the vision he guided her to was adjacent to the one she had about the community garden. He imagined her smile that came with the excitement of her new job. After he was done, he said, "Ravi, do you think what I just showed you is enough to get Lucy's points up past 5,000?"

"I'm not really in charge of the points—the app determines that. I'm just the intermediary between you and the app. From what you showed me, I think she'll get there soon. Keep checking in."

"Okay. Thank you."

When he hung up, his phone began to ping and buzz. He was hoping it was the score, but it was the alarm he'd set to remind him that Lucy would be done with her shift at the garden center. Still carrying the proof with him, he headed to the car to pick her up. As he was driving, he caught a vision of Lucy crying in the office and hoped that he was only catching it because she'd let go of whatever happened, but sped up just in case.

Gabe saw Lucy laughing with Claudia when he walked in and relief swept over him. Lucy spotted him, waved goodbye to several of the employees and smiled as she said, "See you tomorrow."

As they walked to the car, Gabe asked, "So, how'd it go?"

"It was a little rocky at first, but Claudia helped me. I had to tell her about Colt and the restraining order. I need to bring a copy to have here."

"I'm sorry about what happened this morning. That had to be rough."

"It was. I don't think I'll ever fully escape him, but life is going to be a lot better, thanks to you. The rest of the day was great. I helped this woman plan her entire garden!"

"That's wonderful."

As they headed back to the B&B, Lucy's face lit up, sharing more details about her day. "I explained what perennials were several times. I had a blast just helping people, even just checking people out at the register. It felt so good. Part of it was that I wasn't worried about Colt showing up because of the restraining order, and I'm actually relieved now that I was required to share it."

"Sounds like it's going to be a successful path for you."

"Yes, a new start, thanks to you."

Gabe beamed and was sad all at once. As he pulled up to a stoplight, he looked over at her and said, "I'm going to miss this."

Lucy frowned sympathetically. "Well, it's not too late. How's the point situation?"

"Our developer, Warren, found Kai has been manipulating the point system."

"Oh my gosh, but why?"

"I don't know. Warren gave me this big file." Gabe pointed to it sitting in the center console. "I haven't had a chance to go through it all. That's the proof that Kai was manipulating the system."

"Oh wow. Let me look through it." Without asking Gabe's permission, Lucy grabbed the folder. She leafed through the pages and found something. "Did you see these text messages?"

"No, like I said, I haven't had a chance to really look through it."

"But they look like they're between Kai and someone else. What's a Supporter?"

"It's how they used to monitor the quests. There were people who ... wait, he talks about that?"

"Yes, people who what?"

"Kai comes from a family of people who were in the Supporter role. Supporters were kind of like how I'm supporting you and helping you with the memories and pointing you in the right direction. See, you and I are pair bonded and our feelings are so closely linked that it's important to have an impartial party to monitor progress."

"Like a teacher giving you a grade?"

"Sort of, more like a social worker does when they're monitoring somebody. Independently, they'd check in with the Originators. We framed it like a counseling session and they'd also check on them after the quest. Ultimately, though, they'd file an evaluation of the Vision Catcher with the Guild to report on how we did."

"Oh, okay. So where are those people now, if the app is there?"

"Well, some of them took other roles within our community and some had to take jobs in the Originator world to support themselves."

"So it's not a job anymore?"

"No, the Guild eliminated it. Some of them might be ... " Gabe paused for a moment, realizing he was breaking a rule. They could only reveal a little about the process, just enough to get the Originators to trust them. His fingers tapped on the steering wheel nervously. "I'm really not supposed to tell you all about this."

"Well, why not?"

Her question gave him pause, not because he felt he was crossing a line, but more because of her boldness. He looked at her and said, "Lucy, you're coming out of your shell. It's really wonderful to see you so engaged, but we should really focus on you."

"This is exciting stuff—I mean, the garden center is an adventure too, but who knows, maybe if I help you figure out how to solve the app crisis, I can get you points."

Gabe didn't want to discourage Lucy's enthusiasm, but the setbacks earlier in the day had reminded him how fresh her trauma really was. As they pulled into the B&B, he looked over at her expectant face and his heart started beating faster as her passion transferred over to him.

"I suppose you might be right about the points, but ... "

"No buts, plllleeaase." Her hands clasped together as she leaned in, pleading with him. "We can focus on me tomorrow."

Gabe relented and gave into her desire to help. "Fine." He turned off the engine and stepped out of the car.

Lucy followed him with the enthusiasm of a puppy dog.

"Great! What's next?"

He started to open the door and then thought better of it. Aunt Rae could be around and he didn't want her to hear them talk about this stuff. "Maybe we should talk about it in my studio."

"Good idea."

They hurried to the studio. When they entered, it was still a devastating sight, but the dent Gabe had made in his earlier cleaning frenzy had helped. Lucy repeated her question once they'd settled into some chairs.

"What's next?"

"I have no clue. The head of the committee didn't take the proof because he said they spent too much money developing the app. Plus, he doesn't want to look bad if it turns out the app is malfunctioning."

Lucy paused, trying to think of a solution. "But it's not fair. Not just to me, but to Gary. Or that guy Waylon. At least Gary has a new vision for his life."

"Yes, he does, thanks to you," Gabe said, smiling softly at her and realizing that he hadn't transmitted that to Ravi.

"Well, I suppose we don't necessarily need Vision Catchers to turn our lives around. People do it, don't they? But what you contribute has value. So many people lose their way and forget about their creative endeavors or desires."

"Yes, but I feel like we're at an impasse. What am I supposed to do? They didn't cover this in Vision Catching school."

"No." Lucy exaggerated her reaction, leaning back and clutching her chest. "They didn't tell you how to take down an unfair system. I'm shocked."

Gabe shook his head. "Okay, I get your point."

Lucy clasped her hands together and held two pointer fingers up to her mouth, deep in thought. "But they told you how Vision Catchers aided Originators in civil rights movements. What are the key aspects of those?"

"This isn't like that. Vision Catchers aided Originators who were being wronged."

"Well, okay. It's not as serious as that. What I mean is that I'm being wronged, and you are, too. This isn't right. From what you told me, Vision Catchers are supposed to help people meet their potential. The system assigned you to help me, but the system is letting you down. Who's assigned to you? Who's supposed to help you?"

"Well, my VC Rep and the … " Gabe's voice trailed off. He couldn't answer her question fully. He trusted in the system; he hadn't expected to be scored. "Even if the app isn't the best solution. What can I do? I'm just one person and I don't even have full status yet. Now, I need the points for that."

"You're right. You can't do it on your own. There are plenty of VCs that are leading people on quests. I can't be the only victim of Kai's manipulation or someone else's. Look at these texts. Kai's not doing this on his own." Lucy held out one sheet from the file and pointed to a conversation. He took the paper from her and read.

Conversation A123546

Kai: *I did what you wanted. When's my mother going to get her job back as Chief Supporter?*

Anonymous: *In time, in time. You did well, but we need more proof. Enough to convince the new tech advisor to the Guild. Supporters and the old way will never come back into the fold until we crush the tech.*

Kai: *What more proof do you need? You saw what happened at orientation. My Originator was suffering and I'm near the top of the leaderboard. I planted the glasses so he could get on campus. It all worked out. Isn't that proof enough? Now it's your turn to convince the Guild ... show the discrepancy.*

Anonymous: *No, we need you to do it again. And don't get caught. Or your mother and the rest of your family won't ever be Supporters again.*

Kai: *Okay. I don't want this app any more than you do, but my family is struggling to make ends meet. We're running out of time.*

Anonymous: *Then stop wasting mine. I don't care what you have to do. Undermine some other Originators if you have to. Harm a few to save the many.*

Conversation A123547

Anonymous: *What's this I hear about you tanking another Originator's score? When I said do whatever needs to be done, this is not what I meant.*

Kai: *They needed to learn a lesson. The Originator convinced mine to leave the quest. It wasn't the plan, but it turned out to be easier. We don't have time to do it your way.*

Anonymous: *What did you do? You're playing with fire if you did anything to that woman's visions.*

Kai: *Look, the app is as good as gone. I overheard Gabe, the VC of the Originator I damaged, talking to his aunt. He's going to meet with Vance.*

This will all be over soon.
Anonymous: *You're acting like an idiot. The VC police have an entire task force for the black market—that's what you did, I'm assuming. To help your family, how did you put it "make ends meet." They won't just come after you now. They'll come after your whole family. I was going to protect you, but now ...*
Kai: *I just tanked her score. I didn't sell any visions to the black market. I don't know what you're talking about.*

Gabe put down the paper and stared straight ahead, stunned.

Lucy leaned toward him and snapped her fingers to get his attention. "You've got to do something, Gabe. This isn't just about you or me anymore. What happens if this Anonymous guy keeps pulling the strings? What happens when the next person makes someone so miserable and they snap?" She snapped her fingers again. "What if they hurt themselves or someone else? Not to mention all the VC lives they could ruin."

"I don't even know where to start, Lucy. This goes so high up."

"Did you know where to start when you wanted to rescue me from Colt?" Gabe just stared at Lucy. She pushed on. "You did something, though."

"That's different. I was just doing my job. You were just one person I knew, at least somewhere within me, that I could help, because you were ready to help yourself."

"So you're just going to sit back while somebody in the system hurts people. Didn't you take some kind of oath ... like a doctor, to do no harm?"

"In a way, I guess..." He thought back to the word and images he'd projected to Aunt Rae earlier in the day. A little unsteady, he said, "Catch the Vision. Empower the People. Create Lasting Change."

Lucy paused. "That's pretty powerful stuff. I'm not concerned about the points, but you can't hold on to this evidence. What's going to happen to others if this keeps going?"

Gabe opened his mouth to answer, but nothing came out.

"You have to speak up. If not for yourself or for me, then for all the other Vision Catchers and Originators. How are they going to create lasting change if this app continues to malfunction because of bad actors? This Vance guy can't listen to just one person. Of course, he can't bend to every person who brings him a problem." She paused again, looking at Gabe with hope and a touch of idealism. "What if it wasn't one person—one voice? What if it was many?"

Gabe thought back to all the VCs at orientation and The Vibanator. Lucy was resolute, and he didn't want to let her down. He stared at her in awe. She'd changed so much in such a short amount of time. "You really have a fire under you."

"Yes, I do. Where's yours?"

He smiled as he felt her steely determination and energy pass through him. "Okay. Let's gather the troops."

34

The Uprising

Quest Day Thirty-Four

Gabe enlisted Rosa, the gossip he'd met at The Vibanator, to help him gather the other Vision Catchers. The word of the protest spread like wildfire. When they heard of Gabe's troubles with the app and the manipulation of Lucy's score, a deeper dissatisfaction with the system rose to the surface.

Even though most hadn't been affected by Kai, they all had different reasons for being there. The old-timers wanted it to go back to the way it had been. Many just wanted a new system that was more in line with their mission and would create greater change.

There were ladies at a table making signs. There were people gathering in small groups, talking amongst themselves. The Vibanator was probably at capacity. Hundreds of Vision Catchers and Supporters had shown up to take their message to the Vision Catchers Guild.

"Having a leaderboard and pitting us against one another isn't in line with the values we were taught," he overheard one person say. Gabe was so caught up in his own score, he hadn't even thought about that.

People came with stories of how it used to work and how it used to be and their favorite quests, and it was so great to hear from the old-timers. They were so happy and appreciative that Gabe was starting this movement. Lucy had wanted to come, but Gabe told her that Originators weren't permitted in the part of the realm they were entering.

The plan was to march the half of a mile or so toward the head-quarters and stage a sit-in. They marched, with Gabe at the front with a bullhorn chanting, "Catch the Vision. Empower the People. Make Lasting Change." Some people brought drums to accompany the chants. They were channeling Originators' protests in America during the sixties.

When they reached the building, Gabe paused, peering up at the steps that led up to the doorway. The crowd filed in. Someone called out, "Speech! Gabe, Speech." Others joined in "SPEECH, SPEECH, SPEECH." Gabe hadn't planned for this. He was nervous and feeling like a hypocrite. He was aiming to do the same thing as Kai—to shut down the app, at least for now. Kai was going to get his way, and Gabe hated that. He had to put Kai and the mess that he left aside and focus on the task at hand, which apparently, now, involved him giving a speech.

He went through his Rolodex of inspirational and literary quotes trying to find one to start that would fit this moment. He climbed the stairs and turned to the crowd with eyes closed, put the bullhorn to his mouth and spoke.

"I won't lie. I'm scared. Scared of what happens to me personally if this doesn't work, but more of what happens to our culture if we don't stand for what's right. Our task today is to speak up and ultimately, not go back to the way things were, but find a path forward that moves us with the power of our directive. The power of catching visions, empowering people, and creating lasting change. That's what we were created to do." The crowd cheered.

"This may seem impossible, but we haven't had a voice. We've followed ancient rules and then we followed these new ones with the app. We had no real say in how we accomplish our directive. No longer will these discussions be held in silos. By coming together today, we're showing a unified voice. We're saying that the system needs to change for our powers to do the good they were meant to in the world. It's only an impossibility if we believe it is."

Gabe looked out at the many people in the crowd as they cheered again. His adrenaline was pumping and time seemed to slow down as he waited for the crowd to hush. He was at a loss for what to say next, unsure if he could go on. He searched the crowd for familiar faces and his eyes locked with Cecilia's. A familiar energy surged within him. It was like the pride he'd felt from Lucy after he committed to this movement. Cecilia encouraged him. She must have sensed he wasn't sure what to say, so she silently sent him messages, "Tell them your story, why you're here."

The crowd grew silent and waited for Gabe to continue. He breathed deeply and said, "My Originator Lucy has shown me examples over the last several weeks of putting her fears aside and being brave. It's her courage to do what she believed was impossible that's fueling me to believe we can change a broken system. Technology isn't the enemy, but when it judges us and pits us against each other, ranking us instead of aiding us to achieve the mission of our community, it cannot stand." The crowd cheered again for a few minutes before quieting again.

"Even without hacks and malfunctions, the system is broken. Every journey toward achieving a goal, a dream, finding a sense of purpose, being on a path of fulfillment will have both its setbacks and victories. We shouldn't judge Originators on these and score them on each step. We must evaluate progress from where they began to how far they've come. The goal isn't to fix their lives in forty days, but to get them on a path that will not only change their world, but spread their light to others to create lasting change. The Guild must take down the app. We demand a new system now!"

The crowd chanted, "Take it down, no more app."

Gabe had only accounted for a couple dozen people in his plan and thought that they could stage the sit-in in the building's lobby, but now, looking out on the massive crowd, he needed to make a new plan. He asked everyone to take a seat.

Once everyone settled, he put the bullhorn up. "You ready to tell Vance Gunderthorpe what we really think?"

In unison, the crowd screamed, "YEAH!"

"We've been chanting, but the universe has given us a gift. A gift to capture and preserve ideas, but also pass them between one another in a way that no one else can. So together, let's focus all of our mental energy on Vance. With our mind's voice as one, let's let him know what we want—Catch the Vision. Empower the People. Create Lasting Change."

Silently, the crowd focused the idea on Vance. It was like nothing Gabe had ever experienced. Had anyone ever attempted this in Vision Catcher history? The power of the focused chorus swirled around him, and he could sense the heft and weight of their unified power.

Vance must have felt it too because within minutes he came out of the building and shouted to the crowd, "Enough!"

Gabe opened his eyes and looked at Vance, who was pulling at his hair, nostrils flared—anguish on his face from the power of the collective thoughts of the protesters. The weight of it was literally pushing him to the ground as he held himself up on a nearby handrail. He shouted, "I am not the enemy! Will you please stop?!" He covered his ears, grimacing in the silence. He looked at Gabe in desperation and said, "Please, make them stop. It's too much."

Gabe looked at him and felt his pain. He empathized but knew he must stay on mission. "I'll call them off if you hold a hearing about our concerns and the app. You must take it seriously because we'll be back if you don't. We're prepared to screw up the entire system and come every day until you do."

"Yes, yes, anything."

Gabe picked up the bullhorn and said, "Open your eyes and stop your transmissions. He's agreed for us to be heard in front of the Guild."

Slowly, everyone opened their eyes and looked up toward Gabe expectantly. Gabe turned to Vance. He was rubbing his temples, but no longer looked in agony. From the crowd, they heard someone shout, "When?"

Vance, through labored breath, like he'd just run a marathon, said, "Meet here, in Guild chambers, tomorrow morning at nine and we will hear your case. The app will continue for now and the point system is still in place until then. Now make these people leave."

Gabe looked to the sea of protesters and then back to Vance, but he was already in the building.

Gabe was able to get the crowd to disperse eventually, though he thought it reminded him of receiving lines at funerals he'd attended. Everyone was waiting for their turn to speak to him. Most people shared their concerns; he tried to commit these to memory. He tried to forget the few naysayers who just wanted to complain.

Theo was there. Gabe hadn't seen him since the game night. He told Gabe that he'd failed again with Gerald's quest. He was waiting to be assigned a different role in the community. The app was supposed to send him a message in the next few days.

"Gerald was a real jerk. Part of me hated working with him. He made progress. I could see the Infrassin leaving him and being replaced with Feranchin. By the end, he was less greedy. He was just still trying to find his voice. I think if I'd had a Supporter reviewing our work together, I would've passed."

"I'm so sorry Theo. Listen, I don't know if this will work, but maybe if it does, you won't be reassigned."

Theo shrugged. "Yeah. We'll see. It sounded like he heard you."

One old-timer nearby chimed in, "Don't believe him when he says he'll hear you out. I think you did our cause a disservice by believing him."

Gabe would've been fine with engaging in a spirited debate with him about how the key was persistence, but one of the other protesters did it for him—Gabe couldn't get a word in edgewise. As he closed his eyes to take in the gravity of what had just happened and rest briefly, he felt arms wrap around him. It was Aunt Rae.

She kissed him on the cheek and said, "I'm so proud of you. I've always known you were destined for great things." She rubbed his face, grabbing his chin in an affectionate mothering manner. "You're glowing with the power of Feranchin. I can see it."

Gabe smiled and embraced Aunt Rae again. "Thank you." As he peered over her shoulder, he saw someone else approach. Gabe's contentment turned to anger in a flash.

Rae let go, turned around and said gently, "I'll let y'all talk. Remember, everyone missteps, hear him out."

When Kai reached the bottom of the steps, Gabe held the words he wanted to say inside him and instead asked, "What are you doing here?"

Kai hesitated. He looked up at Gabe with what seemed like remorse. He swallowed hard. "Can we talk," Kai looked around at the remaining crowd, "privately?"

Gabe thought about Aunt Rae's urging for him to give Kai a chance. He thought back to the story of her struggle to earn back the trust of the Vision Catchers and reluctantly agreed to step away from the remaining protesters, but not far. Kai was a loose cannon. If he attacked Gabe, he wanted everyone to see.

Gabe glared at Kai in silence for a few moments and then curtly said,

"Well, what … what did you want to talk about?"

"Gabe, I'm sorry. I was trying to ultimately do what you were trying to accomplish here today by myself. I wanted the Guild to see that the app wasn't a viable way to judge Vision Catchers. You know that my family had different roles in the old system—now they're struggling. The system itself needs to change. We need to get back to our roots."

"You didn't have to violate my studio. I mean, killing the chicks and butterflies … you're a psychopath."

"Hey now … I didn't do that. I just messed with her score."

"Yeah right. Who else would do that?"

"Um … the black market mafia or whoever. I mean, you know just as well as I, they've been trying to catch those guys for years. Besides, isn't Lucy doing great? This proves the point everyone here is trying to make. Her points suck, but she's more than fine. I did it the opposite way with my Originators … I made their lives miserable, but their points were through the roof."

"Yeah, serving you more than them. If your little takedown of the app didn't work, you'd get to the top of the leaderboard. Either way, you'd be set." Gabe looked up at the sky and shook his head. The crowd had amplified a fight for justice that coursed through his veins. "You're going down and I've got the proof to put you away for a long time."

Kai looked down at his shoes, turned his head slightly, then shifted his eyes back at Gabe. "I took that risk when I started this. I'm prepared to serve the time or have my powers weakened."

"I still don't believe you that you didn't destroy my studio. I hope they put you and whoever your accomplice was away for a really long time."

"How do you know about … " Kai's voice trailed off, and the blood drained from his face. The revelation that someone had been working with him clearly hit a nerve and he fell silent.

Gabe smoothed out the tone of his voice as if he was trying not to spook a wounded animal. He looked as sincerely as he could at Kai and said, "You want to make amends to me? Show up to the hearing tomorrow. Tell them how vulnerable the app was to hack."

Kai looked back and said with determination, "I will. I want to speak my piece too. I promise."

Gabe relented to this pledge with a nod. He wanted to make sure they'd detain Kai. He made the conscious choice to just believe him at his word. When Gabe turned back to the crowd, there were still a few stragglers, but most had dispersed.

Gabe walked away, still running Kai's apology over in his mind. As he was approaching the B&B, he saw Lucy standing outside the door to greet him. She beamed with excited anticipation, clearly wanting to hear about the events of the day. Exhausted, he took a deep breath in to muster the strength to relay the story. He hoped that his actions had been enough to have the Guild deem her quest as successful and preserve their friendship.

35

The Hearing

Quest Day Thirty-Five

Gabe had changed four times. He wasn't sure what to wear to a Guild meeting. The first time he changed was just because he'd sweat through his shirt. The second two times, he was undecided on what would impress the Guild. He finally chose a mix of comfort and style–a sensible gray button-up shirt with black slacks and nice shoes, but ditching the jacket and tie.

Drawing in a deep breath and closing his eyes, he whispered the mantra that had pulled him through the day before–"Catch the Vision. Empower the People. Create Lasting Change." He wiped his brow with a handkerchief and carried on. The folder Warren had given him was in a safe. After retrieving it, he placed it in his laptop bag and forced himself to head to breakfast. Every footstep felt weighed down by the gravity of the day's procedures. His pace quickened when he smelled coffee. He needed more than nerves and adrenaline to carry him through.

He'd stayed up with Hannah into the early morning reviewing evidence–she'd promised to come and testify. When he'd finally made it to bed, he'd tossed and turned, running through the worst scenarios in his head. What if Vance had just brought him there under false pretenses and they were going to charge him for "inciting a riot"? On the flip side, he imagined them giving him a medal for his courage, Lucy all her points back, and locking up Kai for life.

The thoughts were still swirling that morning, but came to an immediate halt when he reached the threshold of the dining room. To his surprise, Aunt Rae had made a feast and somehow had convinced people to join them at seven-thirty in the morning. A large sign hung across the wall behind the head of the table that read, "Good Luck Gabe." Seated at the table were a few Originators on quests, along with Lucy, Gary, Cecilia, Hannah, and six other Vision Catchers that were Aunt Rae's friends. These weren't just any friends, they were elders that sat on committees and a few that had been on the Guild at one point.

"I can't believe you all came up here? Just for me?"

"It's not every day that someone stands up for our cause in front of the folks in charge," Aunt Rae replied, beaming at him.

He looked at Gary. "You're not on a quest, how are you even ... "

"I invited him," Aunt Rae said, holding up the spectacles that Waylon had used to get into orientation. "With these, he'll even be able to testify at the hearing."

Lucy came up to Gabe and grabbed his arm, pulling him to the head of the table. With enthusiasm and excitement, she ordered him around. "Sit down, sit down. We're hungry! This is a big day and all of us have been waiting and the aroma is so intoxicating its making our stomachs rumble." She looked back at the motley crew. "Actually, I don't know about some of them, but I was about to start without you."

Gabe plopped down in his seat and Lucy immediately spooned a big helping of eggs onto her plate. As they ate, the elders gave him advice for his big day. Some of it he knew, but he listened respectfully for any new nuggets of info. There were eight seats on the Guild, the chair and one representative from each of the seven continents. When it was first formed centuries ago, the community selected members based on merit. At a global meeting of Vision Catchers, they nominated individuals who had led exceptional Originators, crushed tyranny, or who embodied the directive to create lasting change. Since then, when someone on the Guild wanted to leave, they just selected their successor, looking at those merits. This subjective approach inevitably caused some friction and accusations of unfairness among many in the community.

"Now, your most sympathetic member is probably Simone Tallis. Jovial people with a fun-loving spirit have always held her seat. Your Aunt Rae handpicked her when she left the Guild," advised one elder.

"Seth McGuvers—he's been there the longest. I know he was vocal about not wanting the point system, but they outvoted him. I honestly never liked the guy, a little too cocky for my taste ... but he'll be on your side," chimed in another.

"I know him." Gabe said. "He was one of my teachers at school. I doubt he'd remember me."

One elder said, "I'm sure he will. It will be good for you to see another familiar face."

The elders had buoyed his spirits, but he also realized he wouldn't be able to name all the current Guild members if someone quizzed him. As Lucy was retelling her skateboarding experience to some of those seated at the table, he pulled out the app reluctantly to read more about each member. He avoided the point total and just went straight to the members section and filtered by role="Guild Member." One by one he clicked on their profile, read their bio, and studied each face, committing them to memory. He chomped on a sausage biscuit with one hand and scrolled with the other. The Guild's reach was global. He looked at each name and photo with growing unease.

Aunt Rae stepped in behind him, gently touched his shoulder, and gave him insights as he read. "You already know the Chair—Gunderthorpe. He's guided mostly prominent Originators or so he says. If you ask me, he's a little arrogant, but a lot of people in our community think he's the strongest leader the Guild's had."

Gabe looked up from his phone at her and smiled softly.

She had something to say about everybody. He didn't have time to read their bios with her interjections. This mothering behavior on most days would annoy him, but today it was a comfort.

Simone Tallis: North America.

"Like they said before, I selected her to fill my seat. She's got a real knack for revitalizing dying visions, especially in bustling cities."

Seth McGuvers: Europe.

"He's a little intense, but he's often credited with unraveling the intricacies of layered visions. And as the others said, did not want this app or points."

Amara Okoro: Africa.

"She's renowned for nurturing Originators who have had visions ripped from them by hardship."

Tenzin Dawa: Asia.

"Oh, you'll love him. He's serene, but always coming up with creative solutions."

Pilar Escobedo: South America.

"He's got a reputation for embracing unorthodox methods and taking bold risks."

Lars Thorsen: Antarctica.

"He wears a lot of hats. Still actively working to guide Originators, while also being the youngest Guild member. He's one of a small group of VCs guiding Originators in Antarctica."

Moana Te Ariki: Oceania.

"She's deeply connected to the ancestral roots of her people and focused on preserving cultural legacies while guiding Originators toward their dreams.”

Aunt Rae sensed Gabe was still nervous. She offered to lead him through a transdreamosis session to calm him and walk him through what to expect. They went to a quiet space while the group cleaned up the dishes. Gabe took in his aunt's warm presence and held her hands.

“You did so well yesterday, speaking from the heart. I'm going to give you a basic feel of the setup and order of it all, but we'll stop there. For this hearing, you'll be going to the Guild's main hall. Let's start just outside the hall.”

Aunt Rae projected a hallway lined with regular doors and at the very end of the hall was an arched door. Gabe noticed the beautiful carving in the door with swirling lines. The lines coalesced within a silhouette of a human's profile. Within the face there were many spirals and outside were representations of ideas swirling around, waiting to be caught. Gabe touched the door lightly, feeling its smooth edges, admiring the artist's work. He was so intrigued by it he startled a little when he heard Aunt Rae's voice again.

“Open the door.” Gabe pulled on the door handle and hesitated to walk into the room. He was expecting it to be empty, but Aunt Rae was projecting many people into the gallery. “Go ahead, walk in. I'm just trying to prepare you for what to expect.”

He walked in and recognized some observers from the protest. Official looking chairs and tables had been placed in a rounded horseshoe shape.

Aunt Rae's voice chimed in again. “The hall is set up as an emergency panel, which means they'll most likely conduct the meeting in a round to facilitate dialogue. They do this to maintain the idea that while the Guild helps to dictate the structure of our world with an established hierarchy, everyone's voice is welcome.”

The Guild members hadn't entered yet, but as he approached, he saw some of the empty seats had plaques on the tables with Guild members' names etched into each one. He ran his finger over Vance Gunderthorpe's name. Instead of feeling the grooves of the letters, his movement wiped away Vance's name to reveal his own. He smirked, thinking he understood Aunt Rae's point.

"Are you trying to tell me we're all on equal footing?"

"Something like that."

A door in the back of the room opened, and the Guild filed in, each taking their assigned seats. Aunt Rae said softly, "Now go sit in the front. Pick a seat directly across from Simone. If ever you feel lost, look into her eyes. And if you can't catch her gaze, you know Seth McGuvers. Plus, remember what the others said—he was against the points. Try to use your powers to lock in with him too."

Rae's words comforted him.

"This hearing is called to order. We will discuss the VC app specifically. We will review the incident that led to this meeting and then take statements, starting with Gabe Allard."

Aunt Rae let go of Gabe's hands. "Okay. I think that's enough. I'm not sure exactly what they'll say, but I imagine this will be the basic format based on my experience."

"Alright. Thank you, that helped." It was a half-truth. He would've liked a practice run-through of the whole thing, but he knew she couldn't tell the future any more than he could.

Lucy tapped Gabe on the shoulder. "I'm headed off to work, but I want to hear what happens."

"I promise, I have my alarm set to pick you up. Hopefully, we'll know something by then." She gave Gabe a quick hug goodbye and wished him luck again. Over the last few weeks, he'd habitually checked the points when Lucy left for the day. Muscle memory kicked in and he grabbed for his phone, but he stopped himself just short of checking the points. They didn't represent Lucy's true progress or his own. Their journey together had been a success, but if he wanted to help others, he knew he'd have to prove that to the Guild.

Aunt Rae and Cecilia escorted him to the hearing. Cecilia even held his hand as they headed toward the Guild headquarters. A group of Vision Catchers who attended the protest stood outside the building holding signs with the VC motto and "Take it down, no more app." They'd returned to cheer Gabe on.

As Gabe, Cecilia, and Rae approached the steps of the building, he drew strength from the memories of his speech—each step lighter than the next as he soaked in the collective power. By the time he reached the hallway with the arched door he'd seen in his transdreamosis session, his pace had quickened. He was ready and determined to make a difference.

They were chanting, "Catch the Vision. Empower the People. Create Lasting Change." The rhythm of their words pounded out in a staccato, mirroring Gabe's heartbeat.

People were sending him visions of people giving powerful orations in history, but the one that surprised him was one someone sent of his speech from the day before. The VC was able to project it from their view. It was like Gabe was watching a movie of himself. "Every journey toward achieving a goal, a dream, finding a sense of purpose, being on a path of fulfillment will have both its setbacks and victories."

When Gabe paused, Cecilia whispered in his ear, "Are you okay?"

"Yes. More than okay. Let's go." He locked arms with both his aunt and Cecilia as he marched up the steps.

The chanting became a low mumble as they entered the building, but the support permeated the walls, and Gabe's energy only strengthened. He was determined to make things right, not just for Lucy or for himself, but for the ideals their society had been formed around. No point system could measure growth, but as empaths, they could see Originators take steps forward toward a path that lit them up. They could also see them retreat into the darkness and despair. If he hadn't been thinking about the points so much, he may not have made missteps on his own journey, like making Lucy stay in a songwriting class she clearly hated. Before and after the protests, he heard from other first-time Vision Catchers who had felt less sure of themselves because of the points. He was doing this for them too, and he was ready.

When he reached the door, it was heavier than he'd imagined—having to prop it open with his whole body to let Cecilia and Rae through. Gabe got goosebumps when he stepped into the room. Partly from how cold they were keeping the room, but also from the powerful art and symbols that adorned the walls. There were iconic reproductions of prominent artists he'd always admired, like Monet and Picasso, alongside banners of the motto that had become an anthem driving his soul forward. Above Vance Gunderthorpe's seat, the VCG logo was encased in gold.

Just like in the images Aunt Rae had projected to him, there were already people in the gallery. Despite anticipating this, his hands started to sweat because everything was more real. Also, he didn't have a moment to catch his breath because the Guild had already taken their seats. Aunt Rae squeezed his arm and gave him a side hug, whispering in his ear, "It's going to be okay."

The room spun, and his breath quickened. Cecilia gave him a quick peck on the cheek before they parted ways, making his legs even more wobbly. A clerk directed him to his seat, which gave him a reprieve, but not for long. He barely had time to whisper to himself, "Catch the Vision. Empower the People. Create Lasting Change," before Vance Gunderthorpe called the meeting to order. His words echoed the ones that Aunt Rae felt she could predict.

"This hearing is called to order. We are here because of an incident yesterday led by Gabe Allard. He has asked for an audience with the Guild and we've agreed to hear his concerns. After he speaks, we will have a public comment period and members of the Guild can make their opinions known as well." He paused, glaring at Gabe. "I for one will express right now that gathering and torturing me with mind overload will lead this community into chaos and anarchy. While I don't approve of his methods, I have heard enough similar concerns about the app not meeting our mission that I agreed to hear you out. We will look at ways to prevent this kind of thing in the future. Mr. Allard, you have called us here. We are listening." Gunderthorpe crossed his arms and leaned back in his chair, ripe with anticipation and skepticism.

Gabe swallowed and looked toward Simone Tallis for comfort. She smiled and nodded, silently saying to him, "You're going to do fine." He took a deep breath in and pulled the folder of evidence from his bag.

"Thank you, Mr. Gunderthorpe, and thank you to all the esteemed members of The Guild who have gathered here on such short notice. I want to first acknowledge Mr. Gunderthorpe's statement about the methods I used to get this hearing. I recognize they were unconventional, but as I'm on a quest with a time limit where the point system is going haywire, this matter was time-sensitive." He took a deep breath and then continued looking down at his notes and statement he'd pre-written for security.

"But it wasn't just about me. I encountered an Originator, Gary, whose points were high but who had fallen mentally into a deep, dark place. His Vision Catcher, Kai Mori, was being given accolades for his efforts. It didn't make sense that Kai was being praised while Gary was suffering, all because of an arbitrary points system. This may be my first quest, but I've learned from the best that our ultimate directive is to create lasting change. If I'd let the fact that my Originator's points fell without reason and done nothing ... " Gabe paused and choked back tears. "If she didn't reach the point threshold within the forty days, I'd lose my pair-bond with her. She'd lose me as an Originator and be assigned to someone else because of my so-called failure."

Tears broke through and Gabe's voice began to crack as he continued. "I wouldn't get to talk to her again, not even through the alumni network, and I would have to start my first quest all over again. If a Supporter had been with us throughout Lucy's journey or Gary's, they would've been able to document her growth and his despair. Technology can serve us and help us grow, but the point system only hinders Vision Catchers and makes them question every move."

Someone in the audience shouted, "Here, here!" A low mumble of people talking began and Gunderthorpe banged his gavel. Once everyone was quiet, Gabe went on with passion, embracing the confidence of the crowd.

"I'm not saying to take down the app entirely. I've benefited from the words of wisdom from other Vision Catchers in the learning area of the app. I think it's great that the visions I capture are summarized and backed up by a database. Perhaps this can help the police finally take down the black market. But there's no technology that can catch visions yet. Our powers given to us by the Universe are a treasure. We need to take the time to work together as a community and build stronger lasting change. I have evidence that proves that Kai Mori tampered with my Originator's record in the system as well as his Originator's."

Gabe pulled out the document with the text conversation between Kai and Anonymous. "One person encrypted their message, but I had someone in the IT Department who wishes to be anonymous decrypt it for me. This shows that Kai intentionally manipulated the app, which resulted in his own personal gain."

Gasps filled the air followed in quick succession by chants of "Take it down, no more app."

Vance hammered his gavel and echoing his plea from the steps the day before shouted at the top of his lungs, "ENOUGH!" He followed the statement with, "I will have you removed." Low conversations rumbled for a few moments. The crowd quickly conceded and fell quiet.

The Guild member from Asia, Tenzin Dawa, said, "We've invested a lot into this point system that you're claiming is malfunctioning. I have no doubt that there are bugs, but they sound like one-off cases. I propose we re-intake any Originator's journey if their Vision Catcher feels the points are wrong and have these reviewed by the VC Rep to confirm the overall score. Should we find foul play, we will bring the perpetrators to justice."

Simone Tallis piped up. "This sounds like a Band-Aid solution. Gabe has brought up more than just the malfunctions. If the VCs are acting differently and no longer tailoring their quests to the Originators' needs, but catering their decisions to the points, the entire system needs to be reevaluated."

"Here, here," Seth McGuvers chimed in. "I've been telling you all for years that this automation is the wrong path." He turned to Gabe. "You're brave to have brought this forward. Thank you."

Gabe was temporarily thrilled when he heard Dawa's solution. He'd be able to get Lucy's score up and perhaps help the Originators Kai damaged. Kai would finally pay for his crimes. It was hard to focus on the bigger picture of the system, but Simone and Seth's comments made him remember the greater cause.

People from the gallery had locked into Gabe's consciousness. In unison they said, "Catch the Vision. Empower the People. Create Lasting Change." They gave him the courage he needed to press on.

"They're right. Band-Aid solutions won't help. The Guild must address the bigger issue of the broken scoring system."

Gunderthorpe replied, "Is it broken or is this just a one-off? I still contend ... "

Gabe cut him off. "There are others here who have come here today to give testimony to how the points system affected their actions. Many who have been on hundreds of quests. There's no doubt in my mind this kind of pressure will only lead to the growth of the black market. I'm sure some Vision Catchers have purchased visions for their Originators just to gain more points—or at the very least been tempted to. I move we open it up to the floor and I'll leave you with this evidence," Gabe said as he held up the folder.

Vance interjected, "You can not make a motion. You've not earned that privilege, but I move to accept Gabe's evidence and open the floor for comment."

The crowd cheered.

Person after person came up and told stories of how the points made them feel. Gabe had thought he'd been alone in his insecurities, but now felt the community, even old-timers, were right there with him. Gary came forward and spoke about his perspective as an Originator. After all had said their piece, the meeting adjourned, and the Guild left the room to deliberate.

Cecilia stayed by Gabe's side, holding his hand. Aunt Rae had brought along some almond cookies to munch on. Like the day before, Vision Catchers came up to him to thank him, which filled him with pride. As the crowd thinned and a few hours went by, Gabe began to worry. What if this process would take longer than he and Lucy had? Would he be required to help her gain more points? As he sunk into the depths of despair and hope was being drained from his body, the Guild chamber's door opened and the members filed in.

36

A Seat at the Table

Gabe looked intensely at the door as Simone came around the corner, followed by the rest of the Guild, with one exception. Seth McGuvers was missing. Cecilia and Gabe looked at each other, confused. A low hum of whispers traveled around the room.

Gabe looked for Aunt Rae for answers, but she wasn't sitting next to him when they filed in. His heart raced as the anxieties crept in. Could they even rule on this matter without the full Guild? What were the rules? Cecilia, sensing his worry, attempted to calm him and whispered in his ear, "Maybe he just went to the bathroom."

Gabe nodded. Time seemed to slow down as they waited for someone to say something. Vance Gunderthorpe cleared his throat and spoke in a solemn and serious tone.

"You may notice that we have a member missing. While reviewing the evidence, it became clear Seth McGuvers may have played a hand in the sabotage along with Kai Mori. Right now, they're not officially charged, but I'm certain they both will have their day in court. In the meantime, we've put him on temporary administrative leave. He will no longer be a part of these proceedings."

Gabe's eyes grew wide as gasps and whispers came from the gallery.

Aunt Rae had slipped in during Gunderthorpe's comments. She leaned over and grabbed onto Gabe's arm and, with a pinch of excitement, said, "Well, this is a juicy turn. Don't worry, that means they're not just doing this for show … this is good for us." Cecilia was a rock and never let go of Gabe's hand. He took a labored breath, waiting for the crowd to hush and Vance to continue.

"Thanks to Gabe, we have some evidence, but the investigation will be ongoing to understand how this hack happened and who was involved. This appears to have an extra layer of complexity because of the theft of visions from Gabe Allard's studio. With today's ruling, we're attempting to ease concerns about the point system and the app. First, I must say that we will not be taking down the app."

Someone shouted obscenities from the gallery and more people shouted over one another. Gabe didn't join in, trying to remain steadfast, but his blood was boiling.

Gunderthorpe's voice boomed. "Please, let me finish. Disrupters will be removed. We believe the resolution we've come to will ease your concerns." The crowd quieted quickly, and he continued.

"As Mr. Allard pointed out himself, there are educational aspects of the app. Those were in development long before the points system. The contributors and technical team invested a lot of time. Some of you in this room helped in that process. However, from the testimony today, it has become clear that the point system, while well-intentioned, has had a chilling effect on the efforts of many Vision Catchers. Therefore, the point system will no longer be used to judge Vision Catchers. However, we will keep the points for internal use as a tool for Supporters to use as they individually evaluate both Vision Catchers and Originators as part of their caseload. The points will serve as a guidepost, but the Supporters' personal judgment will be the primary factor in determining a Vision Catcher's status and the Originators' progress."

A voice from the back of the room shouted out, "So the Supporters will get their jobs back?" Gabe looked back, searching in the direction of the voice. He spotted him in a dimly lit corner. It was Kai. Gabe had been so laser focused on his role in the hearing, he hadn't noticed him. He wasn't sure, but Kai appeared to be smiling slightly.

"Some of them, yes," Vance replied.

Gabe heard someone say, "I'll believe it when I see it," among the other inaudible mumblings from the gallery. Kai was getting exactly what he wanted. Gabe clinched his free hand in a tight ball at this thought, but calmed himself when he remembered that if the Guild removed McGuvers for suspicion of wrongdoing, they would certainly discipline Kai. He was also comforted by the thought that Kai had shown genuine remorse at the protest and seemed prepared to accept his punishment.

"This will go a lot faster if you remain quiet," Simone chimed in— firm, but encouraging. A minute passed, and the room was silent.

Vance continued, "In regards to the specific Vision Catchers and Originators that were affected by the hack, we will reevaluate the quests, as per Mr. Dawa's suggestion. Those who come forward with claims will be among the first to take part in this revised system."

Gabe felt Cecilia squeeze his hand, and they both smiled widely. This time, the crowd remained mostly silent. Simone Tallis looked directly at Gabe and spoke softly, "Gabe, we're sorry the system failed you, but it took courage to speak up. We would like to appoint you to help any willing Originators who were damaged by the hack. You will need full status to manage more than one person at a time, so this, of course, depends on your quest being deemed successful by your assigned Supporter. I'm confident that it will be."

She paused, then added, "If approved, your promotion will come with more resources, including your own house, and autonomy. We believe you've earned that."

"Thank you. I won't let you down." Gabe's thoughts went to Lucy and her growth.

Gunderthorpe spoke again, directing his words toward Gabe. "You showed gumption in what you organized here, but don't think that this is the way it will be from here on out. Stunts like this are once in a century. If you try something like this every time things aren't going your way, we may reevaluate your status. For now, this hearing is adjourned."

The Guild then stood up and left. The ending was abrupt and left the crowd turning to one another. Gabe heard someone nearby ask, "So did we just win?"

Gabe said softly, "I think maybe we did." He sat soaking in the gravity of all that had passed when Cecilia turned to him and gave him a big hug.

"This is such good news." She pulled back, smiled, and slapped him gently. "See, I told you not to worry about the points."

"Ha, ha." Gabe let out a big sigh, her words lightening the mood. He turned to Aunt Rae, smiled and embraced her. As his second mother held him, his anxieties floated away, and a sense of calm washed over him. He held her tight for a long time, only letting go when his phone pinged.

"Do you have an update on Lucy's status already?" Cecilia asked flippantly.

"No, it's just my alarm. It's time to pick up Lucy at the garden center." He smiled and looked around. "I can't wait to give her the news." He said his goodbyes and as he ran to his car, he hoped she'd had no setbacks while he was at the hearing.

When he pulled up, Lucy was arranging a beautiful bouquet. He watched her from afar as he'd done many times in this journey, but today seemed more final. Though he was eager to tell her about his victory with the Guild, the excitement calmed somewhat when he came near her. His energy now matched the peaceful mood she exuded. As he walked toward her, she looked up and he smiled so hard his cheeks hurt. She smiled back and ran toward him with the bouquet in hand.

"It worked," she said.

"How did you know?" Gabe replied.

"Would you be smiling if it didn't?"

"What? Am I smiling?" Gabe asked jokingly.

She held up the bouquet. "Congratulations."

"I saw you making this bouquet before you saw me. How did you know it was going to work?"

She looked at him, smiling from ear to ear. "I didn't. I was going to give you the bouquet either way. Just one might be a more somber occasion."

"All right," he said. "Well, I have something to give you, too." He pulled out a keychain from his pocket. It was like the one she had left in Booneville with the *Alice in Wonderland* quote—"I knew who I was this morning, but I've changed a few times since then."

"Oh, thank you. I've thought of this almost every day on this journey. It holds so true for me."

His smile softened as he looked at her and said, "I know. For me too. As you've changed every day, so have I. I wouldn't have done any of this without you."

They sat in the moment, then Lucy glanced toward the clock. "Oh, let's go. I'm going to run out of time if we don't get a move on. I got to get ready."

"Run out of time for what?"

"It's a surprise."

He was spent, but her excitement filled him and he drove off to their next adventure.

37

The Last Verse

Lucy came out of the dressing room in the closet wearing a gray knit sweater cinched in a knot on the side, an intricate crocheted necklace, patterned wrap pants that looked like a skirt, and gray faux-suede boots. She felt like one of the models Rae had shown her on the runway. Looking at Daisy, she asked, "What do you think? I absolutely love this one."

"Girl, you're going to freeze. That skirt is thin!"

"They're actually pants." She separated the palazzo pants so Daisy could see. "And I'm wearing leggings underneath."

"Oh," Daisy said. She pouted her lips as she examined Lucy from head to toe. "It's very you, but maybe we should pick something more Emily's style. It's her concert, after all." She turned around quickly and held up a pair of ripped jeans, a plain white undershirt, and a red plaid flannel. "I pulled this from the rocker closet a few doors down."

"Emily doesn't care what we wear. We have to wear clothes that spark joy in us …" She leaned in closer and looked around, then whispered, "Plus, how much longer are they going to clothe us? We really need to take advantage while we can."

"Well, I'm graduated and here," Daisy replied.

"That's different. I invited you. I'm moving out soon, so this may be the end of the line on the free clothes train. Are you sure you don't want to stay in Nashville? We could be roomies!"

"I'm set. Training and learning improv at Second City in Chicago is going to be like a whole new quest. That's where so many of the greats got their start. We've been over this ... oh, but did I tell you that Randy hooked me up with a bartending gig there?"

"OMG, that's great!" Lucy's composure changed when she remembered Daisy's DUI. "Is that going to be hard for you?"

"I can handle it now. My head is in a much better place. And remember, I actually did a little bartending on the quest before I landed on comedy."

"I'm so happy for you. I guess that part of the quest paid off then, right?"

"I guess so. Glad I'm not bagging groceries, even if the monotony of it might help open up my creative juices later."

"Yeah, but you'll probably get a lot of material from drunk folks."

They laughed and then Lucy spotted the last piece to finish her outfit—a wide brimmed floppy cowboy hat. She went to grab it, turning to Daisy. "So, back to the outfit. You can wear what you want, but this one is sooo me. And hey, it's Nashville—this adds a little bit of country." She pulled down on the sides of the hat and tilted her head up to the right with a giant smile across her face.

"I suppose it does. Well, okay, I'll go for this." Daisy ran into the changing room and minutes later came out looking fabulous. She was wearing a magenta silky dress, black tights, and a long pink swing coat with the dress showing beneath. She topped the look off with retro gray heels, long burgundy gloves, and a burgundy beret.

"Is there a portal to the 1950s back there I don't know about? You look great!"

Daisy smiled and curtseyed. "Thank you, my dear." She looked around. "Where's Gabe?"

"I'm not sure." Lucy felt so high on life that she was letting her silly self out. She shouted at the top of her lungs, "GABE, GABE, WHERE ARE YOU? DON'T YOU WANT TO CELEBRATE YOUR BIG WIN TODAY? IT'S ALMOST TIME TO LEAVE."

Gabe came around the corner. "You called?"

Daisy whistled and said, "Well hey there, cowboy!" Gabe was wearing dark blue jeans, a gray undershirt, and a black denim jacket—sleeves slightly rolled up. He was also sporting a giant red belt buckle and a light brown cowboy hat.

"All you need is an American flag in the background and you'd look like the cover of a country album," Daisy said.

He tipped his hat and smiled, doing his best southern accent. "I reckon so. You ladies ready to skedaddle I take it?" They all laughed and headed toward the car.

As she grabbed the door handle, Lucy looked back and said, "Oh wait, I forgot my bag. It'll just take a sec."

She ran inside to grab it and then also remembered the bouquet she'd arranged for Emily was still in the fridge. Before she reached the kitchen, she heard voices and slowed her pace. She listened in and peered around the corner, not wanting to snoop, but also not wanting to barge in.

Someone dressed in a uniform she was unfamiliar with was handing Rae something framed. As he passed it to her, he said, "We found it as part of a larger black market raid. I'm afraid it's one of the only visions from Gabe's studio we've recovered so far."

Rae nodded. Lucy's eyes widened. It was true there was a black market. Was Daisy right? She'd told Lucy she suspected Randy was feeding her jokes that weren't ever hers. Lucy heard footsteps behind her. She turned, and it was Daisy and Gabe. "What happened to just a sec? What are you doing?" Gabe asked.

"I was … " Before she could answer, the man and Rae came to the group now all standing conspicuously at the threshold.

"The officer here was just returning this painting." Rae handed it to Gabe.

He looked at the painting and then up at Lucy and smiled softly. Gazing at it, he said, "I never thought I'd see this again." He handed it to Lucy and her heart felt the yearning to find a fresh path that she'd felt weeks before.

It was the painting of her chasing the sunset. She hadn't told Gabe that it was the only stolen vision to break her heart that it was gone. With watery eyes, she said, "This is where my journey began. Thank you for finding it."

Gabe looked like he wanted to ask more questions, but Daisy chimed in. "Lucy, this is so beautiful, but if we don't leave now, we're gonna miss the show."

Rae let Gabe know she'd fill him in later. Lucy grabbed the flowers for Emily and they left.

Lucy couldn't believe how far Emily had come. In mere weeks, she was getting to showcase some of her songs at a songwriter's circle at the Listening Room Cafe. No doubt Cecilia had pulled some strings, but Emily was joining four other female singer-songwriters. The chairs for the performers were set up in a round. Cecilia and Gary were holding down two tables and seats in the front.

They greeted them warmly as they took in the atmosphere. The warm glow of string lights crisscrossed the ceiling, and soft conversations filled the air, blending with the faint hum of tuning guitars on stage. Lucy felt the anticipation as the intimate crowd settled into their seats, each face turned toward the simple round of chairs waiting at the center of the room.

There was a guitar in front of every chair and women were tuning their guitars and talking and laughing with others. Lucy sensed this was home for many of them. She turned to Gary to steal a word with him before the performance began.

"How's it going?"

"Really good, actually, and I owe it all to you." He looked into her eyes with a mix of sincerity and joy she'd only ever felt from Gary.

"Have you started your business? Are you painting? I want to hear all about it."

"Right now, I'm back to accounting, but I've shifted to part-time temporarily. I've been painting a lot and am interviewing for a job as a painting instructor at Cheers to Art. You know, the place where people drink wine and try to paint? I'm nervous. I'll have to do an instruction class for the interview."

"Oh, that's a lot of pressure. Hey, maybe the talent show and all that crap Kai made you do will actually help."

Gary laughed. "Maybe, but I'm glad to be done with him." Gary put a hand on her shoulder and said, "Seriously, thank you. You pushing me and Gabe believing in me have meant the world."

Lucy smiled warmly at him. They chatted a bit more, but their conversation was cut short by two more unexpected guests. Paul and Flora had shown up too.

Gary wasn't surprised to see Paul. Apparently they'd connected and he was inspired to buy a franchise of Cheers to Art—where he could paint to his heart's content and run the business too. Flora had returned home with a renewed energy, started some much needed therapy, and had begun writing the novel she'd put down years ago. Her Vision Catcher had set her up with regular accountability sessions with someone else who had been on a quest with the same dream. Lucy had so many questions for both of them, but soon the musicians sat down and the performance began.

Lucy was so happy to see Emily. Right before it was her turn, she saw her take in a deep breath and let out a smile. When she sang about

Daniel, the friend she'd shared about in small group, it was gorgeous—the words dripped from her mouth like butter, heartbreak carrying every note toward hope. Others were more seasoned and less nervous, but Emily's healing shone through more than anything.

When Emily's turn came around again, she had a mischievous smile on her face. "Alright, now for something a lot lighter." She looked at Lucy and Daisy and gave them both a wink. The crowd started laughing when she sang the silly "Seafood Diet" song Daisy and Lucy had written with her.

Lucy was cracking up and as she took in the joy on everyone's face, she wasn't the least bit embarrassed or ashamed. She was proud. A light brightened inside her and in that moment, she knew that she'd reached the end of her quest.

A sense of peace washed over her, and she closed her eyes, soaking in the moment. Finally. Herself.

Epilogue

Six Months after Quest Day Forty

The garden center didn't open until eight, but Lucy clocked in at seven. She pulled into the parking lot and when she stepped out of the car; she felt lighter. It was her first shift since the divorce, but she knew that wasn't the only thing filling her with calm.

Dawn had just broken and there was barely a cloud in the sky. As the sun rose over the greenhouse, she was hit with a vision of the painting that hung in her bedroom.

The quest for this moment—when she was one with someone else's sunrise—had been forged in her bones and locked in her mind. She'd become the someone else. At the end of forty days, Gabe was glad that she'd "passed," but the points never mattered to her. He told her they didn't matter to him either. The main thing was to get her on a path to create lasting change. It had worked.

She'd feared Colt would fight the divorce, but she had the upper hand. After the park incident, she agreed to drop the charges if he signed the divorce papers and complied with the restraining order. He was eager to oblige and went back to Booneville with no one at the school catching wind of what had happened. When she gathered her things when he was teaching a class, she bid Garfield a tearful goodbye. The well of tears shed for Colt had dried for the most part. She'd have painful moments in therapy at the shelter, but those were mostly working through the guilt of not leaving him sooner.

She was working through the shame of fracturing the relationships

"

with Anna and her parents. But that felt on the mend, too. Her mom and dad had visited her at the garden center and her new apartment. Anna and she were finally going to go on the birthday trip they'd missed. It was still a few months off, but she'd already asked for the time off.

Still entranced by the sunrise, she barely noticed when Claudia arrived to unlock the employee's entrance. Lucy startled when Claudia shouted, "Good morning!" She tried to maintain her peaceful moment as she hurried in to fetch her apron and start a new day. Claudia asked her to set up a special display of aloe vera plants. Apparently a good seller during the summer sunburn months. Lucy grabbed an A-frame chalkboard sign and chuckled to herself as she wrote, "Aloe You Very Much."

From the privacy of a car, Gabe watched off in the distance. He knew today was her first day back since the divorce was final. He should've known she'd be just fine. Since passing the quest, his pair-bond with Lucy had weakened slightly because she needed less help and his caseload was larger. There were more Originators than they realized that Kai had sabotaged and he was trying to gain their trust.

The Guild didn't allow Gabe to tell the damaged Originators about Kai. How he'd pleaded guilty and was in a Vision Catcher Rehabilitation Center. Seth was still claiming no wrongdoing and waiting for his day in court. Gabe would have to help these Originators with extra sensitivity and a dash of creativity. Aunt Rae had warned that with their frame of mind, the Guild would probably not grant any of the wronged Originators quests. He'd have to wait to see if the adjusted system was working.

In a nearby office building, a man was being berated by his boss. Gabe called the Feranchin drifting out the window toward him, grabbed his sketchbook, and went to work.

EPILOGUE

Acknowledgements

There were many false starts with this novel, where I put it down, and let it rest. But being able to persist and finally join the world of indie authors with a finished product has been a labor of love. I wouldn't have been able to do it without the many cheerleaders by my side.

This book was born out of a lost vision of my own—to be a novelist. It is with self-compassion that I must first acknowledge my twenty-two-year-old self for finishing a completely different manuscript. That book was never published—it was lost many computers and moves ago. But if I could speak to my younger self today, I'd thank her for finishing it. Finishing any large project is never a simple feat, but my memories of writing then, allowed me to know I could do it again. Reclaiming her dream, my dream, has been one of the proudest moments of my life.

The catalyst for recapturing this vision was my husband, Adriel, who volleyed the dream back to me after I had forgotten it. We had a "writing date" a couple of months into our relationship. We both spent an hour writing side by side, with dueling laptops. He read what I wrote then, a version of what turned out to be chapter one of *Chasing the Sunset*. He never let go of his belief in my talent as a writer. When I was feeling lost six years after that date and I told him I wanted to find my purpose, he said, "You should write." He kept repeating this and encouraging me through all the self-doubt until I found the courage to persist.

This persistence was aided greatly by the support of fellow writers.

My cousin Robin, who referred me to her MFA classmate Sara Graybeal, who I hired as my first book coach. Sara asked the right questions in our sessions to help me verbally process where this story was going.

She led me to my critique group, which at the time of this publication has been meeting twice a month for close to two years. Their feedback and reactions to early chapters helped to give this story legs. Khallori, Whitney, Ricky, Veronica, Lori and especially Jen; I'm in your debt.

When I asked for a morning accountability buddy from that group, Jen O'Bryan began showing up every single morning at 8 a.m. She is my writing companion, accountability buddy, and self-doubt slayer. We share in the dream of being novelists together. I could not have made it this far without her.

Grace, Teri, and Jim became my local in-person critique group recently. Their feedback just in the last several months has brought a fresh perspective to the book. I'm grateful for their continued feedback as I take on the second book in this series. (!!!)

I consider myself incredibly lucky to have stumbled upon my editor, Sam Stringert. From our first meeting, I knew she was going to be the perfect person to guide me. With every round of edits, she made this novel stronger.

Finally, I'd like to acknowledge and thank the family and friends who served as beta readers for being my encouraging and honest supporters. Every phone call lit me up and filled my soul—whether it was Emily D. taking the time to give me detailed notes, Emily S. talking to me for an hour about how much the story meant to her after a hard week, or the other calls of support from family members.

As I continue to find my way in endeavoring to create a bit of lasting change, I am immensely grateful to all who were with me for the journey.

What's Next?

If you enjoyed this story, would you take a moment to leave a review on Goodreads? Your honest feedback not only means the world to me, but it also helps other readers discover the Vision Catching Universe.

Leave a review on Goodreads

Book Two in *The Vision Catchers* series — *Stealing the Dawn* — arrives in late spring 2026. Gabe's journey continues as he takes on his most difficult challenge yet—helping an Originator whose dreams were damaged by Kai. But the deeper he digs, the more he's pulled into the dangerous black market of stolen visions...and the secrets it's desperate to protect.

Want to be the first to see the cover, read sneak peeks, and get exclusive behind-the-scenes updates? Join the Vision Catchers Reader List here: https://hopeloschak.com/#sign up

About the Author

Hope Epting Loschak writes uplifting, magical-realism fiction about rediscovering dreams, reclaiming self-worth, and finding light in unexpected places. Her debut novel, *Chasing the Sunset*—Book 1 in the *Vision Catchers* series—blends heartfelt storytelling with a touch of the mystical, following characters on transformative journeys of hope and healing.

Hope chases her own dreams from her home in Georgia, where she lives with her husband. A lifelong believer in second chances, she's passionate about inspiring others to follow the spark that makes them come alive.

Connect with Hope and explore the world of Vision Catching at visioncatching.com.

You can connect with me on:

🌐 https://hopeloschak.com

🔗 https://www.instagram.com/hopechasesdreams

Subscribe to my newsletter:

✉ https://hopeloschak.com/#signup

www.ingramcontent.com/pod-product-compliance
Lightning Source LLC
Chambersburg PA
CBHW030753310726
48969CB00005B/1390